Marguerite K
romances featu
of place and t
Ferguson, Du
bestseller, *Her Heart for a* ...
working on their second book together. Marguerite lives in Argyll on the west coast of Scotland. When not writing, she loves to read, cook, garden, drink martinis, and sew, though rarely at the same time.

Regency Secrets

July 2022
Those Scandalous Stricklands

August 2022
The Governess Swap

September 2022
Penniless Brides of Convenience

October 2022
The Cornish Dukes

November 2022
Breaking the Marriage Rules

December 2022
The Beauchamp Heirs

January 2023
The Wild Warriners

February 2023
Brides for Bachelors

March 2023
Secret Lives of the Ton

April 2023
The Widows of Westram

May 2023
Saved from Disgrace

June 2023
The Return of the Rogues

Regency Secrets:

Penniless Brides of Convenience

MARGUERITE KAYE

MILLS & BOON

First Published in Great Britain 2022
By Mills & Boon, an imprint of HarperCollins*Publishers*
1 London Bridge Street, London, SE1 9GF

www.harpercollins.co.uk

HarperCollins*Publishers*
1st Floor, Watermarque Building,
Ringsend Road, Dublin 4, Ireland

ISBN 978-0-263-30584-5

MIX
Paper | Supporting
responsible forestry
FSC™ C007454

This book is produced from independently certified FSC™ paper to ensure responsible forest management.

For more information visit: www.harpercollins.co.uk/green

Printed and Bound in Spain using 100% Renewable electricity at CPI Black Print, Barcelona

THE EARL'S
COUNTESS OF
CONVENIENCE

For the original Twinnies, my sisters Johanna and Catriona. You are nothing like the twins in this book and, despite what you think, you are neither of you in the least bit musical, but I love you every bit as much as Eloise loves Phoebe and Estelle. Maybe even a wee bit more!

Chapter One

Elmswood Manor—April 1827

Kate, Lady Elmswood, burst into the morning room waving aloft a single sheet of thick writing parchment. '"Lord Fearnoch is most pleased to accept Lady Elmswood's kind invitation to call at Elmswood Manor on Friday April the sixth, with the express purpose of meeting with her eldest ward, Miss Eloise Brannagh, to discuss the possibility of a marriage between the parties on terms outlined in his previous dispatch." Goodness, that sounds as if it was written by his lawyer.'

'Perhaps, but it's just as likely he wrote it himself.' Eloise looked up from her position on the floor, kneeling in front of Phoebe to pin the hem of her sister's new gown. 'Remember, Kate, until he inherited the title, he was merely Alexander Sinclair, some sort of clerk at the Admiralty, so well used to penning memorandums, one would imagine.' She smiled. 'It's certainly not the most romantic proposal I've ever come across. Does he proffer any other endearments?'

'"Should either party conclude that the match does

not fully satisfy their requirements, then negotiations will be terminated without prejudice. Should both parties prove amenable, however, it is imperative that the nuptials are concluded by the second of June, Lord Fearnoch's thirtieth birthday, whereupon, under the terms of the Fearnoch entail, failure to be of married status would result in the Fearnoch title and estates passing to a cousin." And he looks forward…et cetera, et cetera,' Kate concluded. 'What do you think, Eloise? It all sounds a bit cold and heartless. It's not too late to write back and say you've changed your mind.'

'But I haven't.' Eloise inserted a final pin. 'Turn around slowly, Phoebe. Yes, I think that will do nicely. Your turn, Estelle.'

One twin replaced the other on the footstool, Eloise resumed her pinning and Kate dropped into her usual chair by the fire, surrendering the letter over to Phoebe to read. 'You know, you could make a very handsome living if you set yourself up as a modiste. Those gowns are beautiful.'

'Madame Eloise, dressmaker to the aristocracy,' Estelle said in a dreadful French accent. 'You would have a very exclusive little boutique in…'

'Bond Street,' Kate supplied for her, smiling.

'Bond Street. And Phoebe could bake cakes to serve to your ladies while they wait to be fitted, and I could entertain them by playing on the pianoforte. Am I done?'

'You are.' Eloise stood up, shaking out her own skirts and returning her pin cushion to her sewing box before sitting down opposite Kate. 'May I?'

Phoebe handed her the letter. 'I shall bake my special spicy biscuits for Lord Fearnoch. I would have preferred to offer him a fruit cake, but you can't make a good fruit cake in three days, it needs at least a week for the brandy to soak in.'

Estelle threw herself down on the sofa beside her twin. 'I'm not sure the biscuits are a good idea, Phoebe, they're very brittle. Not ideal for a man with no teeth.'

'For heaven's sake!' Eloise handed the letter back to Kate, laughing. 'I'm sure he has a perfectly good set of teeth.'

'Yes,' Estelle said, grinning, 'but the question is, are they his own?'

'Perhaps I should make a sponge cake, then,' Phoebe said, her eyes alight with mischief. 'If he does have wooden teeth…'

'A man as rich as Lord Fearnoch will surely have ivory,' Estelle interjected.

'Yes, but he's not rich yet, is he? Unless he marries Eloise, he'll have to revoke the title and will have nothing but his salary from the Admiralty to his name. So I think perhaps I will make a sponge, after all. What do you think, Eloise?'

'I will leave that momentous decision in your capable hands, Phoebe.'

'You're quite right, you've more important things to worry about. Such as what to wear. I think the cream dress with the emerald trim is your most becoming gown. Lord Fearnoch will be so dazzled by your radiant beauty that he will be rendered quite speechless, and without further ado will fall at your feet and beg you to be his.'

'Now you are being ridiculous,' Eloise said, colouring. 'You know very well that I am the bookish sister.

It is you two who have the kind of looks which cause carriage accidents.'

'That does not make a scarecrow of you!' The twins leapt up of one accord, pulling her over to stand in front of the empty fireplace. 'Take a look in the mirror, for goodness' sake.'

Laughing, Eloise did as she was bid, catching her breath at the reflection of herself flanked by the twins. Though they were not identical, one strawberry blonde and the other Titian, they were both quite ridiculously beautiful. Her own auburn locks were tarnished in comparison, and though all of them had the same hazel eyes, her face was not a perfect oval, and her skin, though the same creamy colour as the twins', was marred by a sprinkling of freckles. What would Mama, the former toast of Dublin society, think if she could see her daughters now, the younger two grown into such beauties as would put her in the shade? Ha! And there would be the rub, for Mama never could bear to be anything other than the centre of attention, the most beautiful woman in any room.

'No one would ever mistake us for anything other than sisters,' Phoebe said, kissing Eloise's cheek affectionately.

'True,' she agreed, 'though no one would deny that I am very much a watered-down version of you two. And besides,' she continued, cutting short her sisters' protests, 'my appearance is quite irrelevant. Lord Fearnoch is not in need of a beautiful wife, but a practical, pragmatic one.'

'Just like Aunt Kate.' Phoebe gave her guardian a quick hug. 'Practical, pragmatic and pretty. And don't say that old married ladies cannot be described as pretty because you are neither old nor married—at least, not in the conventional sense.'

'I am twenty-eight years old, young lady, and have been married to your Uncle Daniel for six years,' Kate retorted. She rolled her eyes. '*Uncle Daniel!* It makes him sound positively ancient, but he has only just turned thirty-four.'

'And despite the fact that he is our guardian, we have never actually met him.'

'That is because he has been overseas ever since we tied the knot, a year before your arrival.'

'Yes, but before that…'

'There were nine years between Mama and our uncle. When I was born, he'd only have been…' Eloise wrinkled her nose as she calculated. 'Ten, I think.'

'And by the time he was sixteen,' Kate said, 'he was already off on his first expedition to exotic foreign climes.'

'The wilds of rural Ireland can't have held much appeal in comparison, I suppose,' Phoebe said.

'No, but even if they had, Papa wouldn't have made him welcome.' Eloise grimaced. 'Any more than we would have been welcomed with open arms here, at Elmswood Manor, when Papa was alive. Even if our grandfather had forgiven Mama for eloping, Papa would not have set foot over the threshold, nor allowed any of us to.'

'*How* Papa loathed our grandfather for implying he was not good enough for Mama,' Phoebe said.

'I don't know about not good enough, but they were certainly not good for each other,' Estelle added.

'Nor for us,' her twin concluded sadly. 'Papa was forever saying he would not darken our grandfather's doorstep again, which was all very well for him, but we were not permitted to darken the doorstep once, while our grandfather was alive.'

'I've always thought that old Lord Elmswood could have said nothing more completely designed to guarantee an elopement, than to forbid your mother from seeing your father,' Kate interjected. 'Though I was too young to know anything of the precise circumstances, I knew Daniel had an older sister, but it was only after I was married and found that portrait of her hidden away in the attics that I realised there must have been some sort of scandal. It is such a shame you didn't get the chance to know your grandfather. I'm sure, if he'd met the three of you, the breach could have been healed.'

'Not if our father had anything to do with it,' Eloise said grimly, recalling Papa's regular, vicious diatribes on the subject.

'No,' Phoebe agreed with a shudder. 'And now it's too late. Isn't it odd, that our only close living relative is a man we've never met. Which makes it all the more peculiar, don't you think, that he offered up Eloise as the perfect wife to a total stranger.'

'You make it sound so dramatic!' Eloise exclaimed, shaking her head. 'Uncle Daniel's letter made it clear that he has known Lord Fearnoch for many years *and* that he is an honourable man whom he would trust with his life.'

'Or, in this case, his niece's life. I've been racking my brains,' Phoebe said, 'and I can't remember him ever mentioning an Alexander Sinclair in any of his previous letters.'

'But Uncle Daniel rarely mentions anyone in his letters to Aunt Kate,' Estelle reminded her. 'Half the time, we don't even know where he is and what it is he's doing.'

'Exploring far-flung corners of the globe! And the more dangerous and remote the place, the happier he is. As the three of you know perfectly well, because you've read every one of his very occasional missives, all he ever writes is a brief scrawl to let me know he is still alive. He never even acknowledges my replies. Half the time, I wonder if he even reads them.'

'Well, there you must be in the wrong of it,' Eloise pointed out, 'for he has read enough to deduce that I might fit the bill for the Earl of Fearnoch's vacancy for a wife. Though he did not *offer me up,* as if I were a dish of stew, he merely suggested, *if* I was amenable, that the match might suit me.'

'And we are all agreed, having discussed nothing else since Lord Fearnoch's first letter arrived three weeks ago, that it will suit you,' Kate said. 'At least,' she added, frowning over at the twins, 'I thought we had?'

The twins gazed silently at each other for a long moment. Eloise knew they were sharing their thoughts in that disconcerting manner they had demonstrated from a very young age. 'We have,' Phoebe said, speaking for the pair of them. 'Truly, Eloise, we haven't changed our minds. Though we were dead set against it at first, and we hate the very notion of losing you, and if there is any chance that you think you would be the least bit unhappy you must not—but we've been over and over this, haven't we, so I won't rake over old ground.'

'Anyway, even if this match didn't make excellent sense, we really had no choice but to agree, did we, Phoebe?' Estelle said irrepressibly, slanting a smile at her twin. 'Because we know that you live in terror, dear

Aunt Kate, of Uncle Daniel returning home and giving you merry hell because his nieces are still cluttering up the place.'

'One down, only two to go,' Estelle chimed in. 'After five years, the Elmswood Manor coven is breaking up.'

'Stop it,' Kate said, laughing. 'You know perfectly well that all of you are welcome here for always, if you wish.'

'The twins are just funning.' Eloise cast her sisters a reproving look. 'Seriously, we've been round the houses on the arguments for and against my meeting Lord Fearnoch, and I thought we were all agreed that it is an opportunity I would be a fool not to explore, at the very least.'

'That's what I just said.' Phoebe's smile was conciliatory. 'Though goodness, do you remember when Kate first read Uncle Daniel's letter out, in this very room, we thought it must be some sort of joke.'

'I must admit, I thought he must have been suffering from too much desert sun when he wrote it,' Kate admitted. 'It seemed so very odd to think of him sitting in the shadow of the pharaoh's tombs proposing Eloise as the solution to Lord Fearnoch's dilemma.'

'And such a dilemma, as we finally discovered when we eventually had a letter from the man himself. Lord Fearnoch, you must marry before you attain your thirtieth birthday, following the death of your elder brother, the Earl,' Estelle intoned in the voice of doom, 'else you will forfeit one of the largest fortunes in all of England.'

'I still find it very odd though,' Eloise said, squinting at the needle she was holding up to the light to thread. 'Why on earth would there be such a condition attached to the earldom?'

'An attempt to ensure that it always passed through the direct line, I expect,' Phoebe replied. 'What is even odder is why an earl with a fortune must ask a complete stranger to be his wife.'

'And I've told you several times,' Kate retorted, 'that it is not an easy thing to do, to secure a platonic marriage. I was the perfect solution to your Uncle Daniel's problems when his father died. By that time, my poor ailing papa had been forced to delegate almost all of his duties as estate manager to me. Having grown up on the estate, I knew the lands better than anyone else.' Kate gazed out of the morning room window to the view of the back gardens rolling gently down to the lake. 'Old Lord Elmswood, Daniel's father, had let this house fall into a sad state of neglect by the time he died. I think the whole sorry business with your mother affected him greatly. When I was a girl, I used to dream of living here. I had all sorts of plans for restoring the place to its former glory.'

'So when my uncle proposed, it was a wish come true?'

Kate shook her head. 'What I'm trying to say, Estelle, is that your uncle didn't propose to me. Daniel balked at the idea of depriving me of children—I was only twenty-two at the time. So I proposed to him.'

'You have never told us that before,' Phoebe exclaimed, startled.

'It has never been relevant until now.' Kate laughed at the twins' identical expressions. 'That is what comes of being practical and pragmatic, my dears. As I pointed out to Daniel at the time, it was an eminently sensible arrangement, with both of us gaining. I would secure my independence, I'd be free to carry on doing the work

I loved and I'd be able to restore this beautiful house, while he was free to pursue his career abroad, knowing that his estates were in the best possible hands.'

'And you have never regretted it?' Eloise asked, though she was fairly certain she knew the answer to the question.

'Never,' Kate said firmly. 'As it happens I would have liked children. But I got them, didn't I, only a year after I was married? All three of you at once.'

'We were hardly children,' Eloise said drily. 'I was nineteen, the twinnies were fifteen.'

'And you were all three of you quite devastated.' Kate shook her head. 'Even now, to think of what you'd been through, losing both your parents and your poor little brother in one tragic accident, with all of them lost at sea. As if that was not bad enough, to be evicted from the only home you had ever known, and packed off from Ireland to come all the way here to live with a complete stranger who happened to be your only relative's wife. If I hadn't already been married to Daniel, I'd have married him then, just to give you all a home. Now for heaven's sake, there is no need...'

But Kate's voice was muffled as the three sisters enveloped her in a hug, and it was some time before they separated, to return to their seats. 'Goodness,' she said, emerging very ruffled, 'I did not mean to upset everyone, dredging up the past. I was trying to explain why I thought that Lord Fearnoch had chosen to speak to Eloise rather than any other woman, wasn't I?'

'Let me, because I think the explanation is quite simple. Think about it,' Eloise said, addressing her sisters. 'We know from our uncle's letter that when he met Lord Fearnoch in Egypt five months ago, he had only just heard of his brother's death and the terms of the will. It will have taken him some time to secure return passage to England, no doubt to become embroiled in a legal wrangle to avoid the need to marry, because we also know from our uncle that he had no wish for a wife. And now, having realised that he either marries or loses his fortune, he's up against the clock and since Uncle Daniel has already presented him with a potentially suitable candidate...'

'Who, thanks to the poor example set for us by our dear departed parents, has absolutely no desire whatsoever to become either a wife or a mother,' Estelle interjected grimly.

'No one who witnessed what we did would ever want to marry.' Phoebe clasped her twin's hand. 'Do you remember, Estelle, how we used to pretend we had been adopted, and that one day our real parents would arrive to claim us?'

'And how we vowed we wouldn't leave unless they promised to take Eloise too?'

'We did. We vowed we would never, ever leave you behind.'

Phoebe's tragic little smile touched Eloise's heart. She had tried so hard to protect the twins from the worst of her parents' vicious bickering and confrontations, and in turn they had tried to protect her, pretending that she'd succeeded. They almost never talked of those days, but they all three of them bore the scars, buried deep. She thought she knew everything about her sisters, but she hadn't heard this sad little story before. 'Thank you,' she said, swallowing the large lump which had risen in her throat and trying for a watery smile. 'I am touched that you were so intent on keeping me with you, though you were by implication disowning me as your sister.'

'No!' the twins called in unison.

'And to think that just a moment ago, you were telling me that no one would ever mistake us for anything but sisters too.'

'We didn't mean...'

'She's teasing,' Estelle said sheepishly. 'Anyway, Phoebe, we knew at the time it was just a pipe dream.'

'Yes. Though we also knew that if someone did come along to claim us, our actual real parents would probably have handed us over gladly,' Phoebe said bitterly.

'Or they wouldn't have noticed we'd gone.'

There was no denying the truth of this, and Eloise felt no inclination to defend the indefensible as she inspected the stocking she had been darning before snipping the cotton and tying it off. But nor was she about to let those skeletons creep back out of the closet and colour the present. 'I think that's enough talk of those times.'

'I agree. Let's talk instead about what it will be like when you are rich beyond our wildest dreams,' Estelle said, taking her cue and rubbing her hands together gleefully.

Phoebe giggled. 'You will be able to buy up a whole warehouse of silks to make gowns.'

'She'll be far too much a lady of leisure to sew. Besides, I'm not sure it's the done thing for a countess to make her own gowns. Do you know how to attach a sprinkling of diamonds to a décolleté, Eloise?'

'Oh, I'll have a maid for that sort of thing. I shall be too busy, just like Cleopatra, bathing in asses' milk.'

'A rather rare commodity in London, I should think,' Kate interjected wryly.

'London!' Phoebe clapped her hands together, her eyes shining. 'And you'll be a countess. To think of our big sister being a countess! Will you go to lots of parties, do you think? And will you live in a palace?'

'A town house,' Estelle said reprovingly. 'Though a very *large* town house. With—oh, I should think at least a hundred bedchambers, and a thousand servants, and a French chef.'

'Who will never be able to bake a cake as delicious as Phoebe can,' Eloise said. She stuck her darning needle into the pin cushion and closed the lid of her sewing box. 'One thing is certain, I will never have to darn another stocking. As for the rest—I am not particularly interested in draping myself in ermine and diamonds.'

'No,' Estelle agreed, 'you're more likely to spend a portion of your immense fortune on your own loom.'

'I don't see me taking up weaving, not even if Lord Fearnoch turns out to be as life-threateningly tedious as his title of Victualling Commissioner suggests,' Eloise said tartly. 'But it is no exaggeration to say that the settlement he is proposing is life-changing, for all of us. If this marriage works out, I will be able to provide Estelle with the funds for her own private orchestra if she likes, and you, Phoebe, could set up in competition to the legendary Gunter's tea rooms. We could travel. We could do anything we want, or nothing at all if we choose to. The future will be considerably brighter than any of us ever imagined.'

'And all you have to do is put up with a toothless, tedious earl,' Estelle said, chuckling.

'Heavens though, what if he turns out not to be toothless but cut from the same cloth as our neighbour, Squire Mytton?'

Kate, Eloise and Estelle gazed at Phoebe in horror. 'Surely there is only one such. I heard from one of our tenants, who heard from his sister in Leamington Spa, that the squire rode his horse into a hotel there. Right up the grand staircase Mad Jack went,' Kate said in a hushed tone, 'and from the balcony he actually jumped down into the restaurant below, then back out of the window.'

'I heard,' Eloise said, 'that he likes to ride a bear around his drawing room to alarm his house guests.'

'He supposedly set fire to his nightshirt in an effort to stop a bout of hiccups,' Estelle added, stifling a giggle. 'Surely that cannot be true?'

'Nothing about that man would surprise me,' Kate said drily. 'But what would surprise me very much would be your uncle suggesting such a man as a suitable husband for Eloise. And although I don't know what a Victualling Commissioner for the Admiralty actually does, I think he'd have to be of sound mind to do it, don't you?'

'That's true,' Phoebe said, heaving an exaggerated sigh of relief.

'I promise you that if I find I cannot reconcile myself to the idea of living under the same roof as Lord Fearnoch, if I consider his nature unkind or in any way brutish, or if I feel that I cannot trust him, our first meeting will be the last. I will not be a sacrificial lamb.' Eloise got to her feet. 'But I will not rule him out as a husband if he has wooden teeth, or a wooden leg, or even if he is simply a stranger to the bathtub. *If* we find we suit—and let us not forget that, astonishing as it may sound to you, he may not take to me—but *if* we do find we suit, this is the chance of a lifetime for us. I have to embrace it.'

'Yes.' Estelle grinned. 'Luckily, if he is averse to bathing, that's the only thing you'll have to embrace.'

'That's more than enough speculation for now,' Kate said, biting back her own laughter. 'We will discover the cut of Lord Fearnoch's jib soon enough.'

'Kate is, as always, quite right,' Eloise said briskly. 'You two, change out of those dresses and let me sew the hems before I become too hoity-toity for such menial tasks.'

Chapter Two

As the ormolu clock on the mantel chimed the hour, a carriage could be heard coming to a halt on the gravel drive outside the drawing room. A cloud of butterflies fluttered to life in Eloise's tummy, intensifying the faint feeling of nausea she'd woken up with. Today could prove to be life-changing.

A cold sweat prickled at the back of her neck. What if Lord Fearnoch really did turn out to be loathsome? What if *he* found *her* repugnant? Now that everyone in the household was reconciled to the idea of her marrying, now that they had all agreed that the benefits by far outweighed the fact that the groom would be a complete stranger, Eloise couldn't bear the thought of the match falling through.

What would it be *like* to be married? How much time would they be required to spend together? Would they be expected to have breakfast and dinner at the same table? What would Lord Fearnoch tell his friends, his colleagues at the Admiralty? She had a hundred questions. And right now, bracing herself for the coming introduction and feeling quite sick with nerves, Eloise was discovering that there was a very big difference between the idea of a convenient and advantageous marriage and the reality, in the shape of the man who might become her husband, a man who was at this very moment descending from his carriage.

She stared at her reflection in the mirror set over the mantel. Her hair was still obediently pinned in the smooth chignon, which had taken her three times longer to do than her usual careless topknot. She looked pale, her eyes betraying her anxious state. Pinching her cheeks, forcing her mouth into a semblance of a welcoming smile, she tugged unnecessarily at her gown. It was the one which Phoebe had suggested she wear. Her own creation in ivory muslin, she was rather pleased with the result achieved by twisting emerald and ivory ribbons together to trim the neckline. Triangles of emerald silk fluttered like little pennants around the high waistline, and she had used larger triangles in the same colour to trim the hem. Green suited her colouring, she knew, but she worried that today of all days it would over-accentuate the red hue of her hair.

The doorbell clanged, making her jump. Her heart felt as if it was in her mouth. Upstairs, Phoebe and Estelle would no doubt be peering down from Kate's bedroom window, which would give them the best, unobserved view of the new arrival.

Alert for the sound, she heard the familiar teeth-grinding grate as the huge front door scraped on the uneven flagstones of the hall. Eloise took several deep breaths in an effort to calm her nerves. Casting her eyes around the familiar room, she first opted to seat herself on one of the chairs at the fireplace, but that seemed inappropriately intimate. She hurried to her favourite window seat, picking up the book she had left there, but that seemed too studied a pose, so she jumped up to her feet again, and was casting about for some other innocuous task to go about when the door opened and Kate's butler announced Lord Fearnoch. Voltaire's *Candide* involuntarily dropped from her hands as a man who bore absolutely no resemblance whatsoever to the abacus-wielding Admiralty bureaucrat her sisters had had such fun imagining walked into the drawing room.

Alexander Sinclair, the Earl of Fearnoch, had cropped dark-brown hair, a high, intelligent brow, wide-spaced brown eyes framed by ridiculously long lashes, cheekbones which were razor sharp and a jaw that made strong seem like an understated description. His mouth, in contrast, could only be described as sultry. His navy-blue coat fitted tightly over a pair of shoulders which would be the envy of a blacksmith, fawn pantaloons encased muscular legs, a fact which she should not be noticing. He was a physical specimen to make any woman weak-kneed and he was in her drawing room, looking at her expectantly.

'How do you do? I assume you are Miss Eloise Brannagh?' He took her hand, kissing the air above her fingertips.

His teeth were pearly white and clearly his own. So much for the twins' wild speculation. He smelled faintly of lemon soap. 'Lord Fearnoch.' Utterly confused, because Eloise wasn't the type of woman to go weak-kneed, she blurted out the first thing that popped into her head. 'I assume you *are* Lord Fearnoch? You don't look at all like someone who works in some rather tedious capacity at the Admiralty.'

'I am indeed Lord Fearnoch, and very pleased to

meet you, Miss Brannagh. If I may respond in kind, you do not look at all like a dutiful mother hen to twin sisters.'

A startled laugh escaped her. 'Good grief, is that how my uncle described me? Then I'm surprised you agreed to meet someone so tiresomely worthy.'

He raised a brow. 'You imagine my predicament must be desperate indeed, to attempt to lure such a paragon from her life of self-sacrifice?'

'I am wondering why a handsome man who is heir to a vast fortune would choose to marry a—a—how did you imagine I would look?'

'Older. Fiercer. With spectacles.'

'Spectacles!'

'Daniel—that is, your uncle—told me that you were the clever one of his nieces. So I imagined eyes weakened by long hours of study. Hence the spectacles.'

Though his tone was cool, there was, she was almost certain, a hint of laughter in his eyes. A sense of humour was another thing that Eloise had not expected. 'I hope you are not now imagining me ill-tempered. I should tell you that I consider myself extremely even-tempered, and if you think that the colour of my hair tells a different story, then you are making a common, very facile assumption. Red hair does not denote a fiery temper any more than the looks of a—a Greek god denote a—a romantic poet.'

'Rhyming cat with mat exhausts my poetic abilities. Shall we sit, or would you prefer to continue trading misconceptions standing up?'

'I do beg your pardon.' Her face flaming, Eloise finally remembered her manners. 'How was your journey, Lord Fearnoch?'

'Painless.' He sat down, seemingly at ease, and studied her overtly. 'It is clear, Miss Brannagh, that your imagination had conjured as inaccurate a picture of me as I did of you.'

If only he knew! Her colour heightened. 'I did not—I tried not to anticipate—after all, it is not as if we are required to find each other—I mean—I mean you did say in your letter that it would be a marriage in name only,' she finished lamely.

This time she was certain she caught a glimmer of a smile. 'Indulge me,' he said. 'How would you imagine an Admiralty clerk, I wonder? Dandruff, or a squint? Ink-stained cuffs? A man with a stoop, perhaps, from spending his life poring over dusty ledgers?'

Eloise laughed. Lord Fearnoch steepled his hands, waiting. She could not possibly tell him. The silence stretched. She wasn't used to silence. 'My sisters, they cannot understand why an earl with a fortune should wish to marry me.'

'How very unkind of your sisters to say so.'

'No, I mean—not me, but anyone. A complete stranger. They think that you must be—' Mortified now, she broke off, shaking her head, but he simply raised an enquiring brow, and waited. Eloise counted out forty-five seconds before she threw up her hands in surrender. 'If you must know, they thought you must at least be averse to bathing, or toothless perhaps. We knew that Uncle Daniel would have said in his letter if there had been some—some physical—defect—so it had to be the sort of drawback that men don't really notice.' She grimaced. 'Sorry. You did ask.'

'I did.'

That silence again. 'You obviously do bathe regularly,' Eloise said, trying for a smile.

He nodded.

'And your teeth are—well, what I can see of them, they are...'

He burst out laughing. 'All there, and in good condition. You sound as if you are inspecting a horse with a view to buying it.'

He had a very attractive laugh. Relieved beyond measure, Eloise relaxed a little. 'But that is precisely what we are doing, in a manner of speaking, aren't we? I hadn't thought—I mean, I was looking forward—but then this morning it occurred to me that it would be—well, it's very awkward. You're looking me over and I'm looking you over, and for the life of me, I can't understand, now you are here—I beg your pardon, but I think the twins—my sisters—have a point. A man like you, surely there must be women queuing up to be your wife?' She stopped abruptly. 'Sorry. You must think I am an idiot, but you are so silent I feel compelled to fill the gaps.'

'I tend to say something when I have something to say.'

'Does that mean you think I'm a wittering fool or don't you have an answer to my question? Or perhaps you think I oughtn't to have asked it, though I must say, I do think it a pertinent question, my lord.'

She would not speak. She would sit here without uttering another word until he answered. Eloise bit her lip. She would not count the seconds. She folded her arms. She unfolded them. 'I don't mean literally queuing, my lord, I meant...'

'I understood you perfectly, Miss Brannagh. Would

you mind calling me Alexander? When you "my lord" me, it makes me want to look over my shoulder for my brother, Walter.'

'You would not be here, if your brother were still alive.'

'I wish to heaven that he was.' He coloured. 'Forgive me, I meant no offence, but I think it is best that we are candid with each other from the outset. I had no ambition to be either an earl or a husband. The truth is, I am obliged to be both.'

'Well! The truth is, I would rather not be married either. At least—I would rather not be *married*,' Eloise added hurriedly. Lord Fearnoch—Alexander—smiled. His smile lit up his eyes, and it acted on Eloise like a punch in the stomach. Their eyes met, and something very odd seemed to pass between them that made her cheeks heat in a way that had nothing to do with embarrassment. 'If you understand my meaning,' she added.

He nodded, breaking eye contact, smoothing the palms of his hands over his pantaloons. Was he nervous? Already regretting his decision to come here? Fortunately, before she could voice this fear, Alexander cleared his throat. 'I think it would be a good idea for us to learn a little about one another before we launch into the business which brought me here. As you will know from my letter to Lady Elmswood, time is of the essence.'

'I understand that you must marry before your thirtieth birthday or forfeit your inheritance.'

'And it is a very large inheritance, though I'm not particularly interested in it for my own sake. I am aware that sounds disingenuous, but it happens to be the truth.'

She couldn't say what it was that made her believe

him, but she did. 'Why, then, are you interested—no, that cannot be the right word, for you are sacrificing your bachelorhood to inherit, so you must have more at stake than an *interest* in inheriting?'

He smiled faintly. 'Very well, let us say that I think it is my duty to marry. No, since you insist on being precise, let me rephrase that. My conscience tells me that I must marry.'

'Why?'

Alexander did not answer her directly. 'I had no expectations of inheriting. My brother's untimely death, and his lack of foresight in providing an heir, have come as a most unwelcome surprise.'

He spoke lightly, but his eyes spoke of a different, more brittle emotion. 'Your brother had no children, then? But he must have been married to have inherited, since the entail—I'm sorry if this is a painful subject to you, your brother has not even been dead a year, but...'

'My brother and I were not close.' Alexander's mouth thinned in the brief silence which followed this interjection. 'There are—were—eight years between us. We were raised very differently. Walter, as the heir in waiting, was fully aware of the terms of the entail, and married shortly after he came of age. His wife died in childbirth along with their son about five years later. The entail did not require Walter to remarry, but I never doubted he would. As a quintessential Fearnoch male, he would have been keen to maintain the proud patriarchal tradition of passing the title directly from father to son—a tradition which his sudden death has put an end to. Unfortunately, the conditions of the entail remain in force, which means I must now marry if I am to become the Eighth Earl.'

'What happens if you choose not to?'

'My cousin Raymond Sinclair will inherit. Unlike me, he has always had an avaricious eye on the title, and duly took the precaution of arming himself with a bride prior to his own thirtieth birthday. Raymond is an inveterate gambler. It would only be a matter of time before he brought the Fearnoch lands and the people who make their living from them to rack and ruin. Most of the Fearnoch estates are in Lancashire. Aside from the many tenanted farms, I understand that substantial seams of coal have recently been discovered. Mining coal is extremely lucrative, but can also be extremely dangerous. I fear my cousin would have far more regard for profit than safety.'

'Good grief, yes. I have read some truly dreadful stories about men being trapped—and not only men, but young boys. And they use children too, to sort the coal. It is an outrage.'

'Precisely my own views.' Alexander smiled thinly. 'I wish to ensure that any mining is done responsibly. I wish to ensure that the profit from the estates continues to be ploughed back—you'll forgive the pun—into the land. My father and late brother cared little for running the estates. Simply put, both were ardent libertines. It is a trait which all Sinclair men have embraced and propagated over the years, and of which they have all been inordinately proud. Needless to say, it is a proclivity that I do not share. However, the estate manager is, I gather, an excellent man, whose family have run the Fearnoch lands for generations.'

'Like Kate,' Eloise exclaimed. 'That is exactly why she married my uncle—because her father was the estate manager here, and Daniel was never interested, and Kate loves Elmswood Manor and—and so you see, I do understand why it is important to you to do what is right.'

'Thank you. There is one other factor which is pertinent to my decision.' Alexander shifted in his chair, frowning. 'If you will bear with me. It is not my habit to discuss such personal matters. It does not come easy to me, but under the circumstances, I think it vital that you fully understand my motives for wishing to make this unconventional match.'

Her instinct was to reach over, to touch him reassuringly, but she caught herself just in time. 'It can't be easy, to be so painfully honest to a complete stranger. Please, take your time.'

'The matter concerns my mother's settlement which I discovered to be woefully inadequate.'

'Your mother! But she is a dowager countess. Your father was a very rich man. Surely when she married him, your mother's parents would have ensured her jointure reflected her circumstances.'

'I have no idea what the original arrangements were. The were amended in the Sixth Earl's will.'

'The Sixth Earl being your father?'

'Her husband. The amended settlement which my mother was granted on his death would be insulting if it were not frankly punitive.'

'Punitive! What on earth can she possibly have done to deserve such shabby treatment?'

Alexander's fingers dug into the arms of the chair. 'The reasons are less pertinent than the net effect, which is that the terms would force my mother to rely upon the goodwill and generosity of others in order to survive. I will not have her reduced to such penury.'

'But your father died almost three years ago. Surely your brother...'

'My brother provided for her, while he was alive, by installing her in the Dower House on the Lancashire estates. Whether he intended to amend the provision made for her at some point is another question that must remain unanswered for ever. The fact is that he did not, and my personal circumstances do not allow me to supplement the paltry allowance to what I consider an appropriate level.'

'And if your cousin, Raymond Sinclair, inherited? No, I suppose from what you've said that you could not trust him to do right by her.'

'Precisely. You understand now, Miss Brannagh, why I believe it is my duty to marry?'

'I do and I think your reasons are extremely laudable.' Though he had not explained why he was so averse to marriage in the first place. Perhaps his Admiralty career rewarded him insufficiently to maintain a household—but he didn't dress like a man on the breadline. He was the son of an earl, albeit the second son, surely his father would have given him an allowance? Though the same father had made a pauper of his wife. And Alexander had been, in his own words, brought up very differently from his brother, the heir. Eloise knew from her own experience that this could only mean that he was treated very much as second best.

Aware that her thoughts had run away from her, she looked up, discovering to her consternation Alexander watching her carefully. 'I was just wondering why you are considering me as a wife, when...'

'There are women queueing up for the privilege?' He smiled faintly. 'Perhaps because there are not. What

I'm wondering is why you are considering my proposal. To put it bluntly, Miss Brannagh, though we will live separate lives once we have established the marriage in the eyes of the world, we will remain legally married. For the sake of appearances, Fearnoch House in London must be your main residence—and I hope you will treat it as your home. For form's sake it must be my home too, during the time when my work does not detain me abroad. So our paths will cross, albeit infrequently, though Fearnoch House is, I gather, large enough to permit us to live under its roof without encountering each other unless we wish to.'

'You gather? I thought you said it was the family home?'

'And has been for generations, but it has never been *my* home.'

For reasons he did not wish to discuss, judging by his tone. 'But—forgive me, your brother died almost a year ago, and though you were abroad at the time, you've been back in England…'

'Until I marry, Miss Brannagh, I have no rights to anything but the title. Fearnoch House has been closed up since Walter died. The family lawyer has been administering the estate. My mother continues in the Dower House in the country, and I have continued in my own lodgings.'

'I had no idea.'

'Why should you?'

Since Eloise could think of nothing to say to this, she decided, wisely, for once to say nothing.

'I can assure you that once we are married—if we marry,' Alexander continued, 'you will be free to live your life as you choose, but—forgive me, but I think it imperative that we are clear on one delicate matter. Since there can be no question of a divorce or even an annulment, you understand that there can be no prospect of your having children?'

Once again, her cheeks flamed. She had not anticipated their discussions becoming so personal. 'I do understand that, and I assure you it's not an issue,' Eloise said hurriedly. 'I am not—I'm not—that more intimate aspect of marriage does not appeal to me. Furthermore, I have never wanted children.'

'May I know why?'

She didn't want to explain herself, reluctant to recall those miserable years in Ireland. Already, she had the impression that Alexander Sinclair was the type of man who saw a great deal more than he let on, and she didn't want him peering into the dark nooks and crannies of her past. 'If we do not have children—I mean, if you and your wife don't have offspring, then the Fearnoch estates will pass to your cousin, I presume?'

'Yes, though I don't see why...'

'My point is, that's what you're trying to avoid, isn't it—his bringing the estates to rack and ruin. I am not suggesting that you will die prematurely...' *As his brother did!* 'What I mean is, that there's a chance, at some point, that what you're trying to prevent might come to pass if you don't have children of your own.'

'No, there's no chance of that.' Alexander said grimly. 'I haven't made myself clear. As far as the estates are concerned, my intentions are first to protect them by preventing my cousin from inheriting, and then to secure them for the future by ridding myself of them.'

'Ridding yourself?'

'I believe that those who have lived and farmed the

lands for generations are far more entitled to profit from them than I.'

'That is an extremely philanthropic point of view to take.'

'It is a question of what is right, as well as what is in the best interests of those concerned.'

There was that tightness in his expression again that made her feel uncomfortable, as if she had inadvertently opened the door on something extremely painful and very private. *Could* he be thinking that he would, like his brother, die young?

'It should go without saying,' he said drily, 'that your settlement would be safe, as would my mother's.'

'That is not what I was worried about!' She stared at him, aghast. 'I was thinking about you, your brother— if he died of some sort of hereditary disease, it would explain why you do not wish for children. To have such a—a cloud hanging over you…' She broke off, blinking furiously as tears blurred her eyes. Alexander looked quite thunderstruck, and no wonder, the poor man. He looked so healthy. Eloise searched frantically for her handkerchief.

'Miss Brannagh, I am in rude health, I assure you. My brother's demise was largely self-inflicted.'

'Oh. I see.' Though she didn't, quite, but she could not possibly embarrass herself further by asking. 'I don't think I could bear to marry you, only to have you die on me. People would think I was a murderess as well as a gold-digger.'

She had meant it to make light of the situation, but his smile faded immediately. 'I have only just met you, but I am absolutely certain that you are not a gold-digger.'

'Well, no, I'm not, but…'

He caught her hands in his. 'As you can imagine, the life of an Admiralty Victualling Commissioner is fraught, danger lurks behind every inventory. There, I have made you smile! But there is an important point to be made. What I'm proposing is a purely—I believe the term is companionate relationship, though we won't be companions in that sense, for I will be away much of the time, as I said.'

'I do understand that, Alexander. I'm not sure exactly…'

'I won't marry you, if you—forgive me if this sounds presumptuous, but you must not become overly fond of me.'

She was mistaken, was reading too much into what he said, he was simply being scrupulously honest, and she appreciated that. Yet there was such a bleakness in his eyes, his expression so earnest, and his grip on her fingers so tight. Then it dawned on her, and she felt extremely foolish. Even she, who considered herself utterly immune to such things, had found herself momentarily attracted to the man and he had sensed it. 'I won't fall in love with you, if that's what you're worried about. I assure you, that sort of thing is anathema to me, so you need have no fears, I will respect both our marriage vows and the terms under which we must live them.'

He studied her for a long moment. She held her breath, realising as she did so, that if he did not believe her, he would leave, and she wanted him to stay. Very much. When he nodded, her audible sigh of relief made her want to cringe. 'Inscrutability is not one of my talents,' she said.

To her surprise, he smiled. 'I would rather say that you lack guile, and I find it charming.'

'You mean I'm naïve.'

'I always say what I mean, Miss Brannagh. You are a surprise. A very pleasant one.'

He lifted her hand to his lips, brushing a kiss to her fingertips before getting to his feet. Wholly taken aback, flustered as much by the unexpected leaping of her pulses as by the odd compliment, Eloise glanced at the clock and exclaimed in dismay, 'I haven't even offered you a cup of tea. Would you like one? Please don't say that you would, simply because you feel obliged to. If you think that perhaps we've said all there is to say and you wish to leave I won't be—this would be a good time to—because there's no point in continuing if...'

'Take a breath, Miss Brannagh, I beg of you.'

He was, to her relief, still smiling. She did as he bid her. 'What I'm trying to say is, if you have formed an unfavourable impression of me, following this admittedly awkward conversation, then it would be best if you said so now.'

Alexander's smile broadened. He really did have a very, very attractive smile. 'I'm not thinking any such thing.'

'I was hoping not, as you have no doubt already surmised.' She smiled back at him. 'It comes of living in a household of four women, this habit of mine of speaking my thoughts without putting them into order. And also, because Kate and my sisters know me so well, of course. They always know if I'm trying to keep something from them. As I do when they try to do the same. In fact, I think I'm worse. I should warn you that I'm the sort of person who—who sees too much, if you know what I mean? I'm painfully observant. I wish I wasn't. It makes me uncomfortable sometimes—I don't mean I spy on my sisters, but I notice things they would rather I did not.'

'Is that a warning, Miss Brannagh?'

'Has it put you on your guard?'

He laughed. 'Actually quite the opposite. I would very much like to continue our conversation, but I think we'd both benefit from some refreshment first, don't you?'

'Yes.' Eloise got to her feet. 'If you'll excuse me,' she said, 'I'll go and organise it.'

Chapter Three

In the kitchen Eloise was immediately waylaid by Phoebe and Estelle, who were sitting at the huge scrubbed table guarding the tea tray which was set out in readiness, waiting to pounce on her the moment she appeared.

'Is he as handsome close up as he looks from a distance?'

'He was immaculately turned out. He does not have the look of a man who is a stranger to soap.'

'You've been closeted away with him for an age. Why has it taken you so long to order tea? Look, Phoebe, she's blushing.'

'Do you *like* him, Eloise?'

'Do you think he likes you?'

She refused to answer a single question while setting Phoebe's freshly baked biscuits out on a plate, and there were a great deal more thrown at her while she waited on the water boiling. 'I'll tell you all about it later, I promise,' Eloise said, picking up the tray.

'Chapter and verse!' the twins chorused in unison.

Returning to the drawing room, Eloise was even more flustered than when she had left fifteen minutes earlier. The fact that Alexander, when he crossed the room to take the tray from her, looked even more handsome on second viewing, did nothing to improve her fractured composure. It was a huge relief, she told herself, nothing more. It wasn't that she wanted an attractive husband, but facing this man over the breakfast table would be no hardship.

'Were you thinking that I had fled the country in embarrassment?' Irked at the breathless note in her voice, Eloise sat down beside him and began to set out the cups. 'Please try a biscuit. Phoebe made them. They are not sweet, but spiced.'

'I take it, then, that you reassured your sisters, while making tea, that I am neither odiferous nor do I have bad breath. They would have seen for themselves that I don't stoop or wear spectacles. I spotted them peering out of the window at me when I arrived.'

Eloise stopped in the act of spooning tea from the walnut caddy. 'How embarrassing. I am so sorry.'

'There's no need to apologise. It's perfectly understandable that they would be protective of their big sister and want to give me the once over.' Alexander helped himself to another biscuit. 'Am I to assume, then, that they endorse your decision to meet with me today?'

'Oh, yes, very much so.' Would he think them all money-grasping harpies? 'Not that I made the decision lightly, you understand. In fact, we discussed it a great deal.' Was that worse? 'What you are proposing—well, it would be to our mutual advantage, wouldn't it? A—a quid pro quo.' She smiled, but it felt more like a wince. 'And it's not an unfamiliar concept to me, of course. Kate—Lady Elmswood—and my uncle have already made a success of a similar accommodation.'

'Yes. Daniel was quite frank with me on the advantages of his own arrangement.'

'You are old friends, I understand.'

Alexander smiled blandly. 'We bump into each other occasionally. Tell me a little more about yourself. I know next to nothing, save what Daniel told me.'

'That I am a mother hen with an overdeveloped sense of duty!'

'Was his assessment correct?'

'No! At least—that makes me sound—I suppose I have been—Kate thinks that my sisters will benefit from being out from under my wings, and I think she might be right. I keep forgetting that they are twenty years old, young women and not children.'

'There are four years between you, I believe?'

'Yes. It doesn't sound a lot, but when we were little it made a big difference.' Eloise set her teacup aside. 'They have been my responsibility since—I was going to say since they were born, but even Mama was not quite so careless as to leave a pair of babes in my charge. We had a nurse, but later, from the schoolroom I suppose, when the first of our governesses left, I have taken care of my sisters.'

'You make it sound as if there was a procession of governesses.'

Eloise rolled her eyes. 'We lived in the wilds of Ireland. Not many genteel ladies could endure the life, and when they left, as they invariably did, it was sometimes a while before Mama noticed. She spent a great deal of time with Papa in Dublin, when the—the dibs were in tune—have I that right?'

Alexander frowned. 'Your father was a gambler?'

'Well, yes, though not in the sense that your cousin

is. He only placed wagers on his own runners—or so he claimed. My mother did not approve of his obsession with the track. He bred racehorses. Papa said that, as an Irishman, the turf was in his blood. Sadly, his obsession outstripped both his luck and his judgement, and he lost a great deal more than he won. When he lost, and had to retrench, then he and Mama would rusticate with us girls.' Suddenly realising that she had been cajoled into discussing the very subject that she wished to avoid, Eloise picked up the teapot. 'Would you care for another cup?'

Alexander shook his head. She was horribly conscious of his eyes on her as she poured herself one, of the spark of anger in her voice which always betrayed her when she talked of those days. 'Your parents,' he said, 'you did not look forward to their visits?'

'It was rather that they did not care for them. Or for us.' Eloise sighed. He was not going to give up, she realised. 'Until Diarmuid, my brother, was born, I would have said that my parents were the sort who were indifferent to their children. They didn't exactly dislike us, don't get me wrong, but aside from Papa and his thoroughbreds, all they really cared about was each other. But then Diarmuid came along. He is—he was five years younger than Phoebe and Estelle and from the moment he was born, Mama and Papa were quite besotted with him. I have never understood why they did not care for my sisters in the same way, it's not as if they were troublesome or demanding children.'

'Sometimes,' Alexander said, 'it is simply that there is room in a parent's heart for only one child.'

His tone was even, his expression neutral, but Eloise was certain he must be thinking of *his* brother who died and she, who had long ago decided she would not be hurt by her parents' blatant favouritism, recognised a similar resolve in Alexander. It made her warm to him. Her instinct was to commiserate, but that would be to recognise a scar that he would not acknowledge existed.

'Well,' Eloise said, 'in our family that child was Diarmuid. The golden child, quite literally—he had a mass of sunny golden curls. Such an endearing little boy he was too when he was very little, with the kind of smile that no one could resist. We all adored him. I often wonder, if he had not been such a favourite, whether he would have been a more endearing little boy, but he was so very spoilt, the sulks and the tantrums on the rare occasions he didn't get things his own way were inevitable, I suppose. Mama and Papa were forever telling him how wonderful he was, it's not surprising that he believed them. Perhaps he'd have grown out of it.'

'You don't believe that, do you?'

'Not really. It's a dreadful thing to say, but though I loved him because he was my brother, I liked him less and less with every year. He was moulded too much in the image of Mama and Papa. Smothered with love, and quite ruined by it, while we girls were utterly neglected and all the better for it. I am sure there is a happy medium to be found, but I have never been tempted to discover it for myself.'

'That is something else we have in common, then.'

Eloise gave herself a shake. 'I'm sorry, I didn't mean the conversation to take such a melancholy turn.'

'Then let us change it.' Alexander took another biscuit. 'These are very good. My compliments to Phoebe.'

'She will be pleased, for they are made to a receipt of her own invention. She is a very creative cook. When she first invaded the kitchens—she can have been no more than five or six—her concoctions were much less appetising. I remember one cake in particular, which she told us had a very secret ingredient. It kept us guessing for a very long time before she finally revealed it to be new-mown grass.'

'What about Estelle, does she also have a particular talent?'

'She is musical. Not in the way people describe most young ladies—she doesn't simply strum the pianoforte or the harp—she can pick up any instrument and get a tune from it. And she writes her own music too, and songs. She is really very talented.' A talent which her parents had been utterly indifferent to. 'She wrote a piece to welcome Mama and Papa home once. My sisters would so look forward to Mama and Papa coming home. They would forget what it had been like on previous occasions and imagine—' Eloise broke off, swallowing the lump in her throat. 'Needless to say, they were suitably unimpressed. I'm sorry—I shouldn't have mentioned it—but it used to make me so angry, you see. It wouldn't have taken much to make the twins happy, but it was still too much for them to make an effort.'

'So you made it instead, is that it?'

There was sympathy in his eyes, but she was embarrassed at having betrayed so much. She had tried so hard to compensate, and to shield her sisters too, from her parents' callousness, her mother's infidelities, her father's cuckolded fury. They never talked of those days now, it was too painful for all of them, but she knew that the twins were as scarred as she by their experiences. 'You're thinking that Daniel was right when he called me a mother hen.'

'I'm thinking that your sisters are very lucky to have you.'

'And they would agree with you. Most of the time.' She smiled, making light of the compliment, but she was touched all the same by it. 'I've told you a great deal about me, it's only fair that you reciprocate.'

'Oh, you already know everything there is to know about me. I'm the younger son who bucks family tradition and does something boring at the Admiralty.'

'What, precisely, is it you do that is so boring?'

'Mainly, I count weevils and anchors.'

'I beg your pardon?'

'Well, technically I don't count the weevils, I count the ship's biscuit that they consume.'

'What on earth is ship's biscuit?'

'It is also known as hard tack—a form of bread, which does not go stale though it is inclined to attract weevils. Weevils,' Alexander said, waving his hand dismissively, 'are a way of life in the navy, no sailor worth his salt minds them. It was the diarist, Samuel Pepys, who regularised victualling, as we call it,' he said, seeming to warm to his subject. 'Pepys came up with the table of rations which we quartermasters use today to calculate the supply required for each of our ships. One pound of ship's biscuit per man per day is what we calculate—that is the weight before the weevils have taken their share, of course. And a gallon of beer. So now you know all about me.'

'I know more about the role of a Victualling Commissioner, at any rate,' Eloise said, biting back a smile.

'There is no one else at the Admiralty who understands the need as well as I do, to ensure that hard tack is made to the same recipe, no matter which part of the world the raw ingredients are sourced in.'

'You mean the correct ratio of weevils to biscuit?'

'I mean the correct ratio of flour to water,' Alexander said reprovingly.

A bubble of laughter finally escaped her. 'I am tempted, very tempted, to ask you for the receipt, but I am fairly certain that if you don't know it you would surely make it up.'

'I do know it, in actual fact. I make it my business to know every aspect of my business.'

'And such a fascinating business it is too.'

'I think so, at any rate. I don't find it boring at all,' Alexander replied. 'Of course my duties will be curtailed for a period while I establish my marriage. I am required to travel abroad a great deal, but I could not, if the veracity of my marriage is to be maintained, abandon my wife within a few weeks of making my vows, and so will work from the Admiralty building in London for the foreseeable future.'

She could not make him out at all, for while she was fairly certain he had been teasing her at first, now he seemed to be quite sincere. 'You would not contemplate resigning, now that you are the Earl of Fearnoch, and all that entails?'

'No. My life is with the Admiralty. I am willing, for very good reasons, to find a compromise for a few months, but give it up—absolutely not.'

His primary very good reason being to make provision for his mother, and his second to *rid himself* of most of the wealth he was marrying to inherit. Not for Alexander, a life of privilege and leisure. He was a man with a strong sense of duty, to his mother and to his country, and a man determined to do both on his own terms. Her admiration for him climbed several notches.

'Miss Brannagh...'

'Eloise.'

'Eloise. From Heloise?'

'I believe my mother rather fancied herself as *La Nouvelle Héloïse.* A free spirit, though I think she radically reinterpreted Monsieur Rousseau's creation to suit her own notion of freedom which meant, by and large, the freedom to do exactly as she pleased and beggar the consequences. And now you will think me disloyal for being so disrespectful towards my own mother, especially since she is deceased. What is it they say, never talk ill of the dead?'

'From what you've told me, Miss Brannagh—Eloise—it is more than justified.'

'Well, it is, frankly, but I cannot help thinking—forgive me, Alexander, but I can't help but contrast my finding fault with my mother and your truly honourable behaviour towards your own.'

'I am merely providing the settlement I believe her entitled to. Do not make a saint of me, I beg you.'

'I imagine your mother must think you a bit of a saint, since you are marrying in order to provide for her. In fact, I've been wondering why she hasn't put forward any candidates for the post? The position, I mean. Of your wife. Or perhaps she has?'

'You are the only current candidate. You have a very inflated idea of my attractions as a husband. First you line up queues of women for me, and now you have me rather arrogantly going through some sort of process of elimination.'

'If you eliminate me, what will you do?'

'I have no idea what I will do if you—if *we* decide *we* don't suit. I will certainly not be asking my mother to, as you most eloquently phrased it, put someone forward for the post.' He was silent for a moment, clearly struggling with his thoughts. 'She would not help me, even if I asked her. She does not believe that the reasons I outlined to you are sufficiently compelling. In short, she disapproves of marriages of convenience, even if mutually advantageous. She was quite vehement on the subject.'

'Despite the fact that it means she will likely starve?'

'It would not come to that.'

'But aside from that, Alexander, and even aside from all the tenants who are now yours but who must have once been hers, are you seriously saying your mother wishes you to hand over the Fearnoch fortune to your cousin?'

Once again, he was silent, painfully silent, his expression taut. Eloise touched his hand tentatively. 'Alexander?'

He blinked, shook his head. 'I can only conclude that my mother, having relied first upon her husband and then my brother to support her, underestimates the impact on her standard of living unless I intervene. Nor, I must assume, can she have any idea of the havoc my cousin would wreak on the estates.'

'But even if she is somewhat deluded,' Eloise said doubtfully, 'surely she would prefer you to inherit rather than your cousin? Is it your plans to rid yourself of the estates, perhaps, that she objects to?'

'I told her nothing of my plans, save that I intended to marry, and by doing so, to secure her future. The purpose of my visit was not to explain myself, but simply to reassure her. I failed. In fact, she became overwrought. Since my mind was set, I saw no point in attempting to reason with her.'

Eloise's heart sank. It was clear to her that Alexander's mother didn't wish her son to marry a gold-digger, and it should be equally clear to him. 'Your mother is to be admired,' she said carefully, 'for putting your interests before her own. Knowing that your preference would be to remain unmarried...'

'She can know no such thing. My mother and I are, to all intents and purposes, strangers to each other.'

'Strangers! What on earth do you mean by that?'

'Like your own mother, mine had interest only in one child. That child was not me. I was packed off to school at an early age, and spent most of my holidays in the country while my parents remained in London with Walter. I joined the Admiralty at sixteen and have spent the majority of my time since then abroad. Though we have met on occasion since—at her husband's funeral, and most recently, when I returned to England after Walter died— they have been only very occasional meetings, and my mother seems perfectly content for that state of affairs to remain unchanged.'

'You are implying that she abandoned you. But why? And now, when she has lost her husband and her only other son, why—oh, Alexander, I'm so sorry, this must be incredibly painful for you.'

'I have long become accustomed to her indifference. I would have thought, after what you told me of your own upbringing, that you would understand that.'

Eloise was nonplussed. There was a world of difference between uninterest and outright rejection, but to say so would be cruel. Alexander might well believe himself reconciled to it, but the way he spoke, the way he held himself, told quite another story. She would not rub salt into the wound. 'You're right,' she said, deciding to risk covering his hand with hers, 'that is one thing we have in common. Your determination to provide for her, despite—it is an extremely honourable and admirable thing to do. Although it strikes me that she might be, as a consequence, disinclined to like your wife,' she added awkwardly.

'My marriage will allow me to right a wrong. I am not interested in my mother's gratitude nor am I interested in her opinion of the woman I choose to marry. As I said, we have never been close, and I see no reason for my marriage to alter that state of affairs. Now if you don't mind, I think we have more important matters to discuss than my mother.'

Alexander was furious with himself. Though he had striven to keep his tone neutral, it was clear, from the sympathy in her voice, in the way Eloise had touched his hand, that his feelings had betrayed him.

'Will you excuse me just a moment?' He strode over to the window, staring out sightlessly at the view of the ordered drive, the neatly clipped yew hedge which bordered it. When Robertson, the lawyer, had informed him in that precise way of his that the Seventh Earl had chosen to abide by the Sixth Earl's terms with regard to the Dowager Lady Fearnoch, Alexander had been first confused, then outraged on his mother's behalf. When he called on her, he'd expected to find her deep in mourning, perhaps bereft with grief, for her beloved eldest son had been dead only five months. Instead she had seemed, as she always seemed, aloof, cold, firmly in control of herself. Only when he informed her of his plans had she become animated, begging him not to marry for her sake, or for any other reason than love. Love! As if he would ever take such a risk. There was no place for love in his life, save the one which had ruled him since he was sixteen, and that was for his country.

He leaned his head on the cool of the window pane, breathing deeply to try to calm himself. His mother didn't want his help. She didn't want anything from him. As if he needed any more evidence of that! Her reaction was irrelevant. She had been wronged. It was up to him to make it right.

Alexander slanted a glance at Eloise, head lowered, intent on studying her clasped hands in order to grant him the semblance of privacy, and his sense of purpose strengthened. It was vital that they understood each other from the very start, if this marriage was to have any chance of succeeding.

As he resumed his seat opposite her, she seemed to brace herself. 'If you're having second thoughts, I'd rather you said so now.'

'I am not,' Alexander said firmly. 'I was thinking the very opposite. I'm very serious about this, but I need to understand if you feel the same.'

'I wouldn't be here if I were not entirely serious.'

He steepled his hands, choosing his words with care. 'When people marry in the traditional manner, it is with the expectation that affection, passion, love, if you wish, will form a bond between them, and that bond will in time be augmented by children. If we marry, we will have neither of those things. And we would be required to stay together, Eloise, albeit in name only, for the rest of our lives. We cannot afford to have regrets, which means we must enter into this agreement with a clear understanding of what we are getting into.'

'And also what we are not getting into.'

'You're quite right,' he agreed with a small smile. 'It is very difficult to be honest with someone who was until this morning a complete stranger, but it is far better that we make the effort now, before it is too late. I have been frank with you, and, as you have doubtless realised, I am not accustomed to confiding my thoughts to anyone. You know why I wish to be married, but I'm not sure I understand your reasons sufficiently. You tell me that you have never wanted children—and now I've heard a little of your upbringing, I can understand why, but what is it you *do* want? I need to know, Eloise, that you're not marrying purely for your sisters' sake.'

'And as I told my sisters, I have no desire to be a sacrificial lamb of a wife.'

'I am very relieved to hear that. So tell me, then, what kind of a wife do you wish to be?'

'Well, firstly, what you offer, a marriage which does not entail any—any wifely duties, is the only marriage I would consider. I've said enough, I hope, regarding my parents' marriage to give you an idea of its nature. Passionate and poisonous in equal measure, an endless round of fighting and making up that shattered our peace, and put all of us girls constantly on edge. If that is love, I want nothing whatsoever to do with it.'

'Why marry at all, if that is the case?'

She looked up at that. 'I could remain single, though don't forget, Alexander, I have the evidence before my eyes every day of how successful a marriage of convenience can be. It would be a lie if I told you I haven't thought of my sisters, because I've spent most of my life putting them first, and the settlement you are offering is very generous, far too much for my requirements. I would share it with them, and I would leave it entirely up to Phoebe and Estelle to decide what use they put the money to. There is nothing worse, I imagine, than to be given a sum of money and then told how to spend it. I am determined not to do that.'

'Even if Estelle spends it on establishing an orchestra and Phoebe on—oh, I don't know, setting herself up in a restaurant.'

Eloise chuckled. 'Neither of those is outwith the bounds of possibility.' She resumed her study of her hands. 'My next reason for considering your proposal is to take the burden of responsibility for the three of us from Uncle Daniel. He has—albeit through Kate—looked after us for five years, and I rather think he spent a significant amount of money paying off Papa's debts too. We owe him a great deal—and when I say him, I mean Kate too, naturally.'

'That is very admirable.'

'Anyone in my position would feel the same, but honestly, Alexander, it was neither of those reasons which persuaded me to meet with you today.' She smiled fleetingly at him. 'My main reason is quite simple. Freedom for myself and for my sisters too. By marrying you, I'd earn my independence, and I'd be able to offer the same independence to my sisters, which is something I could never do were I to find an occupation—as a female, not only are there very few respectable careers, none of them would pay me any more than a pittance. My reward for being your wife will be the freedom to do whatever I want without having to consult anyone else or to be beholden to anyone else—provided I maintain the façade of being Lady Fearnoch, of course. You can't imagine what that would mean to me.'

In fact, he could imagine it very easily. It was one of the most rewarding aspects of his work, to act on his own initiative, to solve the problems he was given in whatever way he saw fit. Only once had he compromised that freedom. The price had been almost unbearable. Never again. 'So,' he said, firmly closing his mind to the memory, 'how will you use that freedom?'

Eloise shrugged, smiling. 'I have absolutely no idea, and that in itself is so exciting I could—I could hug myself.'

Which gave him the most absurd desire to hug her instead. It was because she might just be the perfect solution to his problem, Alexander told himself. Daniel had done him a very great favour in making this introduction. He checked his watch, then checked the clock on the mantel in astonishment. 'I can't believe how long we've been sitting here.'

'Too long? Must you get back to London?'

'Not a bit of it. I noticed a passable inn in the village where I can spend the night, if necessary.' He got to his feet. 'The only thing I'm worried about is whether it will rain, because I'm hoping that we can continue our discussions in the fresh air. That is, if you think there is merit in continuing our discussion?'

Eloise allowed him to help her up. 'I think we have established that we both see merit in it.' She smiled. 'A good deal of merit.'

The sky, which had been overcast when Alexander arrived at Elmswood Manor, had cleared, and now the sun was shining brightly and with some warmth.

'Lovely,' Eloise said, standing on the top step, tilting back her head and closing her eyes.

Lovely was the very word Alexander, looking at her, would have chosen too.

'Isn't it a beautiful day?' She smiled at him. 'I don't think I'll bother fetching a pelisse. Shall we?'

She tripped down the stairs on to the drive. Her gown fluttered in the light breeze, giving him a tantalising outline of long legs, a shapely bottom. She was not one of those willowy creatures who survived on air and water, and who were always, not surprisingly, having fainting fits. Eloise was more earthy, more real, the kind of woman who would, if she must faint, do so into a convenient chair rather than hope that some passing beau would catch her.

She was gazing up at the house, frowning, as he joined her, and he looked up automatically to see what had piqued her interest, catching a glimpse of two female faces at a window. 'Your sisters resuming their spying mission, I presume.'

'I'm afraid so.'

Alexander swept into an elaborate courtly bow, making Eloise giggle. One of the watching sisters had the presence of mind to drop a curtsy before dragging the other out of sight. He turned away. 'Which direction shall we take?'

'This way. There is a walled garden quite out of sight of the house.'

He followed her, feeling slightly dazed, as if he had unexpectedly won a prize, and he wasn't at all sure that he deserved it. Eloise's hair was the colour of polished bronze in the daylight. Her eyes were hazel, wide-spaced under winged brows. She had a sprinkling of freckles across her nose. It made her tawny beauty less flawless and therefore more interesting. There was a determined tilt to her chin that didn't surprise him, now he knew her a little better, but her lips, full, sensuous, quite belied her claim to a cold nature. In fact, he knew, for he had witnessed it, that she was compassionate, and he had overwhelming evidence of her love for her sisters. It was not love which repelled her, but passion, and what little she'd told him of her parents' marriage made her feelings entirely understandable. It should be a crime, the damage parents could do to their children.

Eloise did not trip along taking tiny steps, nor did she try to glide, but walked with a easy gait that he had to make only a small adjustment to match. Though the matter was far from settled, for the first time since he had made the decision to take a wife, Alexander didn't feel utterly dejected. In fact, glancing at the surprising woman walking beside him, he felt—no, not elated, that was absurd, but he really couldn't quite believe his luck.

The walled garden had been a crumbling ruin when Eloise and her sisters first arrived at Elmswood Manor, she informed him as they wandered around the perimeter. 'It was my favourite place,' she said, 'I thought of it as my private domain, because back then the door was stuck fast and you could only get in by climbing over the wall.'

'You must have been very adept at climbing. It's at least fifteen feet.'

'I told you, we grew up in the wilds of rural Ireland. There wasn't much to do save climb hills and trees if you are not the sewing samplers sort, which I am not. I've always thought samplers such a waste of stitches which would be far better served making clothes.'

'You are a needlewoman as well as a scaler of heights! Do you include gardening in your list of impressive attributes?'

'Oh, no, that is Kate's domain. This is her project, though all three of us helped her with the research—poring through the archives in the attics, to see what we could uncover regarding the history of the place. When Estelle found a map...'

He listened with half an ear as they completed their circuit of the garden. Her love for her sisters was genuine and profound, her affection for Lady Elmswood evident too. 'Are you sure leaving here won't be too much of a wrench?' he asked, steering her towards a convenient bench.

'It will be odd, but it will be good for us all in the long run. We can't be together for ever, huddled up like hothouse flowers.' She sat down, staring distractedly out at the gardens, biting her lip. 'Alexander, I have no wish to embarrass either of us, but there is a topic of a delicate nature that I feel I must raise.'

He waited, for it was obvious from her expression that she was girding her loins.

'I've told you that I am not—I told you that I would not consider a real marriage because that sort of—that aspect of marriage doesn't—isn't for me.' Her cheeks were bright red, but she held his gaze steadfastly until he nodded. 'But that doesn't mean that you cannot—you might wish to find some comfort in someone else's arms. I would not—' She broke off, completely flustered. 'Goodness, this is mortifying. Please, I beg you, forget what I said. Let us change the subject.'

He happily would, but unfortunately she was in the

right of it. 'It's better we discuss it now, don't you think, no matter how awkward it is?'

'Awkward is rather an understatement.'

'Then let me see if I can make it easier for you, now that you've been brave enough to bring it up.' Though how to do so, Alexander puzzled. He ought to have anticipated this, but he hadn't, principally because it was a facet of his life that had been a closed book for almost precisely two years. He couldn't tell Eloise the truth, but he owed her a version of it.

'There have been women in my life,' he said. 'though my affaires have always been extremely short-lived. I am by nature a loner, and have never wished for any more intimate arrangement.'

And, even if he had, it would have been contrary to every rule in the book. He'd known that, and yet to his eternal regret he'd allowed it to happen anyway, telling himself it didn't matter because he didn't care enough, succumbing to temptation because he was heartily sick of being alone in a foreign land. He'd taken comfort in her admittedly beguiling company. If only he had put an end to it sooner. Or better still, before it started. The entire episode had been a mistake. The biggest mistake he'd ever made. He'd learned the hard way that the rules he'd so cavalierly broken were there for good reason. The guilt he had carried with him ever since made his chest tighten. He would never risk a repeat. Never!

Perhaps now was not the time for subtlety, after all. 'Love,' Alexander said bluntly. 'That is what I mean. I am not interested in love, I have never been in love, and have no ambition whatsoever to change that. Love is anathema to me.'

Eloise blinked at his fierce tone. 'Well, you are preaching to the converted on that subject.'

'As to the idea of my finding comfort in another's arms—all I can say is that at the moment, I have absolutely no interest or intention to do so.' Which was the truth, and not one he could imagine changing. Was it a life sentence? At this point, Alexander decided the question irrelevant. 'Does that answer your question?'

'Yes,' Eloise said, though she looked unconvinced. 'What is it?'

'The thing is, I can't help but wonder what your family and friends will think of your sudden and dramatic conversion to conjugal bliss, given that you so adamantly do not wish to be married. I expect that this cousin of yours, who stands to inherit all, will be counting the days now, until he lays his hands on a fortune.'

'According to my lawyer, Raymond has been counting the days since Walter died, and for some months now has been borrowing heavily against his anticipated windfall. With only a few weeks to go until my birthday, he will think he is home and dry. He will get a very nasty surprise when he reads the notice of my nuptials.'

'Will he have grounds to challenge your inheritance if he can prove that the marriage is one of convenience?'

'Hardly, considering that half if not more of every marriage which has property at stake is arranged for the convenience of the families concerned. But I've been thinking, Eloise, about what you said.'

'I've said a lot. One might argue that I've said too much. Which of my many utterances in particular has struck you?'

'I should warn you, I have one of those minds which

registers every word. Don't say anything to me you'd rather I forgot.'

She laughed, mock horrified. 'Now you tell me! Good grief, I shall have to wear one of those contraptions like a muzzle that they used to punish women who talked too much. What was it called?'

'A scold's bridle?'

'That's it.'

He burst out laughing. 'What on earth will you say next! I am going to be hanging on your every word, not silencing you, if we are to persuade the world that we have fallen madly in love.'

'I beg your pardon?'

'I think it would be best all round, if we had a—what do they call it?—a whirlwind romance.'

'To have met and married in a matter of weeks is not so much a whirlwind as a tornado.'

Alexander grinned. 'We'll need to concoct a suitably credible story.'

'We'll need more than a story. Are you saying that we will have to pretend to have fallen in love?'

'How difficult can it be, people do it all the time.'

'You never have. I most certainly have not. Why would we do such a thing? You said that marriages of convenience…'

'Are common, and they are, and I meant it when I said that my cousin would have no grounds to challenge our union, but I'd far rather he did not waste my time or my lawyer's time by trying.'

'And if he believed it a love match, you think he wouldn't?'

'I can't be sure, but if everyone else believed us too—do you see?'

'Yes, but…'

'And then there was your remark about the world accusing you of being a gold-digger. I know it couldn't be further from the truth, but—I'm sorry…'

'I'm a nonentity from the sticks with no dowry,' Eloise said wryly. 'Of course it's what they will think.'

'So we must persuade them instead that we are genuinely in love.'

'In love! I am not sure I would know where to begin. How does one stare in a besotted manner, for example?'

He studied her, smiling uncertainly at him, and found himself, wholly unexpectedly and entirely inappropriately, wanting to kiss her. Properly kiss her. Which would be a catastrophic mistake. Because he also wanted, very much wanted, Miss Eloise Brannagh to become his convenient wife.

'I think,' Alexander said, 'that we can discount any besottedness.' He took her hand, lifting it to his lips. 'Small demonstrations of affection will suffice.' He kissed her fingertips. 'There will be shared glances, times when our eyes meet, when it will be obvious to everyone that we are counting the seconds until we are alone.'

'I am not sure…'

He turned her hand over, kissing her palm, felt the sharp intake of her breath, the responding kick of excitement in his gut, and met her eyes. Her lips parted. Dear God, but he wanted to kiss her.

'There will be other glances.' He leaned closer, his voice low. 'Glances that speak of pleasure recently shared, rather than pleasure hotly anticipated.'

'I don't know anything about such things.'

'You don't have to. It will be an act. You have an

imagination, don't you?' He ran his fingers up her arm to rest on the warm skin at the nape of her neck. 'Pretend, when you look at me, that we have been making love.'

'But I don't know how that would—what should I be feeling?'

'Happy. Think of something that makes you happy.'

'When a gown I've made turns out to be exactly as I'd imagined it?'

He bit back a laugh. 'Think of something a little more—how did it feel when you climbed to the top of a tree as a girl?'

'Exciting. Dizzying. A little bit frightening. I always wondered what it would be like to let go, as if I might fly.'

'Imagine you are feeling that now.'

Eloise gazed at him wide-eyed. He could feel her breath on his face, see the quick rise and fall of her breasts beneath the neckline of her gown. She reached tentatively for him, resting her hand on his shoulder. 'In the mornings, in the summer, when the sun is only just coming up, I like to walk on the grass, barefoot,' she whispered. 'It's cool, and damp, but in the most delicious way that makes you want to curl your toes into the grass. Is that what you mean?'

'It is perfect.' So perfect that he could picture the bliss on her face, that he wished, absurdly, he was the grass under her feet.

'Alexander, I've never even been kissed.'

He could have groaned aloud at the temptation. Instead, he forced himself to sit back, to lift her hand to his lips once more, to press the lightest of kisses to her wrist. And then to let her go. 'There will be no need for real kissing. Absolutely no lovemaking. What we have discussed will be the extent of our performance. Do you think we can manage that?'

'Do *you* think we can?'

'Yes, I do.' Alexander shifted uncomfortably on the wooden bench.

'Would you still think so if I had been as you imagined, fiercer, older and with spectacles?'

Would he? The chivalrous answer would be no. But hadn't they agreed to be honest? 'Luckily, I tried to avoid imagining you at all.'

'For fear you wouldn't be able to abide me? It's fine, you can admit it,' Eloise said with a rueful smile, 'for I confess, that I was—I was steeling myself for the worst.'

'And would you be here now, if I had lived down to your expectations?'

'Would the vast sum I will earn compensate for a stoop or spectacles or bad breath?' Eloise grimaced. 'The truth is, when I saw you I was vastly relieved, but—well, we are being brutally honest, aren't we? Then I will tell you that you could have been an Adonis, but if I had taken you in dislike, and felt I could not overcome my reservations, then I wouldn't be sitting here with you.' She smiled shyly. 'The fact that you do resemble a Greek god—a fact that I am sure cannot come as a surprise to you—well, the female population at least will not find it too difficult to believe that I fell in love with your face and not your fortune. Not that I mean to imply that all females are so shallow as to fall in love only with handsome men, but...'

'No, but I fear that the majority of men *are* indeed that shallow,' Alexander interrupted wryly. 'My cousin will find it much harder to question the validity of our marriage when he sets eyes on you.'

'When you meet Phoebe and Estelle, you will realise why I am known as the clever sister.'

'Clever *and* beautiful. I am fortunate indeed,' Alexander said, thinking, as she blushed charmingly, that he was in fact beyond fortunate.

'Clever enough to recognise that you have not answered my original question.'

'I think we are all shallow creatures as far as first impressions go. I would like to think that I'd have overcome any reservations by getting to know you. I am certain that, having come to know you a little, I'd want to know more, and I can also say, as you did, that if I'd taken you in dislike, I would have put an end to the matter. But I am relieved—I can say now, hugely relieved—to discover that while your exterior is extremely attractive, it is what lies beneath that makes me think we will suit.' He cast a worried look up at the sky. 'We should get back inside, it looks like it's threatening to rain.'

Eloise stood up. 'Do you realise we've been talking all this while as if the decision has already been made?'

Alexander considered this. He felt odd. Not afraid, but it was that feeling he often had, at the culmination of a mission, when everything was finally coming together but there was still the danger that it could all go wrong, the thrill of the unknown. He felt as Eloise had described, perched at the top of a tree. 'Have I been presumptive?' he asked.

'Do you really think our natures are complementary?'

'Yes,' he replied, surprising himself with his certainty. 'I think—I really do think that we will suit very well. And you?'

Eloise bit her lip, frowning. Her smile dawned slowly.

'Yes,' she said. 'I think—I think if opposites attract, then we are an excellent match.'

He took her hands in his. 'Miss Brannagh, will you do me the honour of marrying me?'

'Lord Fearnoch, I do believe I will.'

And then she smiled up at him. And Alexander gave in to the temptation to kiss her. Delightfully, and far too briefly, on the lips.

Chapter Four

Six weeks later

The journey from Elmswood Manor to London was made by means of a carriage which Alexander had sent for her. Eloise had been too sick with nerves to notice much, conscious only that each passing mile drew her nearer to the beginning of her new life. She knew she was approaching the metropolis because the roads became crowded, the post houses noisier, the buildings first crammed closer together, then growing ever taller. The well-sprung carriage jolted over cobbled streets. Iron palings, imposing mansions passed in a blur. She could hear street criers, see people jostling for position on the pavements, but little of the colourful city landscape registered. Overwhelmed, she abandoned her futile attempt to work out where she was and where she was headed, and sank back on the seat, trying to regain some element of composure before she arrived at the church.

She had made her own wedding gown of white satin with an overdress of white sarcenet. A broad crimson silk sash was tied at the waist. Redheads should on no account ever wear red, Mama always used to insist. She had never allowed any of her daughters to do so, one of the very few instances of her involving herself with their upbringing, so naturally it was one of Eloise's favourite colours. She had trimmed the neckline and the sleeves with the same crimson silk, and had worked a frieze of crimson flowers along the hem with her tiny, perfect stitches. There was a short velvet pelisse to match. Phoebe had trimmed her poke bonnet with complicated knots of crimson satin ribbon. Estelle had fashioned her a matching reticule. Kate had generously given her the locket on a gold chain, her only piece of jewellery.

How many hours was it since she had bid them all goodbye? Her sisters had been so dejected at first, to be missing out on the wedding ceremony, but Eloise's anxious pleas, endorsed by Kate, to be allowed to focus entirely on establishing herself as Lady Fearnoch without either the distraction of their presence or risk that they might give the game away, had reconciled them. Though at this moment, with the carriage drawing up in front of a church, she'd give a great deal to have them here in person to give her a hug and tell her that she was going to be the best Lady Fearnoch imaginable.

It must be late afternoon. The church, she knew from one of Alexander's flurry of missives, was St Mary-le-Bow in Cheapside. A sudden squall of rain spattered the window pane, and Eloise shivered. Panic kept her in her seat as the carriage door was opened, the steps lowered. It was one thing to agree to a very convenient marriage, another to actually go through with it. Though there had been any number of letters, she had not seen Alexander since accepting his proposal. Was she really going to marry him?

Knees shaking, Eloise stepped out of the carriage and into the shelter of the portico where Alexander was waiting patiently, dressed in a navy-blue coat, fawn pantaloons and polished Hessian boots. He was carrying a hat and gloves. He was every bit as handsome as she remembered. This man was about to become her husband! Her heart lurched, thudded, raced.

'Are you sure about this? There is still time to change your mind.'

Nausea gave way to excitement as she met his gaze. She was terrified, and at the same time oddly exhilarated, as if she had climbed the highest tree and was looking down, astonished at her feat and afraid that she might fall. 'I don't want to change my mind.'

'Good.' His mouth relaxed into a smile. 'Shall we?'

She preceded him through the door. The interior of Wren's church was beautiful in its simplicity, with arched recesses on either side of the nave bounded by Corinthian columns of white Portland stone. The nave was flooded with light, the myriad colours of the stained glass reflecting on the marbled floor, making silhouettes of the two figures who would be their witnesses standing at the altar in front of the vicar. Not quite sure whether she was sleeping or awake, Eloise placed her hand on the man who would very shortly be her husband and made her way down the aisle towards them.

The vows had been solemnly made, the papers duly signed. The deed was done. She was married. Eloise stood on the steps of the church in a daze as Alexander—

her husband!—thanked his witnesses. She was now Lady Eloise, Countess of Fearnoch, but she still felt remarkably like the eldest Brannagh sister.

'The sun is shining on our nuptials,' Alexander said, turning to her with a smile. 'A good omen, I hope.'

'I can't believe we are married.'

'I hope you're not regretting it already.'

'No, no, of course not, it is just—there were moments during the ceremony when I felt as I if I must be dreaming. It's all very strange. I've never even been to London. I have no idea how to behave or what is expected of me or—or anything.'

'You must be yourself, that is all I expect of you. I hope you don't mind that our first night will be spent in a hotel. Robertson—my lawyer—tells me he has had Fearnoch House made ready for our arrival, but I reckoned that today would be momentous enough without subjecting you to the ordeal of formal introductions to the staff. Was I wrong?'

'Good grief, no,' Eloise exclaimed, looking horrified. 'Is that what I must expect tomorrow?'

'Let's enjoy today first.' He took her hand in his. 'Ours is not a traditional wedding day, but there is no reason why it shouldn't be memorable. Your carriage awaits, Lady Fearnoch.'

'My carriage?' She turned, just as a very elegant equipage drew up at the church steps. The body of the carriage was in the shape of a cup, painted glossy black, as were the spokes of the wheels. The hood was folded back to reveal an interior of dark-green velvet. 'You don't really mean that this is *my* carriage?'

'I never say what I don't mean,' Alexander said, smiling at her. 'Do you like it?'

'Like it! I love it. May we go for a drive?'

'That was my intention. Excellent timing, Bennet,' he said to the coachman who, having secured the reins of the two lively grey horses, jumped down, doffing his cap. 'This is Lady Fearnoch.'

'My lady, it is a pleasure to meet you. May I be the first to offer my congratulations.'

'Thank you.'

'Bennet is not a coachman by trade,' Alexander said, as the other man opened the carriage door and let down the steps. 'He is my personal servant. And I assure you,' he added, pre-empting her anxious question, 'very much in my confidence, and entirely trustworthy.'

'Also, be assured, my lady, that I know how to handle the ribbons,' the man said. 'Now, if you will help her ladyship into the carriage, my lord, we can be off.'

'My love?' Alexander handed her, quite unnecessarily, up the steps, jumping in beside her. 'Since this is your first day in London, and the first day of our new life together, I thought you might like a very short sightseeing drive.'

'I would. I can't think of anything more—it's a wonderful idea, especially in a fine carriage such as this.'

'It is called a barouche, and it is yours, as are the horses. There wasn't time to have your coat of arms painted on the doors, but...'

'I have a coat of arms?'

'You are a countess. I am sure there must also be a cloak of ermine and a coronet somewhere, though I'm hoping that King George keeps his fragile hold on this earth for a few more years yet, and spares us the necessity of wearing either at the next coronation.'

'Good heavens, I hadn't thought of that. I sincerely

hope that he does—though I must confess, I do feel that England would be a great deal better off without him.' Eloise covered her mouth theatrically. 'Ought I not to have said that? As a countess…'

'I have married a radical!'

'I am not! Only it seems to me that we expend a great deal of money on keeping a fat, drunken womaniser in luxury, that could be put to a much better use elsewhere.'

'I couldn't agree more,' Alexander said, 'but now you are a peeress of the realm, it might be prudent not to voice those thoughts in public.'

'Would I be sent to the Tower? They would surely not send a countess to Newgate?'

'I'd rather not have to rescue you from either.'

'Ah, but surely you could use your influence to have me released. The Duke of Clarence is the First Lord of the Admiralty, isn't he—and now that he is next in line to the throne—' She broke off, as he looked quite startled. 'I was only funning, Alexander. I don't expect you've even met the Duke, have you?'

A crack of the whip distracted Eloise as the barouche pulled away from the church steps. 'Where are we going?'

'We're headed towards St Paul's Cathedral,' Alexander said. 'If you look back, down river, you'll just about be able to see the docks. That's Southwark, on the other side of the Thames, and that bridge you can see is Blackfriars.'

Craning her neck, Eloise could see the masts of innumerable tall ships on the skyline. The river teemed with traffic, crammed with smaller sailing ships, dinghies, rowing boats and barges. The Thames was wider

than she'd imagined it, a strange colour, somewhere between brown and yellow, and judging by the way some
of the smaller boats were being tossed around, much
faster running than she had imagined too.

The barouche was making its way slowly along a
wide road, also teeming with traffic, with a terrifying
number of people taking their lives in their hands to
dodge from one side to the other. Every street corner
seemed to be alive with vendors shouting their wares,
from candles to shoe blacking, hot-pressed paper to ink,
jellied eels, sugared buns, buttons and buckles. Dray
carts bearing barrels and kegs, stacked high with straw,
were pulled by plodding shire horses. There were carts
drawn by donkeys or pushed by hand. There were covered coaches and open carriages like their own, sport-
ing phaetons, and innumerable riders on horseback, all
of them vying for space. The noise made conversation
impossible.

She did not need to be told when St Paul's loomed
into sight, for the dome dominated the skyline, the cathedral itself starkly white in contrast to the surrounding buildings. As they turned down to drive along the
frontage nearest the river, its distinctive cross shape
revealed itself.

'Ludgate Hill,' Alexander informed her, 'and through
there, the Old Bailey and Newgate. Chancery is nearby,
and all the Inns of Court.'

Lawyers and their clerks now crowded the streets.
The cries of newspaper vendors, trying to outshout each
other with their stories, manned the street corners. The
city was so much bigger than Eloise could ever have
comprehended. Her nose, as well as her eyes and ears,
was assaulted, with the smells of horses and coal, of too

many people in too enclosed a space. There was a yeasty smell from the taverns and the drays delivering to them, some less pleasant smells from the gutters that she tried not to inhale. Then, past the expanse of Lincoln's Inn Fields, they swung down towards the river again.

'Covent Garden,' Alexander informed her. 'That is the Royal Opera House, and down there, that enormous building fronting on to the river is Somerset House, where the Royal Academy exhibits each year. Are you interested in paintings? I believe that there is a vast collection at Fearnoch House.'

'I'm afraid I know almost nothing about art,' she replied. 'Perhaps because whatever I try to draw, whether it's a horse, a cat or a person, they all end up looking the same.'

Alexander laughed. 'Another thing we have in common, then.'

The traffic had eased. The buildings around them had become more spacious, some positively grand, and the people more elegant.

'We're on the Mall now,' Alexander said. 'That's Horse Guards Parade on the left. If you look straight down as we drive through St James's Park you'll see Buckingham Palace. We'll go on through Green Park to the edge of Hyde Park, just where Apsley House is...'

'Wellington's home?'

'Yes, but I think we'll avoid Hyde Park for today. It's the fashionable hour, everyone will be out showing off their horses and their toilettes, and I am not sure that we want to risk meeting anyone I might know, before the notice of our marriage has gone out.'

'I thought you spent most of your time abroad?'

'I am obliged to spend some time in London.'

'So you do have friends here? You'll no doubt have relatives here too? Your cousin, you mentioned, and there will be your brother's friends, I expect.'

'We never mixed in the same circles,' Alexander said. 'It's quite a contrast, isn't it, the parkland from what surrounds it.'

Quite a deliberate change of subject? She could not be sure. Bennet had turned the barouche around and they were driving back along the Mall, with St James's Park on her right now. On her left an imposing sandstone mansion presided over a huge garden.

'York House, home to the late Duke of York,' Alexander informed her. 'Next to it is St James's Palace and next to that is Marlborough House.'

'Heavens, it is like driving through a history book. Where is Fearnoch House from here?'

'In Mayfair, just north. Have you seen enough?'

'For now, I think I have. Thank you, Alexander. If you had asked me, this is exactly how I'd have wanted to spend this afternoon. I think you must be a mind reader. Will we dine at our hotel? Is it nearby?'

'Not far, but if you don't mind, we're actually almost at Whitehall, and I have a small bit of business I have to attend to at the Admiralty first.'

'No, I don't mind. I'd like to see the place where you work.'

The barouche swung round past Horse Guards Parade on to Whitehall, and drew to a stop outside a large building, the pedimented entranceway flanked by two projecting wings, the whole fronted by a pillared screen with an archway at the centre.

'The Admiralty,' Alexander said. 'Though strictly speaking, we're headed for Admiralty House.'

'We?'

'I am hardly going to leave my wife sitting alone in the carriage, am I?' He jumped out, pulling the steps down behind him. 'Come along, Lady Fearnoch.'

She did as he bid her, bemused, a little nervous for fear of being introduced to any of his colleagues, and a little infected by the air of suppressed excitement which she thought she detected in him. Alexander took her arm, leading her through the archway into a courtyard, but instead of heading for the massive portico, he turned left. 'This is the official residence of the First Lord of the Admiralty.'

'Prince William, the Duke of Clarence,' Eloise said, eyeing him in some confusion now. 'We are surely not paying him a bridal call. You said…' She hesitated, trying to recall what he had said earlier.

'*You* assumed I hadn't met him.'

'You're going to tell me that you and he are best friends now, are you? That we are going to dinner with him, a royal duke, without even changing into evening clothes? I know you are teasing me, but…'

'We are not dining with the Duke, I promise.'

The house had four storeys, and was built of yellow brick. As they approached, the door was thrown open, the servant in black livery bowing low as Alexander led Eloise up the stairs. 'Welcome, my lord,' he said. 'If you will follow me.'

'I know my way, thank you, Soames.'

'Everything is as you ordered, my lord, but if there is anything else…'

'I know how to reach you.' Alexander ushered Eloise towards the central staircase, which split into two half-

way up. 'This way,' he said, taking the left-hand side to
the first floor, where he threw open the double doors.

Eloise stood in the doorway, her mouth open in astonishment. A table with chairs for—she counted—
twenty people—dominated the room. The ceiling was
double height, decorated with white cornicing in the ba-
roque style. At the far end, two tall bookcases supported
a pediment which was adorned by a clock, and between
the two sat an enormous globe. Maps and charts were
hung on the longest wall, the opposite consisting of five
bay windows. 'What is this place?'

Alexander gently nudged her over the threshold and
closed the doors behind him. 'It is used for meetings
of the Admiralty board, and sometimes for banquets.
Today, it is our dining room.'

She turned to him, searching for the telltale gleam
of amusement in his eyes. 'You are teasing me. Why
are we really here?'

'Our first dinner as man and wife. I thought it should
be memorable.'

'Alexander, you must be teasing me. We probably
shouldn't even be here...' But they were expected, she
remembered now. 'How did you—I know you work at
the Admiralty, but surely—did you hire this place—
can this place be hired?'

He laughed. 'No.'

'Then how...?'

He shrugged. 'A favour. You're not supposed to ask
how I managed it, you're supposed to be delighted that
I did. Did I get it wrong? Would you rather...?'

'No! I am simply astounded, to be perfectly honest.
And delighted, I promise you.'

'Good. Now, I expect you'll want to take off your

bonnet, tidy yourself up before dinner. There is a room, just here, set aside for you. Take your time.'

The door opened out of the panelling. The room was small, but there was a washstand, a mirror, and even a set of brushes. 'Thank you,' Eloise said, grateful, as she guessed he knew she would be, for the breathing space.

Alexander took off his hat and gloves, summoned the servant to light the candles and the fire, for the light was fading, and made sure that the champagne was chilling with the glasses on the side table by the fire before making for one of the tall windows, gazing sightlessly out at the familiar view of Whitehall. He was married. He was actually married. Earlier, in the church, he had listened to the vicar recite the words of the marriage ceremony with a growing sense of disbelief. The fact that the man repeatedly referred to him as the Earl of Fearnoch only added to the notion that it was not really him standing here, about to make his vows. Then the vicar had joined their hands, and he'd placed the ring on Eloise's finger and calm had flooded him. He was doing the right thing. With a woman who was as perfect as any woman could be for the role. As his wife. Who would not be his wife.

She had enjoyed her carriage ride, just as her sisters had predicted. He was extremely glad he'd had the idea of consulting them, for aside from a determination to mark the day somehow, and to make it less of an ordeal and more of a pleasure, he had been at a loss. He smiled, remembering Eloise's face as she stood on the threshold of this room. It was a risk, for it was ludicrous to imagine that a Victualling Commissioner could commandeer not only the room but the kitchens of Admiralty House, but he had gambled on Eloise being blissfully unaware of the extent of the favour he had called in, and being too astonished to question him closely. He was pretty certain he'd been right about both, and it was worth it. He only hoped she wasn't hiding in that room, expecting at any moment that someone might come along and demand to know why she was trespassing.

The door in the panelling opened, and Eloise peered in. Alexander strode over to meet her. 'I'm sorry I took so long,' she said, 'I've been—I've been fretting about tomorrow.'

Alexander had been too intent on today to think much about tomorrow. 'There's nothing to worry about,' he said blithely, steering her over to the sofa. 'We'll be introduced to the servants. The housekeeper will give you the grand tour.'

'The grand tour.' Eloise looked rather daunted. 'Will she be expecting to take her orders from me?'

He shrugged. 'Only if you wish her to. I assume she is perfectly capable of running the place without your intervention since she has been doing so for my brother since his wife died.'

'The housekeeper will think I'm a—a usurper.'

'Fearnoch House will be your home now, I thought I'd made that clear. You can do exactly what you want with the place—or you can leave it exactly as it is.'

'Is it very large?'

'I believe it is one of the larger of London's town houses. Robertson gave me the inventory and a floor plan. They are at our hotel—do you wish to see them?'

'I wish—Alexander, to be perfectly honest, I am somewhat daunted by the prospect.'

Cursing himself for a fool, he sat down on the sofa

beside her. 'I will let you into a secret. I know as little, maybe even less, of how the household operates as you do.'

'You don't have to exaggerate just to make me feel better.'

'No, it's the truth.' His childhood was a distant country he avoided visiting, but Eloise was his wife, and even if it was in name only, he was responsible for her. It struck him then, the courage it must have taken her to come here alone, to entrust herself to his safekeeping, for in the eyes of the law she now belonged to him. She needed to be reassured. Sharing a little of his pathetic history was a small price to pay.

'I have only very faint memories of my early years which were, I believe, spent in Fearnoch House.' In actual fact they were not memories as such, more a series of vague impressions of emotional states, one segueing into the other. Early happiness, a sort of peaceful calm? Then something like dread. Fear. And pain. There was definitely pain. None of which he could conjure into tangible recollections, or perhaps had chosen not to.

'My first real memories are of school,' he continued, which was near enough the truth. 'I was packed off to boarding school when I was five. After that, my holidays were spent in the country in the charge of a tutor. I was left to my own devices from an early age. It was sink or swim. I chose to swim. When I was sixteen I joined the Admiralty and moved into lodgings, first shared, and then my own. I spend a great deal of my time abroad. When I am in London, I have my own rooms and am quite content in my own company. My family excluded me from their lives, so I created my own. If they did anything for me it was to engender a

strong streak of self-sufficiency. For that I am grateful.'
He recognised that a tinge of bitterness had crept into
his tone. He squared his shoulders. 'Fearnoch House
was their domain, never mine. So you see I truly am
as much a stranger to it as you.'

Eloise took his hand in hers, clasping it tightly. 'To
favour one child, that I can understand, I've experienced that myself, but to ostracise you from such a
young age—'

'Made me the man I am today,' he said curtly, cutting
short her nascent pity. 'One cannot miss what one never
had.' Though ghostly images from his childhood visited
him unbidden sometimes, in the half-awake hours when
he couldn't sleep. Memories or dreams, of those childhood holidays in the countryside. Seeing his brother in
the distance, playing with friends. His mother swooping
down on him to embrace him frantically. An encounter with the Earl, staring at him in disgust. Knowing
what he did now, he was sure that one was real enough.

'I am happy with my life,' Alexander said more
firmly. 'Those early lessons in independence, learning how to rely only on myself, they were invaluable
to my success in my chosen career. Besides, I've never
wished to walk in my brother's shoes.'

'Though now you must.'

He laughed shortly. 'I have no intentions of living
Walter's life.'

She tightened her fingers around his. 'So we will
make Fearnoch House our own, then?'

'We shall banish the memories and conventions of
the old guard. We shall stand on as many toes, tear up
as many customs and traditions as we see fit.'

Eloise giggled. 'But I think we'll draw the line at

inviting a horse into the household. Our neighbour in the country, Squire Mytton, gives his favourite horse the run of the house,' she explained, seeing his confusion. 'He is reputed to sleep curled up next to it by the fireside.'

'You are making that up.'

'No, I assure you, but I think we'll stop short of that.'

'Agreed. But seriously, I don't want you to feel uncomfortable living there, Eloise.'

'I am sure I'll very quickly become accustomed to playing lady of the manor. Shall I be expected to sit round idly all day twiddling my thumbs?'

'I expect there will be trees in the garden you could climb if you get bored.'

'I think I'll confine my climbing to the stairs. Though the Climbing Countess does have a certain ring to it. Thank you, Alexander.'

'What for?'

'You know what for. I will do my best not to be overwhelmed.'

'And I will do my best to help you if you are. That's what husbands are for, after all.'

'Thank you.'

Her smile was wholly unconvincing. 'There's something else worrying you?'

'It's just—at the hotel, will there be a maid? Kate says I will have a dresser at Fearnoch House, and to expect a maid to undress me at the hotel tonight. But I don't want a complete stranger to help me undress. I'm perfectly capable of taking off my own clothes, for heaven's sake.'

'It's your wedding night. If anyone is undressing you, it should be your husband.'

'Alexander!'

What the devil had possessed him to say such a thing! Appalled, he jumped to his feet.

He wished that it had not occurred to him, for now his mind was picturing what it would be like to be slowly undressing his bride, each layer of clothing revealing more of her body. Would he discover freckles, as there were on her nose, or would her skin be flawless and creamy white? And would the fire of her hair be echoed…?

'Champagne,' he said hurriedly, picking up the bottle, banishing the image of Eloise in her underclothes, allowing him to unwrap her like a present.

He attacked the bottle, fumbling with the wire, yanking the cork free with too much force so that it made a loud crack and wine bubbled out over his hands. Turn the bottle, not the cork, he remembered someone in the dim and distant past telling him. He poured two glasses.

'I know you were teasing,' Eloise said.

'It was a wholly inappropriate…'

'We're both nervous. When you're nervous, you say the first thing in your head without thinking. Though actually I do that all the time, but you don't, I've noticed. You are always careful with words, you think before you speak, and so you only say what you mean. Oh.' Her eyes widened.

'I didn't mean it,' Alexander said, handing her a glass. 'I was teasing, as you said.' Touching her glass to his own, he smiled at her. 'A toast,' he said, 'to us, and our own very particular form of married bliss.'

'To us.' Eloise sipped the ice-cold wine, hiccuping as the bubbles burst on her tongue. 'I've never tasted champagne before.' She sipped again. 'I rather think I like it.' She drained the glass. 'I like it very much. Now that I am a countess, perhaps I shall drink champagne every night. May I have some more?'

Alexander obliged her, smiling. 'Take it slowly. What have you eaten today?'

'Breakfast. Phoebe made me a special breakfast. Scrambled eggs with cream. My favourite oatmeal bread, which none of the others like because they say it tastes of horse food, but I love it.' Eloise laughed softly to herself. 'I always say to them, how do you know it tastes of horse food, unless you've actually tasted horse food? Phoebe, being Phoebe, said she has, mind you. Oh, yes, and there were strawberries, the first of the year, from the succession house. To be honest, they were a little tart, but it's the thought that counts, isn't it?

He smiled. 'And it was a very thoughtful gesture.'

'You really do have the most attractive smile,' Eloise said, 'do you know that? You must know that. I'll wager you've been told a hundred, a thousand times. It does strange things to my tummy. Though that is probably the champagne.'

'Or the lack of food coupled with the excitement of the day.' He got up to push the bell by the fireplace. 'You are tired. It's been a long day. You're hungry.'

'You're thinking the champagne has gone to my head, but I meant what I said, I just didn't mean to say it aloud.'

Alexander burst out laughing. 'Thank you for the compliment.' Taking her hand, he kissed her fingertips. 'Truly, I'm flattered. Contrary to what you think, no one has ever told me that my smile did strange things to their tummy. I owe Daniel a huge favour for introducing me to you.' He moved closer on the sofa, putting her hand on his knee. 'I have been remiss too, in not complimenting you on how lovely you look. I'm sure the fashion plates would say that a redhead should avoid red, but I think it a striking combination.'

'My mother agreed with the fashion plates. But since I make my own dresses I am free to make them whatever colour I choose.'

'The green dress you were wearing the first time I met you, that was another of your own creations, you told me. You are a great deal more talented than a mere seamstress. And your mother was wrong, red really does suit you. Not that your hair is red. At the risk of sounding clichéd, I think it is the colour of fire.'

She was blushing. 'There is no need to pay me compliments, there's no one around to hear.'

'I think I told you once that I always say what I mean, Eloise. You look very lovely.'

'Thank you.' Their eyes met. He really did have the most ridiculously long lashes. And then there was his mouth. What would it be like to kiss him? Alexander. Her husband. On their wedding night.

A gentle tap at the door made her jump, pulling her hands free, shuffling away from him on the sofa. He was frowning as he opened the door to several servants bearing trays. Had he read her mind, was he embarrassed by her thoughts? For a moment, she'd been convinced that he'd been wanting to kiss her too. There had been something in his eyes. And she was sure he'd moved, just a fraction towards her. But she must have been imagining it. Thank heavens that dinner had arrived. It was the champagne that was at fault. She would never drink champagne again. At least, not on an empty stomach.

* * *

'Dinner is served, my lady.' Alexander, having dismissed the servants, held her chair out for her. 'What may I help you to?'

Eloise's mouth watered. 'Oysters! One of my favourite foods. I'll start with those, please. It's very late in the year to be eating fresh oysters. Phoebe says that you shouldn't eat them unless there is an *r* in the month.'

She surveyed the table, lifting the lids of several covered tureens. 'Duck with peas. Asparagus with a cheese sauce. Is this Dover sole in burnt butter? And pickled radishes! All my favourite dishes. And this…' She picked up the dish, taking a fragrant sniff. 'Butter-bean puree with garlic. I thought that was one of Phoebe's own unique receipts?'

'I believe it is.'

'How do you know that?' Alexander smiled at her. She narrowed her eyes. And how did you know that these are all my favourite dishes?'

'I didn't, but I consulted someone who did.'

'Phoebe!'

'And Estelle. I told you, I wanted to make this day memorable, so I wrote to the oracles. They were very forthcoming.'

Eloise ate an oyster, closing her eyes as the salty fresh taste of the sea washed over her. 'I can't believe it. This is just lovely, and so thoughtful, and such a surprise. Thank you.'

'Oh, I was only acting under orders.' Alexander poured them both a glass of cold white wine and removed the oyster shells. 'Your sisters were eager to have a say in proceedings, to make up for their absence at

the ceremony, and so more than happy to advise me.'
He pushed the serving dish of Dover sole towards her.

'Please don't tell me they suggested that I bathe in asses' milk.'

'Like Cleopatra?' He laughed. 'Why on earth would they suggest such a thing?'

'Because they possess a singular sense of humour.'

'You wouldn't relish a visit to the silk warehouse, then?'

'A silk warehouse? Really?'

'So you don't want me to cancel that? What about the appointment with Madame LeClerc in Bond Street? It was rather presumptuous of me, I know, since you prefer to make all your own gowns, but if you could select the silk and come up with the designs for your trousseau...'

'Was that my sisters' idea too?'

'Well, no, that was mine. I have no idea how long it takes to make one gown, let alone a wardrobe full of them...'

'I don't need a wardrobe full.'

'I'm afraid that you probably will. If we are to establish ourselves as the Earl and Countess of Fearnoch, we're going to have to do a fair bit of socialising. I'm told that Madame LeClerc, though running one of the oldest establishments on Bond Street, is still one of the most fashionable, but if you have a preference for another modiste...'

'No, I don't. I have no idea—how do you know who is in fashion?'

'I asked the wife of a colleague here at the Admiralty.'

'You must mix with some very senior colleagues,' Eloise said, 'if they mix in the kind of society that an

earl and a countess—I'm sorry, that sounds very insulting, only I thought that your work—to be honest, I
have no idea what your work really is, or who you mix
with, though I did have the impression that it was not
the sort of people you'd be expected to mix with now.
As the Earl of Fearnoch, I mean. Though actually, what
I mean is thank you. For taking the trouble to obtain a
recommendation. However you obtained it. May I help
you to some of the duck?'

'Thank you, yes. And some of the asparagus too.'

She cast him a sidelong glance. 'You're laughing
at me.'

Alexander smiled, shaking his head. 'I'm endeared.'

The candlelight accentuated the sharp planes of his
cheeks. The high starched collar of his shirt accentuated
the decisive line of his jaw. It was the strangeness of it
all that was making her breathless. She was married to
this man, and as well as being the most handsome man
she'd ever met he had been extremely thoughtful, not
only consulting her sisters, but the wife of his mysterious 'friend' who sounded as if he must be rather high up
in the Admiralty, which made her wonder where, in the
echelons, a Victualling Commissioner sat. High enough
to commandeer his commander's house for the evening!

'Now, just when I'd like you to be articulating your
thoughts, you are keeping them very much to yourself.'

'My duck is getting cold.' Eloise picked up her fork.

'For the record,' Alexander said, following suit,
'you're a very unconvincing prevaricator.'

'For the record, my duck was actually getting cold,
and it is delicious. Does Fearnoch House come with a
cook?'

'I believe so.'

'When will the notice of our nuptials be in the press?'

'I've left it with Robertson. We thought it best to inform my mother first, and to let her have the terms of the settlement too. But let's not talk about business tonight. Would you like some cheese? Your sisters told me that you don't have a sweet tooth.'

'I don't, and I do love cheese, but I've had far too much already.' Eloise happily filed away her questions about how, precisely, the Dowager Lady Fearnoch had been informed of her only remaining child's nuptials for another day, and pushed her plate aside. 'Thank you, Alexander. That was a truly lovely meal.' She got up, and automatically began to stack the dishes.

'Leave that.' Alexander removed a plate from her hand and set it down. 'I'll have them come to clear up,' he added, pushing the bell.

'I didn't think. At home, we take turns.'

'You will have a new home tomorrow, and an army of servants to clear up after you. Appease your conscience with the knowledge that you will be keeping several scullery maids in respectable work.'

The dishes were cleared with silent efficiency. The fire was banked up. They were alone again, and Alexander poured the last of the champagne into their glasses. 'It is probably flat.'

'I am not sophisticated enough to care.'

Eloise raised her glass to him and took a sip before settling down on the sofa, curling her legs up under her. Alexander pulled a chair nearer. If he was alone, he'd have long ago discarded his coat and waistcoat. If he was alone, he'd be sitting by the fireside now in his dressing gown. 'Do you mind if I loosen my neckcloth?'

'If I may take off my shoes?' Eloise waited only for his nod to slip her feet out of her satin slippers with a happy sigh. 'When I was younger, I hated to wear shoes or stockings. In the summer, I'd even wander about outside in my bare feet. Save when Mama and Papa were in residence of course.'

He stared, fascinated, as she flexed her toes inside her stockings. Did she tie her garters below or above the knee? Cursing under his breath, he dragged his eyes away, yanking unnecessarily hard at the knot in his necktie. 'I forgot to ask what you like for breakfast.'

'Tea, and lots of it. I should warn you that I am like a bear with a sore head in the morning, until I've drunk the full pot.'

'You promised me, within minutes of our first meeting, that you were extremely even-tempered.'

'And so I am, provided I am left alone to drink my tea.'

'What other foibles do you have that I should take account of?'

'You should have asked that before you married me.'

'Ah, but then you might not have told me the truth.' In the muted candlelight, her hair flickered like flames, her eyes gleamed. He could hear the smile in her voice, was acutely conscious of her curled up within touching distance. He had been alone with other women, but this was a form of intimacy he had never experienced, cocooned in the fading light, sharing their thoughts and not their bodies. It was odd, in one sense enjoyable, in another quite unsettling.

'We haven't decided how we met yet,' Eloise said. 'The story of our whirlwind romance. I must admit, I find the idea that two people could decide to spend the rest of their lives together on the basis of their eyes meeting across a crowded room just a little bit far-fetched.'

'More than a little. I've been thinking,' Alexander said, 'that it would be better all round if our romance was long-standing. What if we met some time ago, and were privately engaged before my brother died.'

'Unrequited love! That would certainly counter any accusations of cupboard love on my part. I presume, since you are looking so pleased with yourself, that you have also worked out how we met, when I have spent the last five years of my life closeted in the country and you have been—wherever it is you have been.'

Alexander moved on to the sofa beside her. 'That is what is so clever about my story, you see. Since I have spent a great deal of the last five years abroad, then who is to say when either of us met, or indeed how often we have met.'

Eloise angled herself towards him. 'But how did we first encounter each other?'

'Why not start with the truth, that I met your uncle abroad, then embellish it so that he asked me to deliver his post on my return to England.'

'Not his post, how about an artefact of some sort?'

'A lamp containing a genie? A mummy with a curse attached?'

Her eyes widened. 'A cursed mummy! I like the sound of that, though it wouldn't really augur well for our romance, would it?'

'Perhaps not. What, then?'

'What about a tribal mask? No, no, wait, I have it, a musical instrument—a set of ceremonial drums, for Estelle's birthday. What do you think?'

He thought she looked delectable, her eyes gleaming with humour, her cheeks flushed from the firelight, her mouth curved into a soft smile. 'A set of drums for Estelle, why not. So I brought them to Elmswood Manor— let's say three years ago—and I met you.'

'Before you set eyes on my sisters, mind, for no one would believe you could fall in love with me if you'd met them first.'

'Rubbish. I knew from the moment I set eyes on you that you were the woman for me. You had been reading a book, and when I was announced you jumped up and it fell to the floor, and I picked it up for you. It was Voltaire's *Candide,* one of my favourites.'

'That is the actual book I was reading when you came to Elmswood Manor!'

'I know, I spotted it on the window seat, lying open. I find that when you're making up a story, it pays to use as many real details as possible, and to ensure that the details are covered. Because my work keeps me overseas, much of our romance was conducted by letter, though I visited Elmswood Manor every time I was back in England.'

'An epistolary romance. My favourite kind to read.'

Alexander grinned. 'Fortuitous. When I visited you in January last year, that is when I proposed, but we kept our engagement a secret.'

'No doubt for a very good reason?'

'I could not possibly become engaged without obtaining permission from the head of the Fearnoch family, of course.'

'Your brother! So you visited him in London?'

'No, alas, I was summoned abroad at short notice, and planned to inform Walter on my next leave of absence.'

'But he died before you could return.'

'And we have kept our attachment a secret until the year of mourning was completed.'

'That is excellent, Alexander. Are you often required to make up stories? I'd have thought your duties here required you to do the opposite, and document the facts.'

If only she knew! For a brief moment, he positively ached with longing for the thrill of the chase, the intellectual challenge of each mission, the knife-edge of danger and the deep satisfaction of a successful outcome.

But she must never know. For the foreseeable future, he had to embrace a different life, and would face very different challenges with Eloise by his side. He'd thought his convenient wife would be a necessary and boring accessory, but he already knew that life with Eloise would not be boring, because apart from anything else, he wasn't planning on it lasting long enough for either of them to become bored. 'I think I'm going to enjoy being married,' Alexander said.

A long tress of her hair had escaped its pins. Her stockinged feet were peeping out from the hem of her gown. One of them was resting on his thigh. If this were a real wedding night, he'd kiss her toes. Then he'd run his fingers up her calves, her knees, to untie her garters. He'd ease her stockings down slowly, and he'd lean towards her as he did so, kissing her carefully, gently, not wanting to alarm her.

Alexander sat up abruptly. 'It's late, he said. 'I think it's time we went to our hotel.' Getting to his feet, he helped her up before brushing her fingertips with his lips. He would not allow himself to imagine that his own desires were reflected in her eyes. 'I'll ring for the carriage.'

'Have I done something to offend you?'

'It's been a long day, that's all, and we have an even longer day ahead of us tomorrow.' He picked up her slippers, handing them to her in order to prevent himself giving in to the impulse to pull her into his arms under the guise of comforting her. 'Go and fetch your hat and we'll be on our way.'

Chapter Five

Eloise lay wide awake listening to the unfamiliar sounds of London at night. She had never lived in a city. She hadn't appreciated it would be noisy, that people would still be afoot at two, three in the morning. And she knew what time it was, because Londoners seemed to find it essential for someone to be employed to wander the streets shouting the hour and informing her that all was well.

She hoped that the disembodied voice knew what he was talking about. She had blown out her candle, but there was a gas streetlamp right outside her window shining flickering light through a gap in the curtains. At home, she slept with the curtains wide open to the night sky. Even on the darkest of nights, when the sky was thick with cloud and there were no traces of moonlight, she could navigate her way around Elmswood Manor without bumping into anything, stubbing her toe on a chair leg or tripping over a rug. She'd spent many nights, in those early days there, stumbling her way in the dark from her own room to the twins' bedroom, soothing their heartbreaking sobs, or simply watching them sleeping or feigning sleep. She hadn't cried, but she'd taken to roaming around the house at night, afraid to sleep.

But it wasn't fear that was keeping her awake tonight, it was excitement. Sitting up, she plumped up two of the mountain of pillows and stared into the gloom. This was her first night as the Countess of Fearnoch. She still didn't feel in the least bit like a countess, but she did feel different. Was Alexander lying awake too?

Their wedding feast at the Admiralty had been delightful and utterly unexpected. She was deeply touched by his thoughtfulness and determination to make the day both special and memorable. In cahoots with the twins, no less! A man capable of surprising her, not least with his revelations about his loveless childhood. She was vastly relieved that there was no imminent meeting with his mother looming. She wasn't at all sure that she wanted to meet the woman. An emotion more powerful than mere indifference to a second son must have caused her to have willingly exiled Alexander, but what on earth could it possibly be? Did he know? He was an intelligent man, but if he knew the answer, he was keeping it to himself. He had a way of avoiding personal questions, of turning the conversation so that by the time she realised he'd done it, it was far too late to wind it back. The reception they had received at Admiralty House, for example, did not square with a mere weevil counter. There was obviously more to him than met the eye.

Eloise's lids began to droop. She snuggled down into the big, comfortable bed. When they'd been funning about how they had met, she'd thought he was going to kiss her, but then he hadn't and he'd been quite brusque when saying goodnight. He hadn't really wanted to kiss her. He must have realised that she'd wanted to kiss him, and that was what had annoyed him. Why was she suddenly thinking about kissing so much? Why was she so fascinated, wondering what his mouth would feel like on hers, not at all repelled by the idea, but intrigued? It must be her perverse streak, wanting what she couldn't have. And didn't want. Not really.

What would it be like to be married? Once they had negotiated the awkward early days, the trials of learning how to live under the same roof, how to act their allotted parts in front of others, what would life be like? Would it ever feel normal? Would carefulness quickly become carelessness? Would familiarity breed contempt? At least it would not breed anger or jealousy. It would not lead to betrayal. They could not be unfaithful to each other. There was no passion to inflame or to scorch. Living with Alexander wouldn't be distressing. There would be no shouting and screaming. No threats and no violence. It might prove boring, but...

Eloise smiled to herself. No, not boring. Not even if he did turn out to be exactly who he claimed to be. He was intriguing and thoughtful and honourable and a little bit too perceptive for her own peace of mind. He had a very sardonic sense of humour. He'd said her hair was the colour of fire. He'd said she was lovely. Was that a bland compliment or an admission that he was attracted to her?

Under the bedcovers, her toes curled into the sheets. She shouldn't be asking herself these questions. But she was attracted to him. It was perfectly acceptable for her to admit that, in the dark, in the privacy of her own chamber, knowing that it had nothing to do with anything. Once she'd accustomed herself to his very, very handsome face and his athletic figure, then this inconvenient and foolish ardour, for want of a better word, would fade.

She was confident of that. She was absolutely confident that she would never, ever, allow herself to be ruled by passion. Passion was a cruel and heartless mistress. Passion made you selfish. It made you vicious. It drove you to heights and it sent you plummeting to depths, and it made you careless of who you took with you. It had always struck her as horribly, painfully ironic, that it was the products of the passion in her parents marriage, herself and her sisters, who had been so thoughtlessly, heedlessly damaged by it.

Her fear of passion was too deep-rooted for her ever to wish to experience it for herself. To marry for love, as her parents had, was a frankly terrifying and repulsive idea. In Ireland, she had vowed never to marry, under any circumstances. Only seeing Kate's marriage, the antithesis of her parents', both contented and passion free, had made her think differently. Which is precisely why she was here, married to Alexander.

So she was being very silly, worrying about her feelings for him. It was the idea of kissing him, not the reality, that's what she was curious about. She'd like to know in theory what it would be like to kiss Alexander. She'd like to know in theory what it was that other people found so irresistible about lovemaking. Happily giving herself permission to imagine, she snuggled under the blankets and at last fell asleep.

'Good morning, my love.' Alexander got to his feet as she entered the sitting room, brushing a kiss to her cheek, presumably for the benefit of the chambermaid, who was setting out breakfast.

'Good morning.'

Eloise took her place at the table, smiling her thanks to the maid, who set out a fresh pot of tea, and watching Alexander as he poured coffee for himself before dismissing the help. He spoke to servants with a casual air of authority, as one accustomed to command, in fact. And why shouldn't he, she chastised her suspicious mind, for though he had not been raised in the London house, his childhood home had been a large country estate.

She cut herself a slice of the bread, which smelled deliciously yeasty. There was butter, jam, a cheese. Alexander helped himself to a plate of sausage and egg from a covered dish, smiling when she shuddered her refusal of the same. 'Did you ask the maid to bring me early morning tea to my bedchamber? If so, I'm grateful.'

'My motives were purely selfish. I had no desire to have a bear with a sore head as my breakfast companion.'

She chuckled. 'Wise man. Do you prefer silence, or would you like to talk?'

'I have no idea. I'm accustomed to silence, since I always take breakfast alone, but since you've come prepared to make conversation, it would be very rude of me to decline your offer.' He took a sip of coffee. 'And, I suspect, ineffective too.'

'I can be perfectly silent if I choose to be!' Eloise sipped her tea and cut another slice of bread. 'Though we do, as it happens, have a great deal to discuss.'

'We do. You know I'm teasing you, don't you?'

'Yes. You are very good at remaining deadpan, but it is there in your eyes.'

'I had no idea I was so transparent.'

'You're not. It's just that I'm very observant.'

'I've noticed. Being so very observant myself.' Alexander pushed his plate aside, pouring another cup of coffee. 'We are expected at Fearnoch House in an hour, but if you want to postpone our arrival…'

'No. Actually, I'm rather looking forward to seeing it, now that I know that you— Now that we have agreed to explore it together. It will be an adventure. I shall think of myself as Uncle Daniel, though without the risk of encountering wild animals.'

'Wild animals?'

'Kate says that my uncle is happiest when he is in the most dangerous and remote parts of the world. I assume that he encounters all sorts of wild animals there, though he says next to nothing of where he is and what he does, in his letters.'

'No, I don't expect he does,' Alexander said. 'On account of not wishing to worry your aunt and your sisters, I presume.' He pushed back his chair, returned to the table with a leather folder and began to flick through the sheaf of papers. 'I've had Robertson open an account for you at Coutts. As you can see, the opening balance shows the lump sum settlement we agreed, and your first quarter's allowance.'

Eloise stared at the figures, then stared at Alexander, then stared at the figures again. 'I have a bank account?'

'I could hardly hand over such a sum in cash. You need to sign here, and some time over the next few days I'll take you in and introduce you, but I thought you'd

probably need some money for day-to-day expenses.'
He handed over a small bundle of notes.

'I don't need all that. I didn't expect an allowance.
The sum…' She eyed the eye-watering number again.
'The sum you've settled on me is more than sufficient.'

'That is yours, as agreed. Your wedding present, I
suppose you could call it, to do with completely as you
please. I don't want you using it for living expenses,
and, of course, your bills must be sent to me.'

'What bills?'

'I don't know, your trousseau for a start.' He put a
finger over her mouth when she opened it to protest.
'It's non-negotiable, Eloise, and nothing more than any
woman in your position would expect. Now, as to a
marriage notice in the press, here is what Robertson
has drafted up.'

Another piece of paper was pushed in front of her,
but she did not read it immediately. 'Alexander, expected or not, you are being exceedingly generous.
Thank you.' She read the notice. 'It seems very odd to
see my name in print like this. What about your mother?
Have you…?'

'I have notified her. My letter went with Robertson's
communiqué regarding her settlement. She should have
it today or tomorrow.'

'Will she—should we expect her?'

'To visit? No.'

He was leafing through the papers again, his brow
furrowed. As far as Alexander was concerned, the subject was closed. As far as Eloise was concerned—oh,
for goodness' sake, she had more than enough to deal
with as it was. 'Shall we be expected to entertain other
visitors?'

'One step at a time! I think we'd better familiarise ourselves with the house first.' He pulled a floor plan from the folder, unrolling it on the breakfast table.

'Good heavens.' Eloise studied it in astonishment. 'I have a dreadful sense of direction. I'll need a guide if I am not to be lost for ever, wandering stairwells and passages.'

'It's not as bad as it looks. All you have to do to orientate yourself is...'

She listened, and she tried very hard to follow what Alexander was saying, but the more she looked, the bigger and more intimidating the house began to appear. Music Room. Library. Large Drawing Room. Small Drawing Room. Ladies' Retiring Room. Gentlemen's Retiring Room. Billiard Room. Garden Room. Morning Room. Breakfast Parlour. And then there were the bedrooms. The servants' quarters. Attics. Kitchens. Her eyes roved over the elevations on the plans. There was a distillery. And three china stores.

'This isn't a house, it's a palace and I am not a princess, never mind a queen. How many servants are there?'

'You don't really want to know.'

'How many?'

He told her. She winced. He pulled her to her feet, taking her hands in his. 'I'll be right beside you—remember, this is all as strange to me as it is to you.'

'No, it's not. I mean this is, this great big barrack of a place, but you were raised in a stately home.'

'You weren't exactly raised in a wattle-and-daub cottage.'

'No, no, that's true, but we had hardly any servants when Mama and Papa weren't there, and most of the house was closed off. When they came, there were servants, of course there were, Mama would not risk breaking a fingernail by drawing a curtain herself, let alone laying a fire, but they were Mama and Papa's servants, Alexander.'

'I thought you said you were nineteen when they died?'

'Yes, but we still lived, my sisters and I, in the nursery suite. How do you think Phoebe became such a good cook? We had to fend for ourselves, most of the time. So you see, it's not the same for you and me. When you walk into a room, no one doubts you are an earl. When you ring the bell, servants jump to obey you, while I…'

'Do you think that I'd throw you in the deep end if I didn't think you could cope?'

'No, but…'

'Think of all the things that you've had to deal with in your life. Looking after your sisters, and then not only losing your parents and your brother, but having to come to a new country, to make a home with a complete stranger—think about how well you dealt with all of these things, Eloise. What you are facing is a walk in the park compared to that.'

She bit her lip, forcing herself to take calming breaths. 'I know you're right.'

'And I know you can do it. It's not an ordeal, it's a voyage of discovery, remember?'

'To a very distant and strange country.'

'Not so distant. It's only a ten-minute walk from here.'

'You expect me to walk! Have you forgotten, my lord, that I am a member of the aristocracy now?'

'Then I shall carry you, all the way over the threshold!'

Her heart was still beating fast, though no longer with panic. She was sure Alexander was teasing her, but there was that strange feeling again when she looked at him, a twisting, churning in her stomach that was close to fear, but a more exhilarating relative. 'You couldn't! You wouldn't!'

The words were barely out of her mouth when he scooped her up, making her shriek in surprise. 'Put me down!' Her arm was around his neck. He held her high against his chest. Their gazes met. Her breath caught in her throat. 'At once.'

He set her back down. Her arm was still around his neck. His arm was around her waist. They were simply acting their parts, she realised with relief. There was no need for her to panic. She could stand here, in the circle of his arms, let her hand touch the skin at the nape of his neck, and it was all pretence, the way her touch made him exhale, as she tilted her face to his. Playacting, as his lips met hers, her head spinning with contrary feelings, a longing to be kissed, a fear of being kissed, wanting him to hold her tighter, wanting to run. She froze.

Alexander released her immediately. 'I'm sorry.'

Mortified, because now she was wishing she had let him kiss her, Eloise strove for composure. 'We were just acting,' she said, though the words which had sounded so convincing in her head sounded hollow aloud. 'You don't need to apologise.'

Alexander was silent for several long seconds, then he nodded and began to fold up the floor plan. 'We should go. The staff will be lined up and waiting.'

'I'll just fetch my hat and pelisse.'

He caught her arm as she turned away. 'I have every confidence in you.'

'You look extremely smart,' Alexander said as they stood at the foot of the steps leading up to Fearnoch House. Before they left the hotel, he'd told her she looked lovely, the truth but a mistake, he had realised too late. What she wanted was to be told that she looked every inch the Countess. 'Modish, but not too frivolous. The feather in your hat is set at just the perfect angle— neither flirtatious nor provocative, but not stern either. The scarf...'

'You can stop now, but thank you for trying.'

'You look perfect, Eloise. I mean that.'

'Thank you.'

'Are you ready?'

'As ready as I'll ever be. What about you, are you ready?'

He shrugged. It hadn't occurred to him that he might not be. There was no reason why he shouldn't be. 'I'm perfectly fine.'

He took her arm as the huge door was flung open. Eloise did not falter, but Alexander did, stumbling slightly as he crossed the long-forbidden threshold. His brother had died in this house, as had several earls before him. Now here he was, forced to walk in their footsteps, live in their shadows. He had a sudden overwhelming urge to run. He didn't want to know if the ghosts who haunted his dreams were real. He didn't want to face the reality of what he had been deprived of, and he didn't want to be faced once more with the question of why, why, why. Though he knew the answer now. He had worked it out for himself, years ago, as the only plausible explanation. The change to the Sixth Earl's will confirmed it.

Eloise tugged his arm gently, forcing him to look down at her. 'I have every confidence in you too,' she whispered.

They would make this place their own, he and his brave wife, he reminded himself, fixing a smile to his face as the butler approached.

'My lord, my lady, welcome to Fearnoch House, and on behalf of the staff, may I offer my warmest congratulations on your wedding.'

'Thank you,' Eloise spoke for them, her grip still firm on his arm. 'Lord Fearnoch and I are very pleased to be here at last.'

'Wiggins.' Alexander recalled the man's name with some relief. 'Mr Robertson tells me that you and the staff have worked tirelessly to have the house ready for us.'

'Thank you, my lord. There is a great deal still to be done, but no doubt you'll want to put your own mark on the place. And your ladyship, of course. Now, if I may.'

Wiggins threw open the second set of doors, ushering them into the main hallway, and now Eloise's steps did falter. Now it was his turn to support her, which he did, urging her forward to face the massed ranks of the servants, which looked to be at least double the number listed on the inventory. The housekeeper, Mrs McGilvery, was introduced first. The upper servants stood in two lines, men on one side, women on the other, like a guard of honour. Two more ranks were formed on the staircase which curved gracefully up from the ground level.

They made slow progress. Wiggins introduced the most senior staff personally, each one bowing or curtsying low. Alexander nodded, shook hands, realised that none of them expected to shake his hand, then realised that having started he couldn't stop.

'Another James?' Eloise exclaimed, startling him from his stupor. She had stopped in her tracks, forcing Alexander to do the same. 'You can't possibly all be called James,' she said, looking back down the row of footmen.

'Excuse me, my lady.' Wiggins intervened. 'You are perhaps not aware that it is the Fearnoch tradition to address all the footmen as James, and all the upper chambermaids are Margaret. It makes things easier.'

'Easier? For whom? Alexander—I mean, my lord, my love—we cannot—James and Margaret! It is an insult. These people are individuals and deserve to be treated as such.'

Eloise looked outraged. Wiggins was looking down at his feet. Mrs McGilvery was smiling grimly. The various Jameses were eyeing their new mistress with a mixture of astonishment, respect and barely concealed amusement. The arrogance of his father and his brother and heaven knew how many of his ancestors before them, to care so little for the people who served them that they couldn't be bothered to learn their names. The situation was utterly preposterous.

Alexander bit back a laugh. 'My wife is perfectly correct,' he said. 'This will be the first of many traditions we intend to change.'

'And while we are making changes, there is no need for the footmen to powder their hair,' Eloise added.

Smiling, Alexander manoeuvred his way out of the

guard of honour, taking his wife with him, to a position in the hall where he could see everyone, and everyone could see them. 'Thank you for taking the time to greet us. I am sure that Lady Fearnoch and I will in time get to know all of you, but for now, you'll understand that we would like to be left to ourselves, to become acquainted with our new home. Wiggins will arrange for a celebratory drink for all in the Servant's Hall. Now, if you'll excuse us?'

'Thank heavens.' As the green baize door closed on the bewildered butler and the last of the servants, Eloise heaved a sigh of relief. 'James and Margaret indeed! I wonder what name they bestowed on the scullery maids.'

'None at all, would be my guess. What would an earl have to do with a scullery maid?'

'That depends on how pretty the scullery maid is, and how much of a sense of entitlement the earl has,' Eloise said sardonically. 'Not that I am suggesting for a moment that your brother or your father would stoop so low.'

'I would very much like to think that they confined their activities to brothels—excuse me for being blunt— but the truth is, I really do know very little about them, save by reputation.'

'Didn't your paths ever cross?'

'You find it surprising to believe that they didn't?' Alexander asked wryly. 'I suppose it is surprising, in a way. London is not that big a city, and I do not spend all my time abroad.' He sat down on one of the many flimsy, gilded chairs scattered about the marble-floored space. 'There is no mystery to it. I avoided places where

I might bump into either of them, and I must assume they did the same.'

'It must feel—I can't imagine how it must feel, then, to be here, in this house...'

'Walking in their footsteps, living in their shadows.' Alexander grimaced. 'I don't know why it didn't occur to me until I walked through the front door.'

'I don't think I'd like to revisit our house in Ireland. I think I'd feel exactly the same, and I at least have the benefit of some happy memories.' She wrinkled her nose. 'Though none of them involve my parents.'

Alexander extricated himself with some difficulty from the chair. 'These are rather more decorative than practical.' He held out his hand. 'Are you ready to survey your new domain, my lady?'

He had changed the subject again. She hesitated only a second before taking her cue, dropping him a curtsy. 'I will follow your lead, my lord. Because if you follow me,' she added, with a teasing smile, 'I don't rate our chances of ever finding our way out of here alive. Which way?'

Alexander consulted the plan. 'That is the grand staircase. There's another, presumably less grand, in the other wing. This,' he said, opening a door, 'is the small parlour, probably used as a waiting room for guests.'

'Reserved for unwelcome guests, going by the furniture,' Eloise said, grimacing as she sat down, 'This is an exceedingly uncomfortable chair. What is next?'

Alexander led the way back out, across the hall, throwing open a set of double doors. 'The music room. And according to the inventory, most of the instruments were collected by the Fifth Earl.'

'That would be your grandfather?'

Either Alexander didn't hear her, or he assumed that his silence was sufficient agreement. 'I believe that some of these are very old.'

'And very beautiful.' Eloise opened the cover of a pianoforte and ran her fingers over the keys. 'My sister would think herself in heaven, here.'

'Estelle?'

'Yes, though Phoebe is not without musical talent. It comes from our mother's side of the family. Our grand-mother used to give recitals, so Kate told us.'

'Does it seem strange to you, to be living in your grandparents' house, but never to have met them?'

'It is sad, not strange. Mama was cut off from her family entirely when she eloped—I can't remember, did I tell you she eloped? And Papa—oh, I don't know for sure, but I think his family probably disowned him. Certainly, none of them came forward to claim us or his debts when he died.'

'Aren't you curious to discover whether you have relatives in Ireland still?'

'No.' She sat down beside him, sliding her slippered foot back and forward on the highly polished parquet flooring. 'You probably think that odd, given that I am so very close to my sisters, but why should I wish to know people who did not wish to know us in our time of need?'

'Why indeed! Though I do wonder if they might choose to know you now.'

'Now that I am Lady Fearnoch and married to a rich man, you mean? I should give them short shrift, I as-sure you.'

'I'd like to see that. Or, no, on second thoughts, I'd rather the occasion did not arise.'

'Phoebe and Estelle don't feel as I do. They don't say it, for fear of upsetting me, but I think they would like to be able to claim a cousin or two.'

'Blood being thicker than water? For what it is worth, I am with you. I see no reason why one should forgive a relative what one would not forgive a friend.'

Eloise reached up to caress his cheek, a habitual gesture of sympathy, of affection that she used so often she was unaware of it, until her skin came in contact with Alexander's and awareness jolted through her. Then the clock on the mantel struck the hour, and a cacophony of other clocks followed at intervals, the ringing and chiming sounding throughout the house, and she yanked her hand away. 'What on earth?'

'The Fourth Earl collected clocks. It seems none of them keep the exact right time,' Alexander said, rolling his eyes as one clock took over just as another ended. 'Shall we continue?'

Two hours later, each grand room was beginning to blur one into the other. Eloise had lost count of the number of drawing rooms and parlours she'd seen, and of the miles of corridors they'd walked, the stairs they had climbed in order to do so. There was a gallery filled with paintings by old masters. There was a billiard room, a ballroom, several dining rooms, and many others with no obvious purpose at all, save to store quantities of outmoded furniture. Every room was elaborately corniced. There were clocks everywhere, chiming almost constantly. And they had explored neither the kitchens nor the bedchambers, nor the attics. The Earls of Fearnoch were collectors of *objets d'art*, of curios, of furnishings and paintings, of anything, it seemed to Eloise, that cost a great deal and was mostly useless.

In one of the morning rooms, there had been a set of five bizarre glass-fronted display cases stacked in a pyramid, each containing two stuffed squirrels dressed as bare-knuckle pugilists, in short trousers with their paws bandaged. Following the display from the top down, Eloise could see that each vignette represented the different stages of a fight, for in the top the rodents were shaking hands, and in the last, one was standing triumphant over the other. Alexander had been confounded when, consulting the inventory, the squirrels were recorded as being Walter's doing. What kind of man was he, who could spend so much time painstakingly creating this grotesque work, with such obvious skill too? A libertine, according to Alexander, a wastrel and a spendthrift, judging by what she'd seen of this house, following in the footsteps of a long line of mountebanks. She found it sad, for all that the various collections showed taste and discrimination, there was nothing else to show for the Earls' industry, save this vast, opulent edifice. Perhaps the estates—but, no, Alexander had said that they were run by a manager.

What was he feeling? He had grown more and more silent as each room unveiled itself. He was so very different from his ancestors. It occurred to her then that there had been no portraits, and she was about to question him on this when he threw open another set of double doors and Eloise was confronted with a room which could have been designed specifically with her in mind.

'A library,' she said, surveying the room with delight.

'A library,' Alexander echoed, staring about him with equal fascination.

It was another vast room but, unlike any of the others, it gave the impression of intimacy. The ceiling was a simple latticework of cornicing, painted plain white. The walls were covered in a rich crimson damask, and lined with bookcases crammed full of books. The wood was oak, carved in the Jacobean style, as was the huge wooden mantel, but everything else in the room seemed to be designed for comfort rather than effect. There were two huge sofas facing each other across the hearth, a desk set in the window embrasure, any number of side tables, footstools, and comfortable armchairs, which seemed to Eloise to be crying out for a reader, a stack of books and a lazy day of reading. There was only one small clock, an exquisite bronze of Venus rising from the waves, and no other artefacts.

She ran her fingers along the spines of the books, which were shelved in no particular order, some unbound, others not even cut. 'There is a real treasure trove here.'

'The Sixth Earl acquired most of it in one job lot,' Alexander said, frowning over the inventory.

The Sixth Earl was his father. His brother had been the Seventh. He referred to Walter by name, but never once could she recall him making reference to any of the other Earls in a familiar manner.

'It seems that none of this has ever been catalogued,' Alexander said, looking up from his study of a large folio. 'I doubt much of it has ever been read.'

'We could work on the catalogue together.' Eloise joined him. The folio was of Dr Johnson's *Dictionary*. 'That looks to me as if it may be a very early edition.'

'It is,' Alexander said, closing it carefully. 'Are you

serious about the cataloguing? There must be thousands of books here.'

She'd thought it would be fun to work together on a common interest, locked away in this lovely room, just the two of them, and all these rarities waiting to be discovered. She'd thought it would appeal to Alexander too, producing a catalogue, creating order out of chaos, because that was what he did as a Victualling Commissioner, wasn't it?

He was smiling quizzically at her. 'Are you thinking that it is a task perfectly suited to my skills as an Admiralty clerk?'

'I was simply thinking that it would be a project we might enjoy together, but I realise...'

He caught her shoulder, turning her back to face him. 'I was teasing you. I thought you could always tell. What was it you said, about my smile being in my eyes?'

'It hasn't reached your eyes at all since we arrived here.'

He grimaced, slotting the folio gently back into its place on the shelves. 'I don't know about you, but I've had my fill for today—the rooms are beginning to merge, aren't they?'

'I remember each by the cornicing, the shape of the room and the colours.' Eloise said. 'I don't have any idea how I'd get to the Grand Dining Room from here, but I know it has a blue ceiling and relief panels on the walls. I loved the harlequin style of the plasterwork in the second drawing room, and the colours, the olive green and terracotta with touches of black, were wonderful. Then in the oval drawing room there were the Roman-style reliefs, and...'

'Enough!' Alexander exclaimed. 'Are there already

plans fermenting away in your head regarding changes you want to make?'

She sank on to one of the pair of sofas facing each other across the hearth, throwing up a cloud of dust that made her cough. 'Replace these, for a start, though aside from that, I think this room is quite perfect.'

'This is your idea of perfect?' Alexander said, sitting down tentatively beside her.

'Perfectly comfortable, compared to almost every other room we've seen so far. Fearnoch House feels more like a vast display cabinet than a home, but if you were happy to spend only a little money, I think it could be made into one.'

'This will be your home, and you can spend as much as you like.'

'It will be your home too, Alexander. Permanently, until our marriage is established, and afterwards—how often do you think you will be back in England?'

'It depends. There is no pattern to where my duties take me. It is impossible to predict.'

'Don't you have any say in the matter?'

He hesitated only briefly. 'No.'

Eloise waited, thinking to try a little of his silent tactics on him, but when she raised her brows enquiringly, Alexander simply drew her a bland look.

'What time will I order breakfast for?' she asked. 'You said—or you implied—that you would be continuing with your work in the short term, though not with the travel, so I assume that will entail a journey to your offices and an earlier start? What time will suit? Eight?'

'Eight.' He shrugged 'Yes.'

'And when should I expect you back for dinner?'

'I have no idea. That is—what I mean is, my work

does not usually follow a strict routine—since I am so often abroad.' He frowned down at his hand, as if he was surprised to see it still covered hers.

'But now, won't the person to whom you report expect you to keep more regular hours?'

For some reason he seemed to find what she said amusing. 'I think I will be permitted a little leeway, as a newly married man.'

'I simply—I don't want to intrude on your life any more than I need to.'

'We've been married a day, and you're already wanting rid of me.'

'You've made it clear how important your work is to you.'

'It is, but right now, there are more important things. More important even than the Admiralty.' He angled himself towards her, his knee brushing her leg, and covered her hands with his. 'Do you think you can be happy here, or at the very least content?'

'I think the question is rather whether you will be happy here, to be honest. I can make Fearnoch House comfortable, I can claim it for my own, because unlike you, there are no memories, no associations.'

'I didn't expect it to be quite so grand.'

'Surely you must have guessed, from the country estate where you were raised, that…'

His fingers tightened around hers. 'I knew the value of my inheritance from Robertson. I knew that this house and its contents were worth a great deal. But it's one thing to see it written down on paper. To see it all in the flesh, so to speak, it's…'

He shook his head. He let her go, throwing himself back on the sofa, stretching his long legs out in front of him, staring up at the ceiling. 'It makes what he did to my mother all the more unforgivable. It would literally have been a drop in the ocean to him, to have made her a decent settlement, but he chose not to.'

'You are talking about the change to your father's will—you think it was a calculated act? The first time we met, you said it was punitive.'

'Did I?'

'Was it?' Eloise persisted. 'Punitive, I mean?'

'I believe so.'

What was her crime? What did she do to deserve such a thing? The questions were so obvious there was no need for her to ask him. Experience had taught her that Alexander would immediately change the subject. She was bracing herself to force the issue, but he surprised her.

'If I'd been raised here, in the bosom of my family,' he said, 'I'd be a very different person.' He rubbed his eyes, sitting up. 'I spent all my time at Fearnoch Manor when I was not at school. Though it is actually the size of several manor houses cobbled together. I think each Earl added his own wing in his own particular style. But I was not permitted in the main house, Eloise. I had my own quarters, a much smaller lodge, complete with my own meagre staff. When my family were in residence, if I happened to be home from school, I was confined to those quarters.'

She stared at him, momentarily confounded. 'Dear God, that is—I don't know what to say.' All her instincts were to hug him, to comfort him, as she would her sisters, but his expression was stony, he was sitting up rigidly, his shoulders stiff with the effort of keeping his

feelings in check. 'I thought, when you said that you'd
been brought up in the country, I thought…'

'I know what you thought, because it's what I led you
to believe. I thought it didn't matter—I had come to believe it didn't matter. Until today. It's not that I feel I have
missed out, believe me. I meant what I said, I have never
envied my brother. It is more that—it's difficult to explain. When you asked me last night what I remembered
of my life here, I meant it when I said virtually nothing.
I don't recognise any of the rooms we've visited today,
there's nothing familiar about the place at all save the
feeling I had when we arrived.'

'You were reluctant to cross the threshold, weren't
you?'

'I was worried doing so might trigger unpleasant
memories, better left undisturbed. You see, I told you
it doesn't make sense.'

'But it does, Alexander. That is why I have no wish
to return to Ireland. My memories of it are bad enough,
but I'm pretty sure there's worse I don't remember.'

'You spent nineteen years at home though. I was
only five when I left for school. My memories of those
days are more positive.'

There was a fine line with him, Eloise recognised.
He would reveal so much, and then he would close the
door. He had already confided in her far more than she
had expected, thanks to the effect this house had had
on him. She did not want to distress him any further.
'So you enjoyed school?'

'I did, does that surprise you?'

'I thought all boys hated school.'

'I was a good student, a rare combination of brain
and brawn,' he said wryly. 'At school, it is important

to have the latter if one has the former. Boys can be vicious.'

'You were bullied?'

He shook his head, smiling faintly. 'No, what I'm trying to say is that I was not.'

'But you had to—are you saying you had to box, like those squirrels?'

'With less finesse, but, yes, I suppose you could say that. Schools, the kind of schools that educate our Establishment, pride themselves on the brutality of their regime. I decided to fight fire with fire.'

'But you were so very young. What about your brother, didn't he protect you? Or didn't he attend the same school as you?'

'Walter didn't attend any school, and even if he had, he was eight years older than I. It was not the done thing, to look out for a younger sibling. A boy must learn to fight his own battles.'

She eyed him, aghast. 'What about the boys who cannot defend themselves? They must have lived a miserable life, poor little souls. And you were—did you say five when you were packed off to prep school? That is barely weaned, for heaven's sake. My mother fought tooth and nail to keep Diarmuid at home, and he was ten. Didn't your mother—? Oh, God, no, she didn't. I am so sorry.'

'It is of no consequence.'

But she could see from the set of his mouth that it was. 'It was one of the few times that my father overruled my mother,' Eloise rushed on, 'insisting that Diarmuid was schooled in England. He said that the most long-lasting connections were those established at school, that my brother would thank him for it later in life, for sending him to a school where the most influential families in England sent their sons.'

'Which school was it?'

'He was enrolled at Eton. They were en route to England from Dublin, my brother and my parents, when the ship went down with all hands in a storm. Poor Diarmuid, I fear Mama's cosseting of him was very poor preparation for what he'd have endured at school. I doubt he even knew how to form a fist, let alone how to use one. Did you attend Eton?'

'Nothing so prestigious, though my school suited me very well. I was recruited into the Admiralty from there. One of the senior masters thought I was a good fit.'

'Because you had a good brain but were also—what is the phrase, handy with your fists?'

'Something like that. Sailors are a rough lot who'll chance their arm if they sense weakness. It helps if they know you will not be taken in or intimidated.'

'But you are a Victualling Commissioner.'

Alexander laughed. 'I am still capable of defending myself if I need to.'

'I had no idea your work was dangerous.'

'It's not, unless you count death by a thousand paper cuts,' he said airily. 'More important even than my ability to defend myself or to write a legible hand, what I learned from being sent away to school at such an early age was how to fend for myself.'

'You mean you can cook? Sew on a button?'

'And even black my own boots. But what I meant was, I'm very resourceful.'

'And you are also happy in your own company. "Solitary by nature" I think is how you put it.'

'Did I? I hope you know that I am more than happy in your company.'

'I hope you know that the feeling is reciprocated.'

'I do.' Alexander took her left hand, turning the wedding ring around her finger. 'It's hard to believe that we've only been married a day. If you counted up the hours we've actually spent together—I feel I've known you much longer.'

'You have. You first met me three years ago, remember. I was reading *Candide.*'

He laughed. 'We shall have to practise telling our story if we are to be word perfect when we recount it for an audience.'

'When will that be?'

'A week or so? I've been thinking that it would be a good idea to hold a formal reception to celebrate our nuptials. We can introduce ourselves to London society, including my cousin Raymond, get it all over with in one fell swoop, rather than an endless round of social engagements. What do you think?'

'I think it would be a baptism of fire.'

'But we would be facing it together.'

He was smiling again. There was so much in what they had talked about that she needed to mull over, so many questions he had, she was sure, expertly fielded, but on such a momentous day as this, she wanted him to keep smiling. 'Then how can we fail?' Eloise said.

Chapter Six

The morning sun poured in through the full-length windows of the ballroom at Fearnoch House, which opened out on to a small balcony overlooking the back gardens. Corinthian columns of black marble and gilded acanthus leaves flanked the room. The same black marble was used to form the door pillars, topped with gilded cupids. Two large fireplaces bookended the huge room for warmth, while three extraordinary chandeliers formed of beaten bronze provided light. The room itself was empty save for the grand piano occupying one corner. Eloise's steps echoed on the polished floorboards as she walked the length of the chamber.

She and Alexander had breakfasted together in one of Fearnoch House's more intimate rooms, a charming parlour with cream walls adorned with painted plasterwork garlands, swags and flowers, the beautiful designs continuing on over the fireplace, the pastel colours soothing. He had called her his love and kissed her cheek, for Wiggins was attending them. It had been astonishingly easy, to sit with her husband at the round rosewood table and map out their day. Which started with planning for their wedding party.

'How many people will expect to be invited?' Eloise asked.

'I have absolutely no idea.'

Alexander, wearing top boots and dove-grey pantaloons, with a matching dove-grey waistcoat, but no coat, threw open the double doors, which led out on to the narrow balcony. He stepped outside, beckoning her to join him. The air smelled fresh and the lawn was still damp with dew.

'Did you manage to sleep, Eloise?'

'Eventually. Knowing that I was *not* sleeping in the same bed as any of the previous Countesses helped, I must admit. Mrs McGilvery was a little surprised when I told her we had no intentions of occupying the state bedchambers, but...'

'I am very relieved that you did. Occupying my forebear's home is one thing, but as for sleeping in his bed...' Alexander winced.

'Did you manage to get some rest?' she asked. 'I will take that as a no, then,' she added, when he rather irritatingly merely shrugged, demonstrating yet again his taciturn nature.

'Look.' He put his arm around her to direct her view. 'More trees than you could ever hope to climb.'

'I would need a set of ladders to reach even the lowest branches of those enormous specimens,' Eloise replied. 'Perhaps I'll have a tree house built, a bolthole where no one can find me.'

'We've only been married for two days, and already you're wanting to hide from me. All jesting aside, promise me you won't be so foolish as to attempt to climb any of them. If you fell you would break your neck.'

She shrugged, playing him at his own game, and then turned to face him. There were shadows under his eyes. He smelled of shaving soap. 'It's not you I'd be trying to escape from, it's the servants. I seem to trip over one every time I move. I counted five on my way from my bedchamber to breakfast. In such a huge house as this, it shouldn't be so difficult to be alone.'

'We're alone now.'

It was absurd, the way her stomach lurched when he said that, as if he'd told her something she didn't know. Something exciting, that made her pulses flutter and her mouth go dry. 'There are probably at least two footmen guarding the ballroom doors. And gardeners—there are bound to be gardeners out there, looking up, catching a glimpse of the newly married Earl and his Countess surveying their domain.'

'The newly married Earl and his Countess enjoying a rare moment of privacy together,' Alexander said. 'Relishing the opportunity too, because once they launch themselves into the preparations for their wedding ball, they are not likely to have many more such moments.'

One of his hands was resting lightly on her waist. The other was at the nape of her neck. Heat was radiating from the point where his fingers made contact with her skin. If they were being watched, it would seem odd if she simply stood there like a wooden mannequin. Eloise put her hand on Alexander's shoulder. Her legs brushed his. She reached up, feeling the smoothness of his freshly shaved jaw under her palm, curling her fingers into his hair. It was as silky as it looked. Her heart was hammering, but she was acting, that was all, she was playing her part as the recently married Countess of Fearnoch, deeply in love with her husband.

She stepped closer. Her breasts brushed his chest. His hand tightened on her waist. If she really was alone with her husband for the first time that morning, she would...

His lips touched hers before she had finished the thought, and her heart began to beat wildly. There was a pause, an aching pause, and she realised hazily that Alexander was giving her time to draw back, but a newly married countess would not draw back from kissing the husband she loved, so she did not. And he kissed her.

But she had never been kissed. She had no idea how to respond. Did you simply press your lips against each other like this? Which was delightful, but surely this couldn't be all? She pulled away. 'I'm sorry, but I don't know how.'

He studied her for a moment. 'Do you want to learn?'

'I don't know. Yes. We should—I mean we would, wouldn't we? Relish the moment, you said.'

His smile was one she hadn't seen before, but she had no time to analyse it. 'Close your eyes,' Alexander said, kissing her lids shut. 'Tilt your head just a little—like that.'

He kissed her again, soft little kisses all the way along her bottom lip. Delicious. So the Countess would think. And if the Countess liked it, then surely the Earl would too. She kissed him back, the same little kisses, and felt his breath quicken. He licked into the corners of his mouth, and when her lips parted in surprise, he moulded his mouth to hers and he began to kiss her and she knew then that this was a real kiss. A tiny moan escaped her as she followed his lead. Her mouth opened to his. Her senses clamoured, her pulses raced.

* * *

Alexander ended the kiss, stepping back, dazed. What the devil was he playing at!

'What did I do wrong?'

'Wrong?' Mortified by his all-too-evident arousal, he could not, for a moment, fathom what Eloise meant. 'Nothing,' he said, belatedly realising how his abrupt termination of their kiss must appear to her. 'On the contrary, you were so convincing that I was in danger of forgetting that we were acting.'

He had completely forgotten, in fact. He didn't know what had come over him. No, that wasn't true. What had come over him was a very urgent desire to kiss her, not because they were playing their allotted roles, but because he wanted to kiss her. And having kissed her, he wanted to kiss her again. Having had no urge to kiss a woman for so long, this was not something he'd anticipated.

'But we were acting, weren't we?'

Eloise looked—frightened? No, but anxious. 'Putting on a show for any watching staff,' he said, because clearly that's what she wanted to hear. 'Of course we were.'

Her smile of relief told him that he'd said the right thing. 'I thought so. Do you think the gardeners witnessed our most excellent performance?'

'I think we'd better concentrate on convincing our expected guests rather than worry too much about the gardeners,' Alexander said. 'If this is to be our wedding celebration, we'll be expected to lead everyone on to the dance floor.'

'Dear heavens, I hadn't thought of that. I can't waltz.'

'You mean you don't think you are very good?'

'No, can't, as in I have never learned, having had no need to.'

He swept her into his arms. 'It is not inordinately difficult, my lady. Put your hand on my shoulder. Now you clasp my other hand like this. The basic steps are very simple. You follow me, mirror what I do, with the opposite foot. Ready? One. Two. Three.'

'Sorry. That was your toe.'

'Several of my toes. Let's try again.'

'I have no sense of rhythm. Ask Estelle. I can't sing—well, no, that's not true, I *can* sing, but I can't hold a tune. I'm very good at remembering the words though. I know the entire libretto of the *Marriage of Figaro*. The one that starts "Say goodbye now to pastime" is my favourite, but it drives Estelle mad when I sing it. I think Estelle would make a very good dancer.'

'I am not married to Estelle. But talking of which, Eloise, I don't think we should invite your sisters to our wedding dance. I am sorry, but...'

'Oh, no, I completely agree. We cannot risk them inadvertently giving the game away. We must maintain a believable façade.'

'As we did a moment ago, when I kissed you. I didn't mean to alarm you.'

'You didn't. I alarmed myself by my reaction,' she admitted bashfully. 'I didn't think I'd like it, and I did, if you must know. Well, not kissing generally, but kissing you.'

Alexander had absolutely no inclination to laugh at this astonishing confession. 'And you don't want to like it too much?' he asked gently, for that was suddenly abundantly clear to him.

'No. I don't. I truly don't.'

'It frightens you.'

'Terrifies me. I don't want to be like my mother.'

'Eloise.' With great difficulty, he stopped himself from pulling her into his arms and instead took her hands. 'You can trust me.'

'I do. I'm wondering whether I can trust myself.'

'Now you know perfectly well you are being ridiculous, don't you?' This time, he did permit himself a small smile. 'We were kissing as Lord and Lady Fearnoch. A performance, for the benefit of the gardeners.'

Eloise nodded. He eased his conscience, telling himself it was more important to reassure her than to admit to the truth. And perhaps the truth was that he had simply become carried away. After two years of celibacy, it was understandable that he had reacted as he had to kissing a beautiful and desirable woman. Nature and instinct had taken over, making him forget, temporarily, the reasons why he had vowed never to surrender to such temptation again. But he remembered now.

Having reassured himself as well as his wife, Alexander clasped her hand. 'Talking of performances, I think our waltz needs a little more practice.'

Their afternoon was spent shopping. Alexander took her first to a silk warehouse in Spitalfields. Though the restrictions on the importation of French silks were now relaxed, the silk produced in the East End of London was still the most sought after for its intricately woven patterns. Stepping over the threshold, faced with bales and bales of fabrics stacked from floor to ceiling, Eloise felt as if she had arrived in paradise.

The plain silks were arranged by colour, the deepest shades on the bottom shelves, with the lightest at the top. Forest green bled into emerald, sea, pea, moss, sage and mint, then a pale hue Eloise had no name for. Mahogany became garnet, segued to vermilion, then scarlet, cherry and rose. The blues took up even more space. There were blues for every colour of sky, from a pale winter morning, to the azure blaze of late summer, the grey-blue of a stormy autumn day, and the indigo of a balmy night. The golds and oranges could be used to construct a sunrise for every season. White became silver became pewter which seeped into dark grey, then ebony. There were silks the colour of every flower Eloise had ever seen and more, an exotic desert garden of colours that made her head spin with ideas.

In a trance, she wandered around the warehouse, caressing chiffon and crepe, georgette and gauze. And then she reached the figured silks, and stopped in awe, as an art lover would before an old master. There were plain silks patterned with one colour, flowers and leaves in the most exquisite of stitches, white figured on silver, blue, green. On others, flowers spilled out in a riot of colour over a white or cream background, vibrant pinks in clusters on green stems or branches of gnarled wood so lifelike that she felt she could pluck them from the fabric, bury her nose in their scent. The most costly and complex were the quilted silks, heavy with silver and gold thread, and the broad bands of finishing silks for hems and sashes which were so densely embroidered very little of the silk base was visible.

'No need to ask if this was a good idea,' Alexander said, appearing at her elbow as she reverently ran her fingers along a bale of emerald green worked with tiny white knots of flowers. 'I only wish I could claim it as my own.'

'Neither of my sisters can possibly have known that this Aladdin's Cave existed,' Eloise said, smiling hazily. 'So a great deal of the credit must go to you. If one could be intoxicated by fabric, then I think I might just be in my cups. Thank you.'

'It is a pleasure, though I fear it presents you with a dilemma. I can tell from your expression that you would love to purchase the entire contents of this warehouse. But even if you changed your gown six times a day and lived to a hundred, there would still be some left unused. So the question is, how are you going to narrow the choice?'

'I can eliminate all of these for a start,' Eloise said, indicating the selection of figured silks. 'They are far too costly and most of them are far too ornate.'

'Must I remind you that you are a countess?'

'You need not worry, I won't embarrass you.' She fingered the emerald-green silk distractedly. It was so fine, the little flowers so tiny that they would not interfere with the flow of the fabric. It would not rustle the way stiffer, more coarsely woven silks would, this would generate the merest whisper. She would make the skirts of a gown made from this silk full, but the gown itself would be plain. Slashed sleeves, perhaps, aw low, scooped décolleté with a lace edging. And underskirts in layers of other shades of green, graduating from dark to pale, like the petals of a flower, which would whirl around her as she danced.

'I take it that you have decided on this one, then?'

'For our wedding ball. It is extravagant, but—may I?'

Alexander summoned one of the attendants, waiting discreetly at the end of the aisle. 'This one,' he said. 'My wife will tell you how much she requires. And she will tell me,' he said to Eloise as the man bustled away, 'what it is that is worrying her.'

'Nothing at all.'

Alexander raised a brow.

'It is only that I have no idea what life will be like for me now,' she admitted reluctantly. 'How can I shop for dresses when I don't even know what I am doing tomorrow, never mind next week, next month, next year?'

'For the immediate future, what you will be doing is planning for a ball. After that—I seem to recall that you told me that having absolutely no idea what you would do was such an exciting idea that you could, to use your own words, hug yourself. What has changed?'

Eloise laughed nervously. 'It is being faced with the reality of it and finding nothing familiar. I'm a bit lost at sea, I suppose, with no anchor.'

'You have me.'

For how long? How long did it take to *establish* a marriage? Once their wedding ball was over, would Alexander consider himself free to resume his old life? But wasn't that what she wanted too? 'I'm being silly,' Eloise said. 'It's only been a few days.'

'Are you missing your sisters already?'

'No,' she said, after thinking about this for a moment, 'it's not that at all. I think that I had become a little too set in my ways at Elmswood Manor. It was a cosy, familiar haven.'

'The perfect refuge after the storm that you were forced to endure for the first nineteen years of your life.'

'I hadn't thought of it in those terms.' She pondered this insight. 'Maybe you're right. It's time for me to step blinking back into the sunlight and stand on my own

two feet without even you to anchor me down. I know
how eager you are to return to your Admiralty career.'

He took her hands in his, drawing her closer. 'This is
our life, for the time being. Let's enjoy it for what it is.'

'I'd like that.' Save for their hands, they were not
touching, but as their eyes met Eloise remembered their
kiss that morning. The way it had made her pulses race,
had seemed to heat her blood, made her body crave
more. She had been pretending, she reminded herself,
and so too had Alexander. He'd said so. But now, as
she looked at him, as he looked at her, it was as if their
bodies had found a role they wanted to perform again,
regardless of whether they were on stage. She wanted
to kiss him again. She knew he was thinking that he
wanted to kiss her because he was urging her closer,
and his head was lowering to hers.

Behind them, the warehouseman cleared his throat,
making them both jump apart. 'Excuse me, my lord,
my lady, I was just wondering if you needed any more
assistance?'

So they'd had an audience, after all. Alexander must
have noticed and played to it, even if she hadn't. She
ought to be relieved, not disappointed, though why he
felt it imperative to prove to a complete stranger that
he loved his wife…

Deciding that there was no merit in pursuing the
answer to this question, Eloise turned her attention to
the question of fabrics and gowns, abandoning herself
to the hedonistic pleasure of shopping without any regard for cost.

They had decided to hold their wedding ball two
weeks on Saturday, which would be Alexander's thir-

tieth birthday, throwing themselves into a wild flurry of preparations that left little time for anything else. The announcement of their nuptials in the press the next day informed the world that the Earl and his new Countess would not be at home to callers until after their wedding ball, but nevertheless an avalanche of visiting cards and invitations arrived at Fearnoch House. Most of the names were unknown to Eloise. Only a very few were known to Alexander from the Admiralty, but, fortunately for the newlyweds, Robertson the lawyer was able to sort the remainder into family, close connections and acquaintances of the previous two Earls, and to advise them on who should and should not be invited to the ball.

Scrutinising Robertson's list, Eloise saw that Lady Constance, the Dowager Countess of Fearnoch, was missing. Warily raising the issue of his mother with Alexander, she discovered, without surprise, that the omission was deliberate and his doing. 'But won't people expect her to be here? It is our wedding ball. Her absence will look extremely odd.'

'We'll tell them that her health is too fragile for her to travel to the city,' he answered after a brief silence.

'Will you tell her that? The first ball given by the new Earl will be bound to be noted in the newspapers,' she pressed, when he looked as if he was about to dismiss her concerns. 'She will surely have friends, acquaintances in attendance too. She's in Lancashire, Alexander, not Africa. Letters can reach her, newspapers...'

'I will have her informed. And I will ensure that she does *not* discuss our nuptials, before you ask. I won't have her spoil the story we have concocted before we have a chance to tell it.'

He would say no more, except to assure her later that day that the matter had been dealt with, and Eloise had neither the time nor the inclination to pursue the matter.

Phoebe and Estelle between them, in a flurry of correspondence, helped her to design the menus for both suppers to be served, and the music to be played for each of the dances. There was too little time for Eloise to fret about how the Fearnoch House staff viewed their new, inexperienced mistress, as she, with Mrs McGilvery's help, embroiled all of them in a frenzy of arranging and rearranging all of the public rooms. Alexander, meanwhile, with Wiggins's help, ordered enormous quantities of wine and champagne, consulted various mysterious authorities to ensure that the carriages arriving with their guests would be supervised, and the waiting coachmen and horses attended to.

In between preparing the house, Eloise had to prepare herself. She expected Madame LeClerc of Bond Street to sneer at her ideas for the very large selection of silks and other fabrics she had purchased. Instead, the modiste was in raptures at her designs, offered several very clever innovations of her own, and promised Eloise that her ball gown would take priority and would definitely be ready in time.

Madame LeClerc recommended that Eloise order her hats from a specific milliner in Piccadilly who also happened to be Madame's particular friend. On the subject of accoutrements, Madame suggested that Eloise pay a visit to Bedford House, which was one of the finest linen drapers, and conveniently close to Oxford Street's wide selection of shoemakers, glovers and hosiers, all of which, Eloise discovered, were essential components of her trousseau.

A shy enquiry into where she might purchase undergarments led Eloise to Number Eighteen New Bond Street, the premises of Mrs Harman, stay-maker, and the visiting card which Alexander had had printed for her caused Mrs Harman herself to attend her illustrious new client. The undergarments Eloise was shown were beautifully made and prettily trimmed, the sort which no lady would be ashamed to be seen in by her sisters, for example, but they were not the type Eloise had in mind. When Mrs Harman's delicate but probing questions established what Eloise *did* have in mind, she was ushered into a small room behind a pair of dark-velvet curtains furnished only with a red-velvet chaise longue reserved, Mrs Harman told her, for very particular customers. Realising too late that the particular customers were likely to be courtesans rather than countesses, Eloise waited in trepidation, and was seriously considering fleeing, when the stay-maker reappeared, bearing her wares, and all thoughts of leaving fled.

The chemises were the most recognisable items, being the simplest, worn next to the skin, though made of the finest lawn cotton, trimmed with cotton lace. Next came the pantalettes, also in finest lawn and cambric, but trimmed more lavishly with lace threaded with ribbons. Then came Mrs Harman's speciality, the stays. There were short stays and long stays, designed to accentuate the wearer's curves or to constrain them. There were stays which were laced at the back and required assistance and stays which laced at the front, which were convenient, Mrs Harman informed Eloise, for both dressing and undressing by a less experienced hand. 'Or should I say a less feminine hand,' she elucidated archly, seeing Eloise's obvious confusion which then

immediately turned to embarrassment as her meaning
sank in. The stays were made of silk, black, red and
jewel colours, too exquisite, surely, to be hidden beneath a gown. Which of course, she realised when she
tried on several, staring at herself in the mirror, they
were not meant to be.

After the stays came the petticoats, confections of
silk and ribbons and lace in a rainbow of colours, some
with sleeves for day wear, some with only the flimsiest
of straps to be worn under an evening gown. Having announced that she would be honoured to make my lady
petticoats of layered green silk, Mrs Harman then produced a selection of stockings. My lady would require
white, naturally, but Eloise was also offered stockings
with embroidered clocks, stockings with coloured garters, a shocking pair in pink to emulate the bare flesh,
and one in black with red rosettes.

When the nightgowns and matching peignoirs were
proffered, she ordered a selection of those too. And just
at the point where her senses were overloaded and she
thought she would never buy another garment as long
as she lived, she remembered her sisters and Kate, and
ordered each a nightgown and a pair of finest silk stockings with clocks of different flowers.

Arriving back at Fearnoch House, safe from any further temptation, she was appalled by her profligacy,
though still in thrall to the sensuous beauty of the gar-
ments. The designs were both practical and flattering, the cut precise, the stitching not only beautiful but
strong. As a needlewoman, she was lost in admiration
for the skill involved.

It was only when the first of her decadent undergarments were delivered and Eloise tried them on, taking

the precaution of locking her bedroom and dressing room doors, that she began to have doubts. The fabrics were sensual. They caressed her skin, they moulded themselves to her form, and they accentuated her curves in a way that made her feel self-conscious, and at the same time oddly excited. Taking out her pins, she let her hair ripple down her back, over her shoulders, and saw a woman she didn't recognise staring back at her. A woman with the sort of siren curves that men noticed. A woman who dressed in anticipation of being undressed, whose silks and laces were designed to invite the most intimate of caresses. Would Alexander find this woman attractive? Would he want to kiss the breasts which were only just covered? Eloise closed her eyes, trying to imagine those kisses, feeling her nipples tighten in response. He would kiss her, and he would touch her, here and here and here. And then he would...

What, exactly? She hadn't the first clue what he would do next! And yet the woman staring back at her, wide-eyed, soft-mouthed, curvaceous, looked as if she were an experienced lover. She looked, in fact...

'Dear God in heaven,' Eloise said, 'I look exactly like my mother.'

It took her less than five minutes to change. Fortunately, among her mountain of shopping she had ordered a selection of more prosaic underwear. Mrs Harman's confections were thrust back into their layers of tissue paper, the boxes retied and thrust to the back of the cupboard.

'I think we're ready.' Alexander brought their waltz to an end with a flourish, twirling Eloise around and making a bow. 'What do you think, Bennet?'

'Very polished, my lord. Most graceful, my lady. You are very well matched. Anyone would think you'd been dancing together for years.'

'Precisely our intention, as you know very well,' Alexander replied, grinning.

'Thank you for playing for us so patiently, Bennet,' Eloise said, as he got up from the piano stool. 'I don't think I could have borne the embarrassment of learning to dance in front of a stranger. You are a man of many talents.'

'Including some I would rather you did not know about, my lady. If you'll excuse me now?'

'What did he mean by that?' Eloise asked as the double doors closed behind him.

Alexander, thinking of some of his man's more lethal skills, merely shrugged. 'Heaven knows. Never mind Bennet's talents, I'm more interested in yours. I don't think you realise how much you've accomplished in less than two weeks, and all without a dancing master.'

'I had *Lowes' Ball Conductor and Assembly Guide* to study,' Eloise said, referring to the volume she had uncovered in the library, 'and I had an excellent tutor in you. You haven't told me where you first learned to dance.'

At the age of twenty in a seedy and very rundown part of Vienna, was the true answer. The waltz he had learned then was a raucous version of the genteel one he'd taught Eloise, danced with abandon fuelled, Alexander recalled, by some potent clear spirit he'd never encountered anywhere else.

'It is expected,' he said, opting reluctantly for another, more sanitised version of the truth, 'that officers in the Admiralty equip themselves with the necessary skills to deport themselves adequately at social occasions such as dinners and balls.'

'Do Victualling Commissioners often attend social events?'

'Regularly, at some of the larger overseas naval bases.'

Looking unconvinced, Eloise wandered over to the piano, flicking through the loose sheets of music. She had asked him several times about the nature of his work, though she was careful never to persist when he resorted to evasion. He wondered if this meant she was more or less curious? The nature of Alexander's real endeavours required him to be an accomplished fabricator, but for some reason he found it difficult to lie to Eloise. Worse than that, there had been a few occasions—now was a perfect instance—when he'd been tempted to tell her the truth.

Contrary to his expectations, he enjoyed their conversations at the breakfast table. He enjoyed seeing Eloise gain in confidence, rising to so many challenges that it was difficult to remember they had only been married two weeks. The servants, inclined from the start to view favourably any mistress who could put a name to every face, were won over by her frank admissions of ignorance when it came to the running of the household. She did not command, but her every request was happily acceded to. It was to be expected that some members of such a large staff would have taken advantage in a house bereft of a master in the months between Walter's death and their arrival here, and Eloise, whose mastery of the account books she attributed to Lady Elmswood's example of careful husbandry, had uncovered a good many instances of pilfering. Alexander would have sacked the culprits. Eloise called an amnesty instead, and he was willing to bet that time would prove her instincts correct.

She had not made Fearnoch House her home yet, but he was confident she would in time. After that first day, Alexander had managed to put aside his own feelings about the place—for the most part. There were moments that still caught him unawares. Not memories as such, still nothing so vivid, but a sudden sense of something, as if someone had just left a room he had entered. And there were rooms he avoided. The master bedchambers. The attics which had been the nursery. The room identified as the study on the floor plan. He told himself there was no need to venture into any of them. Alexander was adept at fooling others. He was not so adept at fooling himself. There would come a time to face his demons, but it was not now.

Eloise set down the sheet music and joined him at the window. 'You are looking very pensive.'

'I am thirty years old tomorrow. I never imagined it would be such a momentous occasion.'

'Our wedding ball. This time tomorrow, there will be an orchestra tuning up where the piano is, and I will most likely be hiding in my room too terrified to come out.'

'That is one thing I am not worried about. I was just thinking how wonderfully you are succeeding in making this place your own. You are making an excellent Lady Fearnoch.'

'I am embracing life, just as you commanded me to. You see, I am a most obedient wife. About to attend my first ever ball and I am actually hosting it! My introduction to London society as Lady Fearnoch, and to your cousin Raymond as the woman who deprived him of a fortune. You're right, I have nothing whatsoever to be afraid of.'

Alexander laughed. 'At least you can have no fears about carrying off the first dance.' He pulled her into his arms in a waltz hold and twirled her around in a small circle. 'You see.'

'I can follow *your* lead.'

They had come to a halt by the piano. He dropped his hold to pull her closer. 'Then you can save both waltzes for me, and dance only the country dances with our guests.'

'Are *you* nervous?'

He hadn't even thought about it, save as a task on his list which must be ticked off. A room full of the great and the good, some of whom would be complete strangers, held no fears for him. It wasn't exactly life-threatening. But for Eloise, it must be daunting. He cursed himself for a thoughtless fool. 'I'm sorry. You have been doing such an excellent job of embracing your new life I didn't realise that it might be taking its toll on you.'

'It's not—well, there are some things I'm struggling with, but—I don't want to let you down,' she admitted.

'That's not possible,' he said fiercely. 'And before you list out every single thing that might go wrong, let me tell you that when we stand at the top of the grand staircase tomorrow to receive our guests, when we take to this floor for the opening waltz, what people will see is what we want them to see—a newly married couple who are madly in love with each other.'

As he had hoped, she smiled. 'Must it be *madly*?'

It had always seemed to Alexander that love was a form of insanity. 'Contentedly? No, that's not right.

Though we've known and loved each other for years, we've only been married a fortnight. That is far too soon for us to be merely content in each other's company.'

'Alexander!'

'Eloise!' He pulled her closer. 'We have waited three years to consummate our love,' he whispered into her ear. 'I would imagine that we would be eager, now that we are man and wife, to consummate it as often as possible.'

She gave a startled laugh, blushing charmingly. 'I cannot imagine how that may have been achieved, with so much to be done for tomorrow.'

She smelled delicious—a new perfume, he wondered, or a scented soap? One of her hands was resting on his shoulder. The other, which had been on his waist during their dance, slid up his back. Her fingers curled into his hair. She was such a delightful combination of innocence and allure, he could not resist teasing her.

'We might start here, for example. We are alone, after all,' Alexander said.

Surrendering to temptation, he kissed her. He had not meant his kiss to be serious, he had not meant it to be a real kiss. Then Eloise kissed him back. And when she kissed him back, he forgot all about teasing her, wrapping his arms tightly around her and kissing her again, kissing her deeply, eyes closed, filling his senses with her scent and her curves and her mouth on his, kissing him back.

He was hard. Their tongues touched, and it made him harder. When she moaned, pushing herself against him, his senses swam. Still kissing, he eased her back against the piano, lifting her up on to the closed lid. Their tongues touched again, and he wrenched his mouth from hers, telling himself that this was enough, but the sight of her, eyes heavy with passion, lips plump from their kisses, was irresistible.

He kissed her mouth again, then her throat. He kissed her breasts along the neckline of her gown. It was high cut. Only a sliver of her delicate, delicious flesh was exposed, but it was more than enough to make his shaft thicken and pulse. He cupped her breast, feeling the hard nub of her nipple through her stays. Her hands slid down his back, urging him closer, and he almost obeyed. Though they were fully clothed, the primal need to press himself against her, to let her know just how much he wanted her...

Alexander ended the kiss, letting Eloise go, helping her down from the piano—from the piano, for the love of God! He was mortified at his own lack of control, appalled by his behaviour. 'I should not have...'

'I see now, how it may be managed,' she interrupted him hurriedly. 'It is as well that I've put an end to having the footmen stand sentry at every door.'

She was making a show of shaking out her gown, turning away from him so that he couldn't see her face. He couldn't begin to imagine what was going through her head. She had not been feigning her desire any more than he had, but it was clear she wanted to pretend that this had been the case. So he took out his watch and shook his head. 'I had no idea it was so late. I have some papers to sign before dinner.'

Her sigh of relief was palpable. 'And I also have a hundred things to attend to. So if you'll excuse me...'

Without meeting his eyes, Eloise fled. Alexander moved over to the window and stepped on to the balcony. Think about something else, he told himself, think about the list of tasks his lawyer had drawn up for him, think about…

What the devil had come over him! Did he really need to remind himself of the dire consequences of getting too close to a woman—any woman, never mind his wife! In his line of work he wasn't even supposed to have a wife, had obtained permission from a reluctant Sir Marcus on the understanding that his marriage was exactly what he had agreed with Eloise, in name only. He could not risk her growing to care for him. He most certainly must not care for her.

Out of the corner of his eye he saw one of the gardeners sweeping up the cherry blossom from the paths. Calm down, he told himself, don't exaggerate. It was a few kisses, nothing more. If Eloise was happy to pretend they had been acting, why couldn't he? His hands tightened on the balcony rails. Because he had not been acting. Because after two years, his body had decided to reassert its needs. Primal, that's all his response had been. It wasn't particularly that he wanted to make love to Eloise, it was simply that he wanted to make love.

The simple solution would be to do just that. Go out, find a willing woman, satisfy his urges and promptly forget about it. He had never done such a thing in his life. The very notion of doing it now filled him with repugnance. It was Eloise he desired. His persistent arousal told him so. Alexander cursed, drawing on his wide vocabulary of naval oaths, expending a great deal of energy and imagination, until finally he ran out of breath. It made no difference. So he tried a different tack.

'Claudia.' He said the name out loud, forcing himself to remember her. The glossy black hair she wore piled high on her head that magically unravelled with the removal of just two pins, to curl down her back. The way she had of looking demure and sultry at the same time. If only he'd ignored her that first night at the Embassy. If only she hadn't sought him out the next day. If only he'd asked her to leave before they made love. But her pillow talk was too useful. Her body too alluring. And he'd thought himself one in a string of many lovers. A passing fancy for her, as she was for him. If only he'd realised how wrong he was sooner, he could have prevented the tragedy that had ensued.

'Claudia,' he said again, summoning up her ghost to exorcise his desire for his wife. It worked, too well. Staring out over the garden, Alexander felt sick to his stomach.

Chapter Seven

Alexander leapt to his feet as Eloise entered the drawing room. 'You look absolutely magnificent!'

She performed an extravagant twirl to show off the layers of green underskirts which had turned out exactly as she had imagined them, the lace-trimmed silk rustling like leaves in an autumn breeze. 'Thanks to Madame LeClerc.'

'She assembled it, but you chose the silks and designed the dress.' He took her hand. 'You are both beautiful and talented, Lady Fearnoch. I am a very lucky man.'

Ah, so they were in character already? Probably a wise move with such a daunting ordeal ahead. Eloise dropped a curtsy, flicking out her fan as her new maid, Agnes, had taught her. 'Thank you, my lord. You look particularly handsome tonight. You are not the only lucky one.'

She allowed herself to study her husband. His evening clothes were black and as ever beautifully fitted, highlighting the breadth of his shoulders tapering to a narrow waist, and the long, rangy lines of his legs. He was *very* handsome. It was perfectly natural that she should find him attractive. And so it followed that it was perfectly natural that she should have enjoyed kissing him, as one would enjoy, say, wearing a beautiful ball gown made from the most exquisite silk.

The emotions were not remotely comparable, she knew that. Aware of him watching her, she turned her attention to the room, though she and Mrs McGilvery had already meticulously checked it and every other room which would be in use tonight. From the cloak-room, to the ladies' and gentlemen's withdrawing rooms and the Grand Dining Room which would be used for suppers, everything was just so. The orchestra were setting up in the ballroom at this very moment. The carpet had been laid out on the steps outside the main entrance, the braziers lit. There was nothing for her to do now but wait. And try to avoid thinking about kiss-ing her husband.

Pulling open the drawer of a side table, she stared down blankly at the array of spare candles. It was sup-posed to be an act, but when he had kissed her yester-day, she'd forgotten everything except the urge to kiss him back. And when he'd touched her—a frisson ran through her as she recalled that particular touch—she had never felt anything like that! She had crossed the line from pretending to experiencing at some stage, and it didn't matter when—the point was that she had crossed it. She'd thought herself immune to the kind of feelings that Alexander had aroused when he kissed her, when he touched her, but on the contrary—she'd wanted more. Was that passion? No, it couldn't be, for it had not transformed her in any way, shape or form. Was it possible to enjoy kissing, to enjoy lovemaking even, without being passionate about it, without it being profound?

Enough! She closed the drawer. She checked the clock on the mantel, one of the few which she had not allowed to run down. Fearnoch House no longer sounded like a school for campanologists when the hour struck. What to do with the vast collection of redundant timepieces— that was one of many items on her list for after the ball.

'In half an hour our guests will start to arrive,' Alexander said. 'Are you looking forward to it?'

'I'm excited and nervous in equal measures. If there is anything I've forgotten to organise it's too late now. I'm as ready as I'll ever be.'

'Not quite.'

The leather case he handed her was slim, fastened with a gold clasp. She opened the case to reveal a collar of diamonds with a large teardrop stone at the centre. There were two matching bracelets and diamond teardrop earrings.

'I had originally planned to give you emeralds, but I was fairly sure you'd be wearing green and so...'

She touched the jewels reverently. 'They are magnificent, so beautiful, but it is too much. I can't possibly accept these.'

Alexander took the jewellery case from her. 'Turn around.'

The stones felt cool on the skin of her neck. Eloise held out her arm, allowing him to fasten the bracelets. He produced a mirror with a flourish, allowing her to fix the earrings. She gazed, rapt at the dazzling effect. 'I did not expect—these are absolutely—I will be very careful with them, I promise.'

'They are yours. There's a chest of family jewels in

a bank vault, but I thought you'd prefer something of your own, for your debut.'

'I do. I—I love them, Alexander.'

'Well, then, there's no need to cry.'

'I'm not. I'm touched. It was very, very thoughtful, and you're quite right, I wouldn't want…' *To wear his mother's jewellery.* She bit her lip. She did not want to let his mother intrude on this special moment. 'I couldn't imagine anything more perfect to set off this gown.'

She put the mirror down. 'And now, I have something for you. A very modest present by comparison.' She retrieved the parcel from its hiding place. 'Happy birthday.'

'I wasn't expecting a gift. You shouldn't have.'

'Open it,' she said, suddenly nervous. It had seemed such a good idea, she had spent so many hours working on it alone in her bedchamber when the rest of the household was asleep. 'It's not—oh, goodness, please just say if you don't like it, I promise you I won't be at all offended.'

Alexander set the parcel on to a table and untied the string carefully. The layers of tissue were folded back with equal care. When her gift was revealed, he stared at it for such a long time, his face quite inscrutable, that she was convinced he was desperately trying to work up a delighted smile.

He picked up the waistcoat, taking it over to the candelabra on the mantelpiece to get a better look, holding it up to study the anchors she had so painstakingly embroidered in gold thread on the black silk. He could have no idea how tricky it was to work with gold thread. He probably didn't even realise that the embroidery was her own work. She wouldn't tell him. She didn't want to make him feel guilty.

He was studying the lining now, which was gold to match the embroidery and the plain buttons. Still he said nothing. He had discovered the tiny insect she had embroidered, concealed under the pocket flap. He stared at it for a very long time. 'A weevil,' he said. 'How on earth did you know?'

'There was a book in the library. An illustrated guide to insects, termites and parasites. I have no idea why anyone would wish to own such a thing—indeed, it was so covered in dust that I doubt it has even been consulted—but anyway there was a drawing of a weevil.'

'And you embroidered it on my waistcoat, burrowing its way into the pocket.'

'Yes.' He understood her little joke. That was something.

Alexander set the waistcoat down carefully and began to pull off his evening coat. He unbuttoned his plain grey waistcoat, casting it carelessly aside, and then picked up her work again, slipping his arms into it before doing up the buttons. 'It's a perfect fit.'

'I used one of your own waistcoats as a template, I hope you don't mind. I'm sorry…'

'Eloise.' He stroked the waistcoat, pulling up the pocket flap, smiling as the weevil was revealed again. 'I don't like it. I am quite lost for words to describe what I feel for this. It is utterly—it is the most thoughtful, most original present anyone has ever given me.'

'Oh.' A lump rose in her throat 'Truly?'

'Truly. The hours you must have spent on this…'

'It was nothing,' she said, blinking furiously. 'Really, compared to what you have given me…'

'Nothing compares to this.' He put his arms on her shoulders and kissed her cheek. 'Thank you.'

She touched his cheek. His skin was smooth, fresh-shaved. She pressed a kiss to his lips. 'No, thank you.'

His breath caught. Their gazes snagged. He dipped his head. Their lips touched again. There was an instant when they hesitated, when they could have pulled apart, but they did not. This kiss was different from their first kiss on the balcony of the ballroom, different from yesterday's passionate kisses after their dancing practice. It was gentle. Sweet. Like molten sugar. Bone-melting. Now she understood that phrase. That's what this kiss did, it made her bones melt.

The clock on the mantel chimed. They did not spring apart, but the kiss slowed, and then it ended, and they gazed at each other, dazed. Alexander took her hand in his. And they made their way out of the drawing room, her arm on his, to the top of the grand staircase.

The double doors in the reception hall below were open. Wiggins stood waiting for the first arrivals, flanked by four footmen. Eloise had butterflies. She felt as if she was dreaming. She touched the teardrop diamond nestling on her breast. She looked at the man by her side, wearing the waistcoat she had embroidered for him. He smiled down at her. Alexander, Earl of Fearnoch. Her husband.

'Time to greet our guests, Lady Fearnoch,' he said. And Eloise smiled back. She was ready.

'My Lord and Lady Rasenby, welcome. May I present my wife, Eloise, Lady Fearnoch?'

'Mr Barrington, it is a pleasure to meet you.'

'Sir Edward, I am so glad you could join us to celebrate our recent nuptials.'

'Lady Teasborough, Miss Teasborough, may I introduce…?'

'Monsieur and Madame Bauduin, if I may be permitted…?'

'My Lord Alchester. Sir, it is with great pleasure that I introduce to you…'

For almost two hours Eloise stood by Alexander's side to welcome the constant flow of guests. Judging by the numbers, it seemed that every person on Mr Robertson's carefully prepared and vetted list had accepted their invitation. She recognised a number of names, having inscribed them herself on the cards, but she knew not a soul. Fortunately each guest was announced by Wiggins as they arrived at the top of the stairs, allowing her to greet them by name, and even more fortunately, Alexander either knew enough or had gleaned enough of each to whisper cryptic reminders in her ear, sufficient to allow her to elevate her conversation above the bland.

'Second cousin. Collects snuff boxes and wives— this is his third.' 'Abolitionist and tea connoisseur. Astonishingly sees no conflict of interest.' 'Breeds lap dogs and children, both in vast quantities.' 'Reformist. Librettist. Gourmand, as you will easily have deduced for yourself,' he whispered as a rotund man in extremely creaky corsets, who smelled disconcertingly of lamb, bowed low over Eloise's hand.

'I've heard of mutton chop whiskers, but mutton chop cologne is a new development,' she whispered back, after he had moved on. Alexander's witty comments were intended to keep her at ease as well as inform, and it was working. She forgot her nerves within five minutes. The ordeal which she had been secretly dreading became an amusing game. Though several people did enquire after the Dowager, they seemed to accept readily enough the story that Lady Constance's health did not allow her to leave the country for the metropolis and merely asked for their compliments to be passed on.

'Sir Marcus,' Alexander said, stepping forward to greet the tall, elegant man who had just reached the top of the stairs and pre-empting Wiggins's announcement. 'I did not dare hope you would honour us with your presence. My love,' he said, turning to Eloise, 'this is Sir Marcus Denby, my most esteemed colleague from the Admiralty.'

'And, I hope, his friend too. How do you do, Lady Fearnoch,' Sir Marcus said, saluting her hand with a courtly kiss. 'Now that I have met you, I can readily understand why Alex was so eager to embrace matrimony.'

'How do you do, Sir Marcus. It is a pleasure to meet one of my husband's colleagues.' The first and only one as far as she could recall, in fact. And there hadn't been another guest who counted Alexander as a friend either.

'Well now, it seems I am the last to arrive,' Sir Marcus was saying, casting a glance behind him at the empty staircase. 'If you don't mind, I'll spirit your new bride away for just a moment, before you get embroiled in the festivities.'

Before either of them could protest, Sir Marcus had taken her arm, leaving Eloise no option but to follow him. He did not make for the open doors of the ballroom, but instead led her into one of the anterooms, informing her that they could have a moment's respite here before she threw herself into the throng.

'Sit down, sit down, my dear, I promise I won't bite.'

'I can stay only a moment, Sir Marcus. Alexander's cousin has not yet arrived, and...'

'Raymond Sinclair!' Sir Marcus sat down on the chair opposite her, crossing his ankles neatly. 'I take it you know the man has been blackening your name all over town ever since the announcement of your wedding went to press? No? So Alex has decided to keep that to himself, has he?'

'Alexander knew about it?'

'Of course he did. London may not be your husband's usual habitat, but he keeps his ear to the ground here none the less. And even if he hadn't heard, I would have informed him immediately.'

'Forgive me, Sir Marcus, but I am not sure I understand...'

'What the devil I'm playing at, dragging you away from your husband before you've even had your first dance together?' He smiled. 'I have known Alex since he first joined the Admiralty at sixteen. I was already established in the same line of business as he is now. I recognised straight away that he was well-suited to the work and would make a fine recruit. I suppose you could say I was his mentor. He was reckless as a lad, and not one who liked to play by the rules. Not that much has changed.' Sir Marcus's brow clouded momentarily. 'However,' he continued bracingly, 'one thing I will say for your husband, he never makes the same mistake twice.'

'No, of course not,' Eloise said, because he seemed to be expecting her to say something. 'I know how important my husband's work at the Admiralty is to him.'

'Your husband is one of our greatest assets, Lady

Fearnoch. He has a very sharp mind and an excellent ear for foreign languages, that goes without saying, but it is his independent streak we value most at the Admiralty. Alex's upbringing was not the most conventional, but it made him the man he is. Self-reliant. Keeps a very cool head in a crisis. A man with few ties, and who is content to keep it that way. I should tell you, unless Alex already has, that it is highly unusual for a man in his position to be married. It may seem extreme to an outsider, but we require our men's loyalty to be first and foremost to their country. Nothing, or no one, must be allowed to interfere with that. I made an exception for Alex only because the circumstances were exceptional.'

Eloise raised her brows quizzically. 'That takes the notion of serving one's country to extraordinary lengths.'

'As I said, it's difficult for those outside the service to understand. Fortunately, it is in my gift to be able to bend the rules just a little, when I deem it necessary.'

'So you know, then, the full circumstances of our—our arrangement?'

Sir Marcus laughed indulgently. 'There is certainly no need to recount the touching little tale the pair of you have concocted between you. Though I must say, it's a good one. Inventive, yet with sufficient grains of truth in it to be believable. And no one, meeting you, could question his ardour, Lady Fearnoch. You are not at all as I imagined you.'

'No? It seems I am destined to confound expectations,' Eloise said, becoming exasperated. The man seemed to speak in non sequiturs. 'Alexander expected me to be older, fiercer and with spectacles.'

Sir Marcus gazed at her over his steepled hands,

treating her to another bland smile. His eyes were very blue. He must be nearly fifty, but he looked no more than forty. Lean, like Alexander, and fit. The Admiralty must keep their men on their toes. 'As I said, Lady Fearnoch, no one, having met you, would question the tale you are putting about, of a love match.'

The Admiralty also trained their men in how to avoid answering questions, Eloise thought. 'I am not sure whether you consider that a good thing or a bad thing,' she said, 'but if you are concerned that I will distract my husband from his duties, then let me assure you, I have no such intention.'

She had the satisfaction of seeing she had surprised him, though his eyebrows were raised only for a fraction of a second. 'I am pleased to hear that, Lady Fearnoch. It would be a great shame if you mistook this little conceit the pair of you are playing out for form's sake as anything other than that. I would hate you to get hurt.'

'What on earth do you mean by that? Are you warning me off?'

'Good gracious, no. I am merely suggesting that for both your sakes it would be better if your arrangement remained on a platonic footing.'

Sir Marcus got to his feet. 'I have detained you long enough. Lady Fearnoch, it has been a pleasure talking to you, but I am loathe to keep you from your guests.'

'Now that you have marked my card, you mean?' Eloise exclaimed, thoroughly rankled.

Sir Marcus, quite unruffled, merely smiled benignly.

'We assumed, my sisters and I, that Alexander was a mere clerk,' Eloise persisted. 'When he arranged for us to dine at Admiralty House on our wedding day, I surmised he must be much more senior than that.'

'Did you indeed?'

'I even speculated, when I realised where he was taking me, that I was to be introduced to His Highness, the Duke of Clarence. I realise that was fanciful.'

Sir Marcus held out his hand, giving her no option but to get out of her chair. 'Not so much fanciful as impossible. You forget that York died in January. Clarence is still technically in mourning for his brother.' He saluted her hand once more, very gracefully. 'Alex is a lucky man, Lady Fearnoch. Now, shall we go and find him before he sends a search party?'

The ballroom was crowded, but even before she stepped over the threshold, Alexander was at her side, and Sir Marcus had melted into the crowd. 'I had the oddest conversation with him,' Eloise said. 'You might have warned me that he knew the truth about us on account of you apparently having to obtain his permission to marry. I had the distinct impression that he was concerned that I might somehow compromise your work, though why he thought that I have no idea.'

'Don't read too much into what he says,' Alexander replied, 'Sir Marcus revels in being enigmatic. It's almost time for our first waltz.'

'What does Sir Marcus do now?'

'Do?'

'He said he was your mentor. Now that you have taken over as Victualling Commissioner, what is his role at the Admiralty?'

'He has no official title. You could say that he's in charge of all our foreign postings. Forget Sir Marcus. The orchestra are striking up the waltz. May I have this dance, my love?'

Alexander's smile was so very distracting. Her

strange encounter with Sir Marcus receded into the background as she smiled up at him just as his loving wife would do. 'It will be an honour, my love.'

The dance floor cleared as Alexander led her on to the floor, holding her at arm's length as he bowed and she curtsied. She was acutely conscious of the crowds of people watching her, and for a moment felt quite sick. She had never in her life performed in public like this. She couldn't even remember the first steps they were to take. Her knees were shaking. She would stand on his toes or trip on her gown or simply stand rooted to the spot.

Alexander pulled her into a hold, his arm on her waist, his other hand clasped in hers. 'You can do this,' he said, squeezing her fingers. 'Forget about everyone else. Remember, my love, you have eyes only for me.'

She did as he bid her. The first chord was struck. And he swept her into a waltz.

'Thank you, Lady Teasborough, it is one of Madame LeClerc's creations.'

Alexander, listening with half an ear to a long and convoluted tale about the near death and miraculous recovery of a prized racehorse, kept a watchful eye on Eloise, surrounded by a group of women who were purporting to admire her dress but who were, he was willing to wager, more intent on discovering how a complete unknown had managed to snare one of the richest men in England. Not that they would admit as much, but he knew what the gossip was. Tonight would hopefully put a stop to it.

He excused himself as soon as the racehorse's owner got to the point of assuring him that any future bets he might make on the creature would be worthwhile, and slipped into the group of women to stand beside Eloise.

'Even for a newly married man, Lord Fearnoch, you are remarkably attentive. We have had your wife to ourselves for barely ten minutes. Lady Fearnoch has been regaling us with the story of your long-distance romance. It seems she has not exaggerated the depth of affection which has burgeoned between you, despite your time together being limited to your occasional visits home.'

'Mere words cannot do it justice,' Eloise said, gazing adoringly into his eyes. She was in danger of over-gilding the lily!

'I suspect Mr Raymond Sinclair, your cousin, is equally lost for words,' Lady Teasborough said waspishly. 'He has just arrived, apparently. I did not think he would have the nerve to show his face, after—oh, I do beg your pardon. I know I speak for all of us, Lady Fearnoch, when I tell you that after tonight, seeing you and your husband together, no one could doubt that yours is a match made by cupid and not...'

'What Lady Teasborough means,' Lady Rasenby intervened, 'is that we are all delighted to see you both so happy. Are we not, ladies? I am sure that you will be inundated with invitations. It is a pity that you have arrived in London just as the Season is ending. Do you intend to retire to the country for the summer? Or perhaps you are thinking of taking a wedding trip to Europe?'

'Our plans are not yet formed,' Alexander said, pulling Eloise closer. 'If you will excuse us now, I am anxious to introduce my wife to my cousin.'

'Alexander,' Eloise said urgently as he extricated

them both from the circle of women. 'Sir Marcus told me that your cousin has been saying...'

'I know what he's been saying,' he said grimly, 'and I intend to put a stop to it.'

'But he's been saying it to everyone. You heard Lady Teasborough.'

'Who is now, thanks to you, completely convinced that my cousin's bile is just sour grapes. As are every one of those ladies and every other person I've spoken to.'

'Perhaps it was our dance that did it.'

'No, I won't have that. It was you. And I. Together. Now are you ready to perform once again? I would dearly love to take my cousin to task in a very different way, but I'd rather not get his blood on my precious new waistcoat. We will put to bed any doubts he has as to the nature of our union, and then he will either put up or I will shut him up.

'Raymond.' Alexander forced a smile as he cornered his cousin. 'Better late than never. Shall we retire to the Blue Room? No need to show you where it is. I am sure you have familiarised yourself with every nook and cranny of Fearnoch House.'

Raymond Sinclair looked taken aback, but he made for the Blue Room without hesitation. Eloise could see no family resemblance between the first cousins. She knew Raymond to be of similar age to Walter, but he looked a lot more than eight years older than Alexander. His hair was mousy brown and lacking any lustre. It was combed forward from far back on the crown in a failed attempt to disguise its receding nature, and then trimmed as if his barber had repeatedly tried and failed to cut a straight line across his forehead. His brows were sparse, his eyes were dark brown, but the whites were a jaundiced yellow. His lids drooped, a fretwork of lines aged him considerably, his nose was overlarge for his face, his mouth too small with a petulant twist to it. When he bowed over her hand after Alexander introduced them, Eloise noticed that his collar was grimy and flecked with dandruff. He was a poor shadow of a Fearnoch male compared to Alexander. It reminded her that she had not yet found the time to explore the portrait gallery, and she made a mental note to do so soon.

'I expect I must offer you my felicitations on your marriage,' Raymond said as he sat down, accepting a glass of brandy.

'What is the point,' Alexander said coolly, taking his seat beside Eloise, 'since you obviously don't wish us well.'

The brandy was inhaled in one gulp. 'Very well, if you prefer the unvarnished truth I will tell you that you would have done much better to carry on counting cannon balls or whatever it is you do at the Admiralty, and left the earldom to a true Fearnoch man.'

'A true Fearnoch man like yourself, I presume?'

Having nursed his empty glass for all of three minutes, Raymond got to his feet and helped himself from the decanter, sparing himself another return journey by bringing it with him when he sat down again. 'Walter and I were very close,' he said. 'We kept the same company, we were members of the same clubs. I dined here at Fearnoch House at least once a week, I'll have you know.'

'I hope you do not expect me to continue the tradition.'

Raymond snorted. 'You've been in residence a fortnight and you've not given a single dinner. As far as I can discover, you've not a solitary friend in our social circle. I have no interest in dining with Admiralty clerks and Irish refugees.'

Alexander stiffened, though his expression remained bland. His hand covered hers in warning, but Eloise was too shocked to say anything. 'An interesting choice of epithets. I would strongly suggest you don't use either again in my presence,' he said evenly.

'I'm only repeating what Walter told me. As to the new Lady Fearnoch—I felt it my duty to enquire into the background of the female who has captured the family fortune.'

Alexander's grip on her hand tightened painfully. 'The only thing Lady Fearnoch has captured is my heart, Cousin.'

'And yet she married you only when you became heir to the earldom.'

'That is where you are wrong. We became engaged to be married eighteen months ago. Our marriage is neither unexpected nor a sudden rash decision.'

Raymond's pallor drained even further, if that were possible. 'Walter never mentioned this to me,' he said suspiciously.

'That's because he didn't know,' Alexander said blithely. 'He died before I could inform him of my happy news. We could have made our betrothal public in April, once the year of mourning had elapsed, but we decided there was no need to postpone the happy event any further, and announced our nuptials instead.'

Raymond downed another brandy and set the glass

down with a scowl. 'Conveniently, just in time for you to qualify to inherit.'

'Convenient? Perhaps. Coincidental, certainly.'

'Your brother would never have wished you to inherit, do you know that? He thought…'

'I know what he thought of me, far better than you.' The change in Alexander's tone startled Eloise as much as Raymond. 'Let us be plain, Cousin. You have been doing your very best to undermine my marriage and more importantly, you have been making some very insulting comments regarding my wife's character.'

'I do not know…'

'Hold your tongue.' Alexander got to his feet. 'Here is how it will be from now on. You will not speak of my wife unless it is with respect—though I would infinitely prefer you did not speak of her at all. Nor will you use our family name to obtain any further credit. You see, I am well aware of your nefarious actions to bankroll your vice.'

Slack-jawed, Raymond was staring up at his cousin, who was quite deliberately towering over him. Eloise would find it comical were she not so astonished at the change in her husband. He spoke as she imagined a general would to a recalcitrant cadet, with a mixture of contempt and authority.

'I assumed it was a safe bet,' Raymond said, staring desperately at the empty decanter. 'Your thirtieth birthday was looming with no prospect of your marrying, as far as I was aware.'

'This safe bet has turned out to be as successful as all your other bets,' Alexander said witheringly. 'You do not deserve it, but I will bail you out as a one-off gesture of goodwill in my brother's memory. I will pay off your debts. Not your gambling debts, those are your responsibility, but I will not have honest tradesmen going unpaid. If you will send every outstanding bill to my lawyer, I will see that the accounts are settled.'

Alexander pressed the bell, which was answered immediately by the butler. 'Goodbye, Cousin. We will not expect you to call on us again. Mr Sinclair is leaving, Wiggins, be so good as to see him out.'

The door closed on Raymond, and Alexander set his shoulders against it. His fists were clenched. Now that his cousin had gone, the suppressed anger was evident on his face, but by the time Eloise reached him it was gone. 'I suppose I should feel sorry for him,' he said.

'It's his wife and children I feel sorry for.'

'I am sorry you had to witness that. I don't think he'll trouble us again.'

'Not after you gave him one of those looks. I was glad I wasn't on the other end of it, believe me.'

'Talking of looks,' he said, his face relaxing into a smile, 'I do believe you managed a besotted gaze while we were chatting to the ladies, you who claimed once that it was quite beyond her.'

'Necessity is the mother of invention. I felt that simply doting wouldn't do the trick.'

'I had no idea there was a difference.'

'You can dote on a lapdog, but you can't be besotted by it.'

'Tell that to Mrs Blessington!'

Eloise chuckled. 'She has twenty-five of the little darlings, she told me. It was only when I did the sums that I realised she must be talking about the dogs and not the children, for she cannot be any more than thirty.

We should get back to our guests, it must be long past the first supper break.'

'In a moment.' He took her hand, lifting it to his lips. 'Thank you. Not only for helping me see off Raymond, but for all the effort you've put into making tonight such a success.'

'It's not over yet.'

'But it will be a success. And so are you, Lady Fearnoch. Thank you.'

He kissed her. Their lips met and held for an achingly sweet moment before he pulled away. 'Let us go and see if our guests have left us any of Phoebe's carefully planned and no doubt delicious supper.'

Chapter Eight

Eloise slept late the morning after the ball, having tumbled exhausted into her bed in the early hours after the last of their guests had departed. His lordship, her maid informed her, had already breakfasted, and had ordered his wife's usual repast to be brought to her room. Having an aversion to crumbs in her bed, she drank her tea at her escritoire while pondering the pile of thank-you notes, invitations and cards which were already accumulating. These could mark the dawn of her new social life as Lady Fearnoch, if she wished. It would be easy for her to fritter away her time shopping, taking tea, making calls and attending parties, the life of a lady of leisure that she and her sisters had joked about, but it held no genuine appeal. She was accustomed to doing something productive with her time.

Pulling her notebook towards her, she flicked through her initial ideas for transforming Fearnoch House. There was plenty there to keep her occupied in the short term, at least. She could always invite her sisters to visit. Though what she really wanted, if she was completely honest, was to get to know her husband better.

Last night had proved how little about him she actually did know. Now that their formal introduction into society had been achieved, would Alexander want to return to the Admiralty? It was wrong of her to want to have him to herself. The Admiralty was Alexander's life, his one and only love, according to Sir Marcus Denby. Eloise shivered, recalling that strange conversation with him last night. It seemed astonishing that Alexander had needed the man's permission to marry. Even more extraordinary that a Victualling Commissioner was not usually permitted to marry at all. What on earth did he do that was so important? Whatever it was, he performed his duties well enough for Sir Marcus to be prepared to bend the rules for him.

The way Alexander had effortlessly slapped down his cousin had been another eye-opener. And the assured way he'd conversed with their guests last night had also been a revelation, so confident and socially at ease. He knew how to talk to everyone in just the right manner, neither condescending nor obsequious, yet he never doubted that he'd be listened to. That natural authority she'd witnessed, of a man accustomed to being obeyed when he put the frighteners on Raymond, which is surely what he had done—where had he learned that particular skill? From Sir Marcus? She remembered, finally, what it was that the man from the Admiralty had said that was niggling her. Alexander didn't like to play by the rules. He'd said it as if that was a positive attribute, but surely a Victualling Commissioner's job was to follow rules to the letter, fastidiously counting his weevils and his anchors! One thing was for certain, that was *not* what he did.

Though her waistcoat with the secret weevil had

been the perfect present. Eloise smiled to herself, setting down her empty cup, recalling with a warm glow just how touched he had been. She pulled the leather box containing his gift towards her, opening it, caressing the diamonds. The kiss they had shared last night had been so delightful, yet so very different from those other kisses in the ballroom, and they had been different again from that first kiss on the balcony. She'd had no idea there could be different kisses, that kisses could make her feel so many different things, that they could have a language all of their own. She had not expected to enjoy kissing so much. To relish kissing. To want more than kissing.

Trying to imagine Alexander touching her more intimately, she realised that she had no idea precisely what that entailed. She was familiar with the crude basics of the actual act, having lived all her life in the country, but until now she'd never understood that there was a lot more to it. Lovemaking. Making love. Words which usually conjured fear and loathing, because she associated them with her mother.

'I cannot change my nature, I am a passionate creature.'

'I am controlled by my passions.'

'I am in thrall to my passions.'

How many variants had she heard of that sentiment, over the years? Passion was her mother's excuse for every aspect of her behaviour, as if she had no will of her own. Was that passion or was it simply selfishness? Mama had always done exactly what she wanted, when she wanted. She indulged her every whim, utterly indifferent to the consequences and the suffering she inflicted on her daughters or her husband or anyone else.

Good grief, Eloise thought, much struck. This was not passion, it was an obsession with pleasing herself.

While Papa—yes, Papa really had loved Mama. Her infidelities had crushed his spirit. Yes, he had shouted and angrily demanded that it never happen again, but he'd made pleading promises too, to try harder, to love Mama more. Had these arguments really been played out in front of all three girls, or was her memory at fault? No, she was sure she wasn't misremembering, though she hadn't realised at the time quite how breathtakingly *wrong* Mama's behaviour had been. How could she ever have worried about being in the least bit like her in nature?

Poor Papa, so hopelessly in thrall to Mama that he must always surrender to her demands, forgive her for the sins it didn't even occur to her she'd committed, worship ever more fervently at her feet. It hadn't occurred to Eloise to feel sorry for him before. Love made a weak cuckold of Papa. Selfishness made a ruthless harlot of Mama. The pair of them had been miserable, and as a consequence so too had all their children, including Diarmuid, the favourite, and as such exposed to even larger doses of their parents' misery than the rest of them. She had always assumed his increasingly selfish nature had been because he was spoilt, that his tantrums and determination to rule the roost when he visited were his arrogant assumption of superiority. Now she wondered what it must have been like for him, to see his sisters so close-knit, to be on the outside of the little signs of affection, the jokes, the very different life they shared. He must have felt excluded. Perhaps he'd been jealous. If they'd made more of an effort with him, would he have made more of an effort in return? But they had all of them been set in their ways, not through choice so much as circumstances, moulded, inculcated by Mama and Papa. Poor Diarmuid must have suffered, in a very different way, but he must have been miserable all the same. Eloise hadn't thought of that before either.

What a mess her parents had made of their lives and their children's. My goodness though, how enlightening it was turning out to be, to look at it all from such a different perspective. Ever since she'd been old enough to understand, she had been afraid of passion. Quite needlessly, as it turned out. A slow smile dawned on her as she stared out the window, where the sun was already up. Why had it taken her so long to realise that her fears of emulating her mother were ludicrous? Because she'd never been kissed before? Because she had not, until Alexander kissed her—oh, those kisses!—understood what she had been missing? Now she did, and she need no longer worry that it was wrong to enjoy those kisses. Or to want more.

Her smile faded. To want more was to breach the terms of their marriage. *The more intimate aspect of marriage does not appeal to me.* Those had been her own toe-curling words. And Alexander had said love was anathema to him. Well, and so it was to her, but he'd also said—yes, he'd said that though he'd had affaires in the past, at this moment in time he had *'no interest in finding comfort in another's arms'*. Yet he'd seemed very interested in finding comfort in hers! True, he had insisted each time that he had been playing the husband when he kissed her, and she had been so desperate to lie to herself that she had gladly accepted that reassurance. But now?

In the ballroom, the night before their wedding party,

there was nothing made up about those kisses, she was sure of it. And last night, before the ball—there was no one watching them, there was no reason for them to kiss, yet they had still kissed. Why would a man so attractive, so evidently capable of passion, vow that he had *no interest* in passion? For how long had he lacked interest? What had happened to make him lose interest? And why, then, was he interested in her? Was it because they were closeted together and she had unwittingly encouraged him?

A tap at the bedroom door roused Eloise from these intriguing conundrums. A new delivery had arrived from Madame LeClerc. Temporarily distracted, she examined the afternoon dress of gold-striped silk. It was beautifully stitched, even more lovely than she'd imagined it when they had agreed the design. Clever Madame LeClerc had enhanced the detailing of the sleeves, which were puffed at the shoulder, but now tied in at the elbow with gold ribbon, tapering down to the lace trim. She had used the same pretty lace at the neckline, but where Eloise would have kept the hem plain, Madame LeClerc had had it worked with a design of leaves and fronds in gold satin which weighted the dress down nicely, and elevated it from a gown which might be worn by a country miss to one in which a countess could happily receive callers. Or go in search of her husband.

She found him, eventually, in the portrait gallery. Alexander did not see her at first, for he was engaged in shooting practice. Eloise stood unobserved by the doors at one end of the long gallery, watching as he primed four different pistols. He was dressed in leather breeches and boots, a shirt open at the neck and rolled up at the sleeves showing his tanned, sinewy forearms, his hair tousled, his jaw rough with stubble. She had never seen him look so dishevelled. He would look like this first thing in the morning. What would it be like to wake up beside him, warm from sleep, to kiss him, feel the roughness of his skin against hers before he shaved?

The retort of the first bullet made her jump. Alexander shot each pistol one after the other in rapid succession at a target set up at the opposite end of the room. She would have been horrified, if there had been time to be horrified, for if he missed, then the bullet would lodge in one of the portraits on the wall behind. But he did not miss, his aim was unerring.

With the last gun smoking in his hand he sensed her presence and turned. 'Eloise!' He was frowning as he set the gun down. 'I thought you would sleep at least until noon.'

'I slept until nine, which is late for me. I didn't mean to disturb you,' she said, as he set about reloading the pistols.

'As I said, I thought you would still be asleep.'

He did not request that she leave, but he hadn't encouraged her to remain either. She hesitated, but Sir Marcus's enigmatic warning had made her curious. 'I know nothing of such things, but you look to me as if you know what you are doing. May I see?' Without waiting for his permission, she made her way down the gallery to the target, astonished to see the inner ring riddled with bullet holes. 'I think that you must be what they call a crack shot.'

'I have a good eye, nothing more.'

'Good enough to hit the middle of the target with

four different weapons. Is marksmanship something else required from a Victualling Commissioner? If so, I am not surprised that Sir Marcus considers you invaluable—there must be very few men in the country qualified to fulfil the role so well.'

Alexander appraised her coolly. Though she held his gaze it was not easy, for there was not a trace of the warmth she had become accustomed to in his eyes. It hurt, because he was studying her as if she was a stranger. 'Very well, don't answer, I don't care, though why what you do is such a *huge* secret, and who you think I would discuss it with even if you did deign to tell me a little about it, I can't imagine.'

Eloise glared, but Alexander remained impassive. Now she wasn't hurt, she was annoyed. 'Sir Marcus told me that Victualling Commissioners are not usually permitted to marry,' she threw at him. 'He seemed to think that I was some sort of threat to your ability to perform your duties.'

Still he studied her. She would not say another word until he spoke! But she would not allow him to wear her down by staring at her. Turning back to the target, she saw that there was a straw bale placed behind it. The bullets must be lodged in it. She traced the bullet holes with her finger. 'These are not even an inch apart. I would certainly not like to face you in a duel.'

'If Walter had been as proficient, perhaps he would be alive today.'

She whirled around in shock. 'What on earth do you mean?'

'My brother was killed in a duel.' Alexander pushed back his hair from his eyes, which she could see now were shadowed. Unlike her, he had not slept. 'I didn't tell you because—oh, I don't know, because it puts him in a bad light. A pretty terrible light. Now I know that there's no other kind of light to view him in. Last night, listening to Raymond, made me realise that I knew very little of his life. I took a look at his personal accounts after you went to bed. Robertson sent me the papers after we were married, but I hadn't opened them. They made sickening reading. Walter was a libertine, a spendthrift and a drunk who considered the likes of my cousin excellent company.'

'Good grief!' So she wasn't the only one who had spent the morning reflecting on her family's behaviour. 'The clubs your cousin referred to last night were gambling hells, I take it?'

'Walter didn't gamble, or if he did he didn't play deep. No, the establishments Raymond referred to last night, clearly documented in Walter's accounts along with the associated fees, are euphemistically known as gentlemen's clubs, though I doubt very much that any gentlemanly behaviour takes place behind their secret doors.'

'I don't know what you—oh! You mean—do you mean brothels?'

'That is essentially what they are, though it would offend the delicate sensibilities of those who haunt them to call them anything so base,' Alexander said, his voice dripping with contempt. 'They would claim to be very exclusive establishments, supplying only the best to the best. The purest, finest-quality goods for the delectation of the most discerning of customers. As if they were butchers supplying fresh meat to a dining club of gourmands.'

It took Eloise a moment to understand his meaning. When she did, she felt sick. 'That is disgusting.'

'You have no idea how disgusting.' Alexander shook his head. 'Enough. This is hardly a fit subject for your ears.'

'Or anyone's ears. You look exhausted.'

'I couldn't sleep last night after my cousin made me realise I know next to nothing about my brother—and given what I know now, I wish I had remained ignorant. Come, let me introduce you to the man himself.' He steered her across to the opposing wall of the gallery. 'This must have been commissioned to commemorate his inheriting the title, as you can see from his ermines.'

Which meant the Seventh Earl had been thirty-six when he sat for Sir Thomas Lawrence, Eloise deduced. Assuming that Lawrence had painted with his usual flattering eye, then Walter had not aged at all well. The same lines of dissipation she'd noticed around Raymond's eyes last night were, if anything, more exaggerated. Though the Earl was still a handsome man, there was a cruel twist to the thin lips, an arrogance in his stance, in the way he thrust his shoulders back, one hand holding out his velvet robe proudly. And in his gaze, there was a self-absorption, a callous concern only for himself, which looked out of the canvas over the head of the viewer. Though she might, Eloise thought ruefully, be reading just a bit too much into the composition.

'Well?'

'He is very much as I imagined. There is something of you in the shape of the chin and the colouring, but the resemblance is not strong.'

'For very good reasons.'

She was puzzled by this, but on reflection thought she understood. 'You have lived very different lives. One doesn't have to know anything about the subject,' Eloise said, pointing at Walter, 'to see that the life this man has embraced has taken its toll.'

'The gentleman next to him is the Sixth Earl, and next to him the Fifth, Fourth, and so on.'

'Your father, grandfather, great-grandfather. My goodness, Alexander, the family resemblance is strong.'

'In more ways than one. What you are looking at is a long line of libertines and spendthrifts. I don't know if all of them were also drunkards, but I don't think I'd bet against it.'

Eloise studied the portraits in turn, working her way back before coming to a halt at the end of the line, back in front of the Seventh Earl, Walter. 'I remember you said that the line has always been passed directly from father to son. Even if I didn't know that, these portraits would confirm it. And yet when your portrait is placed here, it will look as if the pattern has been broken, since you do not resemble these men in any way.'

'I have no intentions of having my portrait hung here. The pattern has already been broken.'

'It certainly has, you are neither a spendthrift nor a libertine nor a drunk.' She couldn't understand his mood. 'But such behaviour can't be inherited, Alexander.'

'Not inherited, no. Rather it was bred into him by his father. I told you, Walter was raised here in this house, exposed, from an early age, to the debauched company his father kept. Introduced, as soon as he was old enough, to those clubs which would, if the damage was not already done, corrupt any innocent. Those are the Fearnoch traditions passed from father to son. I didn't know, until now, just how fortunate I have been to be spared Walter's upbringing.'

'Even though it meant that you were all but ostracised? I'm sorry to cause you pain, Alexander, but it seems to me such a very cruel thing for your parents to have done.'

He was staring at the portrait of the Sixth Earl, his father. 'I am glad it turned out that way,' he said.

'What would your father think of you standing here instead of Walter.'

Alexander's smile was cruel. 'He could never have envisaged that twist of fate.' He turned away and began to pack up the pistols. 'My brother did not confine his amorous activities to professional establishments. He met his end after being shot by a jealous husband. The wound wasn't fatal, but it became infected, allowing the doctor to record that he died of a fever, and allowing the cuckold to escape a murder trial. And they call duels a matter of honour,' he said bitterly, closing one of the pistol cases. 'I don't know what you're thinking of doing with this room, but if you want to take down the portraits and use it for another purpose, then you have my blessing. I could do with some fresh air to clear my head. Will you come for a drive with me?'

'Don't you want to get some sleep instead?'

'I want to escape this house, and all it represents, and enjoy my wife's company. If she is amenable?'

'In that case, she is very amenable.'

Alexander had the grooms harness up the phaeton kept in the stable block while he shaved and changed. His rare forays home from foreign shores had not warranted his owning a carriage, but to one who had negotiated the traffic chaos of Madrid, Lisbon and Cairo, these less familiar but comparatively ordered city streets were child's play. Eloise had exchanged her gold gown for a green walking dress and matching pelisse, her face framed by a straw bonnet. Her smile went a long way to lifting his spirits as he helped her into the carriage.

The sun was shining, the sky was blue with hardly a cloud in sight. It was a nigh on perfect English summer's afternoon as they set out, taking a route through Hyde Park, skirting Holland Park and on through Kensington where the traffic began to ease.

As the city gave way to more open countryside, Eloise gazed at their surroundings with obvious pleasure. 'It is astonishing how easy it is to escape the city. It's silly, but I feel as if I've been holding my breath the whole time I've been in London, and now I can finally breathe.'

'That's more to do with having negotiated the ordeal of the ball, than anything to do with the sweetness of the air,' Alexander said, though it struck him that he felt something similar. In the portrait gallery this morning, he'd had the impression that Fearnoch House was closing in on him. 'It has been a hectic fortnight.'

'But worth it, I hope? Last night paid off, didn't it— at least I think so, if the number of cards and letters I had in this morning's post is anything to go by.'

'You were a triumph.'

'*We* were a triumph,' she corrected him. 'I must confess, I'm glad that we didn't marry in the middle of the London Season. I am not sure I'm either ready for or interested in an endless round of socialising. Is it ungrateful of me to say that I'm actually relieved that most people will be decanting to the country soon?'

'So you've decided against the notion of setting yourself up as a society hostess?'

'That was never one of my ambitions.' Eloise's smile faded. 'I wanted to be free to do whatever I choose. It's somewhat disconcerting to find that I have little idea how to set about discovering what that is.'

'It's not surprising. You've hardly had a moment to yourself since our wedding day.'

'I know, I know. It is a terrible fault of mine, always to be thinking too far ahead, worrying about things that haven't yet happened.'

'An understandable trait, however. You must have lived on tenterhooks, not knowing from one day to the next whether your parents were going to descend on you, or whether your latest governess was going to fly the coop.'

'Or whether there would be something for dinner, sometimes.'

'Surely things can't have been as bad as that?'

Eloise shrugged, staring out at the expanse of fields they were passing as they came to the outskirts of the village of Hammersmith. 'The Vineyard Nursery,' she read as they passed the entrance. 'I recognise that name. I believe Kate has ordered plants from here.'

A taste of his own medicine, Alexander thought, slowing down on the approach to the village. Now he knew what it was like to be on the receiving end of an unanswered question. It wouldn't be fair of him to press her further, when she was usually so careful not to push him. Until this morning, when his dissembling had hurt her, but what option did he have, when he could hardly tell her the truth!

Damn Sir Marcus for raising her suspicions. It wasn't like him to be so indiscreet. Mind you, he'd more or less admitted, in the note Alexander had received in the post that morning, that he had underestimated Eloise's intelligence.

Lady Fearnoch strikes me as an uncommonly observant woman as well as an uncommonly attractive one. Both qualities, I have no doubt, you are aware of and will be wary of.

A clear warning shot across his bows, the parallels between Claudia and his wife clearly drawn. As if he needed to be reminded.

Beside him, Eloise remained deep in contemplation. 'There's a new bridge across the Thames here,' he told her. 'We can cross and carry on to Richmond Park, if you like—I reckon it can't be more than four miles.'

'That sounds like an excellent idea. I've heard so much about its charms.'

She remained unusually quiet, gazing out at the fast-flowing Thames as they crossed the river, though he was pretty sure her mind was miles away. He took a route that followed a bend in the river for a while, turning south at Mortlake, where the vast green swathes of Richmond Park came into view. He entered the parkland through the nearest gate and, following his nose, took one of the paths which he hoped would take them around the perimeter. 'I've never been out here before, but Sir Marcus suggested it as a pleasant country drive.'

'He displays an impressive interest in his protégé's affairs.'

Alexander cursed his mentor once again. 'You surprised him, Eloise, you were not what he expected.'

'So he informed me,' she answered tartly.

'If it were not for him, I would be—I don't know where I would be, to be honest. I know he put your back up, but...'

'What would you have done if he had withheld his permission for you to marry?'

'I honestly don't know. Fortunately, he did consent.'

'Would you have considered resigning?'

'God, no. I have never—no.' Alexander tried to imagine such a scenario. 'That was not an option.'

'So it is as he said, you really are wedded to your country. It is as well that ours is not a real marriage, else I'd be jealous.'

'My duties preclude what you call a real marriage—' He broke off, aware that anything he might say risked raising further questions. He was so used to guarding his secrets it had become second nature. To reveal more would cause her quite unnecessary worry, apart from the fact that to do so was tantamount to treason. Discussing his proposed marriage with Sir Marcus, he had been able to dismiss out of hand any concern that he'd take his wife into his confidence. But that was before he'd met Eloise, when his wife was faceless and formless, a woman who would live a parallel life to his, whom he would care for in an abstract way, but who would remain peripheral. He had had no intention of acting out a love match, of breakfasting with her, dining with her, dancing with her. Seeking out her company when he had no reason to. Taking her for a drive. Talking to her of the past that he had thought long buried. He hadn't imagined it would be so difficult to brush off her questions, to hide behind evasions, to prevent her from getting to know him too well. He hadn't thought that he'd want her to know him. He didn't want to hurt her again with another blunt rebuff.

'My work not only requires me to be abroad a great deal, it requires my complete dedication. I have to be able to react to any crises immediately, and to concentrate totally on resolving those crises without distraction. In that sense, Sir Marcus is right—my duty and my loyalty must be to my country, without compromise. Do you understand?'

'A little. Better than I did, I think.'

Eloise studied the passing landscape for a moment, but he could see that she was debating with herself on whether to pursue the matter. Though his heart sank, he was not surprised when she did.

'Is that why you told me that love is anathema to you? I wondered why, from what you said to me the first day we met, you were so vehement, and how you could be so certain. Then last night, Sir Marcus said that you never made the same mistake twice, and I was thinking about it this morning, and the other thing you told me, that you were not—that you had not been interested in taking comfort in another's arms, and it made me wonder—it made me wonder if you had been? In love, I mean. And that Sir Marcus had forced you to give her up.'

This was what came of exchanging confidences! 'I've never been in love.' It was not a lie. If he had loved Claudia would he feel less or more guilty? But the outcome would have been the same.

His tone was wrong. Too aggressive. Eloise would

think he was lying. 'I assure you,' he said more gently, 'Sir Marcus has never had cause to interfere in my private life.' The absolute truth this time, though only because Sir Marcus hadn't known until it was too late.

'I see I've read too much into what Sir Marcus said. He told me that you are one of the Admiralty's greatest assets. I expect he was simply trying to protect his interests.'

She was studying her gloves, which meant she didn't believe a word of what she had just said. For the third time that day, Alexander cursed his mentor, but there was nothing more he could say that wouldn't amount to treason. As the perimeter path turned north again, Alexander took the next gate out of the park. 'We'll go back a different way,' he said. 'I reckon if we follow the Thames on this side heading east we'll be able to cross at Vauxhall and be back nicely in time for dinner.'

'I've ordered the kitchen to prepare a fricassee with mushroom fritters and asparagus in lemon butter.'

'That sounds delicious.'

'The fritters are made with an ale batter.'

'One of Phoebe's receipts?'

'Who else?' She looked up at him, smiling wanly. 'We didn't go hungry. In Ireland, I mean. There were times when we had bread and cheese for dinner because the butcher hadn't been paid, but that is still more than a good many poor souls around us had on their table. That's not what I was thinking about earlier, when I was so quiet. It was what you said, about my living on tenterhooks and how that explained why I am always wanting to plan ahead. You're right, Alexander. It's so obvious, yet I've never thought of it before. I don't need to rush into anything, do I? I mean, it doesn't matter that

I have no idea what I want to do with my life, does it—not yet, at least? That's what I've been thinking about.' She smiled ruefully. 'That I need to enjoy the moment and stop thinking so much. Where are we?'

'I think that must be Putney Bridge. We'll be passing by the fields at Battersea soon, which I believe is a popular spot for duelling—no, you need not look like that, it's not where my brother was fatally wounded.'

'Does your mother know how he died?'

'Yes. I would have kept it from her, but by the time I arrived back in England, Walter, as you know, had been dead and buried for several months. I don't know how she came by the truth, but she knew.' Glancing over at her, Alexander was unsurprised to see Eloise almost visibly bursting with questions. 'She seemed—resigned, I think would be the nearest I can come to describing her reaction,' he said, enjoying the satisfaction of surprising her with some unsolicited information. 'As you will have surmised from her behaviour to myself as a child, my mother is not the most demonstrative of women.'

'Or she's a woman who has learned from bitter experience not to wear her heart on her sleeve.'

He was startled, as much by the tone of her voice as her words. 'What do you mean?'

'For every one of those dissolute earls who has preceded you, there is a countess. A woman who has been forced to endure the shame and the pain of their repeated infidelities, treated without respect, more likely with complete contempt, her feelings trampled on, mocked, derided. Your mother's treatment of you is indefensible as well as *incomprehensible*, but my goodness, no wonder she appears cold, Alexander. I hope that's how she feels too, because at least then she has been spared the additional agony of actually loving such a man.'

Alexander pulled the phaeton over to the side of the road, quickly tying up the reins, but when he tried to take her hand, Eloise snatched it away. 'I'm sorry. That was completely uncalled for—I don't know where it came from.'

Colour burned in her cheeks. Her eyes were bright with unshed tears. Her shoulders rigid, she was staring down at her gloved hands, now tightly laced, making him think the better of a second attempt to touch her for the moment. What she said shamed him. He had never considered his mother's position, had thought only, always, of the injustice of his own treatment. The extent of his self-absorption appalled him now, though at this moment it was Eloise he was more concerned about and it was blindingly obvious, now he thought about it, where her tirade had originated.

'You're remembering the way your mother treated your father, aren't you? That's the parallel you have drawn.'

'I don't know if there is such a thing as a female rake,' she answered gruffly, 'but that is what she was. She claimed she loved my father, but she can't have, because when you love someone, you'd do anything to avoid hurting them. And my father...' She lifted her head to meet his gaze, her mouth trembling. 'I don't know why I didn't see so clearly before, how dreadful it must have been for him. I feel so awful, because I've always blamed him, every bit as much as Mama, for neglecting the twins.'

'But they *were* both culpable for that. And it wasn't just the twins, Eloise. You suffered too.' He took her hands, and this time she allowed him, her fingers twining around his. 'Doubtless your father was wronged, but that doesn't excuse him abandoning his responsibilities as a parent.'

'Any more than whatever travails your mother suffered excuses her treatment of you, but it does at least go some way towards explaining it.'

'I hadn't thought of it in those terms.'

Eloise freed one of her hands to touch his cheek. 'It's too late for me to attempt any sort of reconciliation,' she said, 'but it's not too late for you. Think about that, Alexander.'

Eloise had dinner served in the breakfast parlour at the back of the house, the least formal of any of the dining rooms at Fearnoch House. They were both subdued, careful with each other, saying little, but the silences were not uncomfortable. When the table had been cleared, the servants dismissed for the night—another of Eloise's changes, for she could not see the point of keeping them out of their beds waiting on orders which neither she nor Alexander ever issued—they opened the long French doors and stepped out into the garden.

It was twilight. With the skies still clear and midsummer approaching, it would not get much darker. The grass was damp with dew, the smell of fresh green sap and early roses scenting the air as they strolled slowly, arm in arm, towards the trees.

'One moment. Look away,' Eloise said, kicking off her shoes, unfastening her garters and removing her stockings. With a sigh of delight, she curled her toes into the cool grass. 'You can turn around now.'

'So it's not only at sunrise you like to walk barefoot?'

'No, I—did I tell you that?'

'Don't you remember?' Alexander took her hand, and they began to walk again. 'The day we met, we were in the garden at Elmswood Manor, and you asked me to help you imagine how you would feel after making love.'

'Oh.' She remembered. 'Like climbing a tree and looking down. Exciting. Dizzying.' And like curling her toes into the cool, damp grass. Delicious. 'You must have thought me ridiculous, to think the epitome of pleasure was to walk barefoot on the grass at sunrise.'

'I never think you ridiculous.'

They had come to a halt under the trees, the new green leaves forming a canopy over their heads. She could no longer see his face, which made her all the more acutely aware of him as they turned towards each other, as he put his hand on her waist, as she stepped closer to him, her skirts brushing against his legs. 'I didn't even know what it was like to be kissed at that point.'

'You were fairly confident that you wouldn't enjoy it, I remember.'

'I was wrong.' She felt him exhale sharply as she put her arms around him.

'Eloise, what are you doing?'

If she thought about what she was doing, she wouldn't do it. But wasn't that the point, wasn't that what she needed to learn, how not to think, how not to plan, how to simply enjoy? 'If you don't want to kiss me, Alexander...'

He groaned. 'You can have no idea.'

He pulled her tight up against him. Her toes curled into the grass as his mouth covered hers. And then she forgot all about her toes. Her eyes drifted closed as she surrendered to the delight of their kisses. She felt as if she were melting, slowly melting from the inside, as their lips clung, moved, shaped and moulded to each other. And then their tongues touched, and she felt as if she was burning, tingling all over, and a sweet ache flared inside her.

More kisses, and she somehow found herself leaning against the tree, Alexander pressed against her, and she was positively flooded with heat in response to the weight of him. And then his hand stroking the side of her breast made her moan, and it made her nipple tighten, and it turned the ache into something else, like a pulse, and when he cupped her breast, when he stroked her nipple through her gown, she felt breathless, as if she had been running.

More kisses. She smoothed her hand down the line of his back, feeling the tension in him, reassured by the layers of clothing between them, but at the same time wishing there were fewer. She was hot, burning inside. She was restless. She felt strung tight. Her body arched like a bow, and her hands found the taut curve of Alexander's rear, under his coat, and all her instincts screamed for her to pull him closer, tight up against her, but he resisted, lifting his head, putting an end to their kisses.

'Eloise,' he said urgently, 'you don't know what you are doing.'

He was right. His words were like a bucket of cold water. Her eyes flew open. She was unutterably grateful too for the lack of light to illuminate her shame. 'I'm so sorry.'

Alexander caught her hands, holding her tighter when she tried to struggle free. 'When I said that you didn't know what you were doing, I was not complaining about your lack of experience, for heaven's sake. I meant that you didn't realise the effect that you were having on me.'

She had only the vaguest notion of what he must mean. Thank heavens for the dark.

'I think,' Alexander said gently when her silence became painful, 'that we had better go in. We are neither of us quite ourselves. Only last night we launched ourselves as the Earl and Countess of Fearnoch. Today has been—well, we've both got a lot to reflect on.'

'And tomorrow?'

'Tomorrow, I think we should try to establish some sort of normality.'

She followed him back up the garden into the breakfast parlour, retrieving her shoes and stockings on the way. Once inside, absurdly conscious of her bare feet, Eloise tried to hide them under her petticoats, watching Alexander as he closed over the French doors and checked the bolts. A wave of exhaustion washed over her.

'Tomorrow, in the cold light of day,' she said, 'we'll wake up and wonder what on earth came over us.'

'Yes.' He sighed, raking his hand through his hair, clearly torn and for once making no effort to disguise the fact. 'I need you to know, that when I told you I had lost interest in lovemaking, it wasn't a lie.'

'I must confess to having wondered what it was that made you lose interest. Will you tell me?'

'No.'

She flinched.

'I can't tell you. Don't ask me. I hate it when you ask

me a question that I can't answer, and then you look so—so hurt!'

She couldn't understand why he was so agitated. 'But how am I to know what subjects are taboo?'

Alexander swore under his breath, raking his hands through his hair again, before attempting a rueful smile. 'How indeed? I have had no desire whatsoever to kiss anyone for some time—I can't explain why, you'll just have to accept my word for it, so this—this attraction between the pair of us is inconvenient to say the least.'

'I didn't think I'd want to kiss anyone at all, ever. It's not only you who finds it inconvenient.'

'Inconvenient, and very wrong.' Alexander gripped her hands. 'We can't allow ourselves to become intimate. It's not what either of us wants from this marriage.'

'To say nothing of the fact that it's against Sir Marcus's rules.'

'Those rules are there for a purpose. I can't risk— they exist to protect us, ensure neither of us gets hurt, Eloise.'

'But we were only kissing, Alexander.'

'You may be innocent, but you're neither naïve nor stupid.' He released her. 'We were not *only kissing*. A few more of those only kisses, and—but we came to our senses just in time, and now we will ensure we not lose them again.'

He was right. A few more of those kisses, and she'd have surrendered to him completely, and the risk of that—it didn't bear thinking about. 'No,' Eloise said, shuddering. 'Tomorrow we will wake up clear-sighted and without regrets, and we will begin our married life as we mean to go on.'

'But first we both need to get some sleep.' He took her hand, lifting it to his lips as he did every night, but tonight, after a moment's hesitation, he kissed the air above her fingertips. 'Goodnight, Eloise.'

'Goodnight, Alexander.' She set out on the long traipse through Fearnoch House to her bedchamber where only this morning she'd decided she would relish becoming better acquainted with passion. And now, less than twelve hours later, that acquaintance had not only been short-lived, it was over.

Chapter Nine

'I'll see you at dinner. Enjoy your day.' Alexander kissed her cheek and departed for the Admiralty, leaving Eloise to finish her breakfast. Outside, the sun was struggling to penetrate a haze of grey cloud. After a beautiful spell of perfect summer days in June, the weather had turned. This first week in July had been persistently muggy, the air oppressive, turning a walk in the park into an endurance test. It looked like they were in for more of the same.

None the less, when she had finished the dregs of her tea, she opened the French doors and stepped outside, making for the shade of the trees at the bottom of the garden where she'd had a wrought-iron table and chair set up. Opening her notebook and her appointment book, she set about the task of mapping out her day. They were hosting a dinner for twenty tonight, for the last remaining stragglers of the Season. She checked the menu, which was more or less as Phoebe had suggested, making notes about flowers, place settings, the dinner service to be used. She had a small list of calls to be returned. She had an appointment at a tea warehouse. Mrs McGilvery was anxious for her to inspect the linen cupboard with a view to a comprehensive clear out. The decorators would finish painting the music room this week. She had to decide whether or not she wanted new hangings, and which room she wished them to tackle next. She had not finished the cushions she was making for the library sofas. And then there was the book catalogue. And…

Eloise set her pencil down with a heavy sigh. If this was the life of a countess, she didn't want it. What was Alexander doing now at the Admiralty? She had tried asking him over dinner a few times. He talked vaguely of auditing, accounts, shortfalls and budget cuts. She didn't believe for a second that he'd spent the day poring over ledgers—there was never a telltale sign of ink on his hands or his cuffs—but it was clear that he didn't want her to know, and since she didn't want to force him to lie, she hadn't persisted.

A bead of sweat trickled down her back under her chemise. Her nape was damp with perspiration and her feet were clammy. To hell with it, she thought, kicking off her slippers and pulling off her stockings. She was screened from the house, and the gardeners worked elsewhere on a Monday. Standing up, she surveyed the cluster of trees. They were mostly oaks. The one nearest to her was *that* tree. She averted her eyes. She didn't allow herself to think about that night, that kiss, that moment. It had been a mistake. It could not happen again. It was completely contrary to the terms of their arrangement.

It usually worked, but today her recitation failed her. Why, when it made such perfect logical sense, did she still pine after more of Alexander's kisses? Her eyes were drawn back to the tree. She leaned her back against the trunk, digging her bare toes into the ground. The earth was baked hard now, not nearly so green, but she remembered that moment with perfect clarity, when she had forgotten all about the delicious feel of her toes on the grass and lost herself in their kisses. In the way Alexander touched her. The sensations his touch aroused. Melting. Burning. Tingling. Aching. Yearning. The moment when her hands curled over the taut muscles of his behind. The moment when she'd arched against him, pulling him closer.

Her cheeks were burning, but there was no one to see her. She stood up, making her way to the darkest point of the tree cover, to the one plane tree in the garden. The bark was mossy grey, the scales that would peel off later in the year like painted swirls of colour. The leaves were thick, leathery, the fruits still spiky. She dragged her chair over to the base of the tree and stood on it. The first branch was a stretch, but she could just reach it. The need to climb was sudden and irresistible. Quickly, she divested herself of all her petticoats, dropping them carelessly on to the ground. The table was higher than the chair. She pulled that over, clambered up and swung herself easily on to the first broad branch. Scrabbling to find purchase with her bare feet, she stood up and tested the next branch. The leaves rustled as she climbed. Her arms and legs ached, but it was a pleasant ache. She'd become sedentary since arriving in London. Concentrating hard, she didn't notice the broken twigs that snagged on her hair, grazing her arms and feet as she climbed ever higher, until she reached the highest limb which would safely support her weight.

Perched there, completely obscured by thick foliage,

her heart pounding with the effort, a sense of well-being filled her. She was on a level with the topmost floor of Fearnoch House. Leaning over, far down below her she could see the white-painted table. The ground rushed up, making her dizzy, and she caught at a branch just in time. It was a very long way down. Alexander had warned her not to climb, but Alexander was at the Admiralty and he would never know. Clinging on, she leaned over again, smiling with elation. A very long way. How astonished her new London acquaintances would be to see her. The Climbing Countess.

Her smile faded as she recalled joking with Alexander on the subject. It had been their wedding day. They were having dinner at the Admiralty. He'd wanted to make the day memorable. She remembered every moment. *'I think I'm going to enjoy being married,'* Alexander had said. Did he still enjoy being married? They were rarely alone these days, attended by servants at breakfast and dinner, or playing their allotted roles as the recently married Earl and Countess of Fearnoch when in company. The kisses they did not share seemed to Eloise to hover in the air between them sometimes. The attraction they must not acknowledge was a constant, haunting presence. Why was it, when she knew it was wrong, that she persisted in wanting him? Why was it that this inconvenient, dangerous passion stubbornly refused to go away? Why shouldn't they kiss each other, when kissing each other was what they wanted to do? Because those kisses would lead to other things, Alexander had said. She knew it was true, but she still had no real idea what those other things were. More kisses? Where would he touch her? How? And how should she touch him? Eloise shivered, excited and afraid in equal measure.

A faint breeze ruffled the leaves of the tree. They had been married two months now. Was that long enough for the world to consider them an established couple? There wouldn't be many people left in London to impress, soon. Would Alexander resume his foreign travels next month, the month after? She ought to be looking forward to that day, because it would force her to abandon her lethargy and decide how she intended to spend her own life. But there were so many things she still wanted to know about him. What had happened to him to make him lose interest in lovemaking? Surely it must involve a woman, despite his very determined claim never to have been in love. She didn't want to think of Alexander in love. She didn't even want to imagine him kissing another woman, forced to do so because it was wrong for him to kiss his wife. Who would very much like him to kiss her.

She had to stop thinking about kissing! What was Alexander doing at this moment? What the devil did a Victualling Commissioner *do*? Victual ships, she supposed was the obvious answer. But victualling ships, though undoubtedly a taxing role, did not require a man to be handy with his fists or a crack shot. A man could victual ships whether he had a wife or not. Assuredly, there would be crises when supplies ran out or weren't in the right place, but were they the sort of crises that demanded a man to be ready to react immediately, to throw himself into resolving them, in Alexander's own words, without compromise? What sort of crises required a self-sufficient rule-breaker with a cool head?

She had known from the first that he was not a mere

Admiralty clerk. Meeting Sir Marcus confirmed that Alexander was a very important man. Married to his country. Not the Admiralty, his country. Something cold clutched at her heart. Sir Marcus had said he didn't want her to get hurt. She'd thought he meant that she would always come second to Alexander's job. She'd thought that, because that was what Sir Marcus told her. But unlike Alexander, Sir Marcus would have no compunction in lying to her.

She swayed, catching the overhead branch just in time, clutching it ever more tightly as her mind raced on. What if Sir Marcus had meant something else entirely? What if he was warning her not to become too fond of her husband because Alexander's job was dangerous?

It was like a curtain lifting. Sir Marcus didn't want her to get too fond of Alexander because Alexander might die. This was why men in Alexander's position were not usually permitted to marry. Alexander undertook dangerous tasks for his country. Alexander was a government spy.

Stunned but certain, Eloise clutched at the branch, staring sightlessly at the speckled sky through the leaves. She was married to a spy. A hysterical laugh escaped her. She had no more idea what a spy did than a Victualling Commissioner. What did he spy on? Who? Where? Did he assume different identities? Did he steal secrets? How dangerous was it?

She must be wrong. She was letting her imagination run away with her. Yet it all fitted so well. Too well for her to dismiss it out of hand.

She would confront him tonight, demand the truth from him. And then what? He couldn't tell her the truth.

If Sir Marcus discovered that she'd forced the truth from him, Alexander might even be locked up. She would have ruined his life, the life he loved. She couldn't possibly ask him. She'd have to keep it a secret from him that she knew about his secret life. Besides, imagine what a fool she'd look if she was wrong.

But she wasn't wrong. Appalled, Eloise stared into space for a very long time, wondering how on earth she was going to live with the knowledge and keep her knowledge from him. The sooner Alexander left the country the better, then. But the moment he left the country he'd be in danger. How was she to get through the days wondering where he was, what he was doing? She couldn't bear it.

Eventually, her panic gave way to common sense. Alexander had chosen his life, and he loved it. She would not spend her life in limbo, waiting to hear whether he had survived his latest mission. She didn't *love* Alexander, she was not about to turn into a copy of her sad, pitiful father, but she did care about him. So she must take control of her own life, and stop worrying about his. Turn her attentions to what made her happy. Her sisters. She would invite them to London forthwith. They were long overdue a visit.

She studied her hands, noticing with dismay the fretwork of stinging scratches. How long had she been up here? It was not like her, to be so—so indecisive. She needed to give herself a shake, she needed a plan. And the first step was to quite literally bring herself back down to earth. Which looked a great deal further down than she'd thought. Her muscles ached. Her legs felt distinctly shaky. Her hands and feet were stiff. If only Alexander did know she was here, he'd help her safely down. Taking herself firmly to task, Eloise reached for the branch over her head and rose cautiously to her feet.

The Grand Dining Room was aptly named, a vast salon with gold-painted walls adorned with an elaborate pattern of cornicing and panels depicting what seemed to Alexander somewhat debauched mythological scenes. Eloise had made no changes to this room, as far as he could determine. The ceiling was painted duck-egg blue and every bit as elaborately decorated as the walls. A huge basket of flowers was arranged in the grate of the immense white-marble mantelpiece. There were matching sideboards ranged against three of the walls, their polished tops cluttered with epergnes, urns, statues and candelabra. The floor was covered in a carpet of dusky pink which must have been woven especially to fit the room, and the curtains, drawn against the murky summer evening, were heavy gold damask. The effect was overpowering and not altogether pleasing.

There was ample room for themselves and their twenty guests around the table. Dinner had been excellent thanks, he knew, to Phoebe's menu suggestions, but he had little appetite. It was the weather. It was the tedium of his days spent idling away at the Admiralty studying maps, reading intelligence reports, staring out of the window at the endless, repetitive, seemingly pointless drilling on Horse Guards Parade, and wondering what Eloise was doing.

At the other end of the table, out of conversational reach, she was listening to Lord Henry Armstrong holding forth. The esteemed diplomat would either be boasting about his clutch of sons or the latest, highly lucrative trade deal the Crown had sealed with Arabia, which he would claim the credit for. Alexander smiled grimly to himself. He had seen the official dossier on Lord Armstrong. That pillar of the community had some very sordid secrets in his past that would ruin him if they ever became public. And as to the lucrative trade deals with Arabia—were it not for Armstrong's enterprising daughters, they would not have been struck. The man had five girls by his first wife, Alexander knew, but to listen to him, you'd think he had only four sons, all of them budding diplomats, if Armstrong was to be believed, raised in their father's image. Poor blighters.

On Alexander's right, the second Lady Armstrong was far too concerned with her dinner to make conversation, save to assure him each time she methodically emptied her plate, that the Countess of Fearnoch was fast becoming known for having the best dinner table in London. And Lady Armstrong would know, if her ample curves were anything to go by. At least she enjoyed her food. He couldn't imagine that life with Lord Henry Armstrong would be much of a pleasure.

Lord, but he was bored. He'd far rather be dining *à deux* with Eloise. Though if they were alone, there would be no need for him to kiss her hand, her cheek, to put a proprietorial arm around her waist. To smile benignly at her down the length of the table as she looked up and caught his eye, the tiny quirk of her brows, just for his benefit, telling him all he needed to know about her conversation with Armstrong. If they were alone, he wouldn't be required to remember how she felt in his arms, the feel of her lips on his, the heat of her kisses, so that their guests could see just how passionately he desired her. If they were alone, she wouldn't return that gaze, blush, look away as if she was embarrassed.

Eloise got to her feet to lead the ladies out. Alexander watched as Wiggins set out the port and the snuff boxes. Another hour, maybe two, and the night would be over. He would kiss his wife goodnight on the cheek. And he'd retire to bed congratulating himself on having endured another boring, frustrating, pointless day.

'Thank you, Wiggins. I will snuff the candles. Dinner was excellent, as usual. Please thank all the staff. Goodnight.'

The drawing room doors closed softly behind the butler, and Eloise smothered a yawn. 'Thank goodness that's over. That Armstrong chap!' She threw herself on to the sofa, kicked off her slippers and began to unbutton her gloves. 'Dear heavens, you'd think that no one had ever fathered twins before. I mentioned my sisters at least three times only to be ignored, but I forgot, silly me, that female twins don't actually count.' She pulled off her gloves and flexed her fingers, which were unaccountably stiff. She remembered too late why they were, and tucked them quickly under her evening gown. Unfortunately not quite quickly enough.

'What the devil?' Alexander sat down beside her. 'Let me see your hands.'

'It's only a few cuts and grazes.'

She granted him a brief flash before trying to tuck them away again, but he was too quick for her, catching her wrist, pulling her to her feet, turning one hand over, frowning over the mass of scrapes and scratches which covered not only her hand but her forearm. 'Please don't tell me you climbed one of those trees in the garden, Eloise.'

'Very well, I won't tell you.'

He declined to be amused by this quip. 'I thought you said that the branches were all too high.'

'There's a plane tree at the back that's more accessible. I used the table to climb up—you know, the little one that I...'

'I know the one. Let me see the other hand.'

'It's just a few scratches, Alexander.'

'Let me see your other hand.'

She sighed dramatically, holding out her arm. 'As I said, superficial, nothing more. Certainly nothing to make a fuss about.'

'Did you tell anyone where you were?'

'Did I tell Mrs McGilvery that I was off to climb a tree? What do you think?'

'So if you'd fallen...'

'I didn't fall.'

'You could have broken your neck. Or you could have been stuck up the damned thing, and no one would have known where the hell you were. What were you thinking?'

'Why are you so angry?'

'I distinctly remember asking you to promise that you wouldn't be so foolish.'

'And I distinctly remember that I made you no such promise. I have been climbing trees since I was five years old and come to...'

'No harm?'

'A broken ankle once, that's all,' she admitted, flustered. 'But I did not come close to breaking anything today, for goodness' sake.'

'I won't have you climbing trees.'

'I beg your pardon?'

'Unlike your parents, I would prefer you not to risk life and limb while you are in my care.'

'I am not in your care. How dare you tell me...'

'You're my wife. I am responsible for your well-being.'

'I am your wife in name only. You have no right to scold me like a naughty child.'

'For heaven's sake, Eloise, all I'm saying is that I would rather you didn't kill yourself.'

'The feeling is entirely mutual.'

'What the devil is that supposed to mean?'

'Nothing.' She could have bitten her tongue. 'I'm out of practice, and the tree is in full leaf. It was silly of me to climb it.'

He took her hand, running his fingers over the scratches.

'Did you enjoy it?'

She laughed shakily. 'Mostly.'

'I had a tedious day. I'd have much preferred to have been climbing trees with you.'

Their eyes locked, and her breath caught in her throat at the heat which flared between them. She thought she might stop breathing if he didn't kiss her, if he didn't, just this once, stop fighting his instincts. They moved together slowly, painfully slowly. Their lips met and clung for a moment as they hesitated, willing themselves to pull apart, but neither did. They kissed. A tentative kiss, as if they had not kissed before, and perhaps they had not, because this time there was no pretence. This was not the Earl kissing his wife. From the moment their lips met, there was no doubt that this was Alexander kissing Eloise. And Eloise kissing Alexander.

At first it was simply a release, the sheer bliss of not having to resist, of succumbing to temptation. He cupped her cheek as he kissed her. She curled her fingers into his hair as she kissed him back. Time slowed and stopped as they kissed, kisses so soothing and so gentle that she barely noticed the heat building inside her, intent only on returning his kisses, on mirroring the way he touched her, stroking, smoothing, soothing. She slid her fingers inside his coat, wanting to feel the heat of his skin. He shrugged himself free of it. She ran her hands over his arms, across his shoulders, down his back. He kissed her neck, her throat, then their lips met again, and they had already crossed the boundary of just kissing.

She tugged at his neckcloth, pulling it free to expose the line of his throat, burying her face into the warmth of his skin, kissing. He kissed her breasts along the neckline of her evening gown. She shuddered. She unfastened his waistcoat, running her hands over his chest, feeling the muscles ripple at her touch, feeling his breath inhale sharply, excited by the effect she had on him. He loosened the fastenings at the back of her gown, sliding the bodice down her arms, and all she cared about was that there was now more of her for him to kiss. She ran her hands through his hair again as he dipped his head, kissed into the valley between her breasts, his hands cupping, his mouth licking, and all of it twisting her tightly inside, that drugging ache she remembered making her breathe fast and shallow.

Taking her lead from him, she tugged his shirt free, smoothing her palms at last over his skin as he pulled it over his head. Hot skin. Muscles rippling on his shoulders. The knotted ridge of his spine. Their mouths meeting again, kisses so deep and so delightful and so delicious. She rubbed her cheek against the soft fuzz of hair on his chest, inhaled the scent of his skin, soap and sweat and something innately male. He untied the laces at the front of her stays and cupped her breasts. A shuddering escaped her. He lowered his head, took her nipple in his mouth, and she moaned. Her body thrummed, twisted, ached. She smoothed her palms over his nipples, felt them pucker at her touch, felt his chest expand, contract, then she stroked lower, the dip of his ribcage.

She kissed him again. He kissed her back as if he was ravenous, desperate to consume her. It was like a hunger, this need she had, a craving that made her anxious, tense, fevered. He eased her on to the sofa and still they kissed. She couldn't lie still, instead twisting under him, her body arching as he took her nipple in his mouth again and sucked. Everything seemed to centre, focus deep inside her. His hand found her other breast, and she had the same dizzying sensation as she'd had at the top of the tree, and then she fell, swooped, unravelled, felt her body shuddering, heard herself crying out over and over, clutching at his shoulders as if he would save her. Which he did. Pulling her hard against him, stroking her hair as she burrowed her face into his chest, keeping her safe until it was over.

She felt weighted down and at the same time as if she might float away. She felt as if she consisted of bubbles or honey or a mixture of both. Dazed, she lifted her head. Alexander's eyes were dark, his lids heavy, his mouth—she touched his mouth. The area around the sofa was scattered with their discarded clothing. 'What happened?'

A laugh shook him. Then he swore under his breath. 'Something that categorically should not have happened.'

She stared at him, trying to make sense of what he was saying. 'You mean that I should not have...'

'No!' He got to his feet, pulling the tasselled silk cloth from the table and handing it to her. 'What happened to you is perfectly natural.'

He picked up his shirt and pulled it over his head. Her bewilderment must have been written over her face, because he sat back down on the edge of the sofa. 'What you felt was a—a natural conclusion to what we were doing.'

'But we did not—I mean you did not—we didn't.' The extent of her ignorance astounded her. 'I thought the natural conclusion was something else entirely.'

'Fortunately, we came to our senses before we reached that stage.'

Curiosity overcame her embarrassment. 'I didn't know there were stages.'

'Well, there are,' Alexander said tersely.

'Are you angry because we did not—?'

'Could we stop discussing what we did and did not do? This is a conversation you should have with another female, if you must have it. Lady Elmswood...'

'Kate is probably even more ignorant on the subject than I am. I'm sorry, Alexander...'

'There's nothing for you to be sorry about. I'm not angry with you, Eloise, I'm angry with myself. I can't understand—I knew, I know, heaven knows, I know—and yet it didn't even cross my mind.' He screwed his eyes shut, clenching his fists. 'How could I have forgotten? I will not be so bloody stupid as to risk repeating the same mistake.'

He didn't seem to realise he was talking out loud. His eyes were closed. He would not have noticed the effect that last sentence had on her. Alexander never makes the same mistake twice, Sir Marcus had said. So she had been right. He had been involved in an affaire and it had gone horribly wrong. That was why he had not been interested in making love to anyone. Until she had tempted him!

Eloise scrabbled to her feet, scooping up items of clothing, pulling her dress up over her shoulder, heedless of the tearing sound it made. 'This won't happen again, I promise.'

'It was not your doing, it was mine. I knew what I was doing, you did not.'

'I am ignorant, but I'm not naïve. I will not allow you to take the blame.'

'I have been wanting to make love to you ever since we agreed that it was out of the question.'

'There, that's the problem in a nutshell,' she exclaimed. 'It is human nature to want what one cannot have.'

'Then the only solution is to remove the source of temptation. I think it's for the best that I return to active service as soon as possible.'

Active service! He must be extremely upset, to have let his guard slip that much. She must not let him see that she'd noticed. She didn't want him to return to whatever active service entailed. She wanted—all she wanted at this moment was to escape before she said something stupid. 'Let's forget this happened,' Eloise said, backing towards the door. 'It meant nothing. It changes nothing.'

'Eloise, you know that's not true.' Alexander scooped up his waistcoat and coat along with her shoes. 'We are neither of us in the right frame of mind to discuss this any further tonight. I think we should get some sleep and talk in the morning.'

He held out her shoes. 'To be honest, I was already thinking that the time was approaching to return to work.'

Work, not active service. He had recovered his poise. Eloise forced a smile. 'I climbed the tree today because I was feeling—not bored exactly, but I feel as if I'm stuck in a rut.'

'There, you see, great minds think alike.' Alexander held the door open. 'Go to bed, Eloise. We'll talk tomorrow.'

They were in the library, sitting on the sofas by the fire facing each other. This was the room where Eloise had made the most changes. Not only were the sofas reupholstered and extremely comfortable, they were strewn with cushions in bright colours, quirkily embroidered—her own work. The curtains were new. The bronze clock on the mantel, with Venus rising from the waves, looked new now that it had been cleaned. The whole room gleamed. Fresh flowers filled the hearth. About half the bookcases had been reordered, the new catalogue lying open on the desk.

'You've done an impressive amount of work here,' Alexander said, looking about him in surprise. She had not, since the first day, asked him for help. Knowing it was her sanctuary, she assumed, he had been avoiding the room.

Eloise waved the compliment aside, pouring him a cup of coffee. She had spent the long night preparing her strategy for this discussion. She was determined to get their marriage back on an even keel. Not because she was being so foolish as to care too much, but because the reasons for this match were still valid. She consulted her notebook quite unnecessarily. 'I think we've rather lost sight of why we agreed to marry in the first place. If we can remind ourselves what is important, then what happened last night won't happen again.'

Alexander took a sip of coffee. 'I reached the same conclusion myself, as a matter of fact.'

'Good.' Very good, in fact! 'So let us remind ourselves, then. You had three goals. A settlement for your mother. A secure future for your estates. A return to your work abroad. My objectives were equally straightforward. Funds to settle on my sisters to allow them the freedom to choose their own future. To relieve the burden on my aunt and uncle. And secure the freedom, and opportunity, for me to decide what I wanted to do. Do I have that right?'

'Perfectly right.'

Alexander's mouth twitched. She wondered if he was comparing her to an Admiralty clerk—a real Admiralty clerk, the sort whose day was not over until he had ticked off every task on his list. 'Excellent,' Eloise continued, keeping her eyes on her notebook. 'And am I right in saying that you feel these goals are still well worth achieving?'

'Of course they are.'

'Then you should know I feel exactly the same. Though my own are considerably—but that is not the point,' she rallied. 'The point is, what happened last night—in the light of these goals—well, it's obvious that we would be extremely foolish to allow it to put any of that at risk. Logically, I mean, it simply makes no sense. Does it?'

'No, it doesn't. But while you're discovering what it

is that makes you happy, I don't want to do anything to make you unhappy.'

'You're providing me with the means to find my happiness.'

'You know perfectly well what I'm talking about.' He joined her on the other sofa. 'Your parents' marriage made you frightened of lovemaking. You thought your disgust of it was ingrained and permanent. I took your assurances on the subject at face value because it suited me to do so. And now that you are married, or more likely, now that you have for the first time in your life had the time to think only about yourself, away from your sisters and all the family associations, you see things very differently. Yes?'

She smiled faintly. 'Well, I know I'm not going to turn into my mother simply because I've discovered that I like to—that I enjoyed what you did last night. I did enjoy it, but I am not a fool, Alexander. I would not risk bringing a child into this world for the sake of a few moments' gratification, especially since you've made it very clear that you do not want children.'

'I have not swerved from that view. Have you?'

She had not considered the question. She forced herself to do so now, aware of his gaze, knowing how important it was to be honest with him. It wouldn't be any child, it would be Alexander's child, and hers. Of course she would love it, as she loved her sisters. Of course she would be a good mother, because she had mothered her sisters, because she had the perfect example *not* to follow, of how to be a bad mother. But did that mean she wanted a baby, when she had only just begun on her journey of discovery? No. Would she ever wish a child on a man who did not want it? No. 'I haven't changed my mind,' she said firmly, meeting his gaze square on. 'I promise you.'

He took his time to mull this over. The fact that they had both, contrary to all their expectations, lost themselves in pleasure, seemed to Eloise to hang over them, an unacknowledged but entirely present unpleasant truth. She desperately wanted to know what had transpired with the mysterious other woman he had last taken his pleasure with, but that was a nest of vipers he clearly wished left undisturbed. It also led them into the murky waters of the real nature of his work—and she had already decided she could never do that.

He still had not spoken. She risked touching his hand lightly. 'So you see, I have thought all of this through. We have made a good match, Alexander. We can make a success of it. What would make me unhappy would be if you had changed your mind about that.'

'I have not changed my mind. I do want to make a success of this, of course I do, but I don't want it to be a sacrifice on your part.'

Eloise stifled a huge sigh of relief. 'No, for we agreed, didn't we, that sacrifice breeds resentment, and we are bound together, for better or worse. There's a difference between deciding that a price is worth paying, and making a sacrifice.'

'You would make an admirable lawyer.'

'Perhaps that's what I will become. England's first female lawyer. Sadly, the law of the land will have to be changed in order for me to satisfy that ambition.'

'Alternatively, you could set yourself up in business as a refurbisher of houses. Use this place as your pattern book, when it's done. You have a real knack for breathing life into a room—like this one. I know there are new curtains and new covers on the sofas but there's more to it—it gleams, and yet it is very restful.'

'Thank you. I have certainly enough to occupy me here for a time, while I think about what I really want to do. I've been considering paying a short visit to my sisters. It's too hot for them to come to London, and besides, Kate won't leave Elmswood Manor until after the harvest.'

'You miss them?'

'Of course, but not as much as I expected. To be honest,' Eloise said, 'it's rather that I thought you and I might benefit from a few days spent apart.'

'To cool our ardour, you mean?' he said sardonically.

'To regain some perspective!' To her horror, her eyes filled with tears. She turned away, blinking furiously.

Alexander cursed roundly. 'My apologies. It must have cost you dearly to speak out as you have, and it has been very much worth saying.' He touched her shoulder. 'I think it's a capital idea for you to get some respite from London and see your sisters.'

She nodded, dabbing at her eyes before turning back around. 'I'm a little overwrought.'

'No wonder.' He made to take her hand, then thought the better of it. 'You are not the only one who has spent the night deep in thought. I have not forgotten what you said to me the day after our wedding ball, the regret you implied at not having the opportunity to attempt any type of reconciliation with your father.'

'Oh.' The change of subject took her aback. 'I did wonder—but then you didn't say anything and I thought...'

'That I had decided to let sleeping mothers lie? No, but it's no small step to take, after all this time.'

'Goodness, I know. Or at least,' Eloise amended sadly, 'I don't. I'm glad though. Tell me what you have decided.'

'I think I must pay her a visit before I go abroad again. There's much that I don't understand. You're right, she must have been miserable. They must all have been miserable down the generations, those faceless females.'

'I've been wondering about that. What happened to the girls? I presume there must have been female children? Your cousin Raymond's mother, for example?'

'Raymond's father was the Sixth Earl's brother. That is why Raymond was raised the Fearnoch way, because that is how his father was raised.'

'But Raymond's father must have been a second son, like you?'

'A second son, but quite unlike me.'

'In what way?'

'I'm not the Sixth Earl's son. I have no idea who my father was, but he's not the man whose portrait is hanging in the gallery upstairs.'

Eloise stared in astonishment. She must have misheard him. Or she had mistaken what he'd said. 'You can't mean—you mean that you are illegitimate? That Walter is not your brother?'

'Walter is my half-brother.'

Eloise shook her head in disbelief. 'So your mother—but good grief, how on earth do you know—what makes you think such a thing could be true?'

'I'm sorry,' Alexander said, 'this has come as a shock to you.'

'That is something of an understatement.'

'I've lived with the truth for so long it seems self-explanatory to me.'

'How you can be so certain? That is, if the subject is not too painful.'

'It's not.' His mouth was set. 'I don't give a damn about the Earl. I'm actually relieved he's not my father. When I told you that I consider myself fortunate to have escaped Walter's upbringing I meant it.'

'It doesn't mean that you can't still be hurt that you were raised as you were. How did you discover the truth of your parentage.'

'Deduced, rather than discovered. I have no tangible proof but it's the only explanation that makes sense. Why else would I have been so ruthlessly exiled? It is a well-established custom for all Fearnoch menfolk to be bred and raised in their father's image. Of course I didn't think so rationally as a child. When I was first sent to school, I was convinced I was being punished for something. I had no idea what I'd done wrong, but I knew it must have been serious, because why else would Walter be allowed to stay at home?'

'It's what children do,' Eloise said, her heart aching for the rejected and bewildered little boy he must have been. 'When my sisters were that age, they saw the world in very simple terms. If something they desperately wished for didn't happen, they blamed themselves.' Even after all these years it hurt her to recall the tears, the looks of incomprehension when some precious story or drawing or cake or sampler the twins had gone to lengths to produce had been ignored, when the visits to the nursery and the goodnight kisses they longed for weren't forthcoming. And what Alexander had suffered was far worse. Tears filled her eyes, but she bit the inside of her cheek to stop them falling. He would mistake her compassion for pity. 'What happened to make you think there might be a different explanation?'

'No one single thing. Aside from the fact that my brother had not preceded me to school, I was treated the same as all the other boys when I was there. The holidays spent alone in the country gave me serious pause for thought. If I was being punished, there would be an end to my sentence, but there wasn't one. Why did my father want rid of me? I remember—I am fairly sure it is a memory—he bumped into me on the estates one day. I suppose I must have strayed beyond my boundaries. If I had done something terrible to offend him, I would have expected him to be furious with me. I was terrified he'd beat me. But he looked straight through me with such disdain, as if I didn't exist.'

'Dear heavens. That is—I can't imagine how you must have felt.'

He shrugged. 'Puzzled. It got me thinking seriously about why I was being treated so singularly. As the less-favoured second son, my father's indifference is easily explained away, but not my mother's. To this day she can barely look me in the eye. She is ashamed of me. My presence would have been a constant humiliating reminder to them both of her infidelity, his cuckolding. It was almost a relief to finally conclude that none of it was my doing. I was an innocent victim.'

'But you bear the Earl's name.'

'Perhaps because he didn't want it defiled. It's all very well for a husband to populate the country with his bastard offspring, but for a wife it's beyond the pale.

He'd have been faced with the choice of a scandalous divorce, or hushing it up.'

'So he chose the latter and accepted you as his own, but then he punished you for it,' Eloise said indignantly.

'I'm not the only one he punished. You remember I told you that the Earl changed the provisions in his will for my mother?'

'You said it was some time ago.'

'It was changed in June 1802. When I was five years old.'

'That was when you were sent off to school.'

'It could be that he thought I was his at first, that would explain why I bear his name. But when I was five, he discovered his mistake. He punished me by sending me away, and he presumably informed Walter of my mother's betrayal, since my brother chose not to remedy the situation in his will.'

'Which is why Walter shunned you, even though he's your half-brother,' Eloise said sadly. 'I presume you being sent away was also intended to punish your mother, by denying her any contact with you.'

'I expect so. I wonder now what other cruel retribution he meted out to her. I think it speaks volumes that the union produced no more children.'

The enormity of what she had heard made Eloise feel as if her head might explode. 'I can hardly believe this. If what you say is true, if this became public knowledge...'

'It won't. I promise you, you have nothing to fear. Your reputation and your settlement are safe.'

'I wasn't thinking about me! I was thinking about you. You could lose everything, perhaps even face criminal charges.'

'It won't come to that.' He covered her hands, giving her a little shake. 'Legally, I am the second son of the Sixth Earl—that's what it says in the parish register, that's how I'm recorded in the family bible. That is why I am, perfectly legitimately, now the Eighth Earl.'

'But in reality you're not legitimate. Good grief, if your cousin Raymond ever found out the truth...'

'He won't. You are the only person who knows, and I trust you implicitly.'

'Then I am very honoured. I appreciate how enormously difficult this must be for you to talk about.'

'I've come to realise that I needed to confront it. You made me see that. Though I must admit,' Alexander added wryly, 'until I actually said it, I wasn't sure if I could. I'm beginning to wonder how much I really know about myself. This house. The things I've discovered about Walter. Your insights about my mother. The very foundations that I have based my life on have been shaken to the core.'

'Has it occurred to you that you might be wrong? About who your father is, I mean. Don't get me wrong, I understand why you've reached the conclusion you have, but you can't be certain unless you confront...'

'That will be—difficult. Verging on the impossible. I described my mother as cold. What I meant was that it's like trying to converse with a stone wall. If she has feelings, she doesn't give them away.'

'A trait her son has inherited.'

'Though you can read me easily enough. Painfully observant, is how you described yourself. Will you come with me, Eloise?'

'She won't want to meet me. I'm the wife she'd rather you did not have. But if you want me to be by your side, of course I'll come. Shall I postpone my visit to Elms-wood Manor?'

'No. You were right, we will both benefit from some time spent apart. Go and see to your sisters. I will write to my mother and inform her we intend to call on her. I thought we could combine the visit with a look around the Lancashire estates. That's another thing I need to make some decisions about.'

'To dispose of the inheritance that isn't rightfully yours? Now I understand why you were so vehement.'

'It's true, I don't feel entitled, but it's also true that I don't want them to end up in my cousin's hands.'

'If Raymond Sinclair does not change his ways, he's likely to die young in a debtors' prison. I don't think you need worry about him outliving you.'

She had spoken flippantly. In the context of every-thing Alexander had told her, Raymond Sinclair and his debts seemed trivial, but she could have bitten her tongue out when she saw the effect they had.

'You can't know what fate has in store for you,' Al-exander said. He reached for her, as if he would touch her cheek, then changed his mind. 'That's why I must put everything in order before I go.'

In case he didn't come back. It took an enormous effort for her not to protest. She fixed a smile on her face. 'You're not going away for ever. You and I, we're not going to be like Kate and my Uncle Daniel. You said that there would be times when you would come back here, that Fearnoch House would be your home in London.'

To her own ears, her voice sounded desperate, but Al-exander didn't seem to notice. 'And so it will be. Now,' he said brusquely, getting to his feet, 'we have a great deal to do. Leave it to me to make the arrangements for your journey into the country.'

'What about this house? The rooms that are currently locked?'

'Unlock them. This is your house now, Eloise, to do with as you see fit. Fearnoch House represents your future, not my past.'

He hesitated before making a show of kissing her cheek, and then he left. Eloise touched her cheek. His lips had barely brushed the skin. Wearily, she sat down at the desk and opened her notebook, but the lists of tasks were a blur. She rubbed her eyes, surprised to find that they were wet. A tear tracked down her cheek and plopped on to the blotter. She couldn't understand why she was crying. She pulled her handkerchief from her pocket, scrubbed her eyes and blew her nose. There was a great deal to be done.

Chapter Ten

The locked and mothballed rooms yielded little of interest. The two bedchambers of the master suite had been stripped bare, the furniture shrouded in dust cloths. There was no trace of the former occupants, no personal items—no clothes, brushes or combs, items of toilette or books. Any papers of interest had been removed from the huge desk which dominated Walter's study by Robertson, and Alexander had already gone through those. Walter did not keep copies of any letters he wrote, and any letters of importance—though Robertson claimed they were few—had already been filed in the family archive in Lancashire. In the attics there had been a nursery, according to the floor plan, but when Eloise opened the doors of the rooms, heart thumping, the rooms were completely empty and thick with dust.

She led Alexander on the same tour a few days later, on a Sunday, when he was not required to be at the Admiralty. It was the first time they had been alone, save for meals, since they had embarked upon what they now referred to as their fresh start. In the study, he stood for a long time in front of the desk. When he knelt down, she thought he was examining the beadwork, until he flinched, his eyes screwed up tight, and she realised he was recreating his child's eye view. When he got to his feet again, he left the room without a word.

In the master bedchamber he stood stock still, staring at the bed where both the Sixth and Seventh Earls had breathed their last, his face impassive. He led the way to what had been the nurseries without the need to consult a floor plan, walking straight through the door of the biggest room without hesitation. 'The playroom,' he said, wiping the dust from the barred window to look out. 'A child's bedchamber,' he said in the next, much smaller room. 'Mine, I think. I don't think Walter slept here. Through there...' He opened the connecting door, nodding. 'Nanny's room. I'd forgotten about her.'

Eloise followed him back to the main room. 'You remember living here?'

'I remember this room. There was a chalk board. A horse. A set of soldiers I was particularly fond of. I remember worrying that they would be confiscated. I don't know why, but I...' Alexander dropped on to the dusty floor, tugging at the skirting by the window seat. 'Good grief!' The skirting came away. He reached in, pulling out a small lead soldier, turning it over in his hands, smiling. 'I hid this one, just in case.'

'Do you remember anything else?'

His smile faded. 'Not a thing. It struck me as odd, the first day we arrived here, that I didn't know my way around. I presume that I was too young to be permitted downstairs.'

'But it was obvious you remembered the study.'

He turned the soldier over in his hand once more,

before putting it into his coat pocket. 'Yes.' He held the door open. 'It's filthy up here. Shall we?'

Wanting to press him but reluctant to force the clearly painful issue, she preceded him out of the nursery, back down the stairs to the library. 'I think I'll continue compiling the catalogue. Would you like to help?'

He thought about it. Then he shrugged. 'This is meant to be my day off from compiling lists, but why not.'

Eloise indicated the open catalogue on her desk with a smile. 'It's a simple enough system, even an Admiralty clerk should be able to follow it. I'll read the titles out, if you can list them in the appropriate section, against the next available number, and I will write it inside.'

'I think I can just about manage that.'

She pulled the ladder towards the next section of the shelves she had been working on and began to climb without checking first that it was stable. It wobbled, it must have had one leg set in a small dip in the floorboards. She continued to the topmost step, reaching for the first volume. The ladder wobbled again.

'For heaven's sake, be careful.'

'I'm perfectly fine.' She tugged at the book. It was jammed in tightly. She pulled again and it came free in a cloud of dust that made her sneeze. The book fell from her hands. She grabbed for it, missed, and the ladder toppled, taking her with it.

Alexander caught her before she hit the ground, kicking the ladder in the other direction, holding her tight against his chest. 'My goodness,' Eloise gasped, 'how on earth did you manage to react so quickly?'

'Are you all right?'

'I can't believe you caught me.'

He set her down gently, putting his hands on her shoulders, giving her a little shake. 'I can't believe you were so careless. You have book dust on your cheek.'

'Book dust. Food for bookworms.'

Alexander smiled, the smile she hadn't seen for days, the one that did strange things to her tummy. She smiled back at him. The air between them quivered with the possibility of a kiss. She stayed completely still, holding her breath. He pulled her to him. She closed her eyes in anticipation.

And then he let her go. 'Please be more careful in future. I won't always be there to break your fall.'

He was making for the door. 'I thought you were going to help?'

'I think we both know that's a bad idea.'

'Yes.' She pinned what she hoped was a bright smile to her face. 'Perhaps you should go for a drive, get some fresh air. You are cooped up at the Admiralty too much.'

'Perhaps.' He hesitated, holding the door open. 'You didn't ask what I was thinking about, when we were in the study.'

She gestured helplessly. 'It was obviously unpleasant.'

'My father used to flog me. That's what I remember. Holding on to the desk, while he beat me.'

'Eloise.' Kate smiled warmly. 'I've been poring over those seed catalogues you kindly brought with you from the Vineyard Nursery. It's given me some great ideas for replanting the walled garden.'

'Order whatever takes your fancy and have the bill sent to me and don't dare protest. It's a small enough token of my affection and gratitude. The twins seem to be thriving, they've barely missed me.'

'That's nonsense and you know it. I've waited days to have a proper chat with you since the girls have commandeered you. Come and sit down, I've just made a fresh pot of tea, and there are some of Phoebe's shortbread biscuits to taste. Flavoured with lavender, I believe.'

Eloise sat down opposite her aunt, snapping a biscuit in two and taking a wary mouthful. 'I think she may have overdone the lavender just a little bit. This tastes like furniture polish.'

Kate chuckled. 'I know we joked about her using the money you have settled on her to open her own restaurant, but I think she may be taking the notion seriously. She's never had her nose out of that receipt book you sent her—*The Art of French Cookery*, I think it is called. To hear her waxing lyrical about the chef who wrote it…'

'Antoine Beauvilliers. He is the chef at one of Paris's top restaurants, according to Monsieur Salois, who recommended the book to me for Phoebe in the first place.'

'Ah, yes, the esteemed Monsieur Salois, who I believe runs the Duke and Duchess of Brockmore's kitchen.' Kate rolled her eyes. 'When you arranged the introduction for your sister, I don't think you realised what Estelle and I would have to suffer. Monsieur Salois sends Phoebe screeds of receipts in every post, or so it seems. Our diet has never been so varied, or so rich. All three of us are in danger of having to let out our clothes. Have you formed a friendship with Lady Brockmore?'

'She's very nice. I've met lots of people who are very nice.'

'But no close friends?'

Eloise shrugged. 'I'm not lonely, if that's what you're wondering. Only I'm not sure that I want to spend the rest of my life in London. I miss the country. I miss—oh, Kate, I'm not cut out to be a lady of leisure.'

Kate laughed heartily. 'You wouldn't be the Eloise I know if you were. But you've earned a little grace and privilege, after all these years.'

'I need to find something constructive to do though. Something more challenging and rewarding than refurbishing a town house.'

'What about the Fearnoch estates? They are extensive, aren't they?'

'And under the care of a very able manager. Though not for much longer. Alexander plans to sell them off. There is coal there, he wants it to be mined safely.'

'Coal mines require a lot of labour. Miners have families who need homes, schooling, food. I was reading up on Mr Owen's New Lanark mill and workers' village recently. You could establish something similar for the Fearnoch mines. That would certainly be a project to get your teeth into, if you could persuade Alexander not to sell.'

'He is set on it.'

'I see.'

'Don't look at me like that. He has his reasons, good ones, I promise.'

Kate poured them both a second cup of tea. 'You've only been married a short while but I see a change in you already.'

'In what way?'

'It's difficult to put my finger on it. On the one hand you seem to be positively blooming, relishing your new life, yet on the other a little distracted, as if you are fretting about something. Perhaps unsettled is a better way of putting it.'

'Alexander will be going back to work soon. Abroad, I mean.'

'Just as you agreed.'

'Yes.' Eloise turned her cup around on her saucer. 'It's for the best.'

'You don't sound convinced.'

She set the cup down. 'Kate, can I ask you—oh, it doesn't matter.'

'It's not like you to be so reticent. What's bothering you?'

'Nothing. Only—did you—do you ever—Alexander kissed me!'

'Oh, my dear! Pray tell me did he—did he force himself…?'

'No! No, I didn't mean that at all.' Eloise pressed her hands against her cheeks, wishing she hadn't brought the subject up, but there was no going back now. Besides, if anyone could relate to her situation, it was Kate. 'Alexander kissed me, and I liked it, and I kissed him back.'

'And he liked it?' Kate asked drily. 'And he wanted more?'

'No. No, he doesn't want more.'

'I'm sorry, but I'm afraid I don't understand what the problem is, then.'

'The problem is that I do!' Eloise exclaimed wretchedly. 'I know it is wrong of me. I know that it is the one thing I didn't want from marriage. And I know that it's the last thing that Alexander wants. We talked about it. We agreed. We have an excellent arrangement, it would be folly to jeopardise it.'

'Would it be such a tragedy if you consummated your marriage—if that's what you are asking me?'

'It is not possible. I'm not asking you that. I'm asking you how you—are you happy, being a wife without—without a husband in the fullest sense?'

Kate coloured slightly. 'The circumstances are very different. Daniel and I have never shared a roof, never mind a bed.'

'And you are content with the situation?'

'I have made my choice and I am happy to live with it.'

There was something in her tone that gave Eloise pause, but Kate never lied, and Eloise had her own concerns to worry about. 'Would it be better if Alexander hadn't kissed me?'

'But he has kissed you. And you liked it, and that has unsettled you. You are going to have to find a way to live without kisses.'

'As you have? Do you ever wish…?'

'No.' Kate began to stack the tea things. 'I never wish for what I cannot have. I already have more than I dreamt of. As do you. It is enough, Eloise, if you make it enough,' she said, giving her a quick hug. 'Trust me.'

Almost two weeks had elapsed since he had written to his mother, but as yet Alexander had received no reply in answer to his request to visit. With Eloise away, despite the constant clattering of tradesmen, Fearnoch House seemed empty, and with the work on his own particular project there complete, he was at a loose end. Sick of kicking his heels at the Admiralty all day, he had taken to wandering the streets of London, and when that had palled, had started driving out, further and further afield each day. July remained hot and oppressive, the constant threat of thunder to clear the air never materialising.

'I see you are in your now customary foul temper,' Sir Marcus said, entering the room which Alexander had purloined without knocking. 'What on earth is wrong with you, man?'

'This damned weather.'

'Then take your new wife to the country, as everyone else does. Or take a wedding trip further afield. Paris, perhaps? No, perhaps not. Paris at the height of summer can be unbearable, remember?

'Especially if you are forced to hide in blanket boxes on a Calais-bound coach. How could I forget?'

Sir Marcus took the chair on the other side of the desk, carefully smoothing out the non-existent creases in his pantaloons. 'Yes, that mission certainly had its moments but all's well that ends well. Anyway, you know you love it, dear boy. Have you told her?'

'What? Who?'

'Your wife, Alex. Have you told her who you are? What you do?'

'Of course not.'

'She struck me as a very observant young woman. Are you sure you've not given yourself away?'

He was not at all sure. Eloise had asked him any number of pointed questions, and though he'd deflected them, or fed her half-truths, he was not convinced she believed him. 'She has said nothing to make me think I have,' Alexander said casually.

He should have known better than to play Sir Marcus at the game he had taught him. He pursed his lips, crossing his legs. 'What happens if you don't come back from the next mission? What happens if you're captured? Or killed? Or executed?'

'What happens? What do you mean, what happens? You will inform her of my tragic death in some sort of accident, as is the way with these things.'

'Lady Fearnoch is a very attractive woman. Intelligence, wit and beauty are a rare combination in a woman. I have heard from several sources that you are a most devoted couple.' Sir Marcus treated him to another of his innocuous smiles.

Alexander smiled blandly back. 'I am delighted to hear that. It means our charade has been successful.'

'You've worked for us for fourteen years now. You are one of our most valuable assets, Alex, I hope you know that. I appreciate that it's a lonely life. We do not expect our agents to be monks.' Sir Marcus's expression hardened. 'But we do expect them to distinguish between—let us say the satisfaction of their more basic urges, and any more profound emotion.'

'You do not have to remind me of that. I will never forget…'

'I would hope not.' Sir Marcus took out a clean white square of linen and dabbed delicately at his brow. 'I hesitate to remind you of what can only be a very painful subject.'

Alexander's hands curled into fists. 'There could be none more painful.'

'I am sorry to contradict you, Alex, but you're wrong.'

'I don't see…'

Sir Marcus held up his hand. 'This is a delicate matter. I would rather not speak of it, but we have known each other a long time. You are not only one of my best men, I consider you a friend. Two years ago, that affaire in Madrid almost destroyed you.'

'I am not the one who paid the highest price.'

'No, indeed not. No. Forgive me, but I must be frank. Your ability to do your job, your judgement, were wholly compromised by the presence of Señora Claudia Palermo. That is why we do not permit our agents to form attachments.'

'I am aware of that, and I—'

'But you were not particularly attached to her, were you, Alex?'

The harsh, pitiful truth, but the one fact he thought he'd kept hidden. Alexander felt as if he'd been punched hard in the gut.

'I am sorry to be so blunt, but it is imperative you understand, this is no time for Embassy-speak,' Sir Marcus said, with a ghostly smile. 'You risked your life and you risked the whole operation in your attempts to extricate that young woman from a situation which should not have arisen. She shouldn't have been there. It was your fault that she was. You took it upon yourself to try to rescue her. You put her first, Alex. Even though you didn't particularly care for her, you cared enough to jeopardise everything.'

'I don't know what the hell you're implying. If you're thinking that I would be damned fool enough to bring my wife on a mission...'

'Don't be so ridiculous. What I'm trying to say is that when you care for someone it makes *you* vulnerable as well as them. You put your country before your own life on a regular basis. You do that, not only because you love your country, that goes without saying, but because you don't and never have placed a particularly high value on your own life.'

For the second time in a matter of minutes, Alexander felt as if he'd sustained a punch to the gut. He opened his mouth to deny the fact, met Sir Marcus's eye, and closed it again. 'I prefer to think of it as living life as if every day was my last.'

'If you let yourself care too much for that wife of yours, you'll stop thinking that. You'll find yourself in the middle of nowhere in a tricky situation, and instead of thinking what is best for the mission, you'll think about how best to preserve your hide lest you ruin her life. And that's before any children appear on the scene.'

'There's no possibility of that!'

'I sincerely hope not. Because it would be bad enough to make a widow, but to leave a child fatherless—'

'You go too far.' Alexander got to his feet, white with fury. 'I broke the rules once. Not a day goes by when I don't regret that. To imagine that I would repeat the mistake...'

'That's not what I'm worried about.'

'No, you're worried that I'll become some sort of lovelorn coward.'

'That is not what I said. Alex—'

'Enough! You've said more than enough. My desire to continue to serve is undiminished.'

'That is good to hear.'

'In fact, I have decided that it is time to return to active service. More than enough time has passed for us to have fooled the world into thinking us a most devoted couple. I have some matters concerning the estates to resolve, but once that is attended to, I will be, as I have always been, at my country's service.'

'I did not intend to offend you, Alex.'

He was furious, but he was utterly determined not to betray himself. 'You have merely reminded me of the rules. It was unnecessary, but I have taken no offence.'

'Good. Give my regards to Lady Fearnoch.' Sir Marcus got to his feet, holding out his hand.

Hesitating only for a second, Alexander shook it. 'I will be in touch.'

The door closed. Alexander strode to the window of his stuffy, temporary office, and hauled it open, only to be assaulted with the pungent smell of horses parading below. The sun was a haze in the sky, which was more grey than blue. Sweat trickled down his back. He closed the window and poured himself a glass of water. It was tepid. Ice was in short supply.

This damned weather was making him ill-tempered. He threw himself into his chair and stared gloomily at his empty desktop. Though he was loathe to admit it, Sir Marcus's accusations were not without substance. He had not come close to loving Claudia. Had his guilt over his lack of feeling fuelled his single-minded determination to save her? He knew it had. He had compromised the mission and himself. But devil take it, he wasn't about to embroil Eloise in any way. He wouldn't dream of putting her life in danger. Look how he'd completely overreacted to her risking her own neck when she'd climbed that tree!

But wasn't that evidence that he was already in danger of becoming too fond of her, Alexander wondered uncomfortably. On the other hand, it was only natural that he should have a duty of care towards the woman he'd married. Besides, there was no chance of him getting too attached. He was not such a fool.

Eloise was coming back to London tomorrow. He smiled to himself, thinking of the surprise he had organised for her. He would arrange to have a bottle of her favourite champagne to be waiting when he showed her around. She'd been away over a week. She would be so eager to tell him all her news that she would hardly draw breath between her various tales. She would get halfway through one, become side-tracked to another, then cover her mouth, her eyes sparkling with laughter as she tried to pick up the thread of the first story.

He would order one of her favourite dinners to be served in the breakfast parlour. Afterwards, they would sit together with the doors open to the garden, because she'd want to be able to view her gift. She'd kick off her slippers, her feet tucked up under her. And Fearnoch House would come to life again.

Alexander looked at the clock. It was only three, but he had no reason to hang around here. He'd go home and set about making everything perfect for his wife's return.

Eloise had come back from Elmswood Manor a day early, having said her tearful goodbyes, promising to have the twins to stay soon. Tuesday was the allotted day off for the senior servants of Fearnoch House. Though she had become accustomed to having a dresser, Eloise preferred to take care of her wardrobe herself, sewing buttons and beads back on, repairing tears, fixing hems and darning holes in her stockings, and this was what she spent a large part of each Tuesday doing. It amused her, that her maid must think her clothes remarkably resilient. Or perhaps it amused her maid to play along with her mistress's foible, she thought today, as she finished her unpacking and set about stitching some petticoat lace back into place.

The house was very quiet. It was lovely and cool here in her bedroom, with a zephyr of a breeze wafting through the open windows, stirring the voile curtains which she had chosen to replace the heavy damask. She finished the petticoat and folded it neatly before putting it back in the cupboard. Her foot hit against something hard, which turned out to be the large box from Mrs Harman, the stay-maker, which she had completely forgotten about.

Placing it on the bed, she opened the lid. The array of undergarments contained within was a veritable treasure trove of silks and ribbons, delicate lace, soft cambric, such a decadent contrast to what she was wearing. The only time she'd tried any of these beautiful things on, weeks ago, she had worried she might turn out like her mother. She knew better now, and it was a shame to have them hidden away, unworn.

She picked up a set of emerald-green stays trimmed with black lace. The silk was like a cool ripple of water against her cheek. Quickly divesting herself of her muslin afternoon gown and various plain white undergarments, Eloise stepped into a pair of pantalettes in mint-green cambric, tied with black velvet ribbons and trimmed with black lace. Rummaging around inside the box, she found a chemise in the same colour, and pulled it over her head. It was a very simple garment, designed, she could see as she stood in front of the mirror, to allow the pantalettes beneath to be visible. Black stockings were next. Why was it that plain black looked positively sinful, compared to white? Next came the stays, which fastened at the front. Convenient, she remembered Mrs

Harman saying, for a less experienced hand. Or a less female hand. A husband's hand. Alexander's hand?

Standing in front of the mirror, Eloise pulled the ribbons tight, making her breasts swell, her waist shrink. She looked voluptuous. She tugged the pins out of her hair. Against the green, it was a blaze of red. She stared at her reflection, waiting for shame to envelop her, but what she saw excited her. She was a sophisticated, dangerous version of herself. A woman who relished the way she looked, and who happily flaunted it. She flicked out her hair, smiling at the effect as it rippled over her shoulders. Her skin looked very white in the sun-dappled light. Her eyes gleamed.

She ran her hands down her curves, enjoying the swish of the silk stays against her skin, entranced by the swell of her breasts, the dip of her waist, the flare of her hips. It was all an illusion, thanks to Mrs Harman's clever designs. She was a sensuous portrait of herself, why shouldn't she enjoy it?

What would it feel like to touch her? Closing her eyes, she trailed her fingers over the swell of her breasts. Her skin was damp, smooth. The lace of the stays was scratchy in contrast. She let her hand drift lower, cupping her breast, remembering how Alexander had done just that, and how her nipple had tightened, and yes, there was that fluttering response inside her. She let her hand slide down the tight lacing to rest on her belly, covering her other breast with her other hand, and imagined that it was Alexander touching her, too lost in her fantasy to notice the door of her bedchamber open softly.

It was Tuesday, and Wiggins's day off. By the looks of things, Alexander thought as he let himself into Fearnoch House, the day off for all the most senior servants. He headed for the library, thinking he might surprise Eloise by doing some work on her catalogue. Her notebook lay on the table by the sofa. Knowing that she took it everywhere, it must mean that she had returned a day early.

His spirits lifted as he set about looking for her, hoping that she had not already discovered his surprise present, but he couldn't find her in any of the main rooms, and the little wrought-iron table and chair where she sat in the garden were deserted. Tuesday. It was her maid's day off. Of course! Smiling, he recalled it was her mending day. He ran up the stairs, pulling off his coat and waistcoat, thinking to find her at her needlework, and gently opened her bedroom door.

Sunlight filtered through the gauzy curtains, which were cream, patterned with a tiny flower he was willing to bet was green. He barely recognised the room from his one and only glimpse when Eloise had first chosen it. The walls had been painted gold, the ceiling white. There was a new bed to replace the four-poster, covered in velvet, tumbled with cushions and a litter of lacy things, like a divan in a harem. She had pulled a full-length mirror into the centre of the room. She was standing in front of it, her back to him. Her hair was down, a thick curtain of glorious, vibrant red. She was wearing black stockings. Pale green drawers, and a matching chemise that barely covered her bottom. A corset of bright green silk trimmed with black.

Alexander's greeting died in his throat. His coat and waistcoat fell to the floor. Blood surged so quickly to his groin that he felt faint. He was trying to assimilate an apology, to will himself to leave, when he realised she hadn't turned around, hadn't even noticed that he was there. What was she doing? Why didn't she see his reflection in the mirror?

Turn around and get the hell out of here, he told himself, as he stepped into the room and closed the door behind him. A flicker of movement in the mirror drew him forward. She would turn around any moment, he told himself, and he would leave, definitely. Her eyes were closed, that's why she couldn't see him. She was touching herself, he realised with incredulity. One hand cupped her breast. The other on her stomach, sliding ever lower. He had never seen anything so utterly arousing.

Every minute since their last kiss after the dinner party seemed to have been leading up to this point. As he crossed the room, Alexander believed he would die a happy man, if only he could have this. His hands where hers had been, his lips on the warm, damp flesh of her shoulder, his body pressed into her back, the throbbing length of his shaft hard against the soft curve of her utterly delightful bottom.

In the mirror, her eyes flew open. For a second, an agonising second, he thought she would turn and push him away and he willed her to do so, steeling himself to leave, but she didn't. She pressed back against him. She whispered his name, and he was beguiled by the dual sensations of touching her, feeling her nipples tighten, her breasts rise and fall as her breathing quickened, and seeing the visible evidence of it in the mirror. His hands covered her breasts, slipping over the satin of her decadent stays, sliding into the gap between her drawers. She threw her head back, moaning, as his fingers slid inside her, dark-russet curls exposed to the mirror, slick heat drawing him in, his name said over and over as he slid higher inside her.

She was watching his actions intently in the mirror. A flush stole over her breasts, up her throat as she viewed the wanton image. He stroked her slowly, making her eyes widen, making her shudder against him, making himself harder. His hand, flat on her belly, could feel her tensing, ready, but his other hand worked slowly, teasing her, making her smile in pure delight at herself, in utter self-absorption, lost in the pleasure he was giving her, in the pleasure she was taking from what she was witnessing, and it was he who couldn't take any more, sending her tumbling over the edge, shuddering against him, and then turning around to him, wrapping her arms around him, seeking blindly for kisses.

Kisses. She craved his kisses. Every part of her was lit up, on fire, desperate for Alexander's kisses, for his touch, for more. She needed more. She had to have more. She wanted to make love to him. Properly and completely. It was inevitable, Eloise thought, as she scrabbled at his shirt, tugging it over his head. These last few weeks, the strain and stress of not touching him, of pretending that they didn't want to touch, and then the separation, the days spent at Elmswood Manor which had seemed far too long, it was inevitable that it end like this. The fates had conspired to put her here, in her bedroom in these scandalous and provocative silks and laces, and to bring Alexander to her. It had to happen. They could not fight an irresistible force.

Their mouths met, and she thought she would swoon with their kisses. She caught glimpses of herself in the mirror and saw a wild, unrecognisable creature and saw the same abandon, the same need reflected in Alexander. With a trembling hand she stroked him, unashamedly, blatantly, beyond caring whether she was doing it right or wrong, her instincts leading her, his reaction reassuring her, emboldening her. She kissed his chest. She licked his nipples. She turned him around, and she kissed his shoulders. She put her arms around him, watching their reflections in the mirror, his chest heaving, her hands, stroking, caressing his bare skin.

He groaned, turning her back to face him, wrapping his arms around her. 'I want you so much.'

'Yes,' she said feverishly, not caring what it was she was agreeing to, only wanting it, needing it. 'I want you too. So much.'

He groaned again, kissing her deeply, and a second wave of pleasure began to gather inside her. Should this be happening? And what about Alexander? She wanted him to feel what she felt. 'What should I do?' she asked. 'Show me.'

'Eloise...'

'Please,' she said urgently, terrified that he would suddenly come to his senses, forcing her back to hers. 'Please.'

His eyes were dark with passion, his pupils dilated. When he kissed her again, it was slowly, his tongue stroking along her lower lip, and he took her hand, placing it over his groin. She could feel his arousal through his pantaloons. Thick. Hard. It excited her, touching him, carefully stroking up the length of him, the sharp intake of his breath, the way his eyes fluttered closed, all the reassurance she needed. But she wanted to see him. To feel skin, not knitted pantaloons. 'Take these off,' she said, astounded to hear the confidence in her voice.

He kicked off his boots. She watched, fascinated, as he stripped himself, unashamedly studying the athletic and astonishingly aroused body revealed in the flesh and reflected in the mirror. When she hesitated, he took her hand again, showing her how to touch him, to stroke him. His skin was surprisingly silky there. She had not expected that. When she touched him, his chest heaved. She was fascinated by his response, by her response to touching him, feeling a jolt of excitement, a fierce longing to be closer to him, entwined with him. She released him, pressing herself against his arousal, and he wrapped his arms around her again, saying her name, his breath hoarse, and their mouths clung to each other, a deeper kiss, a new kind of kiss.

He picked her up, laying her down on the bed, covering her body with his. She could feel his arousal between her legs, against the skin of her inner thighs, and her body arched towards him of its own accord.

And then where there had been hot, hard flesh, there was only cool, empty air. Alexander wrenched his mouth from hers and stood up, backing away from her, his expression something akin to horror. He swore viciously, words she had not heard before. 'This is madness, utter madness!'

She didn't understand at first. It was like waking from a dream. What the hell was she doing? The one thing she knew would be fatal to their marriage, and she hadn't even paused to reflect on that, not even momentarily. Why?

The answer came to her not so much in a blinding flash as in a slow, deathly trickle. No. It couldn't be, mustn't be. Except there was no other rational explanation. Although there was nothing remotely rational about it.

Alexander had already pulled on his pantaloons and boots. 'Eloise, this is my fault. I shouldn't have come in here. I wanted to surprise you, but I should have knocked. If I'd knocked, then I wouldn't have seen— none of this would have happened.'

Slowly, she shook her head. 'No, that's not true.'

'Yes. I saw you. I've never seen you looking so—I lost my head and I couldn't resist, but I should have.'

'No,' she said again, more vehemently. 'It's not your fault.' She needed, desperately, to be on her own. 'I think you should go.' She walked over to the door, holding it open. His waistcoat and coat were on the floor. She picked them up.

He took them from her. 'We will need to talk about this.'

She didn't answer, simply continuing to hold the door open, until he left. Then she closed it and locked it. She stripped off her underwear. She found his shirt on the floor and pulled it over her. She crawled into bed and pulled the pillow over her head.

All her instincts were to run. Pacing her bedroom floor as the humid July day gave way to a heavy, oppressive night, Eloise would have given almost anything to be back in Elmswood Manor, sitting with Kate and her sisters, their coven, as Estelle liked to call it, reinstated. Cocooned, safe, never having met Alexander. Never having falling madly, quite *insanely* in love with Alexander.

How could she have been so stupid! How could she

have missed the warning signs? Why hadn't she taken preventative steps, instead of positively hurling herself headlong towards an unsolvable predicament? At what point along the line had it become too late? When had she stopped pretending? If they hadn't been pretending in the first place, would she still have fallen for him?

She paced the floor between her bedroom and her dressing room. She gazed out of the windows as the lights of London once again seemed determined never to let her see the stars. She threw herself on to her bed and covered her face with a pillow. And then she started the whole process again.

She tried to persuade herself that she was mistaken. She was in lust, not love. She'd been playing another role, dressed in that salacious underwear. That of a seductress. Perhaps it was herself that she had seduced, convincing herself that she was in love since the alternative was that she been carried away by base passion, and therefore like her mother, after all. This was an attractive proposition, but sadly, she couldn't make it stick. She wanted to make love to Alexander. Only Alexander. Always Alexander. She couldn't imagine ever wanting to make love to anyone else.

But how could she be sure it was love? If only she had someone to talk to, but her only confidante was perfectly happy in a truly loveless marriage. Exactly the type of marriage Eloise had thought she was entering into. Kate had warned her. Kate had told her she'd have to find a way to live without Alexander's kisses. And almost the first thing Eloise had done on her return to Fearnoch House was kiss Alexander. Make love to Alexander. Dear heavens, even now, she wished that they had truly made love. Just this once. Kate would be appalled.

Perhaps it wasn't love, but simply gratitude she was feeling? Ridiculous. Infatuation, then? Was it the newness of his kisses, the rapturous delight that her body felt when Alexander touched her? But it wasn't just his kisses or his touch, was it? From the moment she met him there had been something about him. She liked him. She admired him. She was intrigued by him. She was a different person when she was with him. It wasn't that she couldn't live without him, but life was so much better, happier, with him.

That sounded horribly like love. With a sickening feeling, Eloise realised that she sounded horribly like her father. The prospect brought her up short. She was not so needy. She was not obsessed. She could not imagine herself cravenly abasing herself as her father had, begging for attention, tolerating cruelty, ignoring everyone else in her need to hog Alexander's attention. No, that was laughable.

But what if it was the next step? Would she have believed this morning that she would have acted as she had, here in this very room, this afternoon? That she'd have placed her future in doubt, and her sisters' too, by breaking the terms of their agreement so completely? And worse, tempting Alexander to break them? What if the outcome of her seduction had been a pregnancy? Alexander was an honourable man. And he was one who knew what it was like to be rejected as a child too. A child that he didn't want but would never reject would turn his world upside down.

So why, then, had Alexander been so carried away? Why, if the most important thing in the world to him was his precious work, had he even crossed the threshold of her bedroom? Why had he kissed her? Why had he allowed her to touch him—wanted her to touch him, encouraged her to touch him? She knew nothing of such things, but it seemed to her that Alexander had been every bit as enthralled by their lovemaking as she. And every bit as horrified, when he came to his senses. Was it horror, or was he—afraid?

What would he be frightened of? Losing his position at the Admiralty? Sir Marcus had been very clear, Alexander was married to his work, but why must that be such an exclusive bond? It didn't make sense. His work was dangerous, so dangerous she still couldn't bring herself to think about it, but why did it preclude him making love to his wife? She didn't understand, and she needed to understand. She loved him, and she could not afford to hope that he would ever love her back, if he never could.

The dawn light began to filter through the curtains, and Eloise huddled under the bedcovers. If there was a barrier to Alexander's loving her that could not be breached, she had to understand the nature of it, or she would destroy herself, as her father had, by building her life around him in the hope that one day, he'd return her love.

Having established that, it would be better for both of them for him to resume his active service, leaving her to her own devices. He was thirty years old. He'd survived unscathed until now. She was exaggerating the risk. And an extended absence would make her heart grow considerably less fond, she vowed.

Chapter Eleven

Eloise decided to take breakfast in her room, emerging only when Alexander had departed for the Admiralty. She would have to face him at some point, but she needed a breathing space to regain some semblance of composure. It was all very well for her to decide, in the solitude of her own bedchamber, that she must confront him, but how to do so without revealing the depth of her feelings for him, she had no idea.

Her plans were scuppered when she discovered, venturing from her room at shortly after eleven, her husband sitting in the library. He was writing in the catalogue when she entered, working through a fresh stack of books. Her poor, deluded heart leapt at the sight of him. 'Oh.' She stopped short in the doorway. 'I didn't expect to find you here. I thought you'd be in Whitehall.'

'I have been, and shall return later. Will you come in? I have something to tell you.'

She made her way across the room to perch on the edge of the sofa. Alexander finished the entry he was making in the catalogue and sat opposite her. His expression was set. Something to tell her, he'd said, not to discuss with her, she noted with foreboding.

'I've decided to take up a new post abroad with immediate effect.'

'No! There's no need to take such drastic action.'

'There is every need. It is the only sensible solution,' Alexander said implacably. 'What happened yesterday is proof that we cannot trust ourselves to be alone in the same house together. Sir Marcus was not at the Admiralty this morning, but I've left him a note informing him that I am now available. I expect a summons at any moment.'

Eloise felt sick. Her husband, the man sitting opposite her whom she loved more than anyone in the world, was a spy. And spying was dangerous. She didn't want him to get hurt. 'I don't want you to go yet. There is no need to act so rashly.' She must not panic. She had to be rational. Logical. 'There is the matter of the estates to sort out. And our planned visit to your mother.'

'Robertson can see to the estates. As to my mother— she has not even replied to my letter. I must assume she has no wish to see me.'

'But you need to see her, Alexander. You can't go abroad without seeing her. If something happened to you, and your conscience was not clear...'

'What do you imagine might happen to me? You are worried that a ledger might fall on my head, perhaps?'

Looking at him, so cold, so determined to maintain his cover story for her benefit, her heart felt as if it was being squeezed. There was no limit to what she could imagine happening to him. A knife in the back in a dark alley. A fatal blow to the head in the night-time shadows of the docks. A shot to the heart. A fall from a cliff. He could be caught and tortured. He could spend the rest of his life in chains in the dungeon of a foreign power. He had survived thus far, but that didn't lessen the odds of him coming to harm, as she'd tried to reason with herself—it increased them. He'd led a charmed life, but his luck would run out one day. 'I don't want you to go,' Eloise said, her voice cracking.

'We had a bargain. I expect you to honour it with some dignity, at the very least ensure our planned parting is amicable.'

'Amicable! You think we can be amicable after what happened yesterday?'

'There is no need for histrionics,' Alexander said, flinching. 'What happened yesterday, we both know, was a mistake which we cannot risk repeating.'

His tone, the way he was looking through and not at her, further tautened her already jangling nerves. Eloise folded her arms and glared. 'Why not?'

'Why not? You don't need me to tell you...'

'Actually, Alexander, I do need you to tell me. Why is it that you are frightened to make love to your own wife?'

He paled. 'You mean the wife who once vowed that she found the *more intimate* aspect of marriage unappealing.'

His barb had been intended to hurt her, and he had succeeded, but in doing so he had betrayed himself. He cared. 'You haven't answered my question.'

'I am not accountable to you, Eloise. Our marriage is one of convenience, not confidences.'

'You know that's not true!'

He shrugged.

'I demand to know what you are afraid of,' Eloise said, finding his pretence of indifference infuriating.

'You are clearly overwrought. If that is my doing, if it is a consequence of my—my inappropriate behaviour yesterday...'

'Of course it bloody well is! For goodness' sake, Alexander, we very nearly made love. And when you realised just how nearly, you panicked. You looked absolutely terrified.'

'Because it is contrary to our agreement,' he retorted. 'Because my work requires me—'

'I know exactly what your work really involves.' She could have bitten her tongue out, but it was too late. 'You needn't worry, your secret is safe with me. Sir Marcus need never know that I've guessed.'

'Whatever it is you imagine you've guessed...'

'Oh, for goodness' sake, it's obvious that you've never counted a weevil in your life. You're a government spy, Alexander,' Eloise said baldly. 'Deny it if you must, but I'd really rather you didn't lie to me.'

'What makes you imagine such an outlandish thing?'

'My painfully observant nature. Your obvious seniority and Sir Marcus's high regard for you. His not-so-subtle attempt to warn me off. The fact that people in your line of work are not permitted to marry. Your being a crack shot, not the normal attribute of an administrator. Your letting slip that you would be returning to active duty. The mysterious tragedy that has led to you being celibate for two years.'

He looked quite stunned. 'I think you might make a better spy than me.'

'What happened to you two years ago?'

'What difference does it make?'

His determination not to answer her questions was too much for her already severely tested self-control.

'It matters because I love you! For heaven's sake, isn't it obvious? I have committed the cardinal sin of falling in love with my husband, and if he is utterly determined not to love me back, I want to know why.'

He stared at her, his face blank with shock. Eloise stared back, breathing heavily, feeling both relieved and elated. The words were spoken. She couldn't take them back. 'I didn't plan to fall in love with you,' she said, 'it simply happened. I only realised last night. I couldn't understand why, when the last thing either of us wanted was to risk a child, I had been so—so compelled to make love to you.'

'You are—it is natural to—to want what you cannot have. That's what you said.'

'I was wrong. I was looking for excuses. I love you, Alexander.' The words made her smile. 'I love you so much. It is the simple, wonderful and yet terrible truth. If you really are unable to ever return my feelings, I deserve to know why.'

There was a long silence. She could not read his expression, but she could tell from the way he kept it so very carefully empty that he was thinking hard. When he spoke again, his tone was icy. 'Very well, then, if that is what it takes to make you see sense, then I'll tell you. There *was* a woman. Her name was Claudia Palermo. She was my lover. *Because* she was my lover, she died.'

'No! Oh, Alexander...' She made to rise, all her instincts to comfort him, but he put his hands out to ward her off.

'I met Claudia at a party at the Embassy in Madrid. She was a widow, her husband had been a senior officer in the army. She was sophisticated, beautiful and unattached. We became lovers. A temporary affaire, it meant nothing—in those circles, where people move around all the time, it happens all the time. I assumed she felt the same. I didn't ask. My last assignment had been—it had been one of the tougher ones. I was simply relieved that it was over and happy to forget myself for a while.

'I shouldn't have forgotten though, that was my biggest mistake, to forget who I am, what I am.' Alexander leaned his head back on the sofa, staring up at the ceiling. 'It wasn't over, that last assignment, and I had stayed too long in Madrid. They came looking for me, and they found her instead, in my rooms. They left me a note. They promised to free her if I surrendered myself. I knew that regime would never honour such a promise, I knew that they would—that she might already be dead. I should have made good my escape but I decided to try to rescue her. I thought myself invincible, you see. I always had been before.'

Speechless with horror, Eloise waited as Alexander continued to stare bleakly up at the ceiling, his throat working, his hands clenched. 'I tracked them down. I found her, and I almost succeeded,' he concluded roughly, 'I almost got her out alive.'

Tears trickled down her cheeks, but Alexander, now looking over at her, remained stony-faced. 'You loved her.' Eloise's voice cracked.

'No, I didn't love her. I fooled myself into thinking that she felt as little for me as I did her, that it was a fling, nothing more. Looking back, the signs were there, only I chose to ignore them. And she—Claudia—she knew, I think, that if she let me see that she cared, I'd end it.'

His voice cracked. He cleared his throat. 'But that is no excuse. If I'd ended it sooner she would not have been there. If I'd cared enough to worry about her, she wouldn't have been there. If I'd left sooner—but I didn't, and she was there. She died because she loved me. I am responsible for her death and for the fiasco that followed, all the work I'd done in the months before, completely undone. And Claudia dead.'

'What happened to her, Alexander?'

'She was caught in crossfire.'

'And her family?'

'There was a sister, that is all I know, who lived in Seville. To this day, I doubt she knows the truth. I don't know where Claudia was buried, they wouldn't tell me. I don't know what tale they put about in Madrid to explain her disappearance, but I'd guess it was an elopement, since the pair of us left the city at the same time. I have asked and asked, but it's useless. I won't ever know now.'

'So that is what Sir Marcus meant when he said you'd made a mistake?'

'A gross error of judgement. It won't happen again.'

'I'm so very sorry. I don't know what to say. I can't imagine…'

'I don't want you to imagine,' Alexander snapped. 'It is bad enough you know—what you have surmised. You think you know me, but you don't. My work is dangerous, Eloise. I could be killed in action. I could be captured, executed, or simply locked away for life. I might disappear off the face of the earth one day and you will never know what happened to me any more than Claudia's people will ever know what happened to her.'

'No, no, it's different for us. We are married. They would tell me—surely Sir Marcus…'

'Such delicate matters of international politics are

kept tightly under wraps. You would receive a bland official communiqué informing you of my demise— "in the performance of my duties"—nothing more. I warned you before we married not to become too fond of me, for your own good. But it is for mine too. Do you think I want to have you on my conscience when I'm making life-or-death decisions?'

'No, of course I don't. I didn't mean to tell you, I wanted only to...'

'You cannot love me, Eloise. Rid yourself of the notion while I am away, for both our sakes.'

'Please, don't go just yet, Alexander. I need time to think, to...'

'There is nothing to think about. The decision is made.' In the distance, the front doorbell peeled. 'Are you expecting anyone?'

'No. Whoever it is, Wiggins will deal with it.' Eloise searched frantically for her handkerchief, determined not to break down. A soft tap on the library door made them both jump. 'What is it, Wiggins? Tell whoever it is that we are otherwise engaged.'

'It is the Dowager Countess, your mother, my lord. I have taken the liberty of showing her to the drawing room and ordering tea.'

'Your mother is here!' Eloise exclaimed. 'What is your mother doing here?'

Alexander looked as confounded as she. 'I have no idea.'

'But what are you going to say to her? Why must she turn up without notice today of all days!'

Belatedly realising that Alexander was standing stock still, Eloise pulled herself together. Now was not the time for hysterics. His mother was here. She was going to have to find a way to put aside her own feelings and the last awful hour and support him through what could only be a traumatic conversation. 'At least Wiggins had the sense to serve her tea,' she said, getting to her feet and quickly checking her reflection. 'Despite everything that has happened, we need to put on a united front. Would you like me to go ahead and introduce myself? It would give you a little time to think—to prepare yourself.'

'I've had more than enough time to think. But you are quite naturally upset. I can't expect you to...'

'I am absolutely fine.' She smiled up at him in what she hoped was a reassuring manner. 'Where else would the new Countess of Fearnoch be but at her husband's side when he meets his mother for the first time after their nuptials?'

'Thank you,' he said gruffly. 'I don't deserve you.'

'Of course you do.' He wanted her by his side. Despite everything that had just passed between them, Eloise's foolish heart leapt as she tucked her hand into her husband's arm.

'Alexander. Please excuse my calling without giving you due notice. I have been staying with a friend in Kent. Your letter was forwarded to me there, and I thought I would take the opportunity to spare you the long journey to Lancashire.'

The Dowager Lady Constance Fearnoch was a very attractive woman. In her late fifties, by Eloise's calculations, she had a figure that many females twenty years younger would envy and which was complemented by a simple gown of cream-and-coffee-striped cotton. There was no grey in her hair, which was the same very dark brown as Alexander's, and the fretwork of lines at the corners of her eyes did not detract from their rather unusual almond shape.

Alexander bowed over her hand. 'This is Eloise, my wife, Mother.'

The Dowager studied Eloise with cool detachment. 'How do you do.'

'It is a pleasure to meet you at last, my lady.'

'You have not rested on your laurels. You have made some changes here already, I see.'

'A few.'

'Footmen with unpowdered hair at Fearnoch House. Your father will be turning in his grave, Alexander.'

'So he's dead, then?'

'What do you mean? Of course he is dead. As is your brother, else we would not be sitting here.'

'Mother. I know—have known for years—that, whoever my father is, he is not the Sixth Earl.'

Lady Constance set her teacup down with a clatter. 'What on earth do you mean by that?'

'I know that I am not legitimate.'

'You know?' Lady Constance looked quite bewildered.

'Truth be told, I'm glad I'm not the Earl's son. I wanted to talk to you about it, not to blame you or to cause you pain, but simply to hear your side of the story.'

'But why do you—after all this time…?'

'We have my new wife to thank for making me look at things differently,' Alexander said, taking Eloise's hand. 'It was she who made me see that I have judged you very harshly.'

'I doubt you can judge me any more harshly than I

do myself.' Lady Constance smoothed out the skirts of her gown, making an effort to regain her composure. 'I presumed that your proposed visit was a mere formality, to introduce me to your wife. I did not expect...'

'You've had a shock. I'm so sorry. Would you like me to pour you another cup of tea?'

'Tea! A sherry would be more appropriate. No, Lady Fearnoch, do not put yourself to the trouble,' she added hastily as Eloise made to rise. 'I was not serious. Not wholly serious. May I ask, Alexander, what has convinced you that your father is *not* your father?'

'It is the only explanation for the way I was treated by all three of you—you, the Earl, Walter. Not to mention the sudden and significant change to the Earl's will in 1802, to your detriment.'

'Yes.' Lady Constance smiled tightly. 'I should have anticipated that he would seek to punish me from beyond the grave. While he was alive, he was forced to keep me here in the style which I had been raised to expect for propriety's sake, but after he was dead, it was another matter. Walter stepped into the breach to prevent the world from speculating what heinous crime I had committed to make my husband leave his widow a pauper. They would have come to the same conclusion as you did, Alexander, that I had treated him to a taste of his own medicine. But they, like you, would have been wrong. I didn't.'

Confused, Eloise turned to Alexander, wondering if she had misunderstood this unexpected outburst, but he was focused wholly on his mother. 'You're claiming you were not unfaithful to the Earl?'

'Not claiming, asserting a fact.' Lady Constance reached over to touch her son, then changed her mind.

'You are the second son of the Sixth Earl. I was not unfaithful to my husband. But—he thought I was.'

'Why would he think that?'

'Because I told him so.'

Alexander stared at his mother, trying to digest the bombshell she had just uttered, but he couldn't. The man he was so certain was not his father, *was* his father? But his mother had told him he wasn't? 'I'm sorry, but what you said makes no sense whatsoever.'

He waited for her to agree with him. Instead, she asked Eloise if it would be too much trouble for her to have that sherry, after all, and when Eloise poured her a drink from the decanter, his mother downed it in one gulp. What the hell was she having to brace herself to tell him? Alexander had imagined any number of scenarios when he'd first decided to confront his mother, but none of them included this thunderbolt.

'Thank you. I do not usually imbibe at such an early hour, but I did not expect—to be honest, I never expected to have this conversation at all. We have not been close. That is entirely my fault. I will spare you any claims to unrequited maternal affection. After what I did to you, I deserve none and expect none.' His mother frowned down at her hands. She was not wearing her wedding ring. 'But now we are having this conversation, and you wish me to explain. I am not sure where to begin. How aware are you of your father's reputation and standards of behaviour, or rather lack of them?'

His father! 'If you mean the Earl, sufficient to know that you must have been miserable.'

'Oh, I went into the marriage with my eyes relatively wide open,' she said with a grim little smile. 'It was an arranged match, of course. Your father, like the Fearnoch Earls before him, was required to marry before he was thirty. He was twenty-eight to my sixteen, and already well established in his ways. I come from good stock, but my family was rather down on its luck. Marriage would make me a countess, a rich one. My husband's philandering was a small price to pay. Or so I thought. I am sorry to have to subject you to this, Lady Fearnoch, it is a rather sordid tale.'

'Please call me Eloise. Anything that concerns Alexander, concerns me.'

Lady Constance smiled faintly. 'That is much to your credit, my dear, and my son's good fortune. I will be as brief as I can. Needless to say, I discovered I had to tolerate a great deal more than philandering from my husband. I did not love him any more than he loved me, but I had expected to be treated with dignity and respect. I was instead treated with contempt, and being young and strong-willed, I objected. My protests were not well received.'

Alexander had expected this, but it was a very different matter to hear directly from the sufferer of her suffering. His hands curled into fists. 'He beat you.'

His mother made a helpless gesture. 'He would not tolerate what he called insubordination.'

'I remember.'

'Do you?' His mother paled. 'I hoped—you were only five, I hoped you would not recollect too much of that time.'

'I didn't. Not properly. Not until I came to live here. But we were talking of you, before I was born.'

'Yes. It was when Walter was weaned, that was when the real trouble started. That was when your father started to—to teach him the Fearnoch ways, mould him into a chip off the old block, so to speak,' she said through clenched teeth. 'I tried to protect my son, you must not think I didn't try to intervene, Alexander, but—I could bear what he did to me, but when he started punishing my child for what he called my pernicious influence—I gave in. By the time you were born, Walter was eight and long lost to me, set on a course that I couldn't rescue him from. A course I was determined not to allow you to follow.'

His mother was searching in her reticule. Anticipating her needs, Eloise handed her a handkerchief, twining her fingers back around his when she sat back down.

'You were a very different little boy from Walter,' his mother continued, dabbing at her eyes. 'Walter had always run to his father, always preferred his father, but you were mine. I did my best to keep him from you, but it was no good. It's a tried-and-tested process, the making of a Fearnoch man. Nothing and no one must get in the way. But I was determined to save you.'

He had never seen his mother like this. He had rarely seen her show any emotion. Strong-willed, she'd called herself. That was an understatement.

'You were like me,' she said, smiling over at him as if she'd read his thoughts. 'You had a will of your own from a very early age. It cost you so dear in those early days. I couldn't bear the thought of him breaking you. You would not be as malleable as Walter, but I couldn't take the chance, Alexander. I had to get you away from him. He wouldn't hear of sending you to school, so I told him the only thing I could think of that would be guaranteed to cut the tie. I told him that you were not his son. He was surprisingly easy to convince, you were so very different in nature from your brother. But Walter was your brother, Alexander, and my husband was your father.'

How many more revelations would this day bring? He felt as if his world had been turned inside out as well as upside down. 'Are you certain?' Alexander asked, somewhat ridiculously.

'I think if anyone would know it would be me! I can see this is not what you want to hear, but there is absolutely no doubt.'

He swore under his breath. 'So you didn't abandon me, you sacrificed me in order to protect me, at enormous cost to yourself.'

'I take solace from seeing the honourable man you have become. You are so independent of spirit, you might have forged your own path despite your father's best efforts, but it was a risk I could not take. I gave you up, but it was a price worth paying, looking at you now.'

'But after—when he died—there was nothing to stop you putting me straight with regard to your behaviour. We could have been reconciled.'

She flinched. 'Firstly, I didn't want you to feel guilty in any way about my situation. I chose to act as I did willingly, and would do so again. Secondly, I felt I had forfeited the right to play any part in your life. That is not to say I didn't monitor your progress keenly from afar. I was forced to do so by subterfuge. I was forbidden all contact with you at school, but there was a sympathetic master, a friend of a friend. He told me you were a clever boy, and a popular one.'

'But afterwards, Mother. When the Earl—when *my father* died...'

'What would I have said to you, Alexander? Forgive me for a lifetime's neglect, but it was for your own good?'

'You made an enormous sacrifice for me.'

'Do not make a martyr of me. I made my bed and I had to lie in it.'

'You gave him your life, you sacrificed two children to him, and he repaid you with a pittance.'

'That was wrong of him, but it was very wrong of you to marry in order to change matters. Excuse me, Lady Fearnoch—Eloise—but I was very angry with Alexander when he told me that he was getting married in order to make my life more comfortable. A marriage made for any other reason than true affection and esteem is bound to be miserable. Though we've only just met, it's plain to me that I need not have worried.'

'Your son is the most honourable, the most—I could not be more—you should be very proud of him, Lady Constance.' Eloise got to her feet. It was obvious to Alexander that she was overcome with emotion, though she held out her hand, smiling warmly at his mother. 'If you'll excuse me, I will leave you alone to catch up. I'm sure you have a great deal to talk about.'

Headed for her favourite spot at the end of the garden, Eloise was confronted with a newly constructed tree house. A narrow, wooden spiral staircase snaked its way around the trunk of the plane tree, incorporating some of the broader branches for support. Entranced, she climbed the stairs, noting that whoever had installed this stunningly inventive piece of carpentry had been careful to damage as little of the tree as possible. The tree house itself was suspended about two-thirds of the way up, a rustic cabin with a small balcony just big enough to accommodate two padded sun chairs. The resinous smell of newly cut wood mingled with the smell of varnish. The roof of the cabin had been clad with bark so that it seemed to melt into the tree. A window had been cut into one wall, giving her the view directly down the gardens of Fearnoch House. There was a small desk and a comfortable chair, a chaise longue covered in cushions with a soft cashmere blanket, a lamp, a bookcase. The books were all novels, new and uncut. The stationery in the desk was printed with her title. In a cupboard fitted cunningly into the corner, she found a tea set, a kettle and a spirit stove. And on the side table beside the chaise longue, a beautiful marquetry sewing box. Lifting the lid, she found it already stocked with needles, threads, a pair of silver scissors, a thimble, even a pin cushion and pins.

She sank down on the chaise longue. So much thought had gone into every little touch and detail. How long had it been in the planning? When had Alexander conceived the idea? Now she could climb her tree every day in any weather, without him worrying that she might fall. This was not the work of a man who didn't care for her. Quite the opposite.

She went out on to the balcony, leaning over the balustrade to gaze back at Fearnoch House. Alexander had been so sure that he was not the legitimate Earl. What must he be feeling now, talking to his mother, with all that he thought he knew of himself turned on its head? It ends here, he'd said of the line of portraits in the gallery, and he'd been right, but not in the way he meant.

The tree house was utterly beautiful, the most perfect gift for her, a gift only a person who truly understood her could have made. Alexander knew her. He cared for her. He could not resist kissing her, could not quell his desire for her, even though he knew what he was risking. He cared for her, but he would not love her. Instead, he was planning to throw himself back into active service with all its associated dangers, just to get away from her. Sickened, she finally understood why. That awful story he'd told her of the woman, Claudia, had scarred him for ever. His country was his first love and could be his only love. To serve his country he must be free to act without any thought for anyone else. Not even himself. Finally, she understood this too.

But he could love her. The evidence was here, in this tree house. He could love her. If he would stay for another month, six months, a year, give his feelings for her a chance to grow, then...

Then what? He'd offer to give up his life for her? Another week together, never mind a month, would test their resolution to the limit. They would not be able to resist one another. In another six months, familiarity might breed contempt and not love, but by then it would be too late. The result of their passion might be a child that neither of them wanted. She knew Alexander too well. He would stay with her then, for all the wrong reasons. Even if she still loved him—and she knew in her heart that she would—it would be a bitter and twisted love that ruined the loved one's life.

When you love someone, you'd do anything to avoid hurting them.

She'd been talking about her mother's selfishness, her revelation that love formed no part of her parents' marriage. She'd not thought then that the words would ever apply to her own marriage. She loved Alexander with all her heart. If she asked him to stay, it might possibly end up breaking his.

She had to let him go. Though every particle of her screamed in protest, she knew she had to find a way to do so as he'd asked of her, with dignity and with understanding. A farewell which left him feeling no pity for her or guilt. She would have to find a way to put aside her own feelings, and think only of him. Because she loved him. Because she would do anything to avoid hurting him. Even if it meant giving him up.

She would not be her father. She would not abase herself, begging for his love, or worse, waste her days wondering where he was, what he was doing, her heart jumping with fear every time the doorbell rang lest it be Sir Marcus to inform her that she was a widow. She would not be a victim of love, and she would not make a victim of Alexander either, by loving him insufficiently.

She would let him go. It was the right decision, she knew it, could not dispute it. Why, then, did knowing she was about to do the right thing make her feel as if her heart was breaking? Retreating into the cabin, Eloise kicked off her slippers. Pulling the soft blanket over her, she closed her eyes and gave in to tears.

Chapter Twelve

Alexander stood in the doorway of the tree house, gazing down at the sleeping figure curled up under a blanket on the chaise longue. There had been no champagne chilling to greet her as he'd planned. Eloise had climbed the spiral staircase without him. Now he would have to imagine the delight on her face as she explored her little private folly.

Her stockinged feet were peeping out of the blanket. There were tear tracks on her cheeks. His heart tightened in his chest, for he knew he was the cause of them. He had never wanted anything so much as to wake her gently, kiss her tears away and tell her what she wanted to hear, but the very fierceness of his longing made it impossible. She'd said she loved him. He knew, from the tenderness that welled up in him, that he was already falling in love with her. There was only one solution.

Eloise stirred, opening her eyes, brushing her hair from her cheek, and blinked up at him, smiling. 'Alexander. I can't believe you created this magical place for me. I'm so sorry I spoiled the surprise. It's beyond anything I could have dreamt of. Thank you so much.'

She held out her hand to him. He wanted to take it. Her eyes were shining so adoringly he could be in no doubt of her feelings for him. He took a step towards her. And then he stopped. Her face fell at whatever she saw in his eyes. She sat up. 'What time is it? I had Mrs McGilvery prepare the Chinese Room for your mother. And dinner...'

'My mother has already departed. She sends her profuse apologies, but she simply couldn't bring herself to stay at Fearnoch House.'

'That's perfectly understandable. Is she lodging at a hotel, then? Will she be joining us for dinner?'

'She's heading straight back to Lancashire. She'll spend the night at a posting house.' He was aware of her scrutinising him closely. He forced himself to meet her gaze, trying to think of this as a mission, to imagine Eloise as the opposition. 'You are thinking that there is too much to discuss. That I will wish to spend some time with my mother, now that I know— after today.'

'She must love you very much, Alexander, to have made such a sacrifice. To have—to have given you up as she did.'

'It allowed me to become the man I am. If she had not...'

'I understand that, truly, I do. You are the legitimate Eighth Earl. Your father was the Sixth Earl. Your mother did not abandon you. She gave you up in order to protect you. The estates you thought you must rid yourself of belong to you. All those things are true, but in essence you are still the same man, Alexander Sinclair, who lives to serve his country.'

Eloise smiled at him. It was an odd smile. As if she

was trying to reassure him. 'Sir Marcus called here half an hour ago. It seems my country needs me urgently.'

'Then you must go.'

He had come here thinking to do battle with her, to persuade her to his way of thinking. Her immediate agreement threw him off kilter. 'I will have to leave tomorrow. The matter is urgent.'

'Naturally. Do you know how long you will be gone?'

'I have no idea. A year, perhaps.'

'A year!' Eloise exclaimed. 'I had not thought it would be quite so long.'

'It's better that way. In a year, we'll have time to—'

'Forget about each other,' she snapped, then covered her mouth. 'I'm sorry. That was unfair.'

'It's what we should do. Claudia died because of me.'

'And you broke the rules trying to save her. Was it really so wrong to put her life before whatever mission you were on?'

'I compromised myself and my duty to my country by putting her in harm's way.'

'You're not about to put me in harm's way by taking me on an active mission.'

'I thought you understood. I would be taking you with me, Eloise, in my thoughts, and in my heart. I'd be thinking about you. Missing you. And if there came a point where I had to act, where my actions might risk my life, I might hesitate because of you.'

'Because you love me.'

She looked so forlorn, he wanted to sweep her into his arms. Instead, he sank on to the chair by the desk. He did love her, there was no point in denying it. She was right, it could only be love that made it so impossible to resist her. Love that made the idea of lying to her impossible. Love that was making him feel as if the life was being squeezed out of him at the thought of leaving. He loved her. He couldn't tell her so, but it was beyond him to deny it. 'There can be no future for us, Eloise, not as you imagine it.'

She seemed to steel herself. 'No. You're right. I beg your pardon.'

'If I remained here, I'd be giving up the only life I've ever wanted.'

'I would never ask you to do that.' She fixed that odd smile back on her face. When she spoke again, she had her emotions firmly in check. 'Well, then, you must go, and I must get on with my own life, which is the reason I married you, after all.' She smiled brightly. 'I will go to Lancashire, I have decided. I will get to know your mother. I will tend to your estates. You can instruct Robertson to grant me whatever powers I need, assuming that you are not now going to rid yourself of them.'

'I don't know what I want to do with the estates.'

'Then I will look after them while you consider it. I've been thinking, you know, that I am much more like Kate than I thought. I will take her as my role model, and do something useful with my life. There is a mill in Scotland which has a sort of model village attached to it. I think we—I may be able to establish something similar in Lancashire, if we—for the miners and their families. We can make it a sort of joint venture or a co-operative. That way, they can share in the profits, benefit from their labour, just as you wished them to. What do you think?'

'I think it is a marvelous idea, but it is a huge undertaking.'

'I have endless amounts of time to spare.' Eloise faltered. 'I want to do it, Alexander. I've been thinking about it ever since Kate told me about it. I won't do anything precipitate, but…'

'I think it's a wonderful idea.' He should be relieved. Why didn't he feel relieved? 'I'll let Robertson know to give you whatever support you need, and to sort out any permissions for land, funds, whatever.'

'Thank you.' Eloise's smile wobbled. 'I had better go and see to dinner. I don't know what time it is. You omitted to furnish my little kingdom with a clock.'

'It was a deliberate omission. I wanted you to lose track of time up here.' There was a lump in his throat. 'Eloise, I…'

'Actually, I think I'll take dinner in my room. You'll be making an early start, no doubt, so I'll let you get on with your packing.'

It took him a moment to realise what she was saying. 'You mean this is goodbye?'

'Let's not draw it out, it's too painful.' She held out her hand. 'Is it customary to wish you luck?'

He took her hand in his. Now that the moment had come, it felt impossible. He loved this woman. She loved him. Was he really going to walk away from her? But how could he stay, when it would only make their parting more painful, or worse, make it impossible? She was trying so hard to make it easier for him too, he finally realised. Brave, lovely Eloise.

He had made his choice. He let her go. 'Goodbye,' Alexander said, turning his back. At the bottom of the spiral staircase, he looked up, but she was not on the balcony. He squared his shoulders and strode up the garden, resolutely turning his mind to the tasks he had to complete before morning.

Two months later

Alexander slid the telescopic eyeglass back into its case before extricating himself carefully from the look-out. It was five miles across fields stubbled with the remains of the recent harvest to the crudely constructed den in the forest which had been his home for the last fortnight. Though night was falling, he took his customary care not to be spotted, and an alternative route back from the way he'd come. He was weary, hungry and filthy. And sick to the back teeth of being all three.

No less a person than the Duke of Clarence, the Lord High Admiral himself, had requested Alexander's assignment to this mission. Clarence was a most reluctant heir to the throne. There had been times, in the last two months, when the story he'd told, of his brother Frederick's deathbed confession that he had a secret heir, seemed so unlikely that Alexander wondered if he'd invented it. The little girl he'd tracked down was the right age, and so like her mother that there could be no doubting the relationship, but whether the mother was the woman that the Duke of Clarence sought was still up for debate. There were no portraits of the unnamed female who had apparently married Frederick, Duke of York, about five years ago. Alexander had discovered some evidence to suggest a marriage might have taken place, but more would be needed if Clarence's wish, to have the union validated and the child proclaimed heir, was to be fulfilled. He had a number of other leads. It would take him another two or three months at least to follow them up thoroughly. What Clarence would do with the evidence, how the Duke planned to persuade the current King to embrace his plan, Alexander neither knew nor cared. Truth be told, despite the fact that this mission had the potential to change the course of the British monarchy, he didn't give a damn about the outcome.

Reaching his temporary home, he spooned out the leftover stew made from the rabbit he'd caught last night. It was tough, charred on the outside and not far away from raw on the inside. Phoebe would probably recommend turning it into some sort of fricassee. Alexander set the unsavoury plateful aside. He couldn't risk lighting a fire two nights in a row. In any case, despite being hungry, he had no appetite. Sitting cross-legged on the ground in the doorway of his shack, he gazed out at the forest. Which of the trees would Eloise choose to climb? What was Eloise doing now? Where was she? Did she miss him as much as he missed her?

He groaned. Contrary to his expectations, thinking about Eloise occupied more rather than less of his time with every passing day. The pain of missing her was physical. He set about the well-practised ritual of persuading himself that he'd done the right thing in leaving her, recounting every word of the arguments he'd used against her protestations of love, but the more he repeated them, the emptier they sounded. He loved her. Though he had admitted as much to himself before he left, he had not understood the earth-shaking reality of being in love. He hadn't understood that he wasn't only leaving Eloise behind, he was leaving a part of himself that only she knew. He was lonely, the sort of loneliness that no company could cure other than hers. It was ludicrous of him to imagine himself invisible, but there were times when that was how he felt.

What was he doing here? He had never felt so purposeless before. Serving his country had been his life. The thrill of the chase had never palled. The need to think on his feet, the combination of physical and mental agility required had been his lifeblood. He had always been so proud to serve. Knowing that he was needed, that he had been singled out to serve, knowing just how highly the Admiralty valued him, had always made him feel special. He had never questioned the price this demanded. He had never resented the claim his country had on him, body and soul. Until now.

Two years ago he had broken the rules with catastrophic consequences. For two years he'd carried the guilt of his actions around with him. It was his fault that Claudia had been there when they came for him, but was it really so wrong of him to have become involved with her? He was human, after all. And as for the mission—he'd been trying to save her life, dammit! They'd made him think it was wrong. They'd made him believe that Claudia was expendable. As he was?

A branch cracked and broke free from a tree a few feet away, tumbling into the forest. He should have known, that night when he saw the scratches on Eloise's hands and arms, had a terrifying vision of her crashing to earth just as that branch had done, he should have known that he was falling in love with his wife. He smiled to himself, remembering how indignant she'd been at his attempt to exert his authority. She would always make her own decisions, go her own way. As she had done, the last time he saw her. When she must have been breaking her heart, she stood up to him, claiming her life for her own, refusing to weep over him. Doing her best, he saw now, to make the parting as easy for him as she could, once she'd accepted he was going. Had she cried afterwards? How long had she remained at Fearnoch House when he'd gone? She'd be in Lancashire now, whipping the estates into better order, working on her plans. Had she already forgotten him? Did she think of him?

He missed her. What was he doing here, when he could be with her? Why had he chosen this life, when he could be making a new life with her? Because he was afraid, just as she said. He had always had this life. He knew no other. But he wasn't the man he had been before he met Eloise. He was the legitimate son of a libertine. His mother had given him up to save him, and he'd rewarded her with indifference. Even now that he knew the truth, he'd taken evasive action rather than confront it.

This business of Clarence's was not his business. Sir Marcus would claim he was being unpatriotic, but he had nothing to reproach himself about. He had more than done his bit for King and country. Let someone else pick up the cudgel. He could stay, complete this mission, but now that he'd decided, he couldn't wait another day—not when every day apart from Eloise risked her deciding they could never be together.

The relief of having made his decision was momentous. Why had he waited so long! He had to get back to England as soon as he could, beg Eloise to give him one more chance, and to hell with the consequences.

Eloise rolled up the architect's plans for the new workers' village. They were simply outline sketches rather than plans at this stage, but if the latest tests proved the coal seams to be as extensive as earlier trial excavations had indicated, then she would have all the funds she needed to build houses furnished with every modern amenity to provide a school, a village hall and a good deal more. Pulling her notebook towards her, she began to write out a list of tasks for tomorrow. No need to order dinner, she was dining with Constance, as she did two or three times a week, but she ought to think about ordering some supplies for when the twins arrived in a couple of days. Though it might be better to wait until Phoebe got here and commandeered the kitchen.

The ink dried on her pen as Eloise stared off into space. What was Alexander doing now? Where was he? The utter silence, the lack of any sort of communication from him, was the hardest thing to bear. There were no letters. She had expected there might be an occasional update from Sir Marcus. Even an *all's well, fear not* note would have been most welcome, but he had not been in touch. In the small hours of the morning, Eloise had contemplated calling at the Admiralty, but so far daylight had brought common sense with it. She had heard nothing because there was nothing to report. No news was good news, she reminded herself.

Missing Alexander was agony. Even if she had not decided to come to Lancashire, she'd have been unable to remain in Fearnoch House without him. She hadn't climbed the tree house once since that first time, the night before he'd left. It was as if they had both of them left their hearts there. She busied herself, filling every waking moment with tasks, drawing up plans, and whenever she reached a low point, she called on Constance, who was very supportive. She rationed her pining for Alexander to this one wistful hour before dinner—or she tried to. There had been days when she had been angry with him for leaving, but it never lasted. The choice was stark: a real marriage and a new life, or a marriage of convenience and his old life, the only life he knew and the one he loved. She didn't blame him for choosing the old one, even if she wished with all her heart he had not.

But she would not allow herself to be miserable, to wallow in pity she didn't deserve. She was fortunate. She was even happy, for some of the time, mostly content for the rest. Though she was never as happy as she'd been in her all-too-brief time with Alexander.

The dull clang of the faulty doorbell reminded her to add its replacement to her list. It must be Constance, dropping off the transcription she had been working on from a diary Eloise had discovered in the muniment room, written by the first Countess of Fearnoch.

'I'm afraid I can only offer you cold cuts for dinner,' Eloise said over her shoulder as the door of her office opened, 'if you want to join me.'

'Cold cuts sounds like a veritable feast, compared to what I have been living off recently.'

She leapt to her feet, whirling round at the sound of the familiar male voice, knocking over her chair in the process. 'Alexander! Is that really you?' Her mouth went dry. Her heart began to race as he entered the room. 'What has happened? Why have you returned? Are you hurt?'

'Don't worry, I'm still in one piece, just weary from my long journey. Who were you expecting?'

'Constance. Your mother. I wasn't actually expecting her, but I—never mind that.' She hurried over to him.

He had not shaved. There were dark shadows under his eyes. His hair had grown long enough to touch his collar. 'You look terrible!'

He laughed, a sound she thought she'd never hear again. 'Thank you very much. You, on the other hand, are a sight for sore eyes.'

He held out his arms, but as she made to step into them he dropped them again, taking a step back. Trying to disguise her hurt, castigating herself for having been so foolish as to imagine anything had changed, Eloise retired to a chair by the fireside, indicating that he take the one opposite. 'Is your mission completed?'

'In a manner of speaking. My part in it is over, at any rate. I walked out, Eloise. I have come back to beg you for a second chance. I don't deserve one, I haven't forgotten that you told me you wouldn't give me one, but I have to ask.'

'But why?'

'Because I was wrong,' Alexander said simply. 'I am not married to my country, I'm married to you. I love my country, but I'm done with serving it, and I sure as hell don't love it the way I love you.'

Her heart leapt, but she forced herself to remain seated. 'How do you know that? How can you be sure that you won't change your mind?'

'I thought you'd ask me that,' he said, with a wry smile. 'I could simply say that I know, here,' he said, putting his hand over his heart. 'And that's true. I do know—once I admitted to myself—but that's not enough. Do you remember telling me what it felt like to climb a tree?'

'You were angry,' Eloise said, taken aback by the change of subject. 'The first time I did it, in London...'

'I was horrified by the thought of you falling. I should have known then that I was falling in love with you.'

'That's why you built the tree house, to keep me safe.'

'That's one reason, but it's not the main one. You told me, the first day we met, that climbing a tree was exciting. Dizzying. A little bit frightening. You told me that when you looked down, you always wondered what it would be like to let go. If you might fly.'

'I said that?'

'Your very own words. I built the tree house because I wanted you to feel all those things, but to be safe too. When I was away, I thought of you up there...'

'I haven't been able to go there.'

'No?' Alexander winced. 'No, perhaps not. But I thought of you up there. And I thought of what you said, about looking down, through the branches, knowing that you'd crash to the ground if you jumped, but wondering, against all reason, if you might fly instead. And I thought, a leap of faith. That's what love is.'

He smiled at her. 'I can't promise that we won't come crashing to the ground, but I can promise that I won't regret making the leap, if you will jump with me. I love you so much, Eloise, more than I have words to tell you. I'm so sorry that I left you the way I did, but if I'd stayed...'

'You'd never have known if you'd made the right choice.'

'Yes,' he said, looking hugely relieved. 'That is it. I wasn't brave enough to take the chance...'

'So you thought you'd risk life and limb for your country instead!'

'I didn't. Not this time. It took me two months away from you to realise I didn't want to live without you, and for the last two weeks, as I made my way back to you, I've been consumed with fear that I'd be too late.'

Alexander dropped to his knees beside her, taking her hands in his. 'I love you so much. I have never known another life than the one I've lived for the last fourteen years. I have no idea what life holds for me now, or how I will adapt, or even how I feel now that I know that the Earl is my father, but I do know one thing—if I can live the rest of my life by your side, I'll be happier than I could ever be without you. Will you be my wife, Eloise?'

Her heart felt as if it might burst out of her chest. 'I already am your wife.'

'I mean my real, proper, true and very much loved wife. Will you?'

'Yes.' She smiled mistily at him. 'Oh, yes, please.'

'Thank the stars and the moon and all the planets!'

He pulled her out of her chair and into his arms, covering her face with kisses, frantic kisses, as if he was afraid she would disappear, as if he wanted to make sure she was real. She smoothed her hands through his dishevelled hair, twining her arms around his neck, until the kisses became less frantic, and their lips met. This kiss was different, loving, all the sorrow and regret of the last few months melting away in a blaze of delight.

'I love you,' she murmured against his mouth.

'I love you,' Alexander replied, with such tenderness in his eyes that she could never doubt him.

He fell back on to the hearth, taking her with him. His eyes darkened as their kisses deepened. She could feel his breath quickening. Their kisses lost their languor. She could feel his arousal pressing into her belly, feel an answering excitement inside her. She slid her hands under his coat. He wore no waistcoat. His shirt was roughly woven. She didn't want to feel his shirt. She wanted to feel his skin against hers.

'We can't. Not here,' Alexander said. 'Not for our first time.'

He kissed her again. His kisses gave his words the lie. 'Yes, we can,' she whispered. 'Here. Now.'

He groaned. 'I want you so much.'

Eloise, heady with love and with the confidence of being loved in return, chuckled. 'Fortunately, I am all yours to do with as you will.'

'That is an invitation I cannot resist.' His eyes alight with laughter and desire, Alexander abandoned her briefly to lock the door, divesting himself of his clothes as he returned to her, kneeling down on the rug, pulling her back into his arms and kissing her. But when desire subsumed her, he slowed their kisses. 'We have all the time in the world, my love.'

He unfastened her gown, easing it down over her arms, kissing her neck, her throat, her breasts. She wriggled free of her gown, and there were more kisses as he unfastened her stays, and yet more as he pulled her chemise over her head, his mouth warm on her nipples, making them tighten, making her shiver with delight. He removed her slippers and untied her garters. He kissed her knees, her calves, her ankles as he removed her stockings. And then he untied her drawers and pulled them down, and she lay wide-eyed, brazenly naked and gazing up at him.

The light of love and of desire in his eyes caused the knot of tension inside her to wind so tight she could scarcely breathe. He leaned over to kiss her again, his arousal brushing against her belly. When he kissed her again, working his way down her body, she moaned in frustration, and he laughed, and continued to kiss her, gently parting her legs, kissing her thighs, and then between her legs. She cried out in surprise, but he kissed her again, licking into her, and her gasp turned into a guttural moan as his mouth sent her tumbling over the edge and her climax ripped through her.

Lost to everything except an overwhelming, primal need to have him inside her, Eloise tugged at his shoulders, muttering his name over and over. He kissed her deeply, their tongues touching, tangling. His skin was hot to touch. He entered her slowly, easing himself inside her, watching her, careful of hurting her, but there was no pain, only the most astonishingly delightful feeling of rightness, of her muscles closing around him, enfolding him. He kissed her again, his hands under her bottom to tilt her up, and then he began to move. She could not have imagined this. The frissons. The push and the pull. Her muscles. His hard length. The tension inside her building again. The tension etched on his face as his thrusts quickened, as she instinctively arched to take him higher. She moaned, learning a new rhythm, meeting his thrusts, tightening around him, clinging to the building of a new climax inside her until she could hold on no longer, crying out with abandon, feeling his answering moan, the pulse of his own climax, and their mouths met again, their bodies slick.

Eloise smiled hazily into her husband's eyes. 'I had no idea that love could be so wonderful.'

She felt the rumble of his laughter in his chest as he

kissed her again. 'I will let you into a secret, my darling,' Alexander said. 'I had no idea either.'

'Really?'

His expression softened. 'Really wonderful.' He kissed her tenderly. 'And marvellous.' He kissed her again. 'And delightful.'

She twined her arms around him, kissing him back. He kissed her again, more deeply, and she was astonished to feel a response stirring inside her. 'Very delightful,' she said. 'In fact so delightful, Alexander, that I think I might like—unless, is it too soon?'

He laughed. 'It should be. But then again...'

He pulled her on top of him. Her breasts brushed his chest. The soft fuzz of his hair made her nipples tingle. When their mouths met again, their kisses were hungry. She could feel him becoming aroused as they kissed, stirring, hardening. She could feel the answering response inside her becoming urgent, and just as she was beginning to wonder how they could, when surely they were facing the wrong way, he slid his hands under her bottom, easing her up, and it was the most perfectly natural, delightful feeling in the world as he slid inside her.

She moved, a small experimental thrust, and Alexander moaned. Beguiled and aroused by the effect she was having, Eloise thrust again, and he bucked under her. She leaned over to kiss him, her hair brushing his chest, holding him inside her as their tongues touched, and then she moved again. He was watching her, intent, ardent, his eyes dark with passion, yet alight with love. She kissed him again, felt such a rush of love that she could no longer wait, tightening around him, abandoning herself to the need to take him with her, finding a new, urgent rhythm that drove them both to a tumultuous, simultaneous completion and left them panting, wrapped in one another's arms, gazing into each other's eyes in astonished delight.

'I love you,' Alexander said, kissing her again.

A sated kiss. The best kiss of all, Eloise thought blissfully. And the first in a lifetime of such kisses.

* * * * *

Historical Note

In 1827 Frederick, Duke of York and heir to the throne, died. Frederick had no issue from his unhappy marriage. There were rumours that he had secretly married a second time, without the consent of the King—what is known as a morganatic marriage—some time around 1822.

The Duke of Clarence—who became Lord High Admiral the same year—became heir to an ailing George IV following Frederick's death. William wasn't too keen on becoming King.

All of this is historically accurate, but—as far as I know!—Alexander's mission to try to find a lost heir who would spare William the crown is completely my own invention. As it turns out William was a good egg of a king—though it has to be said anyone would have been an improvement on his predecessor.

Mad Jack Mytton—or Squire Mytton—was a notorious Regency character who gave his name to a real pub: the Jack Mytton Inn. His outrageous and eccentric behaviour discussed by Eloise and her sisters are genuine examples, and actually I don't think I've done him justice. Think of a cross between Keith Moon and Oliver Reed! The bear, in case you're wondering, was called Nell, and when he set fire to his nightshirt it did—not surprisingly!—cure his hiccups.

Sadly, I didn't invent the Earl of Fearnoch's tradition of calling every male upper servant James and every female Margaret. It was a practice apparently common in some of the larger households, where the turnover of staff was high, and—presumably—the mental agility of those in charge correspondingly low. Annoyingly, I can't actually remember where I read this, so if it does turn out that I made it up in a fevered dream I apologise wholeheartedly and beg you not to chastise me about it.

I have absolutely no idea whether it was possible to have an entail which required the heir to marry by the time he was thirty. It seemed to me such a good idea for a story, and one which quickly became so funda-mental to *this* story, that I decided not to check. If I'm wrong I will once again apologise in advance and ask to remain happily ignorant.

Admiralty House is obviously a real place, though I doubt that it's open to private diners—not even such high-flying private diners as Alexander and Eloise.

The Vineyard Nursery, which gets a fleeting men-tion, is also real, and originally featured in a scene from my last book, *A Scandalous Winter Wedding*. It was a dreadful scene, which I deleted, but the research wasn't wasted.

And, talking of recycling things, if you're an ob-servant regular reader you'll have spotted a few of my other characters making a reappearance. Lord Henry Armstrong—from **The Armstrong Sisters** series— is a man I keep coming back to lampoon. Madame

LeClerc has been dressmaker to a number of my heroines. And, finally, Monsieur Salois the chef was actually a creation of Bronwyn Scott when we collaborated on the *Brockmore* books. It was her suggestion that I include him in this book as a culinary inspiration for Phoebe—thank you!

A WIFE WORTH
INVESTING IN

For J. My food hero and my everything hero. Always.

Chapter One

Paris—August 1828

Though it was long past midnight, the oppressive heat of the day had not dissipated, having been trapped by the tall, elegant buildings which lined the street down which Owen Harrington wandered aimlessly. He was not exactly lost, but nor was he quite sure where he was. Having crossed to the Rive Gauche at Notre Dame some time ago, the Seine should be somewhere on his right. He thought he'd been walking in a straight line, assumed that he was headed west, but the streets of Paris, as he had discovered to his cost several times in the last week, were not laid out in a neat grid. Instead they veered off straight at an imperceptible angle, often arriving at an unexpected destination. Rather like the locals' conversation.

He had been away from London for less than two weeks, but already felt disconnected from his life there. It had been the right decision. He was not try-

ing to avoid the commitment his late father had made
on his behalf, he planned to honour it, but he could
not embrace it as his sole role in life. He still had two
years' grace, time to be alone to be himself, free to
do as he pleased, to discover a sense of purpose that
would also accommodate his father's wishes. He had
no idea what form this might take, but he was already excited by the endless possibilities waiting to
be explored.

Above him the sky was inky, the stars mere pin-
points. The air, redolent of heat and dust, felt heavy,
forcing him to slow his pace, encouraging him to dally.
A faint beacon of light caught his attention. The lamps
from a café tucked down a narrow alleyway flickered.
Intrigued, for most establishments had closed their
shutters hours ago, thinking a very late *digestif* might
be just the thing, Owen decided to investigate.

The main room of the Procope Café was dark-
panelled, smoke-filled. Two men were frowning intently over a chessboard cleared of all but five pieces.
Around a large table, another group of men were dis-
puting their bill, while a bored waiter looked on,
answering Owen's mimed request for a glass of something strong with a shrug, pointing at the ceiling. He
returned to the foyer and began to climb the rather
elegant staircase. The first floor was silent, the doors
of the rooms, presumably private dining salons, all
closed, their customers either long departed or wishing to be very private indeed. A burst of laughter
lured him to the top floor. The room was built into the
eaves and stretched the full length of the café. Black

and white tiles covered the floor, the narrow windows were flung open to the Paris night, the red-painted walls lined with banquettes which were crammed with late-night drinkers. Lamps were hung from the rafters, their muted light giving a rosy glow to the café's clientele—though perhaps that was the wine, Owen thought, which was in plentiful supply, with large earthenware jugs jostling for space on the tables.

No one paid him any attention as he stood in the open doorway. It was one of the things he liked about this city, being entirely anonymous and quite alone, lurking on the fringes, listening and watching. The French were so much more garrulous than the English. They conducted conversations at top speed, using their hands expressively, talking over each other, spinning off at tangents, around in circles, but never quite losing the thread.

There were no free seats. Disappointed, he was about to leave when two young men got up from their table. He stepped out of the doorway to let them pass, but they had stopped at another table where a woman sat alone. She had her back to the room, facing one of the open windows, and had been writing in a notebook, head bent, making it clear that she had no wish to be disturbed. Though not clear enough, it seemed. The two late-night revellers were hovering over her. He could see her shaking her head forcibly. Her posture gave the impression of youth, though he couldn't say how. Was she a courtesan? In London, there would be no doubt about it, but in Paris it seemed to be acceptable for women to dine in the cafés, to enjoy a glass of wine or a cup of coffee. Though alone, and late at night? Surely even Paris was not that decadent.

Owen looked around, but the waiter now was engaged in an altercation with one of the bill-hagglers and no one else was taking any notice of the woman's plight. One of the men took a seat beside her. She gesticulated for him to leave her alone. The other caught her arm. She leapt to her feet to try to free herself and was roughly pushed back down on to her chair. Owen was across the room before he was aware he'd made any decision to intervene. It occurred to him that he might well be embroiling himself in a dispute between a *demi-mondaine* and her clients, but it was too late to stop now, and whatever the relationship, it was clear the men's attentions were unwelcome.

Though he didn't doubt his ability to see the pair of them off, he was not particularly inclined to get into a fist fight. Hoping that the fair damsel—exceedingly fair, he noted as he arrived at the table—would instinctively follow his lead, he greeted her with a broad smile.

'I have kept you waiting,' he said in French, 'a thousand apologies, *ma chérie. Messieurs*, I am grateful to you for keeping my little cabbage company, but now I am here, you understand that you are *de trop*?'

He allowed his smile to harden as he stood over them, making sure that they could see his clenched fists but making no other move. There was a moment when the decision could have gone either way but Owen knew to wait it out, and sure enough, the man at the table shrugged and got to his feet, clapping his friend on the back and nudging him toward the door.

'Bon nuit, messieurs,' Owen said, standing his ground, keeping his gaze fixed firmly on the men until they had left, before turning back to the woman at the table. 'Will you allow me, *madame*, to keep you company just for a few moments, in case they return?'

'Please, sit down. Thank you very much, *monsieur*. May I offer you a glass of wine? Unless you prefer to drink alone?'

She smiled up at him tentatively, and Owen found himself gazing down into a face of quite dazzling beauty. Her hair was a rich burnished gold threaded with fire. Her eyes, almond-shaped, thickly lashed, seemed also golden, though he supposed hazel was the more prosaic term. She had a pert nose, a luscious mouth, and the hint of equally luscious curves under the demure neckline of her dress. If he'd had a poetic bone in his body, now would be the moment to spout some verse.

He did not spout poetry and he didn't gawk! 'No,' Owen said, rallying, 'it is merely that I did not wish to intrude, *madame*, since *you* clearly do prefer to be alone.'

'I'm waiting for someone, actually.'

'Then with your permission, I would be delighted to act as your chaperon until they arrive,' he said, taking a seat. 'Allow me to introduce myself. I am Owen Harrington.'

'Ah, you are English?'

'As English as you are, judging by your French,

which is excellent but not without accent,' Owen said, reverting with relief to his native language.

'My name is Phoebe Brannagh, and I'm actually Irish.' She poured him a glass of wine. '*À votre santé*, Mr Harrington.'

'*À la vôtre*, Mrs Brannagh.'

'It's Miss Brannagh.'

'Miss Brannagh.' He touched her glass, taking a sip of the very quaffable wine. Her voice was cultured. Her clothes were expensive, as was the little blue-enamelled watch she was consulting. Miss Phoebe Brannagh was most certainly not a member of the *demi-monde*, which made her presence here rather shocking. 'You are waiting for a friend, a relative?' he hazarded.

She snapped shut the watch, rolling her eyes as she returned it to her reticule. 'He is very late. As always,' she said ruefully. 'I'm waiting for Monsieur Pascal Solignac.'

She enunciated the name with such reverence, Owen was clearly expected to know who the gentleman in question was. 'I'm sorry, I'm afraid…'

'The celebrated chef. Perhaps you've not been in Paris long?'

'A week.'

'And you have not dined at La Grande Taverne de Londres? My goodness, where on earth have you been eating?'

'At places like this, by and large.'

'Oh, the Procope is all very well if you like honest hearty fare, but really, Mr Harrington, one comes to Paris to dine, not to eat. Have you heard of Monsieur

Beauvilliers, the author of *L'art du Cuisinier*, the bible of French gastronomy? My sister bought me one of the first English editions. Monsieur Beauvilliers's restaurant closed some years ago, following his death, but La Grande Taverne de Londres has reopened with Pascal at the helm—Pascal Solignac, I mean. He has elevated cooking to another plane and is the talk of Paris, Mr Harrington, I can't believe that you have not heard of him. Perhaps you prefer to drink rather than eat?'

'I eat to live, I'm afraid I don't live to eat, which probably makes me a culinary philistine in your eyes.'

She gave a burble of laughter. 'I love food with a passion. If it were not for the heat of the kitchen and all the running around, and being on my feet for fourteen or fifteen hours at a stretch, I should be as fat as a pig at Michaelmas.'

'Good lord, are you a chef?'

'Not yet, but I hope to be some day. I've been incredibly fortunate to find work in Pascal's kitchen for the last nine months. I'm on the patisserie station at the moment.'

Owen hardly knew what to make of this. 'I'm no expert, but I'm not aware of any female chef working in a restaurant kitchen in London.'

'It's very unusual, even in Paris. In fact, I am the only female in the brigade.'

'And how do the other staff react to having a beautiful woman in their midst, and English to boot—I beg your pardon, Irish—my point is that you are not French. Do they see you as a interloper?'

Once again, she laughed. 'I have earned my stripes

the hard way, peeling sacks of potatoes and chopping mountains of onions—that is a rite of passage in a professional kitchen, Mr Harrington. Fortunately, my eyes don't water, for I've been chopping onions and peeling potatoes since I was this height,' she said, touching the table top.

'You astonish me. It is obvious from your accent that you are well born.'

She gave a pronounced Gallic shrug. 'Oh, I'm born well enough, I suppose, though what matters to me is not the colour of the blood in my veins but my determination to live life to the full. In that sense, I take after my mother.'

'So she approves of your being here?'

Her face fell. 'I believe she would, if she were alive, but I lost both my parents and my little brother six years ago. I hope she would have been proud of me, for I've already achieved far more than I expected in such a short time. In a restaurant kitchen, you know, a strict hierarchy exists. You have to earn your place, and any promotion. To reach patisserie in just nine months is almost unheard of. To be honest, there are days when I have to pinch myself to make sure I'm not dreaming.'

There was pride in her voice and a gleam in her eye. 'You are obviously passionate about your chosen vocation,' Owen said, a little enviously.

Miss Brannagh beamed. 'It is all I've ever wanted, all I've ever dreamed of—and that's all it was, until last year, a pipedream. Were it not for my sister's generosity, I wouldn't be here, learning from Pascal.'

Pascal. It was not only admiration that he could

hear in her voice, Miss Brannagh was in thrall to her mentor. Lucky man, Owen thought. He hoped Monsieur Solignac, who he had already irrationally and instantly taken a dislike to, appreciated his protégée and did not take advantage of her obvious reverence for him. 'The same sister who gave you the famous recipe book?'

'Yes, Eloise my eldest sister. The Countess of Fearnoch.' Miss Brannagh chuckled. 'Goodness, I still find it quite strange, calling her that. She made a most *excellent* marriage just over a year ago, which allowed her to settle a small fortune on myself and Estelle.'

'Another sister?'

'My twin.' Miss Brannagh's smile softened. 'We were a such a close-knit little group until recently—the Elmswood Coven, Estelle called us—myself, Eloise, Estelle and Aunt Kate—she is Lady Elmswood and our aunt by marriage. She very kindly took us in when we lost our parents and there we lived, cosily and very contentedly for five years, until Eloise's wedding.'

'I presume that the appeal of cosy and contented began to wane?'

Miss Brannagh chuckled. 'Though I love Aunt Kate with all my heart, why on earth would I choose to stay in the wilds of Shropshire when I could come to Paris and chase rainbows?'

Chasing rainbows, wasn't that exactly what he was doing, Owen thought, utterly charmed. 'What pot of gold lies at the end of your rainbow, may I ask? Becoming the top chef in Paris?'

'I aim to become the *second-best* chef and part-owner of the pre-eminent restaurant in Paris, along with Pascal.' Miss Brannagh's smile faded slightly. 'The proprietor of La Grande Taverne de Londres is just a little too traditional in his thinking for Pascal, you see. Our intention is to buy him out, so that Pascal's genius can flourish unhindered, and if he will not sell, then we will buy new premises and start from scratch together.'

'You will not mind playing second fiddle to Monsieur Solignac, then?'

'It will be an honour! I will never supersede Pascal, he is a—a maverick genius and what's more, he enjoys being in the public eye—whether it is chatting to diners or talking about his menus to the press. Estelle, my twin, would excel at that sort of thing, and even Eloise—for she is so confident, and takes after Aunt Kate. But I much prefer to avoid the limelight, and am happiest behind a stove.'

'As a lone female in a kitchen though, you must have to fight to hold your own.'

'Oh, that is a different matter all together, for the kitchen is my milieu. But I have never been confident among strangers.'

'I am a stranger, and you seem—forgive me— perfectly at ease with me.'

She flushed. 'You are my knight errant. Besides, there is something about you—but you're probably thinking I have talked too much. I have. I do beg your pardon.'

'I am very much enjoying our conversation. I have

never met anyone like you, Miss Brannagh, you are quite unique.'

'I'm a twin, so actually one of a pair.'

'Are you identical twins, you and your sister?'

'Oh, no, though we look very alike. Estelle is much more talented than I. As well as being an extremely accomplished musician, she is a bit of an actress—a mimic. I'm not any sort of performer.'

'What does she think of your ambition to become the *second*-best chef in Paris?'

'Estelle—oh, Estelle, I have lately realised, has a much more conventional outlook on life than I, but she'll come round.' She took another sip of wine, frowning slightly. 'Do you have any sisters or brothers, Mr Harrington? No? Well, the thing about sisters is that they think they know you better than you know yourself, and in a way they do, but they can also—they assume things, you see. I am younger than Estelle by twenty minutes, which makes me officially the baby of the family, since we lost our poor little brother. They think, Estelle and Eloise, that I need protecting, that my cooking is just a hobby. They have not said so outright, indeed Eloise never would for she was determined her gift came without strings, but I know they both believe my coming here is a mistake.'

'But you hope to prove them wrong? By the sounds of it, you are already doing so.'

'Do you think so? I tell myself I'm doing well. In fact I know I am doing so extraordinarily well, I've astonished myself. I wish my sisters shared your confi-

dence in me, but in time, they will come to see that I've
made the right decision to flee the comfort of the nest.'

'All the same, for one who hasn't been abroad much
in the world, to come to Paris on your own must have
been a daunting prospect.'

'A baptism of fire—the kitchen was, at any rate.
But as for Paris—oh, I fell in love with Paris almost
from the first moment. The way of life suits me, it is
so very, very different from England. I love my sisters and Aunt Kate, but they are such strong women.
I have always lived in the shadow of their low expectations, you know?'

'I do,' Owen agreed wholeheartedly. 'Though I don't
have any close family, I have a reputation which I'm
rather tired of living down to.'

'My own feelings exactly! I hope that Paris suits
you as well as it does me, Mr Harrington. It is the most
beautiful city one could ever imagine. I spend every
Sunday exploring, following my nose, drinking coffee in cafés, sitting in the parks just watching people
stroll by. I play a game with myself,' she said sheepishly. 'I like to guess what their favourite foods are.'

'And what would you guess mine would be?'

'*Rosbif* is what any Frenchman would immediately
say, but you are very far from being a typical Englishman.' She studied him, her hazel eyes gleaming like
gold, her chin resting on her hand. 'I'd say you prefer
breakfast to dinner. Eggs, coddled or perhaps scrambled with cream, delicate but delicious. A ham, boiled
in spices and served cold. Fresh rolls and salty butter.
Coffee. Am I right?'

'Even if you were wrong, you make it sound so delicious that I would change my preference for a dinner of venison stew immediately'

'Now it's your turn. What do I like to eat?'

He took the opportunity to study her as she had him, struck afresh by her lush beauty, which so perfectly complemented her charm. 'Supper,' he said, smiling, 'definitely supper, at the end of a long day when you have finished serving dinner to your clientele. Asparagus with a hollandaise sauce and perhaps a lightly poached egg, and a glass of champagne. Essentially English, but with a soupçon of French flair—though I know you're Irish. How am I doing?'

She laughed. 'I shall return the compliment, Mr Harrington. Even if you are quite wrong, you make me long to have it. You see, it's a good game, isn't it? I can while away hours playing it and don't mind at all sitting by myself to do so. I love the fact that no one knows who I am, far less cares. In Paris, for the first time in my life, I can be completely myself without having to consider anyone else—on my Sundays off, at any rate.'

'You wander Paris alone?'

'Yes, and I love it. Pascal spends his Sundays either experimenting with dishes or catching up on his sleep. Even if I wanted company, I have no acquaintances outside the kitchen, there's been no time to make friends. But I don't need them. It is—it is *liberating*, being alone after always being Estelle's other, younger half. That sounds terrible, I love my sister— both my sisters—with all my heart and I know they are only being protective but they smother me a little and patronise me just a little too.'

'So you want to cast off the shackles?'

'Yes! Exactly! You do understand.'

'I do indeed. I was thinking something similar just before I stumbled upon this café. And I'm very glad I did stumble upon it. Very glad too—if you will forgive my saying—that Monsieur Solignac is so tardy.' Monsieur Solignac, who by the sound of it was more than just a friend to the beguiling Miss Brannagh, Owen thought, his animosity towards this *maverick genius* increasing.

'I take it he does not have the wherewithal to set himself up in business?' he asked.

'No,' Miss Brannagh answered sunnily, entirely unaware of his scepticism. 'Pascal has the reputation, I have the financial means. That is what I call serendipity.'

Almost too good to be true from the Frenchman's perspective, Owen thought as she took out her watch again, frowning at the time.

'He has clearly become absorbed while practising a new dish. It is only after service has finished that he can try out his ideas. Though the dishes he serves are exquisite, they are in essence traditional receipts tweaked with his own flourishes. Classic cuisine with a twist, so to speak, but when we have our own establishment, we will serve food such as the world has never imagined, never mind tasted.'

'And while he creates, you must wait here patiently?'

'Genius must be indulged,' she said, bristling slightly. 'And nurtured too.'

To be nurtured by Miss Phoebe Brannagh was an appealing prospect, Owen thought, regretfully. He had not felt so drawn to a woman in a long time. If only they had met under different circumstances, he'd have made a concerted effort to get to know her better. Captivating, that was the word he'd been looking for, not only in her looks, but in her outlook. She had a true *joie de vivre*, as if she was reaching out and embracing life—a feeling he had lost. He felt jaded, and had travelled abroad to rediscover a sense of purpose, a zest for life, a freshness. She was brave and she was bold. He admired her audacious attitude.

'I wish you every success,' Owen said, raising his glass. The words were a hackneyed toast, but he found that he meant them.

'Thank you.' Miss Brannagh touched her glass to his. He noticed her hands for the first time, the nails cut brutally short, the skin work-roughened, scored with tiny cuts and burn marks. Catching his eyes on them, she snatched them away, hiding them under the table. 'Testament to my trade,' she said, clearly embarrassed.

'Testament to my lack of purpose,' Owen said, holding up his own.

'Goodness, you have a sculptor's hands. Such beautifully long fingers.'

'I don't have an artistic bone in my body. I prefer more physical pursuits.'

Miss Brannagh sipped her wine, smiling. 'It is so nice to converse in English, and though I love being in Paris, I do miss chatting with Estelle and Eloise and Aunt Kate. But I have talked far too much about myself. Tell me what brings you to my adopted city, Mr Harrington.'

'Let me see if I can attract the waiter's attention first and order us another *pichet*. The man seems determined to ignore me. Excuse me, but I think it might be quicker if I go and buttonhole him.'

Phoebe watched the Englishman cross the room and accost the waiter. Had she been indiscreet? Had he guessed that she and Pascal were lovers? Her affaire was so very recent, so much part of her new life here in this exciting city, she hadn't thought how it might appear to anyone else. Had she betrayed her feelings for Pascal in her enthusiasm for him? Mr Harrington had said nothing, but now she wondered what he'd thought of her, sitting alone drinking wine in a café in the early hours of the morning. He had treated her with perfect courtesy. He was certainly surprised to discover her reasons for being here, but he seemed intrigued rather than shocked.

Most people would think her affaire was scandalous. It was why she'd been very careful in how she described Pascal in her letters to Eloise and to Aunt Kate. She had been much more frank with Estelle, thinking that her twin would understand, but to her astonishment, Estelle had taken the very same attitude that she'd guessed Eloise would, if she knew the truth. Instead of lauding Phoebe's daring, she had been appalled, drawing some very unflattering parallels with Mama.

Poor Mama. Phoebe had always known that Eloise didn't understand her, and to be fair, their eldest sister had borne the brunt of Mama's rather careless attitude towards her children. But Mama was a free spirit. Eloise couldn't see how trapped she must have been, by the bonds of matrimony and the expectations of society. It was tragic, for the terrible mismatch that was their parents' marriage made both Mama and Papa very unhappy, and it could not be denied that their children suffered too, but Mama was such a very bright and particular star, it was quite wrong to judge her by the usual standards. To keep such a glamorous, wild creature confined was like imprisoning a beautiful butterfly in a bell jar. Eloise had never understood this but Phoebe had, and she'd assumed that Estelle did too though they never discussed it, out of respect for their elder sister's views.

But Estelle's response to Phoebe's shy confession of her affaire with Pascal had made her position very clear. She imagined Phoebe was in thrall to Pascal rather than in love with him, as if she was blind and had no mind of her own. And she had been rather scathing on the subject of Pascal's involvement too, to the point where Phoebe had even begun to doubt whether he could really be in love with her. She had never in a thousand years expected Pascal to notice her, yet from the first he had seemed to rate her in the kitchen, and he'd made it clear that he found her attractive. She had been hugely flattered, had expected his interest to wane with time, but it had increased. Estelle was wrong. The bond between them was special. It hurt, that her twin didn't understand that, but Estelle obviously hadn't inherited any of Mama's free spirit, so there was no point in trying to sway her. When she came to Paris and saw for herself how deliriously happy Phoebe was, and what a success she was making of her life, she would stop trying to persuade her to come home, but until then, they'd have to agree to differ.

In future, she would be a little more careful in her letters to Estelle. She would definitely not be telling her of this encounter for a start, Phoebe thought, smiling back at Mr Harrington as he returned, armed triumphantly with a new *pichet* of wine. Even though she had eyes only for Pascal, she was not blind to the Englishman's attractions. Although his dark blond hair and cornflower-blue eyes made him look more Norse god than English gentleman, an impression initially formed by the way he'd strode across the room to her rescue earlier, heedless of the fact that he was outnumbered. He was dressed with the kind of careless elegance that only the very rich and the supremely confident can carry off, and there was in his smile a kind of devil-may-care recklessness. Was she being fanciful? No, the term dangerously attractive might have been invented for him.

In fact, if it were not for Pascal, she would be very tempted to spend more time in Owen Harrington's company, while he was in Paris. He had none of Pascal's Gallic flamboyance, a characteristic which Phoebe very occasionally and most disloyally felt teetered over into arrogance. She certainly couldn't imagine Mr Harrington waxing lyrical in the middle of a market over the first ceps of the year, or tearing his hair if they had already sold out, but then she couldn't imagine Pascal rescuing her with such finesse from those two men who had accosted her. Pascal would have come charging over waving his fists and shouting, drawing the attention of everyone in the room to her plight. If he actually noticed she was being harassed in the first place, that is. While Mr Harrington had acted with a quiet self-confidence that was far more effective and infinitely more discreet. Though he was very far from being the stuffed shirt that the Parisians imagined all English gentlemen to be, he was clearly very much a gentleman. Paris would take to him, and he to Paris, Phoebe reckoned. It was a shame, she thought, as he sat back down beside her, that she would not be party to it.

'*Santé,*' Phoebe said, touching her fresh glass to his. 'Now, you were going to tell me what it is that brings you to Paris?'

'To quote the dictionary man, Dr Johnson, when a man is tired of London he is tired of life.' He stared down at his wine, swirling his glass. 'I'm here because I'm sick of both London and my life there, but that makes me sound like an over-indulged, arrogant narcissist.'

'What is the truth?'

'That I'm chasing rainbows, like you, though I don't have any particular pot of gold in mind as yet. I want to—not so much discover who I am as who I might become. Lord, that really does sound pompous.'

'No, it sounds exciting.'

He laughed wryly. 'Excitingly vague. I envy you your certainty and your verve. You know what you want, and you don't care if you have to flout convention to achieve it. I can't tell you how refreshing that is, and how much I admire you for it.'

'You make me sound like a rebel.'

'I think you are, even if you don't realise it. I have always thought myself a bit of a rebel, but I simply behave badly in the conventional manner of spoiled, rich young men. You have widened my horizons already, Miss Brannagh. Until now, I've never had any ambition other than to enjoy myself.'

'Goodness, how lucky you are to be able to indulge yourself.'

'I inherited a fortune from my father, who died ten years ago when I was sixteen. Since I came of age, I have been the toast of society, both high and low. If one pays heed to the scandal sheets I am the richest, the wildest, the wittiest, most handsome, most daring, man in London. My presence can make or break a dinner party or a ball. I never refuse a dare and have never suffered anything worse than a broken wrist in doing so. In a nutshell, for all of my twenty-six years, I've lived a charmed existence. Or so my best friend, Jasper, tells me. What I've come to wonder, these last few months, is whether what I'm living is actually a feckless and shallow one.'

'Good heavens,' Phoebe exclaimed, taken aback and extremely intrigued. 'Are you being entirely serious?'

'I am never serious, unless it's regarding something trivial.'

'Estelle, my twin, does that,' Phoebe said. 'Resorts to sarcasm when she's embarrassed, I mean, or when she's talking about something that she cares deeply about.'

'My problem is that I don't care very deeply about anything.'

'That can't be true!'

'No less an authority than *John Bull* magazine described me as "a dedicated hedonist with a penchant for death-defying dares, who cares for naught but funning."'

Was he teasing her? There was an edge to his smile though. 'Save that you are bored with having fun and have come to Paris to—I'm sorry, I still don't know what specifically you hope to gain from your visit?'

'No more do I, Miss Brannagh, save that it is a very different city from London, and I am already glad that I decided to visit, since I have made your acquaintance. If only you lacked the funds for your restaurant, I would offer to go into business with you, but sadly for me, you can already finance your dream.'

'Then fund your own dream. You must have one, Mr Harrington. Everyone has a dream.'

'Do they?' He threw the contents of his glass down his throat in one gulp. 'I am living most people's dream, and it bores me rigid. I am carefree and I couldn't care less. I'm an *ungrateful* over-indulged, arrogant narcissist, for there is a part of me that wishes I had not been so blessed, then I may have had something to live for.'

'You should be careful what you wish for, Mr Harrington,' Phoebe retorted, 'and grateful for what you have.'

'Well said, Miss Brannagh. You are quite right, of course. I need a purpose in life. Though what form that will take, and whether I will discover it in Paris, or Venice, or St Petersburg or Vienna, I have no idea.'

'Why look so close to home? If you are as rich as you claim, you could try the Antipodes, or Brazil, or Argentina.'

'Or China, perhaps? I'll tell you what, why don't we meet here in—say, a year's time, and I shall unveil the new, improved Owen Harrington to you, and you can then invite me to dine at your new restaurant, which by then will be the toast of Paris.'

'I'm not sure that a year will be sufficient for either to have happened.'

'Two years then. Are we agreed?'

His smile was infectious. 'Two years to the day,' Phoebe said, smiling back. 'You have my word, Mr Harrington.'

He took out a gold case, handing her a card from it. 'And you have mine. Take this, in the unlikely event you need to get in touch before then, to break our assignation, which I sincerely hope does not happen. Otherwise I look forward very much to seeing you again.'

She put the card in her reticule, smiling at the absurdity of it. He poured the dregs of the wine. They raised their glasses in a toast, and their eyes met, and the oddest thing happened. It felt as if time stopped. As if the room and the people in it melted away. And there was only the two of them.

'Phoebe!'

She leapt to her feet, spilling her wine. 'Pascal!'

'Who the hell is this?'

Mr Harrington was on his feet, making a bow. 'Owen Harrington. I met Miss Brannagh quite by accident, but it was a happy coincidence, for I was able to bring her news of her sister, the Countess of Fearnoch, with whom I am acquainted. How do you do, Monsieur Solignac.'

Pascal gave a short bow. He was frowning suspiciously at Mr Harrington. 'Mr Harrington didn't like the idea of my sitting alone so late at night,' Phoebe said. 'He was kindly keeping me company until you arrived.'

'I am grateful to him, but I am here now.'

Mortified by his aggressive tone, Phoebe would have remonstrated, but Mr Harrington was already taking his leave. *'Monsieur,'* he said, making a brief bow. 'Miss Brannagh,' he said, pressing her hand briefly. *'Adieu.'*

He threw some notes on to the table, enough to have paid for all the wine for the entire room for the evening, then with a curt nod, he left.

Despite her lover's arrival, Phoebe was suddenly despondent, and disappointed to have her encounter with Mr Harrington cut short in such a brusque manner. 'I am tired,' she said. 'It's very late, I've had more than enough wine and I want to go home.'

Chapter Two

London—October 1830

Phoebe stepped out of the hackney cab that had transported her from the posting house and gazed apprehensively at the imposing town house. The front door was painted a glossy black, the brass knocker and bell pull brightly polished. She shivered, pulling her cloak around her. It had been sunny when she left Paris, but the rain had set in at Calais, and had poured down relentlessly ever since, reflecting her mood.

She checked her watch needlessly. It was just after ten in the morning. Far too early to be calling on anyone. The shutters of the town house were not closed, which meant someone was in residence, but not necessarily the person she sought. So much could have happened in the intervening two years. He might have changed address. He could be married and settled. It was perfectly possible he was still travelling the world.

He could even be dead, for all she knew. After all,

he hadn't turned up at the Procope café in August as arranged. She'd told herself that it was ridiculous of her to expect him to, that their so-called assignation had been light-hearted banter, nothing more, but she'd gone anyway, three nights in a row. When each night ended without him making an appearance she had been bitterly and quite disproportionately disappointed. She had been so eager to hear what he'd made of his life, fervently hoping it would counterbalance the disaster which constituted her own. She had tried hard not to attach undue significance to his failure to turn up, but it had felt like the last straw, a signal to cut and run. Though she had struggled on for another few weeks, in her head, his non-appearance marked the end of her dream.

Which was one of the reasons why she was here, hoping against hope that Mr Harrington had succeeded where she had so signally failed. Though he probably wouldn't even remember their brief encounter in Paris, she thought despondently. If by some miracle he was in residence and did agree to see her, there was every chance that he'd look straight through her, as if confronted by a complete stranger. Which, in essence, she was.

A footman was eyeing her cagily from the steps of a house across the street. She probably looked suspicious loitering in this genteel locale unaccompanied. Phoebe climbed the first step. If Mr Harrington was not here—oh, God, no, she couldn't bear to think of the alternative. *Please let him be here*, she whispered to herself. *Please.*

The footman was making his way across the street to accost her. Phoebe climbed the remainder of the shallow steps and rang the bell.

The door was opened just a crack by a stern, elderly servant. 'May I help you?' he asked, making it clear that he thought it very unlikely that he could.

She held out the worn card which had lain in the recesses of her reticule for over two years. 'Does Mr Harrington still live here?'

'Yes, but I'm afraid he does not receive visitors.'

Startled, she was about to ask why ever not, when the man made to close the door in her face. 'Please, will you ask him if he will make an exception for me?' Phoebe said urgently. 'My name is Miss Phoebe Brannagh. From Paris, tell him, the young lady from the Procope Café.'

'Phoebe Brannagh,' Owen repeated.

'The young lady wasn't sure if you would remember her,' his butler informed him, careful to keep his expression bland. 'You met in Paris, apparently.'

Not long before his life had changed for ever, in fact. 'Our paths did cross,' Owen said, 'but I can't possibly see her.'

Propped up in bed, his hands hidden under the sheets, he rubbed the extensive scarring on the backs of them compulsively. Phoebe Brannagh! His thoughts often drifted back to their encounter in the Procope. Beautiful, passionate, ambitious and determined, she was unforgettable. He had left the café that night inspired, invigorated, full of optimism for the future, not exactly full of plans but certainly full of determination. He had recalled, many times since, her words of caution when he had so foolishly bemoaned his privileged lifestyle. *'You should be careful what you wish for, Mr Harrington,'* she had said, *'and grateful for what you have.'*

Such prescient words. In the months which followed, in the aftermath, how often he had wished he'd heeded them earlier, returned to London, satisfied with his lot. He might have remained feckless and shallow, but at least he'd have still been himself.

'No,' he repeated, 'I can't possibly see her, it is out of the question.'

'Very well, sir. Shall I convey the usual message?'

The usual message. That Mr Harrington was not at home to callers under any circumstances. Owen hesitated on the brink of assent. What on earth was she doing here, in London? He had wondered, back in August, if she had honoured their assignation. Though it was impossible for him to make the journey he'd still felt guilty, picturing her sitting on her own up in that top room of the Procope sipping wine and waiting for him, just as she had waited patiently, night after night, for Solignac. Had she realised her dream of opening her own restaurant? Were she and the chef who had her under his spell still sharing both a kitchen and a bed? For his part, he fervently hoped not the latter. The little he'd seen and heard of the man had made him certain Miss Brannagh deserved a great deal better.

Why was she here now? It was ludicrous to imagine her concern for him, sparked by his failure to turn

up in August as agreed, had brought her all the way
to England, though if the boot had been on the other
foot, he might well have done just that, for he had
imagined their second meeting countless times. During the darkest days, when the memory of her zest for
life had been a small beacon of light, he had imagined
himself well, fit, successful. Happy. He had dreamed
up endless versions of how his life had turned out, picturing himself recounting them to her in the cosy light
of the Procope, a *pichet* of wine and two half-empty
glasses on the table.

What had she achieved in the last two years? Now
he had the opportunity to find out, was he really going
to pass it up? He was genuinely curious, which was
a refreshing change from his increasing indifference
to the world and its inhabitants. *Miss* Phoebe Brannagh, she had declared herself, though that didn't necessarily mean she wasn't married, merely that it was
the name he would recognise. The chances that she
had abandoned the kitchens for an easier, more prosaic life were high, but Owen hoped Phoebe had remained true to her highly individual self, and beaten
the odds. The more abjectly he felt he had failed, the
more fervently he had hoped that she had found success in Paris.

Though if she had, then why was she here? Her
family lived in England, he recalled. It could be that
she was visiting, and on a whim had decided to look
him up. But why hadn't she written to ask if she could
call, if that was the case? And why call at such an early
hour? In the old days, he'd have been up since dawn,

would have gone for a ride or a run with Jasper while the roads were quiet, or he'd have had a fencing lesson, a shooting lesson, put in some time sparring or at the gymnasium. He could barely recall those days now. When he did, it was as if it was a dream, as if it had all happened to a different person.

Which it had. He was utterly changed in every way. His accident had destroyed him physically. He had battled back for a while, regaining some measure of mobility, but the slough of despond he was sinking into of late was like a pool of black tar, slowly smothering him. His world was muffled, devoid of any feeling, and not even on his best days, when he could just about recognise the importance of not throwing in the towel, did he feel any inclination to take action. He couldn't possibly let Miss Brannagh see him in this sorry and broken state.

Though he wanted to see her. Hearing about her success might just act as a balm for his malaise. It was a ridiculous notion, to imagine that her triumph could offset his disaster, but it might, it just might make him feel a tiny bit better, even give him the kick up the backside he required. And if he didn't see her, he'd always wonder, wouldn't he, what had become of her?

'Wait,' he called to Bremner, who hadn't in fact moved. 'Have her shown to the breakfast parlour. Light the fire there, and in the morning room. Offer her tea. Food. She likes food. Offer her breakfast. Tell her I will join her presently. I need a bath.'

His butler rushed to do his bidding, failing to hide his astonishment, for visitors, Miss Braidwood's dutiful calls aside, were unheard of these days. Owen slumped back on his pillows, already having to fight the urge to change his mind. It hadn't been one of his better weeks. He'd barely crawled out of bed since that last depressing visit from Olivia. He rubbed his jaw, averting his eyes from his un-gloved hands. He needed a shave. He was going to have to work a minor miracle to make himself look even halfway respectable.

Pushing back the bedclothes, Owen placed his feet gingerly on the ground, gritting his teeth as the familiar searing pain shot through his right leg. He had abandoned the exercises prescribed by his doctors. The regime had succeeded to a point, but he'd long ago hit a plateau. He'd been an athlete once. Those simple, tedious stretches, which were the limit of what his doctors thought he could manage, reminded him that he never would be again.

Dammit, he was not using his stick. It was always worst first thing, he simply had to endure it. He took a faltering step, cursing the grinding pain in his hip, forcing another step and another, slowly making his way to the new bathing room he'd had installed, locking the door securely behind him. It was an unnecessary act, as he had no valet, and all the household knew not to intrude on him on pain of death, but it made him feel better all the same.

The breakfast served to her was good plain fare, but though she had not eaten properly for days, Phoebe could only manage a few desultory forkfuls of eggs and ham. She drank an entire pot of tea though. Tea didn't taste the same in Paris, somehow. The different water probably accounted for it. She was gratefully accepting a boiling kettle to brew a fresh pot and wondering what could be keeping Mr Harrington, and why on earth he did not receive visitors, when the door to the breakfast parlour opened and he finally appeared.

She was so shocked that for a moment she couldn't move from her place at the table. He looked as if he had aged ten years. His hair had darkened, he wore it considerably longer than before, and he had lost a good deal of weight. Lines were etched between his nose and his mouth, and more lines fanned out from the corners of his eyes, which were darkly shadowed. Nature had given him excellent bones, and the loss of weight, instead of making him look gaunt, drew attention to his razor-sharp cheekbones, and to the clean lines of his jaw. He was still a very handsome man, but missing the ready smile and easy charm that had previously complemented his looks, the impression he now gave was forbidding, almost intimidating.

Belatedly, Phoebe got to her feet, making her way to the door where Mr Harrington remained stationery. 'Good morning. I'm so sorry to intrude on you so early.' Her smile faltered. 'I wasn't even sure that you'd remember me, until your butler offered me breakfast, which he wouldn't have done if I was a complete stranger.'

'Miss Brannagh, I have never forgotten that night, or you.' Her host sketched a bow. 'Please, finish eating.'

'I have done, thank you, but I am happy to sit while you partake.'

'I have ordered coffee, that will suffice for me.'

She had preceded him back to the table. Only as she resumed her seat did she notice his pronounced limp and the spasm of pain that crossed his face as he put his right foot down. 'You're hurt. Here, let me…'

He yanked a chair out and sat down heavily. 'Thank you, but I prefer to manage for myself.'

The stern butler arrived bearing a silver pot of coffee, which he poured immediately before leaving them alone, and which Mr Harrington drank back in a single gulp, without bothering to add either sugar or cream. He was wearing gloves. Tan gloves, tightly fitted, so she hadn't noticed them at first.

'Would you like some ham? Eggs?' Phoebe said, making a conscious effort not to stare.

He poured himself a second cup, this time taking a smaller sip. 'Thank you, no. I find I do not have much of an appetite these days.' He eyed her half-empty plate. 'Not up to your exacting standards, Miss Brannagh?'

'I'm not very hungry either.'

His complexion was pale. The man she remembered had been glowing with health. This man looked careworn, the lines on his face, she deduced, carved by pain.

'You look shocked. Aren't you going to ask what happened to me?'

'I get the strong impression you'd much prefer that I didn't.'

He drained his cup. 'I had an accident. My recuperation has been prolonged. As you can see for yourself, I am not the man I once was. And that is all there is to be said.'

Or at least, all that he *would* say. He wanted neither pity nor curiosity, that much was clear. Phoebe bit back her questions, opting instead for frankness. 'As you have no doubt deduced from my appearance at your door at this most unfashionable hour Mr Harrington, my circumstances have also changed since we last met.'

'Really?' He pushed his saucer to one side, wincing as he shifted in his chair to stretch his leg out, before turning his attention back to her, his frown deepening as he did so. 'Actually,' he said, 'I can see that you are different. It is as if the light has gone out of you. You can have no idea how sorry I am to see that. I had hoped that at least one of us would have been toasting their success in August.'

'You remembered!'

'Of course I did, and would have been there if it had been humanly possible, but as you can see, I'm in no condition to travel to the other side of the street, far less Paris.'

'I went,' Phoebe admitted sheepishly. 'To the Procope. I hoped—' She broke off, colouring.

'You hoped as I did, that at least one of us would have something to toast. I take it then, that you do not?'

'No.'

'What happened?'

The sheer magnitude of recent events threatened to overwhelm her. She could not possibly ask him for help, not when he was so obviously enduring his own private hell. Phoebe got to her feet. 'I wish you well with your recovery, but I really shouldn't intrude any longer.'

'Miss Brannagh, please wait.'

She was at the door, about to open it when a crash and a shouted oath made her whirl around. Mr Harrington was on his feet, but only just, clutching the edge of the table. His cup and saucer and the coffee pot were on the floor.

'Spare me the indignity of having to call my butler to prevent you leaving.'

'You have troubles of your own. I have no wish to further burden you with my tale of woe.'

He held out his hand, his voice softening marginally. 'Then distract me from mine by recounting yours. If you can bear to.'

Miss Brannagh stepped reluctantly back into the room. Stooping to pick up the shattered fragments of crockery and the coffee pot, she paused, cast him an enquiring look, then completed the task when Owen reluctantly assented. His servants would see yet more evidence of his clumsiness, albeit neatly stacked on the table and not abandoned on the floor, but they were used to it by now. At least the coffee pot had been empty. 'Thank you,' he said as she sat back down across the table from him.

'You haven't eaten anything. It's not good to start the day on an empty stomach.'

'The food won't go to waste, the kitchen staff get any leftovers.'

'I am pleased to hear that, but it wasn't my point.'

'I am not a child who needs cajoled into eating, Miss Brannagh. You cannot fix me with coddled eggs.' He regretted the words as soon as they were out, but it was too late to take them back. Owen sighed, exasperated. 'Very well, I will take some of the damned—dashed eggs.'

She smiled at him encouragingly. 'And perhaps just a sliver of this lovely ham?'

Lacking the will or energy to deny her, he shrugged, studying her as she set about creating a plate of breakfast for him that he had no appetite for. Her smile had momentarily lit up her face, reminding him of the glowing beauty he'd met in Paris, and making the changes in her so much more stark by comparison. She was dressed simply and elegantly in a grey travelling gown, but it hung loosely on her slender frame. He remembered her laughingly telling him how much she loved to eat. He remembered her figure as generous, like her smile. She had lost weight, and he was, unfortunately, willing to bet that it had not been down to working in the heat of the kitchen. As she handed him his plate—like an offering, he thought—smiling at him tentatively, pleadingly, it struck him that what she'd lost most was her confidence. Exactly as he'd said, the light had gone out in her. Ironically, since their paths had parted they had arrived at the same destination, not success but despair.

He eyed the dish she presented him with, the wafer-thin slices of ham curled elegantly into rosettes, the eggs topped with a knob of melting butter, two slices of bread, the crusts removed, cut into delicate triangles. He really didn't want it, but he didn't want to seem churlish by refusing. 'Thank you, Miss Brannagh, this looks most appetising,' Owen said, awkwardly picking up his knife and fork.

'They say we eat with our eyes. Presentation is much underrated by most cooks. It is one of the first things I learned from—shall I have your butler bring fresh coffee?'

He shook his head.

'In Paris, the juice of freshly squeezed oranges is often served in the morning, but the French don't really take breakfast seriously as a meal the way we do. Are you sure you don't want some fresh coffee with that? Or perhaps—perhaps I should simply be quiet and allow you to eat. I talk too much when I'm nervous.'

Her mouth trembled. When she poured herself some more tea, her hand shook. What the devil had happened to her! He'd wager her revered Solignac had some hand in it. He had already taken against the man before he'd finally turned up late at the Procope, and his appearance in the flesh had simply confirmed Owen's dislike. An ill-mannered bully with an inflated sense of his own importance who took his lover for granted.

He forced the last mouthful of breakfast down, and was rewarded with a smile.

'You see, you were hungry after all.'

'Apparently,' he said drily.

'The eggs were a little over. It is very difficult to keep eggs from spoiling, but the simple solution is to add a little knob of butter, I don't know why more people don't realise it. Forgive me, the last thing you need is a culinary lecture.'

Owen pushed his plate away and eased himself carefully to his feet, biting the inside of his cheek as the anticipated fierce stab of pain shot through his damaged hip. 'We'll retire to the morning room, if you are finished with your tea. It is the second door on your left.'

Ushering her ahead of him, he followed her slowly, resisting the urge to use the wall for support, mortified by how vulnerable he felt without his stick. He would not fall over. He bloody well would *not* fall over.

Lowering himself into the wing-back chair by the fireside, he felt as if he'd completed an epic journey, closing his eyes, taking a moment to get his breathing under control, wondering if the doctors had been right after all, and that the pathetic and rudimentary exercise regime at least served to prevent his health from deteriorating further. The footstool was just out of reach, but as Miss Brannagh made to help, he nudged it towards himself with his good leg.

'Thank you, but I'm not entirely helpless.'

He waved her to the chair opposite, where she sat, hands clasped tightly, on the edge of the seat. 'I'm sorry.'

'Stop apologising. Please.' Adjusting his foot on the stool, he tried to force a smile, but it felt strained, and probably looked more like a grimace. 'Now, Miss Brannagh, that we are more comfortable, to what do I owe the pleasure of your company?'

'Well first of all—I know it's silly—but when you didn't show up at the Procope I wondered why. I hoped that whatever your reason for not being there, that you had fared better than me.'

'Then you have been sorely disappointed, I'm

afraid. I assume you are on your way to visit one of your sisters or—did you say you had an aunt?'

'Aunt Kate. Lady Elmswood. She lives in Shropshire.' She gazed down at her hands, which were white at the knuckles, she was clasping them so tightly together. 'I'm not planning on visiting family just at the moment.'

'Then may I ask what has brought you to England—assuming that your concern for my non-appearance at the Procope in August is not the main reason.'

She took a visible breath. 'The truth is that I have lost absolutely everything, including almost every penny of the settlement Eloise made on me. I could not have failed more abjectly and I can't—I simply cannot face my family until I've found my feet again.'

'Good lord! What on earth happened?'

'Exactly what my sister Estelle predicted.'

'Monsieur Solignac,' Owen said, fatalistically.

'You don't sound very surprised.'

'I wish I had misjudged him, Miss Brannagh.'

'You cannot wish that more fervently than I.'

'Tell me.'

She winced. 'It sounds as if you have already guessed. I was dazzled by him. Everyone was, who came into contact with him—everyone that is, save Estelle and by the sounds of it, yourself. I thought myself the luckiest woman in the world to have been taken under his wing as his protégée, to be allowed to train under him, and I thought that I was progressing well.'

'I remember,' Owen said, 'you had reached the

meant, but it seemed to mean a good deal to you.'

'Yes, it did. And I kept progressing, or so I thought. Pascal even permitted me to introduce a few of my own dishes to the menu. The rest of the kitchen brigade treated me as a fellow chef, not a woman. I thought I was earning their respect too. Perhaps I was, but it was more likely they knew me for Pascal's—Pascal's lover.' She coloured violently. 'I expect you will think that a shocking admission—my sisters were both shocked to the core.'

'Miss Brannagh, I guessed when we met that your—your heart was engaged.'

'You did? I thought at the time that I had been discreet, but I should have known better. I'm not very good at disguising my feelings.' She stared at him, her face set defiantly. 'I'm not ashamed of them, or what I did. They view affaires of the heart very differently in Paris.'

'And you were very much in love with Paris.'

'And with Pascal—or so I thought,' Miss Brannagh replied, looking mortified. 'It is probably difficult for you to understand, but in the kitchen, passions run so very high, and Pascal—he was—he is—the most passionate of all.'

'But your feelings were not reciprocated?'

'I thought they were. Perhaps they were a little bit, for a time. Or perhaps I'm just fooling myself. You've guessed what happened, haven't you? I don't suppose it's difficult. Anyone but me would have seen it coming. That's what Estelle said.'

'You were living your dream,' Owen said. 'That stayed with me, your sheer determination, the way you embraced it all, the way you defied convention to do so. Living life to the full, that's what you said you were doing.'

'Did I? That was what Mama used to say. She was rather more successful at it than me.'

'What happened?'

'Oh, it turned out that Pascal didn't covet me at all, only my money. From the first, when Monsieur Salois—he is the Duke of Brockmore's chef—recommended me to his kitchens at Eloise's behest, Pascal knew I was rich. He was so—so—I couldn't quite believe that I was actually there, in La Grande Taverne, working for Pascal Solignac. Not only working for him, but—he singled me out. He admired my work. He admired me—he seemed as fascinated by me as I was by him. Even at the time, I thought, why would a man so famous, so charismatic, with all of Paris at his feet would fall in love with me. I was enormously flattered, and I suppose it went to my head. I should have known better.'

'Miss Brannagh, you do yourself an enormous injustice. If anyone had Paris at their feet, I'd have thought it would have been you.'

She shook her head vehemently. 'Only because I gave you that impression, because when we met, I was still deluded enough to think that I was what I imagined myself to be. Living life to the full,' she said sardonically. 'I don't have what it takes to make a success of that. I should have known better. I was simply basking in Pascal's reflected glory.'

'I think you underestimate yourself. When I saw you…'

'As I said, when you saw me, I was deluded. We shared a common dream, Pascal and I, but only one of us would achieve it, and the other one would pay dearly. You can guess which was which. We spent hours after service talking of our restaurant, planning the menus. Pascal felt his genius was wasted, having to conform to the dictates of La Grande Taverne's owner. Only in our own place would he be free to unleash his true artistry. And I would be there at his side, Paris's best and most inventive *sous-chef*. That is what we agreed. That is what he promised me.'

'But when he had your money, his promises proved to be empty?'

She shuddered. 'The premises were purchased in his name. As a foreigner, I could not own property. As a woman I was apparently not permitted a bank account in France. I don't even know how much of what he told me was true, I never thought to check. I trusted him implicitly. The new restaurant opened in June this year. What should have been the best night of my life turned into the worst. I had always admired Pascal's burning ambition but it hid a ruthless streak, as I found out to my cost. He didn't even wait until the staff had gone home. When the doors closed and the opening-night party began, he took me to one side and told me that he didn't need me any more. I had served my purpose, and he cast me off like a dirty dish rag.'

She curled her lip. 'I had been incredibly naïve not to realise that all he had ever wanted from me was my money, but I didn't take it lying down. I didn't fight for his affections, though I thought my heart broken, but I fought for what was mine. It was futile. Pascal can do no wrong in Paris's eyes, and he wields a great deal of influence. No one would believe the word of a deluded, scorned Englishwoman, against Paris's new culinary king. He made sure of that.'

Her eyes sparked with anger. 'According to Pascal, he took me in as a favour to Monsieur Salois and tolerated me for far too long because as everyone knows, who has ever met Pascal, he is such a soft-hearted fool, beguiled by a pretty face and a well-turned ankle! Also according to Pascal, he covered up my many mistakes in the kitchen, and took me into his bed because I made it so difficult for him to refuse. The fact that it was my bed in my apartment—but that too, he claimed was my idea. Then when my inflated opinion of my own abilities caused me to demand that I had a place in his new venture, he had no option but to disillusion me. And to ensure that every other restaurant in Paris was similarly disillusioned.

'So there you have it, my full, sorry and pathetic tale. I tried, heaven knows I have tried to secure gainful employment in another kitchen since. But no one would take me on, and the only offers I received were of a—a very different nature. Paris is a wonderful city when you are happy, when you feel that nothing is impossible, that the future is bright. But when your dreams are shattered, when you dare not look into the future for fear of what you might see, then Paris feels like living in a nightmare. I could hardly bring myself to stay in that apartment when he moved out, but I had nowhere else to go. Now the lease has run out, and I am quite penniless. If I started as a kitchen maid, perhaps I could scramble my way back up, but not in Paris. I love that city so much, but it is tarnished for ever for me now.'

Though her eyes were over-bright, she had not shed a single tear in the telling of this appalling tale. Owen would have given a great deal to throttle Solignac's scrawny, arrogant neck, but Miss Brannagh was determined to take the blame for the man's ruthless ambition and callous, abominable treatment of her. In fact she seemed to think she deserved it. Not content with stealing her money and her heart, Solignac had also stripped Miss Brannagh of her self-confidence. 'And was he right,' Owen asked tentatively, 'about your culinary ability—or lack of it?'

Her shoulders slumped. 'That is the hardest thing of all for me—he's made me question just that. All I've ever wanted to do is to cook, and it's the only thing I've ever thought I was good at. I was astounded by how well I did under Pascal's tutelage, but I truly believed it was because I was learning fast, that my promotions were all merited. When he told me that I hadn't earned any of it, that he wouldn't ever have promoted me beyond peeling potatoes—I don't know, Mr Harrington, perhaps I was out of my depth. Perhaps I am simply a competent domestic cook. I'd like to think not. I'd like to think that I can cook to a professional standard, but all I know for certain is that I still want to cook.'

'Bravo, Miss Brannagh, you are bowed but unbroken,' Owen said, though he was furious, for it was clearly far from the truth. As he suspected, Solignac had knocked the stuffing out of her.

'I thought I was broken. I hope that I can put myself back together.'

'I am very glad to hear that. You have taken some appalling and undeserved knocks, but your spirit has not been completely extinguished.'

'We'll see. I'm absolutely determined to try again, which is why I'm here. I got myself into this mess and I am determined to get myself out of it without falling back on my family.' She paused to take a visible breath. 'When I met you in Paris, you told me that you were the toast of society.'

'Once upon a time, but I'm afraid I no longer go out in society, Miss Brannagh, and I'm not quite sure—'

'You still have contacts, influence?' she interrupted. 'You see, I need a job, Mr Harrington. I need work. If I have to start at the bottom I will, though I would prefer—but I know I am not in a position to make demands. Only a request. Does anyone of your acquaintance need a cook?'

'You want me to find you a position in domestic service?' he exclaimed, astounded.

'I would be for ever in your debt if you could.'

Undoubtedly he could. His influence was such that he could find her a position in any of the best households in London, if he chose to exert it. 'Why not ask your sister for a recommendation? The Countess of Fearnoch…'

'No! No, no, no. It's not that I can't, Mr Harrington, it's that I won't. I won't be pitied. Eloise would never say I told you so, but it would be worse than that, she'd blame herself for letting me go abroad in the first place. She was very shocked, when she and her husband came to Paris back in April last year, and discovered—I'm still not sure how—my affaire with Pascal. She did not tell me that I was making a mistake in investing the money she had given me in the restaurant, she promised both Estelle and I that we could spend our settlement as we pleased, but I could see she was very concerned. I tried to persuade her she need not worry, but she obviously did, for she sent Estelle to talk sense into me at the end of last year. My twin had no compunction in making *her* feelings known. We parted on very bad terms.'

'And Estelle would say I told you so, if you went to her now?'

'Probably, and she'd have every right to, but she'd reserve her vitriol for Pascal. It may be perverse of me, but I don't relish the idea of being seen as a witless victim. It was my decision to go to Paris, a gamble that didn't pay off. Pascal exploited my passion and ambition, but I—oh, I was easily duped, let's face it. He told me what I wanted to hear.'

For the first time, a tear escaped her eye, though she wiped it hurriedly away. 'I can't get in touch with Estelle. She'll be furious with me for keeping her in ignorance, but she'd drop everything and come running regardless, if she knew I was in such dire straits, and I don't want her to do that. I've never been at odds

with her like this before. We have been out of touch
ever since our arguement. I miss her so desperately,
but I can't—I absolutely *cannot* make up with her until
I've redeemed myself. Do you think you can assist me
to do that?'

'Mr Harrington?'

Owen blinked. Judging by the concern on her face
he'd had one of his episodes, where his mind froze and
went blank. But for how long?

'Mr Harrington, are you in pain?'

Not too long, by the sounds of it, or she'd have rung
for help. 'I've been sitting still for too long, that's all,'
he said brusquely, removing his leg cautiously from
the footstool. Pins and needles made it numb. He had
no option but to wait until they passed before standing up. 'You were saying?'

'Are you sure you are—can I get you anything?'

'No, I thank you,' he said, hauling himself upright.
'I need to think about what you have told me.'

'Oh. Yes. Indeed.' Miss Brannagh got to her feet.
'I expect I'll stay at the posting house tonight, until I
can make other arrangements. You could send a note
to me there, if you think of a suitable position.'

She held out her hand, and he took it in his gloved
one. Though he had lost some of the feeling in his fingers, her touch still sent a jolt through him, conjuring
the fleeting memory of the last time they had held
hands like this, and the way time had seemed to stop.
He looked down at her work-roughened hands, the tiny
healed cuts, the result of constant chopping, the outline
of old blisters from cooking on a hot stove. A perma-

nent reminder, as his scars were, in a very different
way, of her broken dreams. He no longer dreamed, but
if he could help Miss Phoebe Brannagh to pick up the
pieces of her life, then he would have rescued something, for her if not for him. It was scant consolation
but it was better than nothing.

The kernel of an idea began to form in his mind. It
was an outrageous idea. No, he couldn't possibly—or
could he? 'You can't stay in a posting house. I'll have
Bremner organise a hotel for you.'

'Mr Harrington, I'm afraid I don't have the funds...'

'You can pay me back.'

'I can't possibly...'

'What you need is a good dinner and a night's rest
in a comfortable bed,' Owen said firmly, ringing the
bell to summon his butler. 'You'll wake up refreshed,
and much more prepared to face whatever the day may
bring. I will brook no argument.'

'Very well, if you insist, but I will refund you as
soon as I can.'

'Fine. Now, I'm going to hand you over to Bremner.
Eat well, Miss Brannagh, and sleep well. I will send
my carriage for you in the morning.'

She smiled tremulously. 'I don't know how to thank
you. You are very kind.'

Not kind, determined, Owen thought, and already
feeling a hundred times better than when he'd woken
up this morning. 'Until tomorrow,' he said, releasing
her hand as Bremner appeared, his man listening with
well-disguised surprise to his clipped instructions.

The door closed on the pair of them, and Owen

dropped heavily into the nearest chair. It was only just noon but the day, which usually stretched like a vast empty desert in front of him, seemed too short. He had a great deal of thinking to do.

Chapter Three

Confounding her expectations, Phoebe slept soundly in the hotel's huge, extremely comfortable bed. It was delightful to be able to stretch out her limbs, find a cool spot when she was too hot, without worrying she would disturb anyone. *Anyone* being Pascal, a light and fitful sleeper who thought that beds were primarily intended for lovemaking.

She couldn't really remember exactly when and why Pascal had come to move into her apartment. She dimly recalled him mentioning a dispute with his landlady, who wished to charge him for laundering sheets. He had refused to pay, and as a consequence found himself homeless. Why waste time looking for new lodgings which could be more usefully be spent in the kitchen, he'd said, especially as Phoebe's rented apartment was so large it was wasted on just her. Since there was no landlady on the premises to object to their scandalous domestic arrangements, and as the other occupants of the building kept themselves to themselves, Phoebe had come to view their living together as perfectly acceptable. Until Estelle found out.

Estelle had been shocked and furious when Phoebe had finally confessed that she and Pascal were living under one roof—and that Pascal was not paying a *sou* for the privilege. Nothing Phoebe said could convince her sister that such arrangements were acceptable in Paris, nor that the situation could end in anything other than disaster. And Estelle had been proved right.

Right about Pascal, and right about Phoebe's ambition too? Estelle simply couldn't understand why Phoebe was putting herself through the rigorous training and unrelenting hard work of a restaurant kitchen. She couldn't understand why Phoebe wasn't content to cook for her loved ones, why she would put herself through all the effort of serving up food to an unknown public who would have no compunction in deriding it, if it didn't please them. Estelle thought that Phoebe would be much happier spending her settlement on building her dream kitchen in her own home, rather than cooking in someone else's kitchen for complete strangers. Estelle simply didn't understand Phoebe's passion, and this was very difficult to bear, especially since Phoebe completely understood her twin's love of music.

Estelle had a very special gift that elevated her playing above the ordinary. Phoebe had hoped that she had such a gift too, for cooking. Estelle didn't understand that, but she'd hoped Pascal, a culinary genius, would. He'd seemed to, at first, but ultimately she'd either failed to prove herself or he'd been lying to her from the first. Either way, the net result was the same. She had set her sights too high, and she had—predictably— failed. All that was to be done now was to try again, with her sights set lower, to make her own way. Though her heart ached at the wedge which the argument had driven between herself and her twin, she was determined to find a way to re-establish herself before the rift between them could be healed.

What would she do if Mr Harrington could not recommend a suitable post? If he could, she would work night and day to prove herself. *Please*, she said to herself, crossing her fingers, *please let him know of someone.*

Her tummy clenched with nerves. She should enjoy the luxury of having her tea and bread served in bed, ask the maid to have a bath made ready, and make the most of her time in this fabulously indulgent and expensive hotel, not waste it fretting.

She had succeeded in this small ambition, but when a message arrived informing her that Mr Harrington's town coach awaited her convenience, Phoebe was immediately assailed by anxiety. Even if he could not help her, she was glad of the opportunity to see him again. The conversation yesterday had been focused on her plight. She had learned little of his own travails save the sketchy details he had told her. His accident seemed to have made a recluse of him. When had it happened? How far had he got on his travels after he left Paris? Pain had changed him, but she found it dif-

ficult to believe that the charismatic man she had met
two years ago would have given up on the world so
completely. He appeared, on reflection, to be a man
without hope. Though perhaps she had simply caught
him on a bad day.

'Miss Brannagh, how do you do today?' Owen
asked, indicating the chair at the fireside she had occupied yesterday. 'You slept well?'

'Very well, thank you.'

She sat down, making a fuss over the arranging of
her skirts, thoughtfully allowing him time to settle
gingerly in his own chair before looking over at him
expectantly, and Owen was immediately assailed by
doubts. What right had he to ask so much of one so
young and so utterly beautiful? She was unhappy now,
her pride and her confidence had both taken a severe
blow, but she would recover in time. What had seemed
so clear in the early hours of the morning, was now
clouding in his mind. The enthusiasm which had kept
his pain at bay all morning waned, and he became
aware once more of the dull, dragging ache in his hip.
One step at a time, he reminded himself, as he had so
often in the last two years, though this time the steps
were metaphorical and not physical.

'If you had the chance to open your own restaurant
here in London, would you take it?' he asked.

Miss Brannagh's eyes lit up. 'My very own establishment, with my own menus, my own dishes. A place
where men and women can dine together, as they can
in Paris. Just imagine!'

'That would certainly be unique in London.'

'Exactly. Aside from private dining rooms, which are the province of the rich and titled, there is nothing like it at present.'

It was a strange thing, but while his accident had left Owen almost completely numb emotionally, he had discovered that something akin to excitement took hold of him when he sensed a good business deal, a sort of tingling in his belly like an attack of nerves. He felt it now. 'Combine that idea with a female head chef, and you have, if you'll forgive the pun, a mouthwatering opportunity,' he said.

Miss Brannagh's face fell. 'If only, but that will never happen. It's probably just as well too, for I'm not at all sure I am good enough to preside over such an establishment.'

'Not good enough? What happened to being bowed but unbroken?'

'Nothing happened, I'm simply being realistic. It makes much more sense to aim for what I know I can achieve than to even dream of the impossible. I've failed once, I don't want to fail again.'

'Solignac seems to have done an excellent job of cutting you down to size, that's for sure. What if he's wrong?'

'He didn't *cut me down to size*. I was too big for my boots. And it wasn't only Pascal who thought so, it was…'

'Your sister, the musician.'

'Yes.'

Clearly the twin was a very painful subject, Owen,

thought to himself. 'She too could be wrong,' he offered gently.

'I've already wasted all my money and two years of my life trying to prove that, and look where it's got me.'

The same two years he had wasted, trying and failing to recover what he had lost. Owen was now utterly determined to help her, if only to prove her superior twin wrong, never mind Solignac, regardless of whether or not in doing so she could help him. 'Am I right in assuming you would not consider applying to your elder sister for the necessary capital? The Earl of Fearnoch, her husband, is a very rich man…'

'No! Absolutely not. I would not dream of it. I would rather peel potatoes for the rest of my life than do that. I thought you understood, Mr Harrington.'

'Owen. Please, call me Owen.'

'Owen.' She leaned forward earnestly. 'Although my sister is wildly in love with her husband, in fact her marriage was arranged. Eloise never wished to marry, she did so in large part to provide Estelle and I with the means to make anything we wanted of our own lives. The fact that she is so happy is wonderful, but it could easily have been otherwise. Though she swore she would not have married Alexander if she had disliked him, to be perfectly frank, I believe it would have taken a great deal to dissuade her. Eloise has done more than enough for me already. I would never ask her under any circumstances, even if our relationship was not at present strained.'

Owen shifted uncomfortably on his chair. The footstool eased the pain in his hip, but if he sat still too long, his damned foot went to sleep. 'So what you really need is an investor.'

She laughed bitterly. 'The chances of my finding one are about as high as Pascal begging me to come back to Paris. I may not be a *maverick genius*, but I still think I can cook. But Pascal, who *is* undoubtedly a maverick genius, says otherwise, and which one of us would the world believe, do you think? I am about as risky a business proposition as you are likely to encounter. I have no references, I've been sacked from my one and only position, and I'm a woman. Would you invest in me, Mr Harr—Owen? I don't think so.'

'I believe I told you, the first time we met in Paris, that I would and happily.'

'In jest, when you knew that there was no possibility of my accepting.'

'I'm not jesting now, I'm perfectly serious.'

Her eyes widened. Her cheeks flushed and then paled. 'Thank you, you are very kind, very generous, but no, absolutely not.'

'I'm offering to be your backer, Miss Brannagh, not your protector. Believe me, the last thing I'm in the market for is a mistress. I am not Solignac, beguiled by your *pretty face and well-turned ankle*.'

'Forgive me, but no one in their right mind would take such a risk with me, and you know nothing about food—in fact I recall you told me that you are a culinary philistine. If you are not offering me a *carte blanche*, then I can only assume that you must feel sorry for me. The answer in either case is the same. I can't take your money.'

Her refusal didn't surprise him, but his conscience insisted that he press his point. He had to be sure that she believed his final proposition was her best and not her only option. 'Miss Brannagh…'

'Phoebe. Please, call me Phoebe.'

'Phoebe. Just over two years ago, I realised that I was bored with my feckless existence. As fate would have it, my travels were cut short, but my desire for some sort of occupation is one of the few things I didn't lose. Circumstances left me with a lot of time on my hands. I don't sleep well, I rarely go out and I fill a great many of the empty hours with reading. I subscribe to countless periodicals, I read every newspaper, and all the Parliamentary reports. The net effect is that I know what's going on the world I no longer inhabit, and I have discovered that I have an instinct for investment opportunities. It's like a sixth sense. I have a nose for making money. My father left me very wealthy. By investing that money wisely I've made myself rich beyond most people's wildest imaginings. Which is a long-winded way of saying that I have a hunch that you are worth investing in.'

'But you have no evidence to support that,' Phoebe said, becoming agitated. 'I could have a completely inflated opinion of my own abilities. And even if I don't, you are underestimating how *radical* my venture would be. Eating in a restaurant is a much more established tradition in Paris than it is in London—in restaurants such as Le Grand Véfour for example, the clientele is mixed. But as far as I know, the only similar place here is Crockford's and that is for gentlemen only. Imagine the scandal, Owen, if a restaurant were to open in London which served food to both sexes, and had a woman running the kitchen.'

'What you call scandal, I would call priceless free publicity.'

'No, no, no. I want my food to speak for itself, I don't want people to come to gawk at me.'

'Phoebe, your idea is as you said, revolutionary. I hope that your customers would return for the food, but initially, you are going to have to accept that many of them will want, as you put it, to gawk at you.'

'Then it's as well that it's all just a pipe dream,' she said, once again becoming dejected. 'I need to earn my living, not accept charity, no matter how well intentioned.'

Here was a gilt-edged opening. Owen braced himself, taken aback to discover that his heart was hammering, though perhaps it wasn't so surprising, with no less than three lives at stake. 'There is another way,' he said carefully. 'An arrangement which would allow me to invest in you, and for you to legitimately earn my backing.'

'What arrangement could that possibly be?'

Get on with it, Owen urged himself, but now it came to the crux, he was loathe to reveal the true extent of his suffering, and not at all sure he could even explain it without sounding like the madman he had for a while imagined himself to be. His instinct was to get to his feet, to pace, to *move*, but moving entailed pain, and pain interfered with his concentration and induced those lost moments.

'Bear with me,' he said, for Phoebe was starting to look concerned. 'What I have to say is—it is difficult.'

'More difficult than confessing that you are penniless, heartbroken and humiliated, as I yesterday?'

'Are you heartbroken?'

She shook her head. 'I thought I was at first, but I think my pride and my self-esteem were far more damaged than my heart. It's not possible to be in love with a man who loves only himself. If I loved Pascal, truly loved him, I'd want him back, wouldn't I? And I don't.'

'I'm glad to hear it. Wouldn't you like to prove him wrong though, Phoebe? Wouldn't you like the chance to prove yourself right?'

'I don't know. Yes, of course I would, but—'

'Let me help you,' he interrupted before she could once again denigrate her abilities. 'There is a way to secure the funds you need to open your restaurant in an entirely respectable and above-board manner.'

'How?'

'Marry me. As my wife the marriage settlement I would make would be legitimately yours to do with as you saw fit.'

Her mouth fell open. 'You are not serious.'

'I am, deadly serious.'

She looked utterly taken aback. 'You can't be.'

'Hear me out,' Owen said urgently. There was no time for dissembling any more, for Phoebe was making moves to leave. 'It would not be charity, you would be doing both Olivia and myself a huge service. Olivia Braidwood,' he added in response to her blank look. 'The woman I'm going to be obliged to marry, unless I can find a way out of it.'

'You are engaged to be married!'

'I *have* to find a way out of it Phoebe,' Owen said fervently. 'I've already destroyed my own life, I won't destroy hers.'

'You are engaged to be married,' Phoebe repeated, sounding stunned. 'Yet you made no mention of it yesterday. I did wonder if you might have married. That was one of the many possible reasons why you missed our assignation. You are a very attractive man. You are extremely wealthy, you have—I remember when we met in Paris, thinking if it were not for Pascal, because there was something between us, wasn't there? I wasn't imagining it?'

Her words brought such a pang of yearning that it took Owen's breath away. Talk about impossible dreams!

'I am so sorry,' Phoebe said, jerking him back to the present. 'I have embarrassed you. I was simply surprised that you had omitted to mention something of such import.'

'I am not betrothed, not formally,' Owen said, regaining his focus. 'There has been no announcement, though it is well known that Olivia and I have an understanding.'

'An understanding that you think would destroy this Miss Braidwood's life? Why on earth would you think such a thing?'

* * *

'Owen?' Phoebe eyed him with some concern. This was the second time it had happened, this odd blank stare. 'Is there something wrong?'

He started, blinked. 'It's nothing. Nothing serious. I lose concentration, drift off for a few moments now and then.'

'Because of your accident?'

'My doctor told me when I first came back to England that such episodes would pass, given time. I see no point in disillusioning him.'

'Have you also led him to believe that the pain in your leg has passed?'

He shrugged. 'I've tried everything the doctors have to offer. They can't do any more for me.'

His words stirred her compassion. 'Is that why you've shut yourself away from the world, because you believe you won't get any better?'

'I did not make a conscious decision to *shut myself away*. I have a world of my own now, this one, right here, and I'm perfectly content with that.'

'Forgive me, but you don't look very happy.'

'I am not unhappy,' he responded testily. 'I have simply accepted that this is how I am and how I will be. Which is why my proposal requires you to be my wife in name only.'

'Good grief!' Phoebe exclaimed. 'My aunt's marriage is just such an arrangement. My sister Eloise's marriage was also intended to be another such. It seems to run in the family.'

'And are they happy, your aunt and your sister?'

'Yes, though Eloise fell in love with her husband after they married. Their marriage has turned out very differently from the one they intended.'

'But they were happy to sign up to the original agreement?' Owen persisted.

She pursed her lips, recalling the weeks before Eloise was married and the excitement with which she had embraced her changed circumstances. 'Yes, even if they had not subsequently fallen in love—yes, I believe it would still have been a successful match.'

'So are you willing to consider my offer?'

'I still don't understand what it is you are offering and why.'

'But you'll listen? And you'll consider what I have to say? I am, as I said, deadly serious.'

Phoebe hesitated. His words sounded sincere but his demeanour was strangely unemotional, almost detached. His accident had changed him radically, that much was certain, and their entire acquaintance consisted of two brief encounters more than two years apart. But it surely couldn't have changed the essence of him. He was still the honourable man who had come to her rescue at the Procope. A man she could trust. A man now under extreme duress. What on earth had she to lose by listening to him? In fact she'd be a fool not to.

'I remember,' she said, 'when my sister Eloise was considering her now husband's proposal, we talked about it endlessly. We felt, all of us, including Aunt Kate—and she ought to know—that it was extremely important that Eloise went into the marriage with her eyes wide open.'

'You mean you want to know exactly what you'd be getting yourself into?'

'And why. Why do think you would be destroying Miss Braidwood's life if you did marry her? Why must you marry someone else in order to avoid marrying her? And why me?'

'These are big questions.'

'It's a very big decision.'

'It's an outrageous idea, I know, but it is—I truly believe that it could be the answer to both our problems.' Owen shifted on his chair, wincing as he moved his injured leg from the footstool to the floor. 'My accident occurred a little over two years ago,' he said. 'In Marseilles. Not long after we met in Paris, as a matter of fact.'

'Just when you were setting out on your travels! Oh, Owen, how awful. What happened?'

He went quite rigid, staring down at his gloves. 'There was a fire. That's all I know. I remember almost nothing of it and don't want to either. My hands were badly burned. Something heavy, a beam I think, fell on top of me. My hip was shattered. I was unconscious for some weeks afterwards. It was three months before I was well enough to face the journey back to London. Six months before I could walk again.'

Though she could see from the way he held himself, completely still, that saying even this much was an immense effort, his tone was oddly cold, as if he was recounting something that had happened to someone else. Phoebe yearned to comfort him, but she couldn't hug him, and in any case, it was clear the last thing he wanted was sympathy.

'But you can walk now. You must have worked extremely hard,' she said, cringing inwardly at the mundanity of her words. She couldn't imagine how it must have been for him, or how it was even now, to be one moment at the peak of his physical powers, a man who took his athletic prowess for granted, if what he'd told her in Paris of his derring-do was true, and then the next, to be like a baby, learning to walk. But he *could* walk now. So why did he no longer leave his house? And why, more pertinently, was he so certain that he would make his fiancée miserable? 'Does Miss Braidwood…?' Phoebe stopped, floundering. 'I'm sorry, I don't understand how your accident should affect your betrothal.'

'It is a long-standing arrangement made by our respective fathers when we were young. My father and Olivia's father were boyhood friends, so I suppose you could say I've known her all my life,' Owen said. 'The intention was always that we would marry when she reached her twenty-first birthday, which is in January next year. I'm not in love with her, never have been, any more than she is with me, though I had, as she had, always taken it for granted that we would marry when the time came. But I wanted more than that, Phoebe, more from my life than becoming a husband and possibly a father. When you and I first met, I had been living from day to day, enjoying every moment, thinking that the future would take care of itself. It finally dawned on me that I was in danger of frittering my life away. So I decided to go to Europe.'

'And what did you say to Miss Braidwood of your plans?'

Owen shrugged. 'As far as she was concerned, my life was my own until we married, and at that point, our marriage was more than two years away.'

'And then your accident changed everything at a stroke,' Phoebe said, her heart aching with the poignancy of this.

'When I returned to England,' Owen said flatly, 'I told Olivia that she must consider herself free of any obligation. I had all but given up on any hope of walking, but she refused point blank to abandon me in my pitiful state.'

'Well, and so I should hope,' Phoebe said indignantly. 'She would be a shallow person indeed, to do so.'

'Which is almost exactly what she said, and so I suppose you could say, she inspired my recovery, for I determined to walk again.'

'And you did.'

'And Olivia still refused to abandon me.'

Phoebe's nascent smile faltered. 'You learned to walk in order to...'

'Make it easier for Olivia to end our engagement. It is not as ridiculous an idea as it sounds. Everyone knows we have an understanding. She couldn't possibly jilt me when I was confined to my bed, but when I regained the use of my legs...'

'But that makes even less sense,' Phoebe exclaimed,

wondering if Owen was, despite appearances, just a little deranged. 'She had always intended to marry you, and you had always intended to marry her. You didn't wish to tie her to you when you couldn't walk, but now you can—what is to stop you doing what both of you had always expected to do?'

'I can walk, Phoebe, but I lost more than the use of my legs. I am not the man I once was.'

'Oh.' She could feel her cheeks burning as she realised what he must be implying. 'I am so sorry.'

'I don't want your pity. I don't want anyone's pity. You said you wished me to be candid with you, then I will be as plain as I can be. I am not physically incapacitated beyond what you see, but I am—I am much changed by the experience. I have no desire, no passion for anything.'

Such heart-wrenching words, yet they were spoken in that same odd tone, as if he were referring to someone else. 'Nothing?' Phoebe said, struggling to understand.

'And no one. You could say I have lost my appetite for life. Mostly, I'm indifferent.'

'Is it an illness? Did it happen as a result of your accident? Did you—I don't know, did you hit your head?'

'I don't know how it happened. I didn't wake up one morning and think, "I don't give a damn about the world", it just settled over me and I cannot shift it.'

'So you detached yourself from the world?'

'But I have signally failed to detach myself from

Olivia. The more reclusive I've become, the more determined she has become not to be seen by that world as a callous jilt. But she can see I am changed for the worse. The privileged and exciting life she imagined for herself as my wife and the dutiful penance of a life she would have to endure if she married me now could not be more different. I'm a stranger to her these days, I can see her looking at me and wondering who I am. But she can't contemplate *not* going through with it, because she is at heart a deeply conventional and dutiful young woman who would do anything to avoid the scandalous label of jilt, even if it means being trapped in a miserable marriage.'

'So you intend to take the decision out of her hands by marrying someone else?'

'Then she can be the wronged party and free, with a clear conscience, to get on with her life.'

'That is a very noble thing to do.'

'No, it's not. I don't want to marry a woman who feels obliged to stand by me. And her parents,' Owen said, his lip curling, 'are doing their damnedest to ensure that the poor girl does just that. I am a very rich man, and the marriage settlement my father agreed is extremely generous. Olivia doesn't consider it material, but her parents most certainly do, and apply their own particular pressure on her to strengthen her resolve any time it might seem that I have weakened it.'

'Are her family poor?'

'Not at all. Merely avaricious.'

'I don't know what to say. I can't imagine how you must feel.'

'Desperate,' Owen said. 'But determined. Olivia deserves a man who cares for her, who will give her the family she wants. I can't provide that, but I can give her the freedom to find someone who can. That aspect of my life is over, I am reconciled to that. All I ask of you is that you go through with the ceremony. Once I have made it impossible for Olivia to marry me, she will be free of all obligation towards me. In return, I will provide you with the funds to make your dream a reality, and in addition put my business acumen at your disposal.'

'I am not sure what to say,' Phoebe said, her head whirling.

'Then say yes.'

'It's an outrageous idea.'

'That should be no barrier. You are not exactly convention personified, are you?'

'No, but—do you really think Miss Braidwood will think she's had a lucky escape?'

'I am absolutely certain of the fact, and society's sympathy will be entirely with her too.'

'I am not a respectable woman, Owen. If the details of my life in Paris were ever discovered, it would cause a huge scandal for you.'

'I personally don't give a damn about that. Aside from the fact that my own former reputation was colourful to say the least, I no longer go out in society.'

'But if I launch my restaurant, I'll need society to sit at my tables, to eat my food.'

'Phoebe, in my experience notoriety whets the appetite.'

'But what about your family—I know your parents are both dead, but do you have any brothers or sisters?'

'No, I don't. But you do. What will they say if you marry me?'

'That with my reputation—or lack of it—I am fortunate to find any man to marry me.' Phoebe wrinkled her nose. 'No, that's not fair. I don't know. If they felt I had done so out of desperation rather than going to one of them with my tail between my legs, they would be very upset.'

'I don't want you to marry me because you're desperate. I want you to marry me only because you think it's an excellent idea.'

'A excellent idea!' She laughed nervously. 'It is the most preposterous notion, though no more preposterous than my own, to open a restaurant when I have absolutely no idea how to go about such a thing, I suppose.'

'You know all about food. I have the business sense. We will make an excellent team.'

'Dare we? No, no, it's impossible.'

'We have both already lost everything. We quite literally have nothing more to lose.'

'When you put it like that! I can't believe this—are you sure you're not teasing me?'

'I would not be so cruel.'

'No, no, of course you wouldn't.' She stared at him, quite dazed. 'You are offering me my dream. Yet you are asking so little in return.'

'You're mistaken. By setting Olivia free, you'll be

giving me a peace of mind that I've not had in a very long time. One thing I'm not asking of you, Phoebe. It's a delicate matter, but you wanted to know precisely what you'd be letting yourself in for, so I'm obliged to mention it. With regard to your private life.'

She blushed violently. 'I have not—I would not—'

'My interest in such things is over,' he interrupted her, 'but you are a beautiful, and sensual young woman. You were badly hurt by Solignac, but you'll get over that and when you do, all I ask is that you are discreet. It has always seemed to me one of the great hypocrisies of so-called respectable society, that an unattached woman is expected to remain chaste and you will, in that sense at least, be unattached.'

'Owen, my only and overriding attachment would be to my restaurant, my only desire to repay your faith in me by making a success of it.'

'At present, but time, they say is a great healer. As I said, all I ask of you is discretion.'

'You don't think time will heal you?'

'If I can be the catalyst to your success, then there will have been a positive outcome, after all, to our encounter at the Procope. Then I might feel better.'

His words and the memory of him, so full of vitality and hopes and dreams brought a lump to her throat. 'My heart is telling me to say yes, but I followed my heart once before, and look where it got me.'

'I, on the other hand, think only with my head. Being quite literally heartless,' Owen said with a small, mocking smile, 'has made me an excellent businessman. But I won't push you. Take your time, think about it.'

Phoebe thought about it for all of thirty seconds before her smile burst through. 'Let's do it,' she said. 'How quickly do you think we can get married?'

Chapter Four

One week later

Phoebe looked on, slightly stunned, as Owen shook hands with the clergyman before he and Bremner, who had been pressed into service as one of the witnesses to their marriage, left the room to show him out. The other witness, Owen's friend Jasper Forsythe, was in the process of opening a bottle of champagne. Black-haired and with striking hazel eyes, Mr Forsythe was immaculately turned out and rather haughtily handsome, but the warmth of his smile, the genuine pleasure he seemed to be taking from the occasion, had gone a long way towards putting Phoebe at her ease.

'Thank you, Mr Forsythe, that's most welcome,' she said, accepting a brimming glass from him, 'I confess I found that more nerve-racking than I had anticipated.'

'May I be the first to offer my congratulations, Mrs Harrington. And please call me Jasper. I can't tell you how delighted I was when Owen told me he was about to tie the knot. You may just be exactly what he needs.'

'Thank you. I hope our union will prove to be mutually beneficial.'

Jasper smiled. 'He told me that you met in Paris just over two years ago, and he'd never forgotten you. He kept that one under his hat! Having made your acquaintance, I can understand why you made such an impression on him. I've not seen him so—so animated since he returned to England.'

'You are his oldest friend, I gather.'

'And the only one of our circle he remains in contact with,' Jasper said, his smile fading slightly, 'though I'm hoping that now you have entered his life, things will change.'

'Oh, we have no plans to launch ourselves into society.' Not in the manner you might expect, at any rate, Phoebe added to herself for Owen had not, she knew, confided their plans to Jasper.

'That's a shame. I had hoped—before his accident, Mrs Harrington, Owen was…'

'Phoebe, please. Tell me what he was like in those days.'

'Oh, brimming with life. He never stood still for more than five minutes. From the crack of dawn he'd be up and about. Most mornings we'd meet up to go riding, long before anyone else was around, you know, so that we could actually get some proper exercise, but sometimes we'd go running instead.' Jasper grinned. 'You should have seen the looks on the faces of anyone we did come across then, the pair of us dressed in just shirts and breeches, running full tilt around St James's. We'd start at the park there, then into Green Park and round Hyde Park and back again—though some days Owen insisted we took in Regent's Park too. *"Clears the tubes, old man, sets one up for the day,"* he used to say. I was in awe of his boundless energy.'

'Do you still run, Mr—Jasper?'

He shook his head. 'I was never really that keen on the actual running, to be honest, though it certainly helped work off the effects of overindulgence the night before. It's not the same without Owen. I still box and fence, but it's all such a serious business with the younger set these days. That's the thing I miss most about Owen—he never took anything seriously.'

'You must see a very great change in him, then?'

'I hardly recognise him, to be perfectly honest. He's still in there somewhere, my old friend, but it's as if—you'll think me fanciful, as if there's a glass wall between us. It's the pain, I suppose. He doesn't complain, but it must be constant. Has he told you what happened?'

'Not in any detail.'

'No, he never refers to it.' Jasper gave himself a shake. 'Anyway, enough of that. This is a fresh start for you both, and I'm honoured to have been able to witness the dawn of it.'

He smiled as the door opened and Owen came back in. 'Good timing, I was just about to raise a toast,' he said, handing his friend a glass of champagne. 'To my best friend and his lovely new wife. Wishing you good health and happiness. Cheers.'

* * *

Phoebe's meagre wardrobe did not run to evening gowns. She'd had no time in Paris for shopping and scant opportunity to dress up. The dress she wore tonight dated from her one and only visit to Eloise and Alexander in London in the first year of their marriage. Eloise had designed it, and Madame LeClerc, the famous modiste had made it up. Copper-coloured organza silk was embellished with full sleeves of chiffon, puffed at the shoulders, tied tight with satin ribbons at the wrists. The décolleté was plunging, and Phoebe's curves were generous, but Madame LeClerc had cleverly satisfied both current fashion and modesty by using chiffon to create the illusion of a high neckline. A wide sash drew attention to Phoebe's waist, and a broad-hemmed border of ruched ribbon that reminded Phoebe of waves, weighted the gown, giving it a satisfying swish when she walked.

She sat down at her dressing table to tackle her coiffure. The prevailing fashion for regimented ringlets suited neither her hair nor her temperament. She gathered her rebellious tangle of curls into a loose knot, fixing it in place with a satin ribbon and allowing a few stray curls to soften the effect, knowing that many more would follow soon enough.

She had been married—she checked her watch—for the grand total of four hours, and resident in this town house for just over five. It had taken less than half an hour for the simple ceremony to transform her life. Not that she felt transformed, precisely. She felt, frankly, terrified. She had the means to achieve her dream now, but precisely *how* she was to set about achieving it, she had absolutely no idea. She hoped that Owen would know where to start, though how a man who didn't leave the house could help, she was at a loss to understand.

Jasper assumed that marriage would change Owen. Phoebe sincerely hoped so too though not in the manner Jasper suggested. She wished for Owen's sake that he hadn't become such a recluse, but she was grateful for her own sake that he was, since the idea of playing any sort of role as a London society hostess was anathema to her. As to what London society would make of such a hostess, if they discovered how she had lived in Paris—Phoebe shuddered at the very thought.

She studied the plain band of gold that Owen had placed on her finger. She was no longer Phoebe Brannagh, she was Mrs Owen Harrington and her husband was a virtual stranger whom she had met a total of four times before today. Once in Paris. Twice a week ago, when her arrival at his door prompted his proposal. And then yesterday, briefly, to agree the final arrangements.

The drawing room where the ceremony had taken place, thanks to the special licence Owen had obtained, had been cold, and though it was perfectly clean, it smelled musty, with the slightly forlorn air of a room only just brought out of hibernation. Now his town house was her home. His servants were hers to command. Tonight, she would sleep in this bedchamber, which had clearly not been in use for just as long as the drawing room. But before that, she was about to have dinner with her husband.

Gloves! She rummaged in her trunk, which she had not had time to unpack yet. The household appeared to be bereft of female staff, she had discovered with surprise when Bremner, clearly embarrassed, had arrived in response to her ringing her bedchamber bell. Did one wear gloves to dine at home? Owen certainly would be wearing gloves. He had even kept them on when signing their marriage certificate. Did he wear them when he was alone? When he slept?

What would their life together be like? She had absolutely no idea, and that, Phoebe realised, was actually a very liberating thought. Owen had no expectations of her as a wife, but he believed wholeheartedly in her as a chef, even though he had never tasted her food.

Her new husband's confidence in her was a huge antidote to the damage Pascal had inflicted. Though it made her toes curl in her evening slippers to think of him, she forced herself to do so, just to test how well the scars had healed. On reflection, her falling in love with the man was inevitable. He had from the moment she stepped into his kitchen been the very centre of her world, a bright, blinding sun for her to worship, whose attention she craved, whose admiration she would do almost anything to win. She had handed him her heart on a plate. And it had been a dish, she thought whimsically, that Pascal had found distinctly unpalatable, though he'd put up a good show of pretending otherwise! She had been from the first his most fervent admirer. One word of praise from him would keep her going for hours, days on end. One word of censure would set her back for much longer. When he paid no heed to her at all it was, quite literally, as if the sun had departed from her world, and she never doubted that it had been her own fault for failing to hold his attention.

Was it her fault? Was she simply not very interesting? Phoebe gave herself a shake. This morbid musing was serving no purpose. Pascal was in the past. Owen was her future, and her future started today. A future happily, as far as she was concerned, free of the messy complications of love and passion which, albeit for very different reasons, both she and her husband had forsworn. She twisted the wedding ring around on her finger. She wouldn't let him down, she vowed to herself. She would be a brilliant success, and all of London would vie for a table at her restaurant. Then finally Estelle would be forced to eat her words.

The thought of her twin brought a familiar pain to her heart, but tomorrow, Phoebe reminded herself, she would be able to share her news with both her sisters and with Aunt Kate too. They'd be shocked, but she hoped they'd be pleased for her too. She would tell them—what? The truth would bring at least one of them hotfoot to London, sure that she'd leapt out of the frying pan—ha, how apt!—and into the fire. No, she couldn't tell them the truth—but a version of it, such as the one Owen had evidently told Jasper? Smiling, Phoebe recalled the story that Eloise and Alexander had concocted to explain their marriage to the world. Why shouldn't she take a leaf out of her sister's very successful book and spare herself and Owen too, from her family's overly protective enquiries? She resolved to discuss it with him over dinner.

Talking of which, she was in danger of being late. With a sigh of relief she finally found a pair of long evening gloves and quickly pulled them on before giving her hair a final check. Heart thudding, she blew out the candles and headed down the stairs in search of her husband.

The dining room was far too grand for two people, Owen thought as he opened the double doors to inspect the room, but it was too late to change the arrangements now, and Bremner, unable to disguise his delight at having a mistress to breathe new life into the household, had gone to great efforts to make it welcoming. The leaves of the table had been removed to make it smaller, the curtains drawn against the dank October day, and the places set nearest the fire, though it was still screened. The crystal glasses gleamed, the wine Owen had carefully selected was decanted, and there were flowers on the table.

He made his way through to the morning room, which he'd decided to use for *aperitifs* instead of the vast acreage of the drawing room. It had been a mistake to have their ceremony there, for the room had a sad air of neglect, its cavernous nature emphasising the paltriness of their wedding party. Poor Phoebe, without either of her sisters or even her aunt by her side, had looked quite overwhelmed, though the decision not to have them there had been her own. He hoped fervently that she wasn't crying her eyes out in her bedchamber, already regretting her decision. While he was still slightly stunned by the speed at which his circumstances had changed, his overwhelming emotion was one of relief. And gratitude. Something else he'd not expressed nearly enough.

He would try to make amends tonight. He would wine her and dine her. He would do what he could to put her at ease, to make her forget that she was in a strange house married to a virtual stranger. Tonight he would forget the man he had become, the self-pitying hermit, and try to remember the man he had once been, the man she had met in Paris, charming and excellent company. Surely he could manage that, for a few hours? He certainly owed it to his new wife to try his damnedest.

He really was married! The proof was currently upstairs and about to join him for dinner, putting an end to his not-so-splendid isolation. This house was no longer a male bastion, but the implications of that hadn't even occurred to him until this moment. There wasn't a single female servant, so that would have to change. He'd assumed that life would go on as it had for the last two years, his world bounded by his own suite of rooms, while Phoebe did—what? He had no idea. He knew next to nothing about her. And vice versa. Yet here they were, starting out as a married couple and—and he had no idea what that meant.

Whatever happened, it meant change, and any alteration to the stifled, oppressive life he'd been living could only be a good thing. He'd been thinking of himself as the catalyst for Phoebe's success, but could his wife be the unwitting catalyst for changes in him? He wouldn't be able to hide away in his rooms any more. He wouldn't be able to take to his bed for no other reason than that he couldn't bear to get up. He would have to put on more of a show. They'd work together on the plans for the restaurant. They'd eat together—dinner at the very least. He'd not be spending his entire day in a chair or at his desk any more. He'd have to find a way to manage his pain. Return to those wretched exercises? The very idea made him want to scream with boredom, but when he pictured himself limping about the house in Phoebe's wake—damned if he would! So a return to the exercise regime it must be, he resolved, starting tomorrow morning.

He had the oddest feeling. Thinking at first it was hunger pangs, for he'd eaten next to nothing all day, as Bremner arrived, hovering in the doorway with a tray, Owen realised it was nervous anticipation.

'The champagne you ordered, sir.'

'Thank you. If you will set the tray down there. No need to open it, I will do that, but please put a few more bottles on ice for the staff,' Owen said, smiling.

His butler blinked, returning the smile with a watery one of his own. 'Thank you, Mr Harrington, that is most kind of you. We will be pleased to toast this most auspicious day.' Bremner permitted himself a wider smile. 'We were hoping—that is I expect there will be changes in the household, now that the house has a mistress.'

'I expect there will be,' Owen said. 'In fact I'm sure of it.'

* * *

Owen had dressed up for dinner, in a fashionable black tailcoat with a broad shawl collar and deep cuffs, and fitted grey trousers. His waistcoat was double-breasted, dark grey silk with silver buttons, his neck-cloth white, his only adornment a plain gold fob watch. His coat was not quite so tight-fitting as fashion decreed, but it was clearly new, presumably made by his tailor to previous measurements. Though her heart was now and for ever well and truly her own, her passion reserved for cooking, Phoebe was not blind. Whatever Owen thought of himself, however he might have changed since she had first encountered him, at an elemental level he was still a dangerously attractive man.

'I'm so sorry,' she said, 'did I keep you waiting?'

'You did not, but even if you had, the wait would have been worth it. You look ravishing.'

She blushed at the unexpected compliment. 'Eloise designed this gown. She has an excellent eye. I've only worn it a couple of times. I wasn't sure whether it was too much for tonight, but I am glad I put it on now, for you are all dressed up—I mean, you also look very well.'

'Like you, I don't have much call for evening dress these days. Will you take another glass of champagne?'

'Yes, please. I was too nervous to enjoy the one I had earlier.'

She watched Owen from under her lashes as he set about expertly opening the bottle, turning the cork carefully so that it came off with a quiet hiss and not a showy pop that spoilt the bubbles.

'To new beginnings,' he said, handing her a frothing glass.

'New beginnings.' She clinked her glass to his and took a sip.

'I was very remiss earlier,' Owen said, indicating that she take a seat on the sofa by the fire, easing himself into a chair opposite. 'I didn't tell you how very grateful I am.'

'That implies that I am doing you a favour. I thought we had agreed that our marriage benefitted both of us. Don't be grateful, be—I don't know, relieved?'

'I am very relieved. Jasper has offered to hand-deliver my letters to Olivia and her parents.'

'Is he acquainted with Miss Braidwood?'

'His sister was at school with her, but if you're worried that Jasper thinks that I've done Olivia anything other than an enormously good turn, you're quite wrong. He knows better than anyone other than Olivia herself, how miserable I'd make her. He took to you, I could tell.'

'He doesn't know me, Owen. What he'll think of me when he finds out about our plans...'

Owen gave a bark of laughter. 'I'll make sure to have a large brandy on hand when I tell him. For all he likes to kick over the traces, Jasper's a bit of a traditionalist.'

Phoebe's eyes widened. 'His approval of me is going to be very short-lived.'

'Oh, he'll come round. All you have to do is offer him a table at the opening night. Jasper likes to be at the forefront of fashion. You don't regret what we've done, do you, Phoebe?'

'Already! Hardly. I've no real idea what it entails— I mean aside from the restaurant—but I'm excited by the uncertainty, if that makes any sense? I don't suppose it does.'

'You can't imagine what the future holds, but anything is possible?'

'Yes, that's it.' She beamed. 'By marrying you, I've wiped the slate clean. Now I can start again. And no doubt make a whole lot of brand new mistakes,' she added, wincing. 'But I will have you to advise me on the financial and business aspects, to ensure that I don't make a disaster of the whole enterprise, won't I? There is little point in a restaurant that serves lovely food but doesn't make a profit. I'm a chef, I know nothing of commerce. I think—I hope our skills will complement one another. But let's not talk business tonight.'

'Very well. Tell me instead, if your room is comfortable?'

'Yes, thank you.'

Owen raised his brows. 'You're not a very good liar.'

'It is rather cold from being unused, that is all.'

'You are free to make whatever changes you see fit to the house, provided you leave my rooms as they are—I have my own suite on the ground floor. Bremner will be delighted to help, I am sure.'

Owen finished his champagne and made to rise, but Phoebe pre-empted him, jumping to her feet and topping up both glasses. 'Force of habit,' she said apologetically. 'I like to feed and water people. I don't just mean professionally, I mean it's what I've done all my life—but you don't want to hear about that.'

'But I do. We're married, and I know almost nothing about you.'

'Nor I you. It's very strange, isn't it?'

'Then in the interests of becoming better acquainted, tell me where your passion for cooking stems from.'

'Necessity, in the first instance. I cooked for my sisters—but you know, I don't really want to look back on those days, Owen. My parents had what you might call a tempestuous relationship, which meant we didn't see much of them. Eloise said that Mama was a social butterfly, trailing my father in her wake. I don't agree, I don't think she understood Mama, but I can see why she thought it and even I would admit that we were—oh, it doesn't matter. Today is about the future, not the past.'

'You're quite right. We have just toasted new beginnings. Let us live up to that and consign the past to ancient history, where it belongs. I am more than happy to look forward, but I think we should do so over dinner. Shall we?'

Phoebe preceded Owen, intuiting that he preferred his impaired gait to go unobserved, along the hall to the double doors where the eponymous Mr Bremner stood waiting for them. She took her seat at the table as her husband made his way into the room. Like the drawing room it was cold, but it was also very beautiful in precisely the kind of understated way she preferred, with pale green walls and white cornicing unadorned by gilt or gold leaf. The table had a highly polished

walnut veneer, a matching sideboard where their dinner was set out on heated trays, and long curtains of
dark green velvet drawn against the winter evening.
Bremner poured the wine and served the soup, before retiring.

'Chestnut soup,' Phoebe said, savouring the delicious
smell, then taking a spoonful. 'It is quite delicious. In
Paris, they set up braziers on all the street corners and
roast the chestnuts. I love the taste of them, piping hot
and fresh out of their shells.'

'They have such vendors in London too. I take it that
you are not well acquainted with the capital?'

'I have spent very little time here. I shall have to
buy a guide book to help me find my way around.'

'Are you keen to see the sights?'

Phoebe chuckled. 'Not the kind which most people
come to London to see. I want to explore the markets,
to see the range and quality of fresh produce available.
In Paris, we were very spoiled.'

'London has Smithfield for meat, Billingsgate for
fish and Covent Garden for fruit and vegetables, so I
don't think you'll lack for ingredients.'

'Good, then I can start to think about compiling my
menus. Though before that I'll need to decide what
kind of food our restaurant is going to serve. And after
that—or perhaps at the same time—I'll need to think
about who I'm going to serve it to. And where. That
is one of my biggest worries, because I don't know
London, and I don't even know who I'll be competing
with—if anyone at all. You can probably understand
now, why I would never in a thousand years have found

anyone to invest in me. You are probably already thinking you have thrown your money away.'

'*Your* money, not mine. Stop thinking about how much you have to do, Phoebe, the prospect is bound to be overwhelming. It's not one big leap you have to take, it's a whole series of small steps.'

'That is a much more sensible way to approach it.'

'Although that's easier said than done, when you are desperate to achieve your objective.'

He was staring down at his almost untouched soup, a grim look on his face. Phoebe set her own spoon down, tentatively putting her hand over his. 'But you've kept going,' she said. 'If I falter, then I'll have you as an example to follow.'

'I don't think I'm a particularly good role model. I certainly haven't been lately.' Owen slipped his hand from under hers and picked up his wine glass, taking a large sip. 'But that's something else I plan to change. Is the wine to your liking?'

'White burgundy,' Phoebe said, taking a sip. 'It is excellent.'

'It is from the Chateau Montendre, the Duc de Montendre's estate.'

'You know the Duke?'

'No, but my father did, back when he was plain Monsieur Bauduin, wine merchant. These days, he spends most of his time on his estates, where he produces his own vintages, but he continues to supply to a select few customers, including myself. I consume very little of it,' Owen added with a wry smile. 'I have a very full, and probably very valuable cellar as a result.'

'Perhaps I'll appropriate it and populate the restaurant wine list with it,' Phoebe teased.

Bremner arrived to clear the plates, making no comment on his master's lack of appetite, but granting her one of his grimacing smiles when she asked him to pass on her compliments to the chef.

'Oysters grilled with parsley and shallots,' she said appreciatively, picking up her fork for the next course, hoping to set an example with her own appetite. 'I adore oysters.'

Owen shuddered. 'I'm afraid I don't share your enthusiasm for them. I am ashamed to say that I once, for reasons I cannot now fathom, took part in an oyster-eating competition for a wager. It was more than ten years ago, but I haven't been able to face one since.'

'I assume you won?'

'Of course, but it all but did for me!'

'The ones you ate were most likely brined. These are very different. Won't you try one? They really are quite delicious.'

'I thank you, but no. Is there any food you don't enjoy?'

'I'm not particularly fond of turnip or parsnip. They are not even improved by being made into a cake.'

'You are teasing me, surely. I may be a philistine when it comes to food but that sounds just plain wrong.'

Phoebe giggled. 'Oh, no, I've made cakes with almost every vegetable you can name. I even once made one with grass.'

'Now I know you're joking.'

'I like to experiment with unusual flavours. I make

excellent lavender biscuits—though Aunt Kate says they taste a little too much of furniture polish for her liking. And I've made ices flavoured with herbs— thyme, rosemary, camomile.'

'And will your customers be able to taste any of these delights?'

'Who knows? I do know these oysters are delightful. And the vol-au-vent look delicious. They are called *bouchée à la reine* in France. The filling in these is chicken and mushroom, though you can put anything you like in them.'

'Including grass?'

'Perhaps not quite anything. Would you like one?'

'I'll save myself for the main course. And while I remember, I'll have a word with Bremner about hiring some female staff. I should have thought of it earlier.'

'Thank you. What about our—our domestic arrangements, Owen? Shall we dine together? I would like to, but I don't want to disrupt your—your routine.'

He laughed shortly. 'You will be a very welcome interruption. My *routine* has become quite tedious.'

'When I was working gruelling shifts in the kitchens, I used to long for a few days of idleness, but these last few months, doing nothing—save for the fruitless task of trying to find new employment—has been chastening. And very lonely. To be perfectly honest, Pascal wasn't exactly riveting company. He could be fascinating when he talked about cooking, but he wasn't interested in much else, and he certainly wasn't interested in me.' Looking up, she smiled. 'In fact, I have been quite starved of conversation since our Elmswood Coven broke up. Let that be a warning to you—you'll be sick and tired of my endless chatter before the week is out.'

'I doubt it.' Owen surprised her by touching her hand. 'Perhaps it's because you don't know me and have no expectations of me, but I find I'm enjoying your company.'

'Thank you. The feeling is mutual.'

Bremner appeared once more, and Owen released her hand while the braised beef and spinach ragout was served. He took a small bite before setting his cutlery down. 'You must speak to Murray, my—our cook about menus, he'll be delighted to be consulted.'

'Shall I be expected to—will there be callers, Owen? I don't even know if our marriage will be formally announced.'

'I'll put a notice in the press, but I thought you'd want to inform your family first.'

'I do. I was thinking though, I am not sure that I want to tell them the truth. Not yet.'

'You think they'll disapprove?'

'I think they'll worry, and I don't want that.'

'So what will you tell them?'

'What did you tell Jasper? Not the truth, I don't think. He was far too—enthusiastic,' Phoebe said. 'He seems to be under the impression that I will launch you back into society.'

Owen laughed harshly, 'Jasper thinks that a few nights on the town will cure me of my doldrums. Not that he put it quite like that.'

'He obviously cares about you a great deal.'

'I told him that we'd met in Paris, which is the truth.

I implied that my accident had prevented me from wooing you, and you had come in search of me,' Owen said. 'I hope you don't mind, but he does care, and I am tired of disappointing him. He thought it very romantic.'

'You mean he thinks that we are in love?'

'I didn't say that, but he leapt to that conclusion, obviously. I'm sorry if I've embarrassed you.'

'You haven't. In fact the same story might suffice for my sisters,' Phoebe said. 'If you don't mind?'

'Why should I? Do you think they'll believe you?'

'Owen, despite what you think, you are a very attractive man. And more importantly, you have faith in me, which I shall be sure to tell my sisters. I'll reassure them that you are rich enough to invest in a dozen failed restaurants and not even notice the losses.'

'I'm only investing in one, and what is more I know that it won't fail.' Owen picked up his glass of burgundy. 'They will be toasting our future health and happiness below stairs as we speak. I'd like to propose a toast too. To Phoebe. For being brave enough to take me on, and for continuing to dream her dream. I thank you, and I wish you every success.'

Touched, she had to swallow a lump in her throat. 'I will need all your best wishes and more.' She lifted her glass. 'To Owen. For being brave enough to take me on, and for allowing me to dare to hope that I might one day realise my dream. Here's to making a success of this—this convenient marriage of ours.'

'Fortuitous,' Owen said. 'I prefer to think of it as fortuitous.'

'Very well then, here is to our fortuitous marriage.'

They touched glasses, their eyes meeting as they each took a sip, remaining locked as they set their glasses down. Owen took her hand in his. He lifted it to his mouth, pressing a kiss to her gloved fingertips. Something crackled between them, an awareness of themselves as husband and wife on their wedding night, and the ghost of themselves in Paris over two years ago, looking into each other's eyes in just this way. Then like now, knowing that nothing could come of it. Experiencing again that brief moment of inexplicable, but unmistakable sense of longing. Owen's fingers tightened on hers. And then he let her go.

'I'm afraid I keep early hours these days,' he said.

'No, of course, I mean please don't let me—I'm very tired, anyway.'

Phoebe got to her feet at the same time as he did, and then they both stood, hesitating, as if unwilling to part after all. 'Goodnight, Owen.'

He reached out, as if he would touch her cheek, then dropped his hand. 'Goodnight, Phoebe.' He opened the door, and she brushed past him into the hallway, picking up her candle from the table and lighting it. She was aware of him watching her as she climbed the stairs, and it was only as she turned to climb the second flight that she heard the dining-room door close softly, and the slight dragging sound of her husband's footstep as he made his way slowly to the opposite end of the house and his own bed.

Chapter Five

Owen jerked back into consciousness with a start, his sheets a tangled knot around his legs, his body clammy, a sheen of sweat making his nightshirt cling to him. The room was pitch black. The muscles in his shoulders and his arms ached, which meant he'd been having what he called his reaching dream. He had no memory of what it was he was reaching for, no idea how he came to be reaching for it in the first place, but he always woke at the same point, when it became hopelessly clear that he would not succeed, no matter how hard he strove, and the high-pitched wailing which accompanied his desperate attempts to stretch those vital inches further came to an abrupt halt.

Hands shaking, heart pounding, Owen struggled to sit up, fighting the overwhelming sense of despair and terrible sorrow, the enormous weight of guilt at his failure, which made his chest heave as he suppressed a violent sob. Forcing himself to breathe deeply, he counted each breath in, held it, breathed out, several

times before his hands had stopped trembling enough
to light his candle and check the time on his watch.
Three minutes past three. The night was only halfway through, but he couldn't face yet another failed
attempt at sleep, knowing from bitter experience that
the nightmare was lurking like a lone wolf tracking
its prey, waiting to claim him again.

Shivering, he pulled on his dressing gown and
headed for his workroom where, unlike the cold ashes
in the grate of his bedroom, the fire would still be
smouldering behind the screen, ready to be rekindled.
He threw on a few coals before replacing the screen,
settling himself in his chair with his leg on the footstool. His violent tossing and turning had caused him
to wrench his damaged hip. The constant, grating ache
which he sometimes thought was his shattered body's
way of punishing him for the trauma he had put it
through, was now a sharp stabbing pain. In the past,
he had turned to opium to help him endure such torrid
nights. Only when he caught himself deliberately in-
ducing oblivion to prevent such nights occurring, had
he realised how reliant he had become on the drug. He
couldn't give in to that temptation even if he wanted
to now, for he had had the presence of mind to ensure
his resolve was not tested by the simple expedient of
refusing to give it house room.

Why had it happened on this night of all nights? His
wedding night! The first night in a very long time when
he was not burdened with thoughts of Olivia, when he
had surely earned a peaceful night's sleep. And yet
here he was, shivering, aching, the hazy memory of

his nightmare taunting him, the details as always just tantalisingly out of reach.

Closing his eyes and resting his head against the chair-back, Owen sighed with frustration. He was heartily sick of himself, of the front he was forced to put on for the benefit of his staff and now his wife, of being inured to his injuries, of accepting that his recuperation had gone as far as it could go.

He was far from content with his lot. Seeing his stern butler begin to thaw, basking in the warmth of Phoebe's smile over the course of the day, made Owen realise, guiltily, how much his own mood had affected the household, how dour he had become. And in Jasper's eyes there had been hope that perhaps Owen was finally on the road to recovery.

Was there hope? Tonight, he had made conversation, he'd even laughed, over dinner with Phoebe. He had forgotten what it felt like to enjoy the simple pleasure of being in another person's company. He had been reminded tonight, but the memory was bittersweet because although there had been moments that could be mistaken for spontaneity on his part, looking back over the evening, maintaining his side of the conversation had been an effort. He'd had to imagine how the old Owen would have responded, taking his previous self as his role model. He had pulled it off, by and large, although there had been a couple of occasions when Phoebe's smile froze as she studied him carefully. They had passed, and she had probably put it down to the strangeness of the situation.

But there had been a moment when he had stopped

being self-conscious. Saying goodnight to his beautiful wife, taking her hand in his, he had fleetingly remembered what desire felt like. He screwed his eyes shut, trying to recapture that elusive moment, the simple pleasure of proximity, the sweet, dragging tug of attraction, the anticipation as their eyes met, and the possibility of a kiss hung between them. He ached with the bittersweet delight of it, yearned to experience it again, longed to be able to touch her, skin on skin, wanting that even more than the kiss they had not shared.

Owen dropped his head into his hands. What was he doing, torturing himself like this, imagining what he knew to be simple fantasy? Just a few hours ago, he had toasted new beginnings. So why not turn his mind to actually thinking about a fresh start instead of looking over his shoulder regretfully at the past and what he had lost for ever. He could not be the man he had once been, but he could try to make the best of the one he was now.

For a start, he could do a damned sight better than blithely wave Phoebe off to explore London's fresh produce markets unaccompanied. London was not Paris. The areas around Smithfield and Billingsgate were not safe, especially in the early hours when market trading was at its peak. He wasn't fit enough to wander around on foot with her, but he could get Jasper to purchase some fresh horses on his behalf since his stables had lain empty for years. He'd have his town coach or the barouche cleaned up, and he could give her the grand tour of London himself.

The heavy, black cloud that permanently hung over him began to lift. Something like a flicker of excitement kindled in his belly. What's more, if he did resume his exercises as he'd planned, he could conceivably escort her to one of those damned markets she was so keen on. It wasn't as if he'd need to worry about meeting anyone he knew there. All he had to do was work on his strength and his stamina—and if he worked hard, he could be ready in as little as a few weeks.

Almost immediately, his enthusiasm flagged. He had followed the prescribed exercise regime diligently for a while, but he'd reached the point where it made no difference, he reminded himself. His doctors, who already thought Owen had worked a small miracle by getting back on to his feet, told him to lower his expectations. But his doctors had only ever known him after his accident. Owen had been an athlete. The rush of pleasure came not from besting anyone, but from challenging himself to run faster and longer to push himself to new limits, the more taxing the better, because what was the point in achieving an easy victory! That was what he'd loved so much about gymnastics. He smiled, remembering the Russian acrobat who had sparked his interest telling him, in that condescending way of his, that it took dedication to master even the most basic of moves. He'd been right, it had taken months, but he'd been wrong in imagining that Owen would give up. He never had, managing to practice even when he was on his travels, rarely missing a day. Until that day.

He missed it. He missed the complete control he'd had over his body. It was bloody hard work, but worth it, when he finally held a position, when his muscles, which had resisted and resisted a particular move, suddenly found the knack. God, he missed that. Once, and only once, a tentative enquiry of his doctors had produced astonished looks followed by vehement admonitions that he must never attempt anything so taxing. He must accept that there were some things he would never do again.

But what if they were wrong? Instead of focusing on what he couldn't do, why not try to explore what might be possible? Owen got to his feet, rolling back his shoulders. He could not control his sick mind, but he could try to reclaim his damaged body. It was an appealing idea. It would at least give him a purpose, and a goal. But he mustn't look too far ahead, nor expect the impossible of himself. Small steps, as he'd said to Phoebe. Though not too small. He'd had his fill of the tedious exercises his physician had prescribed, he needed to do something he enjoyed. He couldn't contemplate going back to the public gymnasium in his condition, but it might be possible to have a small gymnasium constructed here.

To hell with the doctor's regime, he was going to try his own. Casting off his dressing gown, he cleared a space in the middle of the floor and began the slow process of warming up his neglected muscles.

'Are you sure you want to do this?' Phoebe asked.
'We are going for a carriage ride, I'm not setting

out to scale Ben Nevis,' Owen retorted, making for
the front door.

'Oh, you've had the hood put up,' she said, disappointed, thinking it would spoil the view, then realising almost immediately why. 'Excellent idea,' she
amended.

'It is, because I think it might rain at some point,'
Owen said testily, 'not because I am not worried someone might recognise me. Now, shall we go?'

'Please.' She preceded him down the front steps into
the dank October air. She had not been outside in the
six days since they had been married, occupying herself
with putting the few rooms in the town house which she
wished to use to rights, and establishing herself with
Mr Murray, the cook. Owen was carefully making his
way down the steps, wearing a greatcoat, a hat and a
look of grim determination. She eyed the waiting barouche, wondering how on earth he was going to get up
the steep steps and into the carriage, sick with nerves
lest he fall and deciding the best course of action would
be to accept the coachman's invitation to climb in first.
But Owen, as she observed while pretending very hard
not to, got in with surprising ease.

'I would normally have taken the reins myself,' he
said, sitting down beside her, 'but since this is my first
outing in some time, I decided discretion was the better part of valour.' Owen nodded to the coachman to
drive on. 'I thought we'd take a drive along the river,
and if the rain holds off, round Richmond Park. Seeing the city from the outskirts gives you a better sense
of it, and the air is a lot fresher.'

'I miss the countryside, though I love the excitement of the city—not that I know any city save Paris, mind you.'

'You'll get to know London soon enough.'

'Don't you miss enjoying what it has to offer, Owen?,' Phoebe asked impulsively. 'Owen?'

He blinked, and her heart contracted, for he looked for a moment utterly lost. The enormity of what he was doing struck her afresh. The last thing he'd want would be for her to draw attention to the strain it was putting him under. 'I had a letter from Eloise this morning,' she said. 'I think there were more exclamation marks than words. To say that my news came as an enormous surprise is something of an understatement.'

She was rewarded with a faint smile. 'I hope a not-altogether-unpleasant surprise?'

'It appears Alexander, her husband, seems to have put in a good word for you. "A most enterprising and well-respected investor" was how he described you to my sister, though how he knows that, I've no idea.'

'I have a certain reputation in the financial world,' Owen replied.

'I didn't realise. I thought—oh, it doesn't matter, I know nothing of such things.'

'You thought that because I see no one, no one is aware of my success? My success speaks for itself, unfortunately—I am a "name" in the city.'

'Do people seek your advice, then?'

'Often, and offer to pay me handsomely for it, but the whole point of the game I play is risk, a question of odds. I can easily afford to lose. Others can't.'

'But you don't lose.'

'Not often, but I have done, quite spectacularly too.'

'Really? But then why don't you stop, keep what you have safe?'

Owen shrugged. 'Because I enjoy the game.'

'Something for which I am extremely grateful, though I hope I won't be one of your spectacular failures.'

'I wish that you'd have a bit more faith in yourself. Stop looking over your shoulder at what happened in Paris. I thought you were determined to prove Solignac wrong?'

'And my sisters too. Though I didn't tell Eloise about my plans. I'm afraid I allowed her to think that we had fallen in love. She's so besotted herself, to be honest, I think that even if I had told her the truth she'd have persuaded herself that we fell in love at first sight but—well anyway, I thought I'd better let you know.'

'Why? Is she planning to visit?'

'Oh, goodness, no.' Phoebe beamed. 'I quite forgot, Eloise is expecting a baby. I'm going to be an aunt! I think I forgot because I can't quite believe it. She never wished for children, but I think she has revised her opinion given that piece of news garnered the most exclamations marks in her letter. So she won't be coming to London any time soon, though she has invited us to visit her in Lancashire.'

'When will you tell her about the restaurant?'

'When there is something to tell.'

'Fair enough. And has Estelle replied to your letter?'

'Briefly, to offer her congratulations. I can't tell whether or not she meant it.'

'Did you tell *her* the truth about the terms of our marriage?'

Phoebe shook her head. 'I will when the time is right.'

'Are you fretting about her?'

Phoebe considered this. 'I don't like being on bad terms with her but we will resolve our differences. We always do. Anyway, she's probably enjoying being on her own. Being a twin is lovely, but it can be quite suffocating, you know? No, how could you. I can't imagine being without my sisters.'

'Even though they suffocate you?' Owen teased.

Phoebe shook her head. 'It's not exactly that, but they are over-protective. No one knows you as well as a sister. They know all your foibles, they remember all the embarrassing moments one endures while growing up. And when you have a twin especially, they know your thoughts, sometimes, even before you have a chance to voice them.'

'Your dinner conversations were conducted in silence, then?'

'Our dinner conversations were a noisy rabble! Living in a house with three very opinionated women—well, it was a case of she who shouts the loudest.'

'And I'm willing to bet that your voice was often the quietest. It's obvious that you hold your aunt and your sisters in a great deal of awe.'

'Respect,' she corrected him, frowning. 'And rightly

so. Aunt Kate took the three of us in when she was the same age as I am now.'

'I had no idea. I imagined someone much older.'

Phoebe giggled. 'If you meet her—when you meet her—you'll be astonished. She is extremely pretty and she's quite petite, one of those women you think would struggle to lift her fork to eat, until she turns those eyes on you, and you realise there's a core of steel running right through her. She and Eloise are very alike. My eldest sister was forced to grow up far too quickly—I'm afraid Mama was not a very maternal kind of mother.'

'People who are determined to enjoy life to the full, as I remember you said your mother did, tend to be rather selfish creatures, I'm afraid.'

'Mama was not selfish! Although that is what Eloise believes.'

Owen held up his hands. 'I only meant—'

'There are some people who simply break the mould,' Phoebe interrupted him, glowering. 'One shouldn't judge them by conventional standards.'

Clearly not, he thought, taken aback by her vehemence. 'The little I recall of my own mother,' he said, in an effort to mollify her, 'leads me to believe she wasn't particularly maternal either. I remember being brought down from the nursery to be cooed over before dinner, and when I was at school, she would occasionally accompany my father to sports days. "All that mud, and sweaty, smelly little boys,"' Owen mimicked. 'She was very beautiful, and as I recall, delighted when those sweaty, smelly little boys gazed upon her as if she was an angel descended from heaven to the playing fields of Eton.'

To his relief, Phoebe relaxed. 'How proud you must have been when she did visit you. All the other boys must have been so envious.'

Owen, who recalled simply being mortified, shrugged.

'What age were you when you lost her?'

'Ten, I think, perhaps nine.'

'As young as that? Oh, Owen, you must have been devastated.'

Once again he shrugged. She was drawing parallels that did not exist but he didn't want to disillusion her with the truth. 'I was away at school. It's not the done thing to be upset at school, one must take it like a man.'

'Our little brother, Diarmuid, was on his way to Eton with my parents when their boat sank in a storm in the Irish sea, and we lost all three of them.'

'All at once! That's dreadful. *You* must have been devastated.'

'We all were, though Eloise as usual put a brave face on. That's when Aunt Kate took us in. I don't like to remember those days. We felt as if our world was turned upside down.'

'It was. Poor Phoebe.'

'And poor Estelle and Eloise too. But we had each other, and Aunt Kate too. And though no one could ever replace Mama, even I can see that Aunt Kate gave us a much more stable home. And a happy one too.'

'The Elmswood Coven?'

Phoebe laughed. 'You remember.' Her smile became

whimsical. 'Only to think that my little brother was headed for the same school you attended—though your time wouldn't have overlapped, for Diarmuid was four years younger than Estelle and I. Mama didn't want him to go, but Papa said it would be the making of him. Diarmuid was adorable, but he was terribly spoilt and dreadfully lazy, which I don't think would have been in his favour at school.'

'They do rate brawn considerably higher than brain. I was fortunate enough to excel at all sports.'

Owen, Phoebe thought, would have been popular however good or bad he was at sports, a charismatic little boy, just like the man he had become. And an athlete. Jasper had told her so, but she'd not realised how much a part of Owen's life it had been. No wonder his accident had brought him so low.

'So your brother was the favourite, I gather?'

Phoebe started, wondering if her thoughts had been written on her face, as they so often were. Owen did not like anyone to feel sorry for him. 'Diarmuid,' she said, trying to recall the thread of their conversation. 'Yes, indeed. The only son, and much longed for. I think they had all but given up hope, and I do know Mama dreaded having another girl. I remember her telling us so.'

'How very thoughtful of her.'

'Oh, she didn't mean to be unkind,' Phoebe said. 'But children are not good for a woman's figure, she said, and Mama's figure was—she was quite simply the most beautiful woman I've ever seen. When she entered a room, she drew everyone's attention—you simply couldn't take your eyes off her. She was the toast of Dublin, and would have been the toast of London too, if Papa had taken her there.'

'But Papa was rightly cautious.'

Phoebe frowned at his tone. 'It wasn't Mama's fault that she was so beautiful, or that so many people sought her attention. That was why she had so little time for us girls—there simply wasn't enough of her to satisfy everyone.'

'And she chose to satisfy herself. No, don't leap to her defence, Phoebe, my mother was the same, content to hand me into the care of my nurse or my tutor or my school.'

'Well then, you do understand,' Phoebe said, though she didn't really think he did, any more than Eloise understood their mother. 'Though actually,' she felt obliged to add in defence of her eldest sister, 'it was mostly Eloise who took care of us. We lived in the wilds of the Irish countryside. Our constantly changing governesses didn't much enjoy the isolation.'

'Any more than your mother did, I presume.'

She shrugged uncomfortably. 'Anyway, that is how Eloise comes to be such a strong person.'

'With a dominant voice at the dinner table?'

'Exactly.' She smiled at him, relieved.

'And Estelle too?'

'Estelle is the family comic. She is so funny, Owen, she used to have us in fits of laughter. She could easily take the London stage by storm, if she does not choose to lead an orchestra instead.'

'Which leaves Phoebe to be the quiet one—or are you the peacemaker?'

'No, I simply make sure the rest of them are well fed. They are very appreciative, I assure you.'

'But they think you are overreaching yourself in wishing to make a career of it?'

'What if they're right? They think I need protecting.'

'And in doing so they inadvertently stifle you,' Owen said. 'You don't need protecting. If you did, you'd have run to Eloise, instead of which...'

'I ran to you.'

'You asked me to help you to help yourself. There's a big difference.'

Phoebe considered this. It sounded very feasible. 'Perhaps.'

'Definitely,' Owen said firmly. 'You're perfectly capable of standing on your own two feet, and of springing back from adversity.'

She smiled. 'I like that. I shall spring up from the depths of failure and surprise them all with my success, like a jack-in-the-box.'

'A very beautiful jack-in-the-box.'

'Oh. Thank you. I'm nowhere near as lovely as Mama though.'

'I won't argue with you because it would be futile.'

'Well it would.' Which sounded rather defensive, Phoebe realised, even though it was true. 'I've talked far too much, and likely bored you to death. You'll have to learn to do what my sisters do, and talk over me.'

'I happen to enjoy your conversation. I happen to

find you interesting. All that complicated sibling rivalry, to an only child, is fascinating.'

'It's not rivalry. You don't understand.'

'Oh, I rather think I do, but we won't argue. Tell
me, has your aunt added her congratulations to those
of your sisters'? We've been married nearly a week,
we really should put a notice in the press.'

'I haven't heard directly from Aunt Kate. Eloise told
me that she was away somewhere on urgent business. I
can't imagine where, Aunt Kate never goes anywhere.
But anyway—if you must tell the world, then you can
safely do so now.'

'I must. I doubt the world will be much interested,
but Olivia is eager to have the announcement made,
according to Jasper.'

'He's spoken to Miss Braidwood? And how is she?'

'As I hoped, quietly relieved. She will make a be-
lated formal debut next Season.'

'And her parents?'

'Owen shrugged. Their congratulations read like
condolences, but frankly I've never given much of a
damn about what they thought.'

They were crossing the Thames, and Owen turned
to look out at the river. One of his hands still covered
hers. Phoebe wondered if he had forgotten, and decided
not to draw attention to the fact. What was he thinking? How did it feel, to be out in the open air like this
after—how long? He had admitted at dinner one night
that his 'disconnection' from the world, as he called
it, had been a gradual thing, not a sudden decision.
Why? she longed to ask him. Why had he lost his ap-

petite for life? And what had killed it? It didn't take a genius to work out that his accident had involved a fire. He certainly displayed an unnatural wariness of it, for every fire in the town house was screened and meagre. To have come so close to losing everything, she thought, should surely have made him more determined to embrace life rather than abdicate from it. She couldn't understand it, but she did know that this trip he was making for her, with her, marked a significant step forward. And she also knew better than to say so.

So she held his hand, and she inched a little closer to him on the seat of the barouche, and she watched his profile, trying not to let him see that she was watching him, and at some point her concern for him and her gratitude and her admiration for his courage changed into awareness of him. Of the length of his leg against hers. Of his booted foot against hers. And of his hands, covering hers.

The clouds had scudded away on the breeze, leaving a sky that was bright blue, and a weak sun that was almost lemon in colour. As they turned into Richmond Park, a small herd of grazing deer lifted their heads to watch them pass, a stag, two fully-grown hinds and four youngers, gazing haughtily and quite unafraid. Russet leaves still clung tenaciously to the trees. The air was sharp as she inhaled the fresh grassy scent of the countryside. Phoebe lifted her face, closing her eyes, suddenly, for the first time in an age, relaxed and content. Opening them again, she found Owen gazing down at her, and smiled. 'This is so lovely,' she said.

'It is,' he agreed, raising his free hand to smooth

back a curl which had escaped from her bonnet and
clung to her cheek. The brush of his fingers on her
skin, even in his gloves, sent a frisson shivering down
her spine. She smoothed her cheek into his hand, turning her face so that her lips brushed his palm. She
heard the sharp intake of his breath. Saw the flare of
awareness in his eyes. Then the barouche drew to a
halt, and the coachman turned to enquire which direction they should take home, and Owen dropped her
hand. The moment was gone, over so quickly Phoebe
persuaded herself that she had imagined it.

The weather turned wet and miserable over the next
few weeks as November settled in. The announcement
of their nuptials had brought a surprising number of
letters and cards of invitation, considering that most
of London society would have retired to the country
by now. Owen, reading names he had confined to his
past, did what he always did with such communications
and left them unanswered. Beside him at the breakfast
table, Phoebe was sipping her tea and frowning over
the latest sheaf of commercial properties available for
lease which his lawyer had sent for their consideration.
There had been three trips over the last ten days in the
town coach to visit a selection of them, but she had
been surprisingly unenthusiastic about all of them.

'What's wrong?' Owen asked. 'Don't you like any
of these?'

'They all have merit.'

'But?'

'There are too many unanswered questions to be

able to make a decision. I don't know what would be the best location because I don't know who the clientele will be. I don't know how big it should be because I don't know how many covers I'll be serving. I don't know what I want the interior to look like. I don't know—I don't know anything,' she finished, her lip trembling. 'I think you've made a big mistake.'

Owen pushed aside his coffee and his empty plate to reach over for her hand. 'It's not like you to sound so defeatist.'

'I'm not. Only a little. You've found all these properties and personally taken me to view them. Don't think I don't know what an effort that has been for you, and I feel dreadful, Owen, offering so little in return.'

'It's not an effort. I have enjoyed our little expeditions.'

'Have you?'

'Why would you think otherwise?'

'I can't tell, sometimes, whether you really are enjoying something or simply acting as if you are. You're very adept at it.'

He released her hand, taken aback by this. He knew that it had been an act that he put on every moment of the day, but it had become so easy for him to be with her that he didn't have to think, most of the time, about how to behave. When he disappeared into himself as he did occasionally, Phoebe rarely remarked upon it, allowing him to pretend she hadn't noticed. And then there were the moments when he became so caught up in the act that he fooled himself into thinking that what he was feeling was real. Wanting to kiss her. To touch her. To hold her. Imagining that her touch could bring him back to life.

It seemed to him that he paid for such foolishness with his nightmares which, though less frequent, had taken a new turning. His usual reaching dream had ceded precedence to another, more sinister scenario in which he wandered the corridors of some sort of hospital or asylum opening door after door on to empty rooms. He was as desperate in this nightmare as in his other dream to find something, as overwhelmed with grief and guilt when he awoke. And there was the same high-pitched wailing too, which jolted him awake when it stopped. He had always assumed that his reaching dream had something to do with his mind's distorted memory of his accident, but this dream, which he'd had again last night, made no sense at all.

Phoebe folded up the stack of papers and wandered off to the window to gaze out at the rain-drenched street. She thought he was having another blank moment, Owen realised, and was giving him time to recover. He joined her at the window, where she was tracing the path of a particularly plump raindrop with her finger. She wore her hair in a simple knot on top of her head, her copper curls trailing down over her shoulder. Her gown of dark blue wool was trimmed with a ruffle of white lace leaving the long line of her nape exposed. She didn't wear perfume, but smelled of lemon soap. Before his accident, he'd have put his arm around her waist and drawn her back against him. Her hair would have tickled his chin. Or he'd have buried his nose in the warm, soft skin of her nape, his hands sliding up from her waist to cup her breasts. She'd press the soft rump of her bottom against him, and she'd feel that he was hard, and then she'd twist around in his arms, her mouth curved into a sensual smile, and she'd kiss him.

Phoebe turned around, bumping into him, and Owen instinctively caught her.

'I didn't realise you were so close,' she said.

'I'm sorry.'

She smiled up at him, shaking her head. 'What for?'

He made to let her go, but she caught his hand. 'Do you ever take these off?'

Completely thrown, still half-caught up in their imagined embrace, he shook his head. 'Only when I go to bed.'

'Wouldn't they benefit from a little air now and then?'

'The scars are healed.' He snatched his hand away.

'Alexander, Eloise's husband, calls her painfully ob-servant, and she is, but it's a trait we all three sisters have to a degree. We notice everything.' She coloured. 'I have no right to comment on your behaviour. You are coping admirably with something which would defeat most people, including me.'

'Am I? By acting out a part?'

Phoebe sighed. 'To be honest, I feel like a bit of a fraud myself. Maybe Estelle was right after all when she said that I should stick to cooking for friends and family. The last time in Paris—when we argued— that's what she told me. She finds the idea of me cook-ing for complete strangers incomprehensible.'

'She aspires to be a musician. Surely that involves playing for complete strangers?'

'It's not the same thing. That would be a performance, my cooking...'

'Is also a sort of performance,' Owen said, 'with you taking the roles of both the conductor and the composer. Think of the entire meal as a symphony or an opera.'

'With the *amuse-bouche* as the overture, and the dessert as the finale.'

'And as many acts or courses in between as you care to compose. You are as much an artiste as your twin, Phoebe.'

'You are very good at making me feel better. But Estelle is the genuinely talented one, I'm merely well practised.'

'You are certainly well practised at denigrating yourself,' Owen exclaimed, exasperated. 'You readily admit that you were stifled by your sisters' over-protectiveness. So much so, that you fled all the way to Paris.'

'I did not say that!'

'Not in so many words, but it's what you did, Phoebe. Yet despite the fact that you don't want to wear the label they've attached to you, you never question their rather humble opinion of your considerable talents.'

'Every time we discuss my family, I feel as if you are undermining all I know about them.'

'I am questioning your assumption that you were at the end of the queue when it came to handing out talent.' Owen sighed. 'All I want is for you to start believing in yourself. It pains me, how easily you fall prey to self-doubt.'

'But it's hardly surprising is it, after what Pascal said and did?'

'If your family hadn't already eroded your fragile confidence, it wouldn't have been so easy for him. I know you won't hear a bad word said about your sisters, especially not your twin, but please, Phoebe, just think about what I've said. You underestimate yourself. As to your restaurant—do you remember what I said, about taking a step at a time? Never mind what it will look like, who will frequent it or where it will be. Think about the most important element.'

'The food?'

'Precisely. What food do you want to cook? And in order to establish that, you need to know what ingredients are to hand, don't you, what is available, what the quality is like?'

'Yes. You're right.'

'Which means a visit to London's markets is long overdue, don't you think?'

'Yes, but even I know it wouldn't be proper for me to go myself. I suppose I could ask Murray?'

'You could, I'm sure he'd be delighted to accompany you, but why not ask your husband instead?'

'Owen!' Phoebe's eyes lit up, but almost immediately her smile faded. 'No, it's too much to ask.'

'Then don't ask. I shall offer. Would you like to accompany me to the fruit and vegetable market at Covent Garden early tomorrow morning?'

'Truly? It will involve a good deal of walking about.'

'I am sure I can manage.'

'It's true, I have noticed…' She covered her mouth, her eyes wide. 'Sorry.'

'You may as well say it now.'

'I have noticed that you seem to be in less pain of late, and you're certainly walking much more freely. I was wondering if you had restarted the exercises your doctor prescribed?'

It was ridiculous to be flattered by this, but he was, and he had been working extremely hard, though he wasn't yet prepared to admit it. 'Not as such,' Owen said, which was true. 'So, tomorrow morning then?'

'Will we take the carriage?'

It was a relatively short walk, no more than twenty minutes, half an hour at a saunter, but Owen wasn't convinced he could manage that quite yet, not if he was going to be trailing around the market stalls too, so he nodded reluctantly.

'Are you sure—that you want to go, I mean? I would much prefer you to accompany me than Murray.'

'From you, that is a very great compliment.'

Phoebe laughed. 'Why would I not prefer the company of my very attractive husband to his bluff and craggy Scots chef? I am not the only one who underestimates themselves.'

'Perhaps not.'

'Then we will make it our business to bolster each other's confidence.' Her hand crept up to his cheek. Her fingers fluttered over it, caressing the line of his jaw, before she blushed and snatched her hand away. 'Talking of Murray, I had better go and discuss the menus for the rest of the week with him. He is overly fond of spices. I'm surprised he has not tried to serve us porridge with chilli pepper.'

The door closed behind her, and Owen sat back down at the table, pouring himself a cup of cold coffee. His muscles ached from his gymnastics this morning, but it was the pleasant ache resulting from hard work, not over-taxed injuries, save for the dragging pain in his hip, and even that was easing. If only he'd thought to return to his own regime earlier in his recuperation. He took a sip of coffee, grimaced and put it to one side. He'd been following doctor's orders not to take risks. Besides, he'd had no incentive to follow such a punishing schedule until Phoebe came back into his life. It was Phoebe who had inspired him, Phoebe who had, metaphorically, given him the much-needed kick up the backside.

And now his body was recovering in more ways than one. Desire had been absent from his life for so long, he had hardly recognised it when it had flared a minute ago. He allowed himself a moment of pure, sweet, unutterable relief, at this evidence that his accident had not wholly unmanned him. But it was short-lived, for there was no way in hell he could do anything about it. It was a sign that he was improving, physically, that was all, and really, he should have been expecting it. Phoebe was a very beautiful, extremely sensual woman. She had been the last woman he had found himself wanting, prior to his accident. It was no coincidence that she should be the first. After.

What's more, she found him attractive. She admitted it freely enough, though that was most likely because she knew—because he'd told her—that nothing could come of it.

And nothing could. Though he couldn't quite bring himself to wish he was still numb, this new development was a poisoned chalice, for the only outcome could be frustration, where before there had been indifference. Owen peeled off his gloves, forcing himself to study the backs of his hands, the fretwork of scarring, the pale pink colour of the tenderest skin, the hard callouses where the worst blisters had been, the permanently swollen middle knuckle. Flexing his fingers, he reminded himself that he'd been lucky that the damage had not been more extensive. They were ugly, they looked to him like the hands of an old man, but it wasn't vanity that kept them covered. It was fear.

He couldn't remember exactly what had happened, but it made a cold sweat break out on his back simply looking at his hands. Something too awful to bear lurked beyond the black wall of his memory, something that made him want to curl up on himself. Something terrible had happened and it had somehow been his fault. He could feel it building now, exactly the same feeling that he awoke with after his night sweats, an agony of grief and guilt.

He was attracted to his wife, but he dare not allow himself even the indulgence of imagining what it would be like to make love to her. Whatever had happened that day of his accident, his every instinct was to keep it walled up behind the emotional dam he had built. To let down his defences, even for the sweet delight of lovemaking, would be to release something that might make an emotional as well as a physical wreck of him.

He would not inflict that creature on Phoebe. Owen pulled his gloves back on. Phoebe was a naturally sensual woman, who probably had no idea of the effect she was having on him. Besides, he reminded himself, she wanted only one thing. Her restaurant. Her dream. He had married her in part to help her realise it. It would be madness to muddy those waters with anything more intimate. And despite his mental turmoil he was not, yet, barking mad.

Chapter Six

At just after five in the morning and in the pitch dark, Phoebe and Owen descended from their town coach on the edge of Covent Garden. Braziers lit up the market and surrounding streets. Housed in a new building, its neo-classical façade of columns and a balustraded second floor facing out on to the piazza, the market was already alive with traders and customers. Dray carts and their horses jostled for space to unload. Wooden crates tossed carelessly down were expertly caught and carted into the market by an endless stream of porters in leather aprons. Horses whinnied, wheels grated on the cobblestones, and men called out greetings, warnings and prices in a cacophony of sound that transported her back to the fresh-produce markets Phoebe had visited in France.

Putting her basket over her arm, she huddled close to Owen, intensely grateful for his presence, quite overwhelmed by the noise and the bustle. 'It's even bigger than I had imagined.'

'There's even more to it than you can see. It extends

into the surrounding streets,' Owen said, 'or it used to. I don't know how much of a difference this new building has made.'

'You are familiar with the market, then?'

'I've never bought so much as a potato, but I've walked home through it in the early hours many times.'

'When one commercial enterprise is shutting up shop and the other opening?' Phoebe said with an arch look. 'I do know, Owen, what other kind of business goes on here. It's like the Palais Royale in Paris.' She swept her gaze around the piazza, imagining a very different type of business being transacted in the cloisters where flower sellers were setting up. 'It even has the look of it, a little. In Paris, you know, courtesans—the more exclusive ones—are very much respected. The most famous of them dined at La Grande Taverne. Their presence was very good for business, for they set the fashion.'

'I hope you're not thinking of trying to attract London's most famous courtesans to your restaurant?'

'I wouldn't know who to invite,' Phoebe said, eyeing him speculatively. 'Would you?'

'It makes no difference, because it would be a sure-fire way of ensuring that you failed.'

'But you said that scandal was good for business.'

'Yes, but customers who don't pay their bills are not and neither London's most notorious courtesans nor their protectors are inclined to do that. They would expect you to be satisfied with the honour of their presence. Now, can we stop discussing Covent Garden ladies and focus on a different sort of fruit which is also ripe for the plucking?'

Phoebe giggled. 'Yes, I think that would be wise.'

The market hall was enormous and brightly lit, with stalls occupying two storeys built around a huge central area. Phoebe was immediately entranced, her senses swimming with the smells, the colours and the bounty, her brain busy concocting ideas for every single ingredient. Boxes of seasonal greens were stacked high, each vendor vying for trade by calling out the quality and price. Everything, they claimed, was freshly picked that morning, though on closer inspection she could see that the freshest produce was on full display and artfully sprinkled with water to resemble dew, while underneath more wilted specimens lurked, ready to be passed off on the less discerning customers, or those with a smaller purse.

'I will have to be careful when it comes to my own purchases,' she said, pointing out this practice to Owen.

'Once they learn that you are a regular customer and a good one, you'll find them easier to deal with,' he replied, frowning. 'Though I'm not sure that it will be such a good idea for you to do the buying. Have you noticed, it's nearly all men here?'

'I expect the housewives come later, as the market winds down, looking for bargains.'

Phoebe pulled out a notebook and pencil, and began to scribble notes as her basket filled up with samples, muttering about prices, dishes, and comparing what she saw with what she knew of Paris. Owen watched her, delighted to see that her enthusiasm had been rekindled, but not quite so delighted at the notion of her transacting business here on a daily basis. No, she couldn't possibly come herself. He already knew her too well to suggest that she delegate what she'd see as a vital task, so he would have to think of a strategy to ensure that she had an escort.

Adding this to the mental list of tasks he'd already assigned to himself, Owen listened with half an ear to his wife's essay on the various merits of one variety of carrot over another, careful to keep an interested look on his face. Until he met Phoebe, he'd had no idea there were different varieties, let alone different colours—and though it was always a pleasure to see her enthuse, he had to admit to himself that there was a limit to his interest in this particular subject, and he had reached his at the mention of the rare Scarlet Horn and Long Orange.

As they reached the fruit market, Phoebe's musings switched to desserts. She was dressed very simply in a long, enveloping cloak over a plain dress, but she had pushed back the hood in her excitement, and she wasn't wearing a hat. As usual, she was utterly oblivious of the effect her beauty was having, bestowing her generous smile on every trader who offered her a sample from his stall, leaving a trail of dazzled vendors in her wake. They'd be vying for her business, he reckoned, charmed into selling her their best wares at their keenest prices.

'I'm not much interested in flowers,' she said, as they reached the end of the fruit market. 'I think I've seen more than enough. My head is brimming with ideas. You've been very patient.'

'It has been a pleasure,' Owen said.

She chuckled. 'Half the time you haven't listened to a word I've said, but it's of no consequence since I'll doubtless repeat myself endlessly over dinner tonight.'

'Then if you've really had enough, we should be able to pick up a hackney cab in Henrietta Street. I didn't ask our coachman to wait, since I didn't know how long we'd be.'

'And how long have we been here?'

Owen consulted his watch. 'Longer than you think. It's after seven. Time for breakfast.'

'I've kept you on your feet for more than two hours. I am so sorry. Are you…?'

'I'm perfectly fine, Phoebe,' he said, surprised to discover that he was. 'Put your notebook away and let's get out of here. I'm hungry.'

'Is Rules nearby?'

'Rules? Oh, you mean the chop house? Yes, it's just down there.'

'May I take a look?'

'It won't be open at this hour.'

'I know. I just want to get a feel for what a London restaurant looks like.'

'You want to peer in the windows? I think you'll find that they are curtained.'

'Please?'

Owen laughed, shrugged and took the slight detour to Maiden Lane. As he had expected, the place was in darkness, with curtains drawn over the windows, the door barred. Phoebe, to his amusement, jumped up to try to peer through a crack in one of the curtains, then put her eye to the door. 'There's no menu,' she said. 'In Paris, all the restaurants and cafés have a chalk menu outside.'

'There's no menu because it never changes. Oysters. Puddings and pies. Game. It'll probably still be the same a hundred years from now.'

'You've eaten there?' she exclaimed. 'Why on earth didn't you tell me?'

'You didn't ask. Inside it's plush and ornate with velvet banquettes. Now can we return home? There's a hackney stand over there.'

'Yes, let us—why is that man staring at you?'

Thinking that he was more likely staring at Phoebe, Owen turned around, only to be confronted with a very old acquaintance.

'Owen Harrington, as I live and breathe. It is you, isn't it?' Hugo Burnes-Smythe crossed the narrow lane towards them, his hand held out in greeting. 'Good lord. I thought I was seeing a ghost.'

'Hugo.' Owen eyed his former friend with some misgiving for he was clearly three sheets to the wind. 'How are you?'

'More approp—approp—question is, how are you?' Hugo took a tottering step back. 'You're on your feet. I heard you'd lost your legs.'

'No, mislaid them temporarily. I have them both back in my possession as you can see.'

'Excellent news, excellent. I've just remembered something else,' Hugo said, peering over Owen's shoulder at Phoebe. 'Heard you'd tied the knot. 'Scuse me, Mrs Harrington—oh, excuse me, *not* Mrs Harrington. Was pretty sure Olivia Braidwood was a blonde.'

'I didn't marry Olivia Braidwood, Hugo.'

'I remember now. Lucky escape for her, that's what they are saying, though you look remarkably well to me.' Hugo shook his head. 'Where was I? I'm a bit befuddled, if you want the truth. The Running Footman race was today—race that you called your own, too, now I come to think of it. Your record time still stands, you'll be pleased to know. Now that you're back in town, maybe you'll show 'em a clean pair of heels next year?'

'I rather think race running is a bachelor's sport. Now, if you'll excuse me, Hugo, my wife and I are heading home for our breakfast.'

'Of course, of course. Could do with a bite to eat myself. I'm off to an Early House.' Hugo pumped his hand again, made an uncertain bow in Phoebe's direction and staggered off.

'What on earth is an Early House?' Phoebe asked.

'A tavern that opens for the market traders and porters. Not a place you'd care to eat, I assure you. Come, let's go before I meet any more ghosts from Owen Harrington's past,' he said, ushering his wife across the road where, to his relief, a cab had just arrived.

'Who was that man?' Phoebe asked, once they were comfortably settled in the hackney.

'Hugo Burnes-Smythe. I didn't think it was a good idea to formally introduce you.'

She chuckled. 'I doubt he will even remember meeting you, never mind me. What on earth is the Running Footman race?'

'There used to be a tradition of hiring a footman to run alongside your coach—I mean a tradition amongst the upper echelons who liked to demonstrate their superiority to mere mortals,' Owen said sardonically. 'The Duke of Marlborough was one such. He raced his own footman from Windsor to London—he was driving a coach and four, the footman was...'

'On foot! Against a coach and four! That is preposterous. I presume the Duke won the race?'

'Only just. The poor footman died from his exertions. The race was set up in his memory,' Owen said, cringing. What had once seemed to him a fitting tribute, now seemed, recounting it to Phoebe, not only insulting but ludicrous.

'Jasper told me that you were a talented runner.'

'I used to be. I loved the sense of freedom it gave me, and I did enter that race and won it several times. But even if I could, I can't imagine doing such a thing now.'

Or any of the things he'd done in the past, Owen though—save his gymnastics. If he had remained in England instead of setting out for the Continent two years ago, he'd probably have been with Hugo tonight, celebrating another win. He'd have been wandering aimlessly through Covent Garden, half-cut, half-awake and half-aware, and when he woke up later, he'd look back on the day as one well spent. Seeing Hugo was a reminder of the sort of man he had been, and he didn't like it one bit. Which was exactly why he'd left London in the first place.

The hackney dropped them at the door, and Phoebe, after checking as usual that he was not in need of assistance while pretending that she wasn't checking at all, bustled off to the kitchen to hand over her basket of fruit and vegetables to Murray. Owen made his way to his own room to take off his hat and coat, deep in thought.

He had so dreaded meeting any of his former friends that he'd closeted himself away. He'd become so accustomed to thinking of himself as an object of pity, yet Hugo had seemed to him the pitiful one, a fossil locked in amber. The life that Owen had lost was a pretty worthless one. Did that mean he'd rather be as he was now, even if it meant his nightmares would continue to haunt him, living with the blank space in his mind and his blank moments? He didn't know the answer, but it wasn't as straightforward as it used to be.

Certainly not since Phoebe had entered his life. He wondered what she would have Murray cook up with her harvest from this morning. Smiling to himself, Owen quit his rooms in search of breakfast and his wife, to find out.

Phoebe had spent the two days following their trip to Covent Garden working on compiling draft menus. This morning, she planned to try cooking some of the dishes and, wanting to have the kitchen to herself, had given the staff the day off. Pulling an apron on over her day gown, she decided to start by making both a beef and a vegetable stock. But as she began to assemble the ingredients on the huge scrubbed pine table which took up the centre of the room, her mind went completely blank, and her heart began to flutter in her chest so fast that she was compelled to sit down.

Stock, she mouthed, beef stock. The most basic thing to make, she'd done it a hundred, a thousand times, but she could not for the life of her think what else went into the pot save the roasted bones. It had been her responsibility to put the various stocks on first thing in the morning at La Grande Taverne. They simmered all day on the big range, and had to be skimmed every fifteen minutes for the first hour, then every half-hour after that. A good stock was the base for so many sauces. She knew how to make a good stock, for heaven's sake.

Though Pascal had claimed she didn't. Pascal had said that her stock was like dishwater and her pastry was like leather. But he'd used the stock every day, and surely if it was like dishwater then he wouldn't have put it anywhere near his precious dishes? And as for her pastry—but Pascal had always been a bit derisory about pastry and patisserie, claiming it was women's work and that was why she hadn't made a complete pig's ear of it.

She could cook. She knew she could cook, and it was time to stop questioning herself—something she hadn't realised she did quite so often, until Owen pointed it out. But since he had, she'd been thinking about it a good deal. She *was* very guilty of running herself down, expecting to fail, and astonished when she succeeded. It wasn't so much that Estelle undermined her as such, she just felt so inferior in every way to her talented, beautiful and charismatic twin. Owen was right, she had fled to Paris to escape the unflattering comparison, but he was also right when he said that it had been easy for Pascal to destroy all the confidence she'd built up over her two years in the city—because she'd never really believed she was worthy of his attention in the first place.

Well, no longer. Phoebe picked up an onion and began to chop furiously. She was a *damned* good cook and she would prove it to everyone, starting with Owen. Who knew nothing of such matters. But who believed in her, which Pascal did not. And who understood that her cooking deserved an audience, which Estelle did not.

Owen believed in her enough to emerge from his self-imposed isolation to go shopping with her. He'd done it for her, and she hadn't told him nearly enough, how grateful she was, or how much she admired him for doing it. When he had proposed, he'd been adamant that he was gaining as much from their marriage as she was, but thinking back over the weeks since they made their vows, Phoebe found that difficult to believe. The confidence he had in her was immense, to say nothing of all the practical help he'd given her. And she'd repaid him so far with doubts and indecision.

He deserved more than that. He wanted her to succeed. He wanted to be part of her success. She owed it to him and to the fates which had brought them together at the Procope, to have a bit more confidence in herself. She was only twenty-three, and she had made a disaster of her first job, and the best chef in all of

France, the culinary capital of the world, said that she couldn't cook, and her twin said that she shouldn't, but she would prove them wrong and she'd prove Owen right!

Phoebe put the lid on the vegetable-stock pot, and looked with surprise at the beef-stock pot beside it, bubbling away. She didn't remember making either, but that was a good sign. Cooking was instinctive, it was in her blood. She might be neither mature and confident like Kate and Eloise, nor talented and entertaining like Estelle, but she was born to be a chef!

Two hours later, with dinner prepared and the kitchen tidied Phoebe, excited and inspired, decided to seek out Owen. After a brief check of the main rooms downstairs, she concluded that he must be working in his study. He had never forbidden her from visiting his suite of rooms, but nor had he ever invited her. Pushing open the door, she found herself in a square hallway, tiled in black and white marble, and the choice of three doors. One would be Owen's bedchamber. One would be his study. She couldn't imagine what the third one would be. A soft thud from behind the nearest door made her jump. Listening carefully, she thought she could hear him moving about, so she knocked. There was no answer, but the noise of movement continued. Opening the door carefully, Phoebe peered in.

The room faced out on to the back gardens of the town house, the curtains not yet drawn against the fading light. The walls were lined with bookshelves overflowing with books. A comfortable sofa faced the fireplace, there were more books stacked on the floor beside it, but here convention ended. The polished floorboards were bare save for a large rush mat, on which lay a set of heavy-looking metal weights. A bar was suspended about four feet high between two supporting poles at the other window. And in the middle of the room, his back to her, was Owen, working on another set of bars.

She knew immediately that she was intruding on a very private space, but Phoebe couldn't move for fear of disturbing him. Positioned in the middle of the bars, he was stripped to the waist, wearing only a pair of loose cotton trousers, his feet bare though he still wore his gloves. As she watched, he took hold of the bars and began a series of lifts and dips, his legs tucked up under him. He moved fluidly, with apparently little effort, the muscles on his shoulders and arms flexing rhythmically. Moving smoothly on from one exercise to the next, he continued to dip while holding his legs straight out in front of him. His skin was damp with sweat, but his breathing remained regular. She could see, from the way he moved, that this was a regular routine. His upper body would delight a sculptor, Phoebe thought, pretending to an artistic appreciation that she was very far from feeling, for she was in thrall to something far more feral, fascinated by the sheer athletic power of him. He'd told her he had resumed his exercises but this was akin to acrobatics.

His arms straining now, he was holding his upper body quite still and working on his legs, straightening them, then lifting them together until they were at right angles to his body. His breathing was becoming laboured, sweat trickling down his back, but still he continued to work, ten, fifteen, twenty repetitions, until he finally let his legs fall, clinging to one of the bars to support himself, and breaking the spell Phoebe had fallen under. She moved, meaning to back out of the room without him seeing her, but he whirled round, and she froze to the spot.

'Phoebe! How long have you been there?'

'I'm so sorry, I didn't mean to spy on you, I did knock, but you clearly didn't hear because you were— you were—and then I started watching because it was so—goodness, I've never seen anything like it, you are so strong, and so graceful, and it was like a dance, and I—' She broke off, flushing. 'I should leave.'

She was backing out of the door. 'Wait,' Owen called. 'I'm finished for the day. Was there something important you wanted to ask me?'

'No, I—yes. Do you do this every day?'

'That was your burning question?'

'No, of course it wasn't. I didn't even know that you did—do these exercises have a name?'

'Gymnastics. From the Greek, meaning to exercise naked. Fortunately for the sake of your modesty,' Owen said, picking up his cotton gown and pulling it on, 'I'm not a purist.'

'But you are most certainly an athlete.' Closing the door behind her, Phoebe smiled at him. 'To be so—so accomplished, you must work very hard.'

'I can't do half of what I used to do. Years ago, when I was fourteen or fifteen, I saw a performance by

a Russian brother and sister called the Flying Vengarovs. They were acrobats, most renowned for their rou-
tines on the tightrope. I was utterly entranced by them,
and the next day, I sought the brother, Alexandr, out
at the theatre where he was practising on equipment
just like this. I knew that I *had* to learn to do what
he could do. He knew of a place I could get lessons.'

'And you proved an apt pupil?' Phoebe ran her hand
over the smooth wood of one of the bars. 'What is this
apparatus called?'

'Parallel bars.' Phoebe was flushed. Embarrassed,
Owen assumed, though the way she was looking at
him, the softness of her smile, the fact that she was
looking at him and not at the floor or the ceiling or
even the bars made him wonder. 'This is called a pommel horse,' he said. 'Unfortunately I have no use any
more for the vaulting variety.'

Phoebe followed him across the room. She studied
the piece of equipment, smoothing her hands over it
as if she were stroking a real horse. 'What do you do
with this?'

She could not possibly realise the effect she was
having on him. He could not quite believe the effect
she was having on him. Contrary to what he had come
to believe, that side of his nature was very far from
dead. 'It was originally used to help soldiers practise mounting and dismounting from their horses.
A skilled practitioner can support himself on these,'
Owen said, indicating the pommels, 'and then swing
his legs around underneath him.'

Phoebe frowned. 'I can't imagine how you even

mount this thing, never mind swing about like a pendulum.'

'What you do is...' But it was much easier to demonstrate than to explain, and if he focused on demonstrating, he'd be able to ignore Phoebe and the disturbing effect she was having on him. Owen divested himself of his robe. 'Let me show you.'

Holding on to the pommels, he mounted the horse smoothly—something he couldn't have done a month ago—and positioned himself, legs stretched outwards and together, arms braced. The strength, he had learned, came not from the arms but from the centre of his body. He clenched his stomach muscles. Closing his eyes as he concentrated, relishing the new, solid muscles his dedicated training had developed around his abdomen, he began to swing his legs around anti-clockwise, which was marginally easier on his right hip. To move with such freedom was still so new to him, Owen gave himself over to the pleasure of it, barely noticing the pain of his protesting hip as he changed direction, then finished with a forward-balancing handstand before dismounting.

He had forgotten all about Phoebe until he opened his eyes again to see her gazing rapt at his sweating body and it felt so damned good, that raw appreciation, and he'd worked so diligently these last few weeks, he felt he'd earned it.

'I've never seen anything like that,' she said, 'but you are obviously very good.'

'Not bad,' Owen said, 'for a few weeks' work.' His training regime, so radically different from the one his doctor had prescribed, had begun painfully, for he had launched himself into the exercises as if there had not been a gap of more than two years. Forced to go back to basics, progress had been frustratingly slow at first, but as he had started to improve, he had come to enjoy his new regime. 'It's as much about technique as strength,' he said to Phoebe. 'It's easy to achieve a basic level of competence when you have nothing else to do.'

'I think you are being extremely modest. I couldn't even climb on to that thing without a mounting block to boost me.'

He didn't think. He forgot who he was now, and he acted on impulse, just as he would have done if he'd been the man he was before, in the presence of such beguiling beauty, putting his arms around her waist and sitting her up on the horse effortlessly.

Phoebe gasped in surprise, laughing. 'Owen! My goodness, it looks a long way down from up here.'

'Hold on to the pommels.' He let her go as she did so, stepping to the side. 'Straighten your arms and sit back a bit. You won't fall,' he said as she hesitated, 'and if you do I'll catch you.'

'Promise?'

'Promise. Now, hold your tummy in tight.' Phoebe took a deep breath and Owen, his eyes on a level with her bosom, was momentarily distracted. 'Not like that,' he said, dragging his eyes away, 'as if you are trying to press your navel into your back.'

'What a strange thing—oh, yes, I see.' She was frowning in concentration. 'What now?'

What now? He hardly knew where to look, for all the most delectable bits of her body seemed to be straining at her gown, which was wrapped tight around her bottom and riding up her legs. 'Try to lift yourself up,' Owen said, 'not just with your arms, but from your middle, here.'

'I can't—I don't…'

'Stop talking. Save your breath and concentrate. Imagine there's a rope pulling you up from your middle.'

'That is—oh!' Phoebe swung precariously, but there was a tiny gap between her body and the horse. 'Look, Owen, I'm doing it.'

Her delight was infectious. He laughed. 'Stop talking.'

'It's really difficult.'

'Even more difficult when you don't save your breath. Just breathe, and hold everything in.'

'That is easier said than done when you are as fond of food as I am!'

'Phoebe, shut up and breathe.'

She pursed her lips and breathed exaggeratedly, but her eyes were brimming with laughter.

'Now,' Owen said, 'try to lift your legs up just a little.'

She opened her mouth to protest, then closed it again, her expression becoming focused as she tried—and failed—to move her legs. After taking a brief rest at his suggestion, she balanced and tried again with limited success, her face florid with the effort, but shaking her head violently when he told her that was enough. 'One more time.' She took a deep breath and lifted herself up. She screwed her face comically tight, and for a brief second, lifted both legs.

'Well done.'

'I did it!' Her eyes flew open. Her arms and legs collapsed and Phoebe fell straight into Owen's arms. 'I did it,' she said again, triumphantly. 'I did do it, didn't I?'

'You did.' His arms automatically tightened around her. She was flushed, her eyes gleaming, her lips parted as she smiled up at him, her arms twined around his neck. Her body, pressed against his was so lush, sensual and utterly beautiful, that his senses swam, and he dipped his head, feeling her breath on his face, drinking in the sweet scent of her.

Their lips met. He knew it was wrong, but he couldn't resist her. It was a soft, tentative kiss, for he had all but forgotten what kisses were like, but as her mouth yielded to his, as she sighed and kissed him back, he stopped thinking and gave himself over to the pleasure of it. The taste of her. The touch of her tongue. The soft whisper of her breath on his, the little sighing sound she made, and the delight of her body, the sheer otherness of her body, the very definite indent of her waist, the curve of her bottom, her breasts pressed against his naked chest.

Her kisses went to his head. They inflamed him. They made his blood zing in his veins. Her hands were on his shoulders, his back, smoothing down his spine, curling into his behind, making him hard. Their tongues touched again. Their kisses deepened and he was filled with such longing, such an intense yearning to touch her, skin on skin.

Owen broke the kiss, breathing heavily. Phoebe staggered as he released her, leaning against the support of the pommel horse. She was flushed, heavy-lidded and delectable. And he was aroused, confused and—and very aroused! He swore under his breath. 'I'm sorry.'

She gazed at him, looking as dazed as he felt. 'Are you?'

'No.'

'Nor am I.' A laugh escaped her that had an edge of hysteria to it, then her face flooded with colour. 'That will be a lesson to me to come seeking you out in the middle of the day. I should go. Dinner,' she said, backing away from him. 'I'm making dinner. I must see to my pots.'

Owen made no attempt to stop her. Utterly shocked, he stared at the pommel horse, as if it was to blame for his throbbing erection and his wildly beating heart and the sheer elation that was making him grin like a lunatic. He felt as euphoric as if he had made love. His whole body tingled and pulsed. If there was a vaulting horse in the room, he was convinced he'd clear it with several feet to spare. Leaning back against the pommel horse, he closed his eyes, reliving the taste of Phoebe's kisses and the way Phoebe's body had melted into his, and the way his body had responded. The surge of blood to his groin, the throb of arousal, and the unique sense of anticipation that accompanied it, imagining the slow slide into slick heat that felt like nothing else on earth, and then the rhythm building…

He cursed under his breath, sweat sprinkling his back, his heart racing. Another few moments of thinking like that—dear God, if she had stayed, if he had not broken their kiss, would they even now...

Owen picked up his dressing gown, tying the sash in a ruthless knot, striding out of the room across to his bedchamber and into his bathing room. He needed a bath. A cold one! Catching sight of himself in the mirror, his hair dishevelled, his cheeks flushed, his pupils dark and dilated, he was startled into a laugh. He looked almost like himself. Though older.

Wiser? He swore again, sitting down on the rim of the bath, turning the tap which allowed the hot water to fill it, temporarily distracted as he was every time by this innovation. He had lost himself in Phoebe's kisses, but he had not disappeared into himself as he'd feared he might. Was he getting better? Taking a deep breath, he peeled off his gloves and forced himself to stare down at his hands, but all he could think about was how much he wished he'd not been wearing his gloves when he held Phoebe in his arms.

Was he getting better? He still had nightmares, but the moments when he disappeared into himself were much less frequent. Being with Phoebe was easy, no effort at all. And with others too, sometimes, he felt— well, something approaching normal. Did that imply that he was getting better? He was too afraid to hope. A step at a time, he reminded himself, just as he'd cautioned Phoebe.

Bloody hell, Phoebe. Owen turned off the tap and quickly stripped, catching his breath as his body hit the tepid water. It was because he hadn't kissed any woman in over two years, he told himself, that Phoebe's kisses felt to him like no other kisses, like the best, most arousing kisses he'd ever shared. He knew that, but it made no difference. They *were* the best, the most arousing kisses he'd ever shared.

But he had no right to be kissing Phoebe, even if she was his wife. Kissing Phoebe had not been part of their agreement. In fact he'd assured Phoebe that he would never have any interest in kissing her or any woman. And Phoebe had assured him that she had no interest either. Yet she'd kissed him back with—with abandon! Perhaps she felt sorry for him? No, those were not pity kisses. It was the gymnastics, then? He wasn't and would never be as good as he had once been, but there was something mesmerising about the movements, a sensuality, a—a primal connection between muscle and man.

Was he being fanciful? He was procrastinating. He had no idea why Phoebe had responded the way she had to his kisses, but the simple fact was he shouldn't have kissed her. She was his wife in name only. He was her investor, not her husband in any real sense, he had no right to kiss her, and the only reason he was fit to kiss her in the first place was because he'd got himself fit! In order to help her with the restaurant! So he'd better bloody well concentrate on that.

Owen lay back in the bath, putting a wet flannel over his face. He would. He'd concentrate on their business venture. Just as soon as he got out the bath.

* * *

Back in the kitchen, Phoebe tied on her apron and tended to the stock pots before sitting down at the table, staring sightlessly at her notebook where she had written out tonight's menu. Kissing Owen had been—no, she was most certainly not going to compare him to Pascal. There was, she thought with a satisfied smile, no comparison. Kissing Owen had been quite simply delicious. She shivered, remembering the way his mouth felt, the touch of his tongue, the way he'd smoothed his hands over her, clearly relishing her curves. If she had needed proof that Pascal was confined to history—which she didn't—then her response was more than sufficient. Kissing Owen had been like eating an ice, the sharp burst of awareness, the mingling of hot and cold as it melted, then the lingering sweetness, and the craving for the next taste. Kissing Owen was, like watching him exercise, a sheer, sensual delight.

But she didn't have any business kissing Owen, and Owen—goodness, Owen certainly hadn't kissed like a man who had lost all desire. He hadn't been acting, when he kissed her. Or had he? When Pascal told her he'd never loved her, she hadn't believed him. How could he have made love to her with such passion—and so often, right up until the night before he ended their affaire!—if he hadn't loved her. But it was different for men, he'd told her disdainfully, especially a man ruled by passion such as he. And she had been so very eager, he'd said. Had she? She hadn't thought so at the time, she'd thought—but what was the point of going over it, when she'd decided just a few moments ago to confine Pascal to the past.

Had she been too eager with Owen? Seeds of doubt began to sprout in her mind. She was not in love with Owen, but did that make her kissing him worse or better? Would he be angry with her, for awakening feelings he'd thought dead? But he'd said he wasn't sorry. He hadn't looked angry, he'd looked as dazed as she. What was she to think? Perhaps she oughtn't think.

She had kissed her husband, and her husband had kissed her back, and that was the end of it. Save that her husband's kisses were vastly superior to Pascal's kisses, she thought, mentally thumbing her nose at her former lover and making herself smile. Owen was getting better—better enough to want to kiss her—and a *lot* fitter too. Goodness, that physique!

No, she mustn't think about that either. Owen was getting better because he had a purpose in life. She was getting better because she had a purpose in life too, thanks to Owen. So she'd better stop allowing herself to be distracted by kisses, and concentrate on what mattered, and right at this moment, it wasn't superior kisses but superior cooking.

Phoebe scraped her chair back and headed for the pantry to assemble the rest of the ingredients for dinner. Happily turning her mind from one sensual delight to another, she set about constructing what she hoped would be the best dinner Owen had ever tasted.

Chapter Seven

O wen set his napkin down and picked up his wine glass. 'That, I can say without fear of contradiction,' he said, 'was the best meal I've ever eaten.'

Phoebe chuckled, touching her glass to his. 'Well, I was never going to go far wrong by serving venison, was I?'

'How so?'

'Back at the Procope, don't you remember? When we played my game of guessing favourite foods. I guessed that your favourite dish was a hearty breakfast of ham and eggs, and you told me that you preferred a dinner of venison stew.'

'How very ungallant of me. Stew does not adequately describe the fragrant dish you served tonight.'

She rested her chin on her hands. 'You cannot remain a culinary philistine if you are investing in London's newest and most popular restaurant, Owen. I intend to educate your palate, starting now. Tell me what you think was in the dish, besides the venison.'

'Mushrooms.'

'Very good. What else?'

He frowned in exaggerated concentration. 'Chestnuts—yes, there were definitely chestnuts.'

'Think of the flavours, remember how it smelled. What other ingredients spring to mind?'

'I feel like I'm back at school and I'm about to fail a very important exam. I'm sorry Phoebe, I haven't a clue.'

'There was bacon, to give it richness and a little fat because venison is a very lean meat. The warmth comes from cinnamon—though I used a very little of Mr Murray's extensive spice store—cloves and a pinch of nutmeg. The sauce is a reduction of red wine, the good beef stock I made this morning, and the pulped flesh of a tomato for a little bit of tartness. Oh, and bay, onion, salt and pepper of course, those go without saying.'

'Of course they do,' Owen said. 'And what it added up to was the best plate of venison I've ever tasted. I mean that.'

'Thank you. I won't bore you by dissecting the other dishes, I'm just happy that you sampled all of them.'

'I am certainly enjoying my food a great deal more these days—no doubt due to the excellent company provided by my dining companion. I'm also very honoured to be the recipient of the first dinner you've cooked since you returned to England, though it was much more homely fare than I was expecting from a top chef.'

'I reckoned that you're not fond of overly refined and elegant food.'

'Not particularly, to be honest, but isn't that what restaurants like the one you aspire to open serve?'

'I cooked this meal just for you, as a thank you. When I sought you out earlier and interrupted your training—' She broke off, for despite her determination not to think about it, she remembered the kiss and felt the heat stealing over her cheeks. 'I should have knocked more loudly.'

'I'm glad you didn't, but I want to assure you that what transpired was furthest from my thoughts. Or would have been, until very recently.'

'There's really no need…'

'Oh, but there is.' Owen picked up his wine glass, changed his mind and set it down. 'Let me explain, or attempt to. It is a delicate subject. You've inspired me to—to look at life afresh, I suppose. To haul myself out of the doldrums, is another way of putting it. I feel better. I'm fitter. And as a result I discovered today that I—I am no longer without urges,' he said, colouring. 'Our marriage has provided me with an unexpected, but very welcome sense of purpose, thanks to you. But I want you to know that's more than enough for me. Today was a—it happened, but it would be best if we concentrated on the matter in hand, which is the restaurant, don't you agree?'

Phoebe heaved a sigh of relief. 'I was thinking much the same thing. It wouldn't be a good idea at all for us to mix business with pleasure—I mean—oh, goodness, you know what I mean.'

'I do.'

'Good. I haven't told you properly, Owen, how very grateful I am for the help you've been giving me.'

'I said I would, Phoebe, I've simply been keeping my side of the bargain.'

'No, I don't mean the practical help you've given me—or not only that. You've made me see that I've not been helping myself. What you said, about under-estimating myself—I do that, I see that now, and I'm going to try to change.'

'Phoebe, I…'

'No, let me say this. It's very difficult for me to hear any sort of criticism of Estelle because she's my twin, and it was even more difficult for me to accept what you said about her. She doesn't mean to run me down, she's trying to protect me but—well, the effect is that I do have a fairly low opinion of myself.' Phoebe took a reviving sip of wine. 'You know me better than myself or my sisters do, it seems. So thank you, Owen. I've re-warded you with nothing but doubts and worries so far, but that is going to change. I won't let you down—or at least if I do, it won't be for the want of trying. And as to that, I have an idea I'd like to discuss with you.'

'Good, I'm all ears. Shall we take our wine through to the parlour?'

Phoebe jumped to her feet. 'You're in sore need of a more comfortable seat. You should have said. Did you overstretch yourself with your gymnastics today because of me? I'm so sorry.'

'I didn't. No, actually I probably did, but it wasn't your fault. I was showing off for your benefit,' he admitted sheepishly.

And she had appreciated it. Very much. But she must not think about that! 'You go on,' Phoebe said, turning her back on him to look for a tray. 'I'll bring the drinks.'

She took her time putting the decanter and glasses on a tray, and by the time she reached the parlour, she had supplanted thoughts of those kisses with the subject they had agreed must take precedence.

She handed Owen his glass and took her usual seat on the sofa, curling her feet under her. 'Do you know of a place called Crockford's Club?'

'You mean the gambling club in St James's?'

'You do know it then.'

'I don't frequent it, never have. Cards don't interest me.'

'It has a restaurant,' Phoebe said, 'with Eustache Ude, no less, in charge of the kitchen.'

'Another culinary hero of yours, I gather from the gleam in your eyes.'

'His father worked in the kitchens of King Louis the Sixteenth.'

'Who gave his head to Madame Guillotine. There are doubtless a great number of gentlemen who have lost their shirt at Crockford's tables who would wish Monsieur Ude Junior's employer a similar fate.'

'If I had to lose at the tables in order to sample Monsieur Ude's menu, then it would be a price worth paying.'

'A moot point since females are not permitted to cross the threshold. No respectable female, that is. I'm not sure what Crockford's rules are regarding light skirts.'

'I could pass for a light skirt,' Phoebe said.

Owen raised a quizzical brow. 'It conjures an image not without its attractions, but it would be to no avail. I am fairly certain that the dining room is a strictly male-only preserve.'

Phoebe rolled her eyes. 'As I had assumed. Well in that one sense our restaurant is going to be very different, since I am determined it should serve a mixed clientele. But I would dearly like to taste the food.'

'Why is it so important?'

'Aside from the fact that Monsieur Ude is one of the most famous chefs in the world, you mean? We need to understand the competition in London, so that we can then make a judgement on whether we set out to serve the same but better or whether we serve something different altogether. I have always dreamed of a restaurant very much like La Grande Taverne, but what if I'm wrong? What if I discover that the last thing I want to do is serve food that reminds me of Paris and my humiliation.' Phoebe sighed. 'If you were not such a culinary philistine I would ask you to go on a—a tasting mission to discover whether it really is as good as they say, or whether it is a case of style over substance, you know?'

'Clearly you don't consider that I am up to the task.'

'I'm so sorry. I didn't mean to insult you.'

Owen got up, picking up both their glasses to put them on the tray, before sitting down on the sofa beside her. 'I'm teasing, Phoebe,' he said gently.

'Oh. Am I being tediously intense?'

'You are simply being determined.'

'Determinedly tedious, you mean. I am though, determined I mean. To make a success of our venture. To prove that you were right to believe in me.'

He shook his head, smiling softly. 'When I first saw you in Paris, I was dazzled. I've seen more classically beautiful women, but you—you were so bright and so full of life. You can be that person again.'

'You rescued me that night. And now you've rescued me again. No, that's not right. I need to rescue myself. You've taught me that. Not being able to visit Crockford's is a setback but I won't let it defeat me.' She leaned over to kiss him on the cheek. His skin was fresh-shaved, smooth but rough at the same time. She sat back very reluctantly. A lump rose in her throat. 'Thank you for being my inspiration.'

'You give me too much credit, Phoebe.' He touched her cheek, cursed, looked down at his gloves.

'Why do you wear these? Are your hands so very badly damaged?'

He shook his head. 'It's more that they are a constant reminder.'

'I thought you didn't remember what happened?'

'I don't, but when I look at them I feel—that I don't want to remember. That whatever happened—that it's better for me if I don't try. So I prefer not to look at them.'

'I'm so sorry, I won't ask again.'

'But the strange thing is,' Owen said, still staring down at his gloves, 'today, after you left me in the gymnasium...' He looked up. 'After we kissed, and I realised that I wasn't entirely dead inside—I took them off. And it didn't happen, Phoebe. I looked at my hands, and all I felt was—it doesn't matter what I felt, what matters is that I didn't feel what I'd always felt before.'

'So you think you really are getting better?'

'I dare not raise my hopes. But—small steps, yes? So perhaps now's as good a time as any to risk another one.'

Owen began to take off one of his gloves and Phoebe's heart began to pound as she watched him. Slowly, he eased each finger free, until his left hand was exposed. He didn't look at her, his gaze remained concentrated on his hand.

'May I?' Phoebe, bracing herself, gently took his hand to study it. She traced the fretwork of scars delicately. There were patches of pale new skin, hard patches of darker skin where the scarring was deeper. His middle finger was swollen at the knuckle, giving it an odd shape. Aware of him sitting stock still beside her, holding his breath, she lifted his hand to her mouth, pressing the lightest of kisses to the scars before turning it over and kissing his palm. She gingerly removed the other glove. easing the fingers free, no longer apprehensive, only touched to her heart, seeing the history of his suffering mapped out so clearly, and knowing that he had never before revealed it to anyone save presumably his doctors.

His right hand bore the same scarring, the same patches of rough and tender skin. His little finger jutted at an odd angle, having obviously been broken and badly mended. Phoebe kissed these scars too. Then she pressed his hand to her cheek. Owen inhaled sharply. His fingers fluttered on her skin, tracing the line of her jaw, her neck, then releasing her, to clasp her hand between his. He stared, frowning deeply, at their twined fingers for a long time. She couldn't fathom what he was thinking, though she had the oddest impression that he was waiting. Then he released his breath in one long sigh and looked up, meeting her eyes, and smiled.

'Thank you.' He got to his feet, holding out his hand to help her. 'I think we've had more than enough excitement for one day.'

Phoebe nodded, suddenly overwhelmed. 'Goodnight, Husband.'

He touched her cheek again. 'Goodnight, Wife.'

Lying in bed, Phoebe wrapped her arms around herself and snuggled down into the pillow. Something momentous had occurred tonight, much more significant than the kisses they had shared earlier. Owen had changed, had been changing almost every day since their marriage. The moments when he went quite blank were becoming far less frequent, and he seemed more natural and at ease with her, reserving what she had called his acting for conversations with strangers. With her, he was, as far as she could see, himself. His laugh was rarely forced. He teased her. He smiled at her. Today he'd kissed her. And tonight, he had taken off his gloves in her presence. She would not be so foolish as to fall in love—again!—with the man who was pivotal to her achieving her ambition, but the emotions that were now churning up inside her were unsettling.

Owen was not Pascal, he could not be more different. He had married her when he was by his own admission in the slough of despond, when his glittering aura was tarnished, the flame which had burned so brightly in him before his accident, all but extinguished. When they had married, they had been two lost souls hoping to heal one another. But Owen was no longer a lost soul, and he was healing himself. He had promised to support her in her business venture and he was an honourable man, he would honour that commitment. But one day soon, he would want to take up his position in society again, and society would embrace him like a prodigal son. Then, he'd have little use for a tarnished and food-obsessed wife.

What was the phrase they used about racehorses? She wasn't up to his weight. So she'd better make sure that she kept her heart to herself and focus on the reason they'd married, just as he'd said they should earlier. Had that been an oblique warning? When he took off his gloves, had be been trying to tell her that he was ready to go out in the world, ready to leave her behind? It was a deflating thought, but she would do well to bear it in mind.

'Mr Forsythe apologises for calling at such an early hour, but he says the matter is urgent.'

'*Extremely* urgent,' Jasper said, striding into the breakfast parlour.

'Another setting for Mr Forsythe, if you please, Bremner,' Phoebe said, raising an enquiring brow at Owen, but he shook his head, clearly as in the dark as she. 'Won't you sit down, Jasper? May I pour you a cup of coffee?'

'Thank you, Phoebe. Coffee would be very welcome. Owen, apologies again for the intrusion.' Jasper took off his hat and gloves, placing them an a spare chair before taking a seat at the table.

'Do you wish to speak to Owen in private?' Phoebe asked. 'Shall I...'

'No, don't get up. I'm afraid the matter concerns both of you.'

'What matter?' Owen asked, when Bremner arrived with the extra place setting and a fresh pot of coffee.

'Well?' Owen prompted again, when the butler quit the room.

'You're looking very well. Marriage obviously suits you.'

'You didn't come here to compliment me, Jasper. Cut to the chase.'

Jasper took a sip of coffee, looking utterly wretched. 'Truth is, I'm not quite sure how to put this. You're going to be furious with me, but I swear to you, Owen, I had no idea that the man was a journalist. He gave me the impression he was a relative of Phoebe's. In fact I'm almost sure that's what the fellow said, that he knew Lord Fearnoch, though he might not actually have been so specific. I don't recall. I'm so very sorry, Phoebe.'

'What in devil's name are you talking about?'

'Jasper,' Phoebe interrupted, a horrible premonition making her feel sick. 'What did you discuss with this mysterious relative?'

'I'm so sorry. I had no idea...'

'Just spit it out, dammit,' Owen said, his mouth set.

'It was about two weeks ago. I was taking a glass at the Cock Tavern in Holborn as usual, to brace myself for dinner with my Aunt Clementine. Terrifying woman,' Jasper said to Phoebe. 'She must be about a hundred and twenty-five by now, filthy rich, and I'm her heir as well as the only relative she claims to be able to tolerate, so I have dinner with her every Thursday. My uncle, who has long since departed, was a prominent lawyer, and my aunt still lives near Chancery, which is why I drink at the Cock.'

'Get to the point, for the love of God!' Owen exclaimed. 'Phoebe isn't interested in your Aunt Clementine. She would far rather hear, as I would, what it is you've been saying to her relative.'

'I'm nervous. I always talk to much when I'm nervous. The chap wasn't Phoebe's relative, that's the point. Came up to me in the Cock, knew my name, shook my hand and bought me a drink before I had said a word. "You're a good friend of Owen Harrington," he said, "who has married a relative of mine." Or he implied as much, as I said. Mentioned Lord Fearnoch. I had no idea you were so well connected, Phoebe, and I said. It turns out that your sister is a countess.'

'I think you'll find she's aware of that,' Owen said, pouring his friend another cup of coffee.

Phoebe, by now feeling as if she was about to lose her breakfast, picked up her own tea, but her hands were shaking too much. 'My sister Eloise, the Countess of Fearnoch, she is in the country, in Lancashire. What did this man have to say about her?'

'Nothing at all,' Jasper replied, much to Phoebe's relief. 'He didn't seem much interested in her. He was much more interested in how you and Owen had met, so I told him that it had been in Paris, two years ago. I didn't think that it mattered—I mean it's the truth, isn't it?—and I must confess that I found your story— well, I'm not the romantic type—or not usually—but anyway...'

'You told him that we'd met in Paris,' Phoebe said, her relief short-lived. 'What else did you tell him?'

'Nothing, I swear. I didn't know there was anything else to tell until this morning.' Jasper reached into his pocket and pulled out a newspaper. 'My man drew my attention to it. I don't read the scandal sheets, but he does. I'm so very sorry.'

Owen took the newspaper from him. 'The *Town Crier*,' he said, eyeing it with disgust. 'Shall I do the honours?'

Phoebe nodded, feeling rather like an aristocrat waiting for her turn at the guillotine. She had never heard of the *Town Crier*, and knew that her sister wouldn't read such rubbish, but she didn't doubt some kind thoughtful soul would send a copy to her. At least it sounded as if they had not actually tracked Eloise down. Which was a very small consolation.

'"Speculation has been rife,"' Owen read, '"since the rather restrained announcement in the press informing the world that Mr Owen Harrington has tied the knot with Miss Phoebe Brannagh. Though we all know the reclusive Mr Harrington as one of London's most successful investors and speculators, of his new bride, next to nothing was known—save that she was not the bride we all expected him to marry!"' Owen broke off to curse before continuing.

"'As you know, it is our mission at the *Town Crier* to keep you fully informed. When we discovered that Miss Phoebe Brannagh is the sister of the Countess of Fearnoch, what joy we felt on Mr Harrington's behalf that he had made such a well-connected alliance. Alas, our joy was short-lived. Dear reader, if you are of a delicate disposition, we would suggest that you read no further, for what we have to reveal is of a most scurrilous, scandalous and shocking nature.'"

Once again Owen broke off, cursing fluently while Phoebe, horribly conscious of Jasper's presence, wished that the ground would open up and swallow her.

"'Miss Brannagh and Mr Harrington first encountered each other in Paris. It was, we were told by the groom's close friend, love at first sight.'"

Jasper groaned.

Owen continued reading in clipped tones. "'Following our own investigations in Paris, we can reveal that alas, these two hearts who longed to beat as one were denied a happy ending at this point by a prior claim. Not, we hasten to add, the well-known arrangement which Mr Harrington's parent had agreed for him, but a claim of a foreign nature! *Oh, là-là*, Miss Phoebe Brannagh had given her heart to a Frenchman. A common cook, no less, though Monsieur Pascal Solignac does not charge common prices at the restaurant where the former Miss Brannagh peeled potatoes, we hasten to add, lest any of our readers are tempted to sample his wares for themselves." Which means,' Owen said viciously, 'they must actually have talked to Solignac.'

Phoebe, now mute with horror, watched as he turned the scandal sheet over, wondering how much more if it she had to bear.

"'Broken-hearted,'" Owen continued to read, "'Mr Harrington fled Paris and at some point prior to his return to England, as London society is all to well aware, met with a tragic accident which deprived him of the use of his legs. His heart, however, remained true to Miss Brannagh, and she, it seems, finally saw the error of her ways, abandoning her garlic-infused paramour for a slice of English roast beef."

"'How much did Mr Harrington's fat purse have to do with her change of heart? A little bird, with an ear to the ground in the London property market, tells us that despite Miss Brannagh's singular lack of talent in the kitchen—a fact on which Monsieur Solignac was most vociferous—now she is reincarnated as Mrs Harrington, she will be making an assault on London's stomachs at her own restaurant some time in the new year. Yes, dear reader, you heard it here first. Rejected by Paris, the gourmet capital of the world, Mrs Harrington, nothing daunted, is currently looking for premises in which to set herself up as the doyenne of British cooking, right here in London. What dish will she serve? It is to be hoped that it will not contain any trace of garlic."' Owen crumpled up the scandal sheet and threw it in the fire. Phoebe dropped her head into her hands.

'I cannot apologise enough,' Jasper said.

'It's not your fault,' Phoebe said, lifting her head. 'It's mine.'

'If there is anything I can do,' Jasper said, looking helpless. 'Anything.'

'Don't speak to any more journalists.'

'That goes without saying. If I'd had any idea…'

'But you didn't. Stop apologising, man, it's not your fault.' Owen tugged the bell, demanding a fresh pot of tea for Phoebe as soon as possible.

'I don't need…'

'You do.' He pulled his seat closer to her, putting his hand on her knee. 'It's disgusting and slanderous, but it's not a tragedy, Phoebe.'

'But it's not slanderous it's true, Owen—well, aside from the bit where they refer to Pascal as a "common cook". It's all true.'

'Good lord. Beg pardon, but—all of it?'

Jasper looked quite astounded. Mortified, Phoebe could only nod and hang her head.

'I don't know what to say. None of my business of course, but—well, none of anyone's business what you did before you married Owen,' Jasper said, the tips of his ears burning bright red. 'But they must have made up the bit about opening a restaurant, surely?'

'No, it's true enough,' Phoebe said dejectedly. 'That was our intention, but now…'

'That remains our intention,' Owen said firmly.

'How can we, after this? Owen, you must see that this changes everything,' Phoebe said wretchedly.

'I don't see why. You've done nothing to be ashamed of.'

'As I said, nobody's business but yours, what you did before you were married,' Jasper added valiantly before catching Owen's eye, holding his hands up and mouthing, *Sorry.*

'You're very kind, Jasper, but this rag has made it everyone's business,' Phoebe said. 'Now my sister's name and more importantly Owen's, have been dragged through the mud because of me.'

'My name's been dragged through the mud so many times I have lost count and long since stopped caring.'

'Scrapes you got into when you were younger, no doubt. This is very different.'

'Phoebe, I was never anywhere close to being a saint. Was I, Jasper?'

'Nowhere near. But this…'

'We can turn it to our advantage,' Owen said firmly.

'How?' Phoebe asked.

'I don't know, but we will.'

'Owen, you must see…'

'In a moment, Phoebe. Drink your tea, and you'll feel better. Jasper, could I ask a favour of you?'

'Ask away. Anything to make amends, old chap.'

'Would you visit Olivia and let her know about this unfortunate development? That rag doesn't mention her by name, but it's best she is aware of it. Sorry if it is a bit of an imposition.'

'It's the least I can do, in the circumstances. And no

imposition whatsoever. Seeing her later today anyway, as it happens. Drive. Fresh air. That kind of thing.'

'Fine. Good.' Owen got up, pressing Phoebe's shoulder. 'We'll talk, but I'll just see Jasper out.'

'I'm so sorry, Phoebe. If there's anything...'

'I've told you to stop apologising, and I've told you what you can do to help. Now go and do it.'

'You're not limping.'

'No.' Owen held the door open.

'You sound different. And you look well. I meant what I said when I arrived.'

'Thank you. I will be even better after a chat alone with my wife.'

It took Owen another five minutes to finally rid himself of his best friend, whose surprised delight at his much-improved appearance would have amused and pleased him were he not anxious to get back to Phoebe. He found her white-faced, exactly as he had left her, her tea untouched. Sitting down beside her, he clasped her hands between his. 'It's not the end of the world. We'll find a way to turn this to our advantage.'

She slipped free of his grasp, her mouth wobbling, her eyes stricken. 'I'm so very, very sorry.'

'There's no need to apologise. There was nothing in that piece of bilge that you haven't already told me.'

'There is every need. If I chose to behave in a way that the world sees as scandalous, I must expect to be judged accordingly. But to have inflicted the shame and scandal on my sisters and my aunt! And you, worst of all, that is unforgivable.'

Phoebe dropped her face into her hands and burst into tears. Appalled, for he had never seen her cry, Owen pulled her to her feet, wrapping his arms around her. 'What is unforgivable is exposing someone's private life in order to sell newspapers.'

'You've been so kind to me, and this is how I reward you.'

'Phoebe, stop it. Please don't cry.' He tried to tilt her face up, but she buried it in his chest, sobbing as if her heart would break. All he could do was hold her, after tugging off his gloves so that he could smooth her hair, until her sobs became hiccups and then finally stopped.

'I've made your coat all wet.'

Owen pulled out his handkerchief. 'Here, use this instead.'

She caught his hand, rubbing it against her cheek. 'I really am sorry.'

'Stop apologising, you've even less reason to do so than Jasper.'

'Jasper was hoodwinked by a journalist. I have no one to blame for this mess but myself. You shouldn't have married me.'

'Phoebe.' He gave her a little shake. 'That's quite simply nonsense. Come on, let's retire to the parlour,' Owen said, 'and see if we can turn our new-found notoriety to our advantage.'

But to his dismay as they sat down, fresh tears sprung from Phoebe's eyes. 'I have been selfish and thoughtless. Eloise was right after all.'

'Your sister surely didn't accuse you of any of those things.'

'Not me,' Phoebe said, wringing her hands. 'My mother.'

'Your mother! What on earth has she to do with this?'

'I think I told you that Mama was a—a free spirit—or at least that's how I've always thought of her. She was so very beautiful, and so popular and so passionate—that's what she always used to say, "I am a passionate creature."'

Which certainly did sound, Owen thought, like the words of a woman determined to have her own way. He tried to recall what else Phoebe had said of her mother. Not very maternal—yes, he remembered drawing the comparison there with his own mother, but while he had been well cared for by a host of other responsible adults, Phoebe and her twin seemed to have relied on their elder sister. 'I'm sorry,' he said helplessly, 'I can understand why Eloise would think your mother was selfish, thoughtless even, to have preferred a career as the toast of Dublin society to looking after her children, but you don't even like going to parties.'

'I thought she was bold and brave enough to refuse to be bound by convention. I admired her for that. Eloise and Estelle think very differently, so I kept my opinions to myself, but when I went to Paris, I felt as if I'd been brave and bold too.'

'You were.'

'It was a huge step to go, but when I got there, instead of concentrating on working hard to achieve the one thing that I wanted, I was dazzled by the city and seduced by the life I was leading. I knew that it was wrong of me to have an affaire with Pascal, but I wanted it. So I—this is so mortifying—I told myself that *I* was a free spirit like my mother, and was emulating her. I pretended to myself that she'd be proud of me for doing as she did, for bucking convention. Mama had countless affaires. I thought I was finally doing something that would have made her notice me, something that would have met with her approval. You see, that's how pathetic I am. So I blithely carried on, thinking of no one but myself, heedless of the impact my behaviour might have on anyone save myself. And now it's not me who has to pay, it's you and my sisters.'

'So, naturally you have concluded that your sisters were right about your mother. And if you are like her then it follows that you are also selfish and thoughtless.' She had it so wrong, and she looked so woebegone, he wanted to wrap his arms around her, but he'd done that already and it hadn't helped. 'Women like your mother don't care who they hurt, do they, provided they get their own way?'

'She always said that Papa was trying to suppress her true nature.'

'And you felt that your sisters were suppressing yours, in a way, didn't you? Because in their misguided attempts to protect you from what they thought was certain failure, they were trying to stop you from becoming a chef?'

'I don't know. I suppose. But...'

'So you went to Paris, all on your own, and for the first time in your life you were free of them. There was no one to watch over you, no one to advise you.

It's not surprising that you went a little wild, Phoebe. I certainly would have.'

'No one cares if a man has an affaire. It's expected of them.'

'You weren't married to anyone else. You weren't promised to anyone else. And it wasn't just any old affaire, it wasn't a meaningless fling. You thought you were in love. You thought that you and Pascal had a future together.'

'You make it sound as if what I did was perfectly acceptable.'

'It's completely understandable. I won't insult you by pretending that the world won't see it as scandalous, because the world does judge men and women very differently. But you knew, Phoebe, even when you were relishing every moment of your life in Paris, that your sisters would be shocked.'

'And yet it didn't stop me!'

'But you did your best to keep it from them. Not because you were ashamed but to protect them, shield them from what for them would have been an unpalatable truth. Would your mother have done that?'

'No, because she didn't—' Phoebe broke off, looking stricken.

'Go on,' Owen said gently.

'Because she didn't care,' Phoebe whispered.

'But you did, enough to try to keep your sisters in the dark.'

'She guessed anyway. Eloise sees everything. That's why she sent Estelle to Paris. If I had only listened to Estelle...'

'Phoebe, as far as you were concerned at the time, Estelle was asking you to abandon your life-long ambition.'

'If only I had, we wouldn't be at odds as we are just now. Do you think—Owen, do you think Mama simply didn't care for any of us girls?'

'I think,' Owen said carefully, 'that perhaps she cared for herself first and foremost.'

'That's what Eloise believes.'

'If that rag had written a story about your mother, how do you think she'd feel?'

'I don't know. Not like this. She was forever declaring that she wouldn't apologise for her behaviour. I used to think that was brave of her to thumb her nose at convention.' Phoebe winced. 'Poor Papa. And now I'm inflicting the same thing on you. Like mother like daughter!'

'You went to Paris, the culinary capital of the world, because you passionately wanted to learn how to be a chef. Your passion is something you do have in common with your mother—though I suspect it's the only thing. You had the courage of your convictions, you were determined to chase the pot of gold at the end of your rainbow. So tell me, what is there in that to be ashamed of?'

'I failed.'

'There is no shame in failing. Failing to even try would have been a much bigger crime.'

'But I didn't consider the consequences.'

'There would have been no consequences if some

low-life hack hadn't dished up your broken dreams as salacious gossip.'

'And now everyone will know that you're married to a hussy and a failure.'

'Then there is only one thing to be done.'

Phoebe's face fell. 'Oh! Of course you would be well within your rights if...'

'Not that, silly. We must simply prove them all wrong.'

She opened her mouth to speak then closed it again. He waited, watching the emotions flit across her transparent countenance, delighted to see the way she set her shoulders, braced herself as if readying herself for battle. 'Do you think we can?'

'Of course we can, but we're going to ride out this storm first. We are the scandalmonger's dish of the day. I could pull strings, have a denial printed, make them retract it even, but that would simply lend it credence, fuel the fire. They will have other fish to fry soon enough, and then we will be yesterday's news.'

'Leaving you married to a—a fallen woman, as far as the world is concerned!'

'Do not ever say that!' Owen jumped to his feet. 'Do you hear me, Phoebe?' He pulled her to her feet, forcing her to meet his eyes. 'I am proud to call you my wife. In fact I'd go so far as to say that I can't think of any woman I'd rather call my wife than you. You don't have a selfish or thoughtless bone in you're body. You don't trample over your nearest and dearest—or indeed neglect them—just to get what you want. You are not your mother's daughter. Are you listening to me?'

'I'm just terrified I'll let you down.'

'The only way you could let me down would be if you threw in the towel. Stop living in your sisters' shadow, Phoebe and once and for all, put that bas— put Solignac's opinion of you out of your head. If the restaurant fails, it won't be because you haven't put your heart and soul into it.'

'I won't fail. We won't fail.'

Owen smiled. 'That's the spirit.'

'What was it you said, notoriety whets the appetite? If our restaurant was open tonight, we'd be left with a roomful of plates scraped clean! I'll have to write to Eloise.'

'Would it be better if I wrote to her?'

'Prove to her that you're standing by me? No, thank you, then I'd actually be hiding behind you. I'd better do it today, then I may even pre-empt her seeing that article. I can reassure her that it makes no difference to our plans, that you stand foursquare behind me. As to her name being mentioned in the press—there's nothing I can do about that save to apologise to her and to Alexander. At least I don't need to write to Aunt Kate, she's still away.'

'What about Estelle?' Owen asked tentatively.

'The chances of her seeing that story are remote. I have enough on my plate as it is.'

'I think that's wise. Time enough for that when the dust has settled.' A tear trickled down her cheek. He brushed it away, forgetting that he wasn't wearing his gloves. Her skin was warm, soft, damp. His fingers tingled.

'Is my nose red?'

'Yes.' He kissed it.

He felt her inhale sharply. He let her go, taking a step back, but she caught his hand, lifting it to her mouth, pressing a gentle kiss to his swollen knuckle. 'Thank you. I am so proud to be able to call you my husband. In fact,' she said, smiling up at him, 'I'd go so far as to say that I can't think of any man I'd rather call my husband than you.'

A bittersweet compliment if every there was one, for her kiss, just a silly little kiss, had set his senses alight, and right at this moment, he wanted to be the kind of husband he'd promised he would not be. 'Thank you, but do try for a little originality in your compliments.'

'This, from the man who appropriated Benjamin Franklin's words as his own!'

'Touché.' Reluctantly, Owen extracted his hand from her grasp. 'I haven't done my exercises today, and I want to be fighting fit if we're going to brazen this out.'

'If only we could lock ourselves away from the world for a month or so—oh, good heavens, I didn't mean...'

'It's fine. Don't look so horrified, Phoebe, I can't pretend that I didn't do exactly that. But I'm not doing it again. We're going to face this down.'

'How?'

'I've no idea, but we'll find a way. Do you think you are ready to face the world?'

'If you can do it, then I can.'

She was so brave, and so lovely, all he wanted was

to sweep her into his arms and kiss her. God, he really wanted to kiss her. 'Good,' Owen said, stooping to pick up his gloves. 'Go and write to Eloise. We'll talk later.'

'Thank you. For everything. Just one more thing,' she called as he reached the door. She pointed to his discarded gloves which were sitting on the table. 'It's likely to be a bare-knuckle fight, isn't it? I don't think you should wear those any more.'

Chapter Eight

'Are you teasing me?'

Owen shook his head, concentrating on peeling an apple for Phoebe. 'One sure-fire way to stop that rag digging up more dirt from either of our pasts is to give them something new to write about.'

'So we'll give them a new scandal.'

'Of our own making. What do you think of my daring plan?'

'I thought that only men were allowed to dine at Crockford's?'

'They are.' He finished cutting the apple into thin slivers, laying it out like a fan on the plate the way she liked it. 'Would you like some stilton with that?'

'No, thank you. Well, just a smidgen. Do you intend that I dress up as a man? Or do you plan to smuggle me in?'

Owen guffawed. 'I'd very much like to see you in breeches…'

'Owen!'

'You wouldn't fool anyone, Phoebe,' he said, looking quite unabashed. 'You will go as yourself. It will be our first formal appearance in society as Mr and Mrs Harrington.'

'Yes, but how?'

'Before we got married, I told you that I was a bit of a "name" in the city? Well, another man who has an eye for investments is William Crockford—Crocky to those who think he is their friend. In his case, the "investors" are the poor deluded souls who play at the tables. They say he can predict to the pound and to the hour when a man will come into his inheritance, and that's how he times the invitations to grace his tables. He has become one of the wealthiest men in London by knowing how to calculate odds. He also likes to see the money he makes working for him. And I can help him with that.'

Phoebe frowned. 'Didn't you say that you never give investment tips?'

'I'm happy to make an exception if it suits our purpose.'

'You'll bribe him!' She clapped her hands together gleefully. 'Really? And then he'll let me eat in the restaurant?'

'If I also have a word in the ear of the most esteemed member of the club too, I reckon so.'

'And who is that?'

'The Duke of Wellington.'

Phoebe choked on her apple. 'You are acquainted with the Iron Duke?'

'Our paths have crossed.'

'Goodness. I had no idea you moved in such circles.'

'We were never exactly friends, but London is a small village.'

'Did you ever come across the Earl of Fearnoch—not Eloise's husband, but his brother, the previous earl?'

'He was a bit of a loose fish by all accounts. Not my set. I was feckless, Phoebe, but I was never a libertine.'

'I never thought for a moment that you were.' Her eyes widened. 'Do you mean that Alexander's brother was?'

'And his father, too. He has a cousin, Raymond Sinclair, who seems to be trying his best to keep up the family tradition. Rumour has their coat of arms features a codpiece. I've never met your sister's husband though—which is odd.'

'Alexander spent all of his time working abroad until he married Eloise. He was something in the Admiralty.'

'That explains it. The family won't be strangers to scandal though, will they? No, I don't mean that as a consolation,' Owen added hastily, 'just a fact. And I know it's your sister you're more concerned about than her husband. Did you write to her as planned?'

'I hope I said enough to stop her from worrying. As to her name being dragged into that horrible story—well, at least she and Alexander spend hardly any time in London. Now that she is expecting a baby, she'll spend even less time here.'

'When is the child due?'

'Late spring. Goodness, I wonder if she'll have twins! I shall have to take time away from our restaurant to visit her—but I'm not sure if I'd trust anyone to deputise for me, when the business is so new.'

'We haven't even found the perfect premises yet,' Owen chided her, 'and you're already thinking of closing up!'

'I will not rise to your bait,' Phoebe said with a grin. 'Do you honestly think you can get us into Crockford's?'

'Wellington considers himself something of an epicure. Combine that with the fact that he has an eye for a beautiful woman, and I reckon his curiosity should see us gain entry.'

'I can't believe it. I'm going to taste Louis Eustache Ude's food.'

'Phoebe, you're going to have to do so with the eyes of everyone else in the room fixed on you, you do know that?'

Her excitement fizzled out. 'Can't we request a private room? In fact, if you are so influential—couldn't you simply ask Monsieur Ude to come here to cook for us?'

'But the point of this exercise isn't only to allow you to see what our competition may be.'

Phoebe pushed her plate of untouched cheese and half-finished apple aside. 'We'll be giving them exactly what they want, you mean—playing up to what they expect of us—a scandalous couple, daring to thumb our noses at society's conventions.'

His eyes gleamed. His smile was mischievous and quite irresistible. 'I have to admit, it's an enticing idea,' Phoebe said. 'Monsieur Ude will know from the recent revelations in the press that I am contemplating setting up in competition.'

'That will only serve to put him even more on his mettle. How dare an English person presume that they can cook as well as a Frenchman,' Owen said in a preposterous accent, 'It is an outrage. That a woman think such a thing is a sacrilege. It is unnatural.'

Phoebe collapsed in a fit of giggles. 'You are mocking one of my heroes.'

'He certainly has an inflated opinion of himself. I've heard that if his diners fail to be appreciative enough, he emerges from the kitchens to chastise them.'

Just as Pascal had, Phoebe thought. Though he would never admit it, Pascal had revered Monsieur Ude and been extremely envious of his success, but she'd had no idea he took his admiration to the point of emulation. It made Pascal seem rather pathetic, but she decided not to mention the fact. She did not want him, even as a subject of derision, to pollute the conversation. 'When will we go?'

'You think it's a good idea then?'

'I think it's outrageous. Will it work, do you think?'

'At the very least, you'll get to eat dinner prepared by your food hero.'

'A dinner made by my food hero, eaten with my husband hero. I hope I won't be too nervous to enjoy it.'

'In all seriousness, Phoebe, if it's too much…'

'Don't forget that this will be a big step for you too, Owen.'

'I'll have you by my side to prop me up.'

'And I'll have you, to prop me up.'

'It will probably take a week, perhaps ten days to make the necessary arrangements with Crockford and Wellington. You'll need to order a new gown. Expensive. Chic. Something that treads the line between *à la mode* and *oh, là-là*. You know the kind of thing.'

'I don't. Pray tell me.'

'For a start, nothing pale. It should be bright, vibrant, emerald or sapphire or ruby, the colour of a jewel, drawing attention to the jewel wearing it.'

'Mama always said that redheads should never wear red,' Phoebe said, entranced by this new, charming, flirtatious version of Owen. 'That's why it is Eloise's favourite colour. A scarlet woman. Why not give them exactly what they expect?'

'Tempting, but a bit too obvious, don't you think?'

'Which is why I've not to dress demurely in white, yes?'

'And why you should make the most of your quite delightful figure, but by hints and allusions rather than brazen display.'

'Can a dress hint and allude? How do you know such things—no, don't answer that I don't want to know. I know there have been other woman. I didn't mean I wanted to pretend there haven't been, I meant that I really don't want to know. Or to think about—any more than I wish to think about my own past, to be perfectly frank.'

'Do you wish it undone?'

'No, but I'm not that Phoebe any more.'

'I like the new Phoebe.'

'Do you? There's certainly more of me! I've been eating too much.'

'No. When you left Paris, you'd been eating too little.'

'Mama always said that Estelle and I would run to fat.'

Owen rolled his eyes. 'You once told me that your mother was the kind of person who drew every eye in the room when she walked into it. That's what you do. It's not just the way you look—you are undoubtedly a very beautiful woman—it's something in you. You are captivating. I suspect that your mother recognised that and I'm sorry to say that a woman as vain as she was, would not have wanted her daughters to outshine her.'

'Oh, we didn't.'

'Perhaps not then, you were too young. But if she could see you now—' He broke off, shaking his head. 'She's not here to defend herself, and she's your mother. It's not for me to tarnish your memories of her.'

'I'm beginning to think that my memories of her were—oh, never mind. We were talking about my gown for Crockford's.'

'You could walk in wearing a flour sack tied around the waist and every man in the room would still know the moment they clapped eyes on you why I married you. I've embarrassed you,' he added, seeing her blush. 'I'm sorry. I enjoy your company, I just sometimes forget that I shouldn't be enjoying it quite so much.'

'Don't be sorry. I feel exactly the same.'

'What are you saying?'

'I don't know. Would it be so wrong for us to enjoy each other's company a little bit more?'

Owen set down his wine glass. 'Not if you don't think it's wrong. And not if you're absolutely sure. I don't expect…'

'That's why I'm sure,' Phoebe said. 'Because you don't expect. That's why I'm sure.'

He laughed, pushed back his chair and pulled her into his arms. 'I've never met anyone like you.'

'That's the other reason.' She smiled shyly up at him. 'I've never met anyone like you either.'

Owen fluttered his fingers over the nape of her neck. 'You've no idea how good it feels, just to touch your skin. Lovely Phoebe.' He dipped his head to kiss the hollow of her collar bone. 'Delightful Phoebe.' He trailed kisses up the column of her neck. 'Delicious Phoebe.'

Their lips met. Heart thudding, she closed her eyes and surrendered to the sweet, drugging pleasure of their kisses, twining her arms around his neck, opening her mouth to him, melting, slowly melting. They kissed, and kissed, and kissed some more, breaking off to breathe, to stare wide-eyed with wonder, and then falling back into each other's arms to kiss and kiss and kiss again. They kissed as if they had only just discovered kissing, finding new ways for their mouths to taste and to tease, small fluttering kisses and long, deep kisses. He ran his fingers through her hair, smoothed his hands over the exposed skin at the back of her evening gown, and all the time they kissed. She felt as if she could float away on a cloud of delight, as if she would melt, as if she had turned into something molten and hot and sweet.

And then there came a point when their kisses could have changed. When they hovered on the brink of delight and desire. And they stopped of one accord, silently agreeing that it was enough. For now it was more than enough. And that's when Phoebe knew she'd been right to trust him. That he really was different.

'Goodnight,' Owen said, kissing her gently one more time.

'Goodnight,' Phoebe said, pulling his face down for one last kiss. 'Sleep well, husband of mine.'

For Mr and Mrs Harrington's somewhat unconventional London debut, Phoebe wore an evening gown of bronze silk with a black-net overdress, and a black-velvet bodice edged with bronze-satin ribbon. The sleeves were full but not so full as to require the newly fashionable plumpers, and the décolleté was low enough to accentuate the curve of her bosom but not nearly low enough to show off her cleavage. The hem of the overdress was edged with black-satin leaves embroidered with bugle beads to weight it down, the skirts were full, tightly pleated, and swished alluringly when she walked. It was not a dress Phoebe would ever have chosen for herself, but it was, she thought, exactly what Owen had requested, treading the line between *à la mode* and *oh, là-là*. Talking of which! She unfurled the fan of black ostrich feathers and after peeping over the top of it coquettishly at her reflection, burst into a fit of giggles.

'I think this might be a step too far,' she muttered to herself.

'Oh, no, madam, it works beautifully with the gown.'

She still wasn't used to having a maid, and often dispensed with Jennifer's services altogether, but the undergarments that had been delivered with this gown were impossible to deal with single-handed. 'If you're sure,' Phoebe said, a little dubiously.

'Let me fasten your gloves.'

They were long, white, very tight and brand new, Phoebe was already worried about spilling her dinner on them. Owen had insisted that she didn't ask the price of anything when shopping, but she could guess, and the number made her eyes water. A velvet stole completed the outfit. She gave herself a little curtsy in the mirror and made her way down the stairs, her heart fluttering with anticipation.

Owen was waiting for her in parlour, dressed in black evening clothes with an embroidered silver waist-coat. His hair had been cut short, and looked fairer against the high black collar of his coat. He had filled out in the two months of their marriage, and no lon-ger looked gaunt, but it was the way he held himself that had changed the most. He was confident, com-fortable in himself, and though he still walked with a slight limp, which was more pronounced when he was tired, there was an agility in his movement and a supple strength that could only be attributed to his gymnastics. Beneath the stylish evening clothes, his body was hard-packed muscle.

'You look absolutely divine,' Owen said, breaking into Phoebe's reverie to kiss her softly. 'I'm glad you decided not to be a scarlet woman. This suits you perfectly—you are a bronzed goddess.'

She giggled, opening out her fan and fluttering her eyelashes. 'A scandalous, bronzed goddess.'

'A seductive one. I beg you not to look at me like that in Crockford's or we'll cause an even bigger scandal than the one we've already planned, because I won't be able to resist kissing you in public.'

Phoebe waved her fan slowly in front of her face. 'We're not at Crockford's yet.'

Owen pulled her into his arms and the fan fell to the floor as he kissed her swiftly. 'If we don't leave now, we'll miss dinner. It is served strictly from half past four until six, and it's already after four.' He picked up the fan and handed it to her. 'Ready?'

She was immediately serious. 'As ready as I'll ever be. What about you, Owen—this is a very big step for you?' She scanned his face. 'Are you sure you'll be able to cope?'

He visibly braced himself. 'I'm about to find out.'

It was already dark when the town coach deposited them outside Crockford's. The impressive red-sandstone building with its portico frontage dubbed Fishmonger's Hall by those whose fortune was insufficient to gain them entrance, was opposite White's Club and right in the heart of St James's. Phoebe was creating a scandal by her simple presence in this male enclave, though Owen refrained from reminding her.

In the carriage, she had been unusually silent, but her hand had trembled in his.

Two months ago, even a few weeks ago, he'd have considered this an ordeal—or more likely he wouldn't have contemplated being here at all! Would it trigger one of his episodes? Was he asking too much of himself? Though he'd been out of the house regularly of late, traipsing around London's markets, exploring commercial properties or taking Phoebe on sightseeing drives was very different from mingling with society. He was about to walk into the lion's den now. If something went wrong, then the gossip in tomorrow's rags would be very different from what Phoebe and he had planned.

He had a moment's panic, but taking several covert, deep breaths, he reminded himself of how well he'd been over the last few weeks, without a single nightmare for more than two. Thanks to the woman sitting beside him, who was depending on him now, to support her through this ordeal.

'Remember,' she said, as the coachman let down the steps, 'I'll be right by your side.'

He preceded her out of the carriage and helped her down. 'And I'll be right by yours,' Owen said. 'Every small step of the way.'

A blaze of light emanated from the beacons in the club's entranceway. Crockford's thugs stood aside to allow them to pass into the massive entrance hall which was randomly peppered, it seemed to Owen, with Doric and Ionic columns. It was quiet at this time of day, the real business of the club would not get underway until much later, but beneath the smell of burning oil from the huge chandeliers Crockford was so proud of, the lingering smell of sweat, stale perfume and defeat could be detected. 'Crockford has spared no expense on his decor,' he said to Phoebe, who was gazing up at the domed ceiling.

'It is like a palace,' she whispered, 'though a rather tawdry one. Versailles on a budget.'

Owen bit back a laugh as a servant approached them, informing him that they were expected. Which explained the deserted entrance hall, he thought. Everyone else was already seated and awaiting their arrival. He took Phoebe's arm as they ascended the stairs to the dining room, smiling down at her in what he hoped was a reassuring manner. The steps were shallow and wide, an easy climb, but none the less one he'd have struggled with a few short weeks ago.

'Brace yourself for a baptism of fire,' he said, keeping a firm hold of her arm as the double doors were thrown open and Phoebe obediently took a deep breath.

The dining room was long and rather narrow, with the look of a ballroom. The ornately corniced ceiling was painted in muted tones, as were the walls, which were panelled well above head height, then decorated with rows of yet more interspersed Doric and Ionic columns rising to meet the ceiling. There were no windows but the room was very brightly lit, with a central chandelier and any number of sconces burning, making it stiflingly hot. Tables were set in three regimented rows, far too close together. There was only one free, in the very centre of the room.

Phoebe's fingers were digging into his arm. The eyes of every single person in the room was upon them. What on earth had he done! But it was too late to back out now, and Phoebe, bold Phoebe, was rising to the occasion, her head held high, a faint smile curving her lips which only he could tell was rigidly held in place.

'This way, Mr Harrington,' the major-domo said, leading them needlessly to the table. The silence was dagger-sharp. He could hear the rustle of Phoebe's dress as she sat down, but when his own chair was pulled out, Owen stood his ground, taking his time to survey the other diners. He recognised many but none were among his friends, most from an older generation— presumably Wellington's cronies. Some looked away from his gaze, some met it. A very few nodded. Owen made a flourishing bow, then took his seat.

'That's the worst part over,' he said softly to Phoebe, 'forget the audience, and let's see what Monsieur Ude has to offer us.'

'Every one is watching.'

'That was rather the point, but it won't last. If they don't turn their attention to their food, Monsieur Ude will have something to say. Try to forget they are here. I'll order the wine, you concentrate on memorising the menu. Order whatever takes your fancy and as many dishes as you want to sample.'

'It is eye-wateringly expensive, even compared to La Taverne.'

'As is the wine,' Owen said, scanning the huge leather-bound tome he had been handed. '"Our cel-lars boast more than three hundred thousand bottles of the best that France has to offer,'" he read. 'Presumably so that Crockford's diners are well lubricated before they try their luck at the tables later. We should start with champagne, I feel our audience expects it of us.'

A bottle appeared with impressive speed, with two glasses. As soon as they were poured, Owen raised his glass, first to the room, and then, theatrically, to his wife. 'Well done,' he said as she copied him. 'Now, why don't you try really hard to forget our audience, and try to make the most of this unique, never-to-be-repeated experience.'

'We did it!' Phoebe danced into the parlour, casting off her wrap. 'We braved the lion's den and lived to tell the tale. Owen, you were magnificent.'

He laughed, following in her wake and closing the door. 'Thank you, though I'm not sure what I did to merit such fulsome praise.'

'You mean aside from gaining us unprecedented access to London's most exclusive restaurant.'

'Yes, apart from that,' he said, pulling off his gloves and pulling her into his arms.

'I know that can't have been easy for you,' Phoebe said, 'though no one would have guessed since you looked so perfectly at home, as if you had never been away. And the way you raised your glass to everyone at the start of the meal with such—such panache! While I took one look into that dining room and would happily have turned tail.'

'You carried it off every bit as well as I did.'

'I didn't want to let you down.'

'More importantly, you didn't let yourself down. Was it worth it?'

'Yes. It was invaluable. Though it's not an experience I'd ever want to repeat.'

'The main thing is we've achieved what we set out to do. You have run the rule over the competition and we have given the *ton* something new to tittle-tattle about other than your Parisian past. And here we are, unscathed.'

'Are you? Really?'

'I am. You gave me a reason to get better, Phoebe. Tonight—I really think that tonight was proof that I can.'

'Owen! I can't believe it.' With a muffled cry, she threw her arms around his neck, covering his face with kisses.

Laughing, he pulled her tighter, and their lips met. And then they kissed, as they had kissed every night since the night they had planned this Crockford's coup, slow kisses, deepening until they were verging on the frantic, before they forced themselves to stop. This was where Owen would say goodnight. This was the point where they always stopped, because if they didn't it would change everything.

Their eyes met, and suddenly Phoebe couldn't breathe. She wanted everything to change, and she could see in his eyes that Owen wanted it too. Though he would not ask. So she pulled his face back towards her and kissed him again, a long, languorous kiss whose meaning could not be mistaken.

Owen was panting when this kiss finished, his eyes dark with desire. 'Phoebe?'

She nodded.

'Are you sure?'

She didn't hesitate. 'I'm sure.'

The fire in Phoebe's room was burning brightly. She hastily pulled the screen over it, confirming, as he had suspected, that she knew it was his orders which kept the other fires in the town house burning low, though she had never once commented on the fact. Owen pretended not to notice, locking the door, and as she turned back to face him, he forgot everything else.

Wrapping his arms around her, he could feel her trembling. 'It's not too late to change your mind,' he said.

'I'm nervous. I don't want to dis...' She bit her lip. 'I won't say it.'

Owen laughed softly. 'If one of us should be worrying about disappointing the other, don't you think it should be me?'

'I didn't think! Perhaps we shouldn't...'

'Phoebe, I'm teasing you.' Though he wasn't, not completely. He was nervous. He kissed her softly. 'You are so lovely.' He kissed her again. Kisses were definitely an excellent remedy for nerves. 'I want you so much.'

This kiss was deeper. Blood rushed back to his groin. He needed to be patient, there was no rush. He had waited more than two years for this, he could wait a few minutes longer. He dragged his mouth away from hers, scattering kisses down her neck, across the swell of her breasts. Turning her around he tugged at the laces of her gown, kissing the nape of her neck, her shoulders, the knot of her spine, as he eased the dress down her body and she shivered.

The laces of her corsets were tightly tied, but his fingers were much more nimble these days, from practising—ironically—tying knots. Dropping the stays to the ground, he pulled her back against him, his erection pressed against the plump curve of her bottom, cupping her breasts. She moaned, a guttural sound that made him harder. Her nipples were erect. He circled them through her chemise, and she wriggled against him. This time it was he who moaned.

As Phoebe twisted around in his arms, her mouth sought his, and he surrendered to the clamouring need to kiss her again, shrugging out of his coat. More kisses, while her hands tugged at the buttons of his waistcoat, and he pulled the pins from her hair, until it rippled down her back, over her shoulders in a glorious wave of burnished gold.

He ran his hands down her back to cup her bottom, then back up again. Her hands were yanking his shirt free of his trousers, smoothing over his back, making his muscles clench, the sensations she was arousing in him making him shudder. His waistcoat fell to the floor. She pulled his shirt over his head, but when he would have kissed her again, she shook her head. A sensual smile curved her delicious mouth as she touched him, stroking his chest, his shoulders, back to his chest down to his belly, her eyes widening as his muscles flexed, her delight in his muscled body so patently obvious.

'You are so lovely,' she said, sounding awed, and his engorged shaft throbbed in response.

Not yet, he cautioned himself, not yet. He kissed her again—he could kiss her for ever and never tire of her—and undid the ties of her petticoat, leaving her in her chemise, drawers and stockings, a sight that temporarily deprived him of the ability to breathe. The chemise went next. He lost long, delightful minutes kissing her breasts, taking her nipples into his mouth in turn, becoming ever more aroused by her response, the way she moaned, clutched at his shoulders, shuddered against him. His self-control was pushed to the limits.

One more kiss, and Owen scooped her up, making her cry out in surprise, making for the bed, setting her down on it before he'd had time to consider whether or not he was even capable of such a feat. Tearing off the rest of his clothes, he lay beside her on the bed, pulling her tight against him, skin melded to skin. Their kisses were feverish now. He rolled between her legs and she arched under him. He eased himself into her. She was slick, hot, and dear God in heaven he was hard. He pushed higher, feeling her clench around him, and he thrust. Pain seared through his hip, drawing a hoarse cry from him.

'Owen.'

'Wait.' He breathed deeply, shaking his head when she made to move, kissing her again, deeply, until it eased. 'This way,' he said, rolling on to his back, still inside her, the surprise on her face telling him that this was a novel experience for her.

She moved, carefully, tentatively at first, but the

way she clenched around him, the visible shivers that ran through her as he pushed higher, made her bolder. She needed no urging to go faster, to rock backwards and forward, crying out as she reached a juddering climax, sending him over the edge so quickly that he only just managed to free himself, before his own release ripped through him.

'Phoebe?' Owen shuffled over in the bed, wrapping his arms around her, burying his face in her hair, heaving a deep sigh that was unmistakably satisfied 'Oh, Phoebe.'

She curled into him, pressing her cheek to his chest. 'Oh, Owen.'

She felt the rumble of his laughter, and thought that her cup might brim over with happiness. Everything about what had just happened felt so new and so perfect. The kissing. The delicious, delightful kissing that went on and on, as if they were starving and couldn't get enough of each other. And the way Owen had looked at her, devouring her with his eyes, leaving her in no doubt about what he thought of her, how much he wanted her. And even right at the end, the way he had thought of her, of protecting her—when it was her responsibility to take care of such details. Or so Pascal said.

No, she wouldn't think of him. She had not once thought of him, she realised now with quiet satisfaction, pressing a kiss to Owen's chest, breathing in the scent of him, clean sweat and soap. Nothing that Owen had done had reminded her. Nor anything she'd felt ei-

ther. It wasn't like the first time—now that was something she really didn't want to think of—but it felt new.
Delightfully new.

Owen trailed his hand down her back, to rest on
her bottom. She wriggled closer, resting her hand on
his flank, encountered a hard ridge of scarring and
his hand, which had been drawing little circles on her
bottom, froze. 'Is it painful?'

'Not the scar.'

Phoebe lifted her head. 'May I look?'

He shrugged, which was what he often did when
he was embarrassed, and rolled on to his stomach.
She sat up, pushing back the sheet he had pulled over
them. The scar ran in a jagged line from halfway up
his thigh, all the way up his flank to end at the top of
his hip. 'How did you get this?'

'Not in the accident. It was afterwards. An operation to piece together the shattered bone.'

'Dear heavens, Owen, that must have been an agony.'

'I barely remember. I think they poured a bottle of
cognac down my throat.'

'Did it make it better or worse?'

He laughed grimly. 'The big question. I will never
know.'

Phoebe traced the line of the scar with her fingers.
'Can you feel that?'

'Not really.'

She leaned over, pressing a line of little kisses along
it. 'Can you feel that?'

'A little. Perhaps if you tried again.'

She did, this time with more lingering kisses, using

her tongue and her lips. Owen gave a muffled groan. 'Did you feel that?'

'I definitely felt that.'

There was laughter in his voice. Something else that was entirely new. Phoebe kissed her way along his scar again, then carried on, kissing up his back, sliding down the bed to lie by his side again, pressing a last kiss to his ear. 'Did you feel that?' she whispered.

He rolled over, wrapping his arms around her, his eyes alight with laughter and desire. 'What do you think?'

His erection was pressing into her stomach. Her breasts were pressed against his chest. Her body was already starting to clamour for more in a way that astonished her. Another novel development, she thought, answering him with a kiss.

They made love for the second time that night, more slowly this time, savouring each other. Their kisses were languorous. Owen devoted long, exquisite minutes to her breasts, licking, kissing, sucking, so that she thought she might have fainted with the bliss of it. And he wanted her to touch him, to wrap her fingers around the thick, silky length of his erection, to stroke him, his pleasure at what she was doing written so clearly on his face that she gained confidence. And then he touched her too, slow strokes, without urgency, aiming not for completion but only to draw out the pleasure—dear heavens, such pleasure. And all the time, their eyes locked, between kisses, communicating silently.

Their lips met again, and of one accord their kiss

deepened, and with a speed that left her breathless, Phoebe went from floating on a cloud of delight to a swooping, shuddering climax, and Owen pushed inside her, hitching her leg over his, and his slow, deep thrusts stretched the pleasure out further, making her cry out with each one, clutching at him to pull him deeper inside her, murmuring his name over and over, until he pulled free with a hoarse cry.

And afterwards, once more wrapped tightly together, her back to his chest, he nuzzled her ear. 'I have never felt like this, Phoebe. Never.'

Owen left for his own room, leaving her alone in the dishevelled bed. She would have preferred him to stay with her, but had not said so. In this new world order, she had no idea what the rules were. Tonight had been perfect beyond her wildest dreams already, she didn't want to spoil it. She wanted to wake in Owen's arms, but he was accustomed to sleeping on his own, so she must not read anything into his leaving her. And besides, she told herself sternly, she had always preferred to have her bed to herself too. She liked to stretch out, didn't she?

She normally did, but not tonight. Instead, she curled up into the warm space that Owen had left, and nestled her cheek on the pillow where he had lain. She could not compare tonight with any other night, because there was simply no comparison. She hadn't realised until tonight that Pascal was a selfish lover. She hadn't known that making love was a conversation as well as an act. She certainly hadn't known that desire could be rekindled so easily by shared laughter. She hadn't had to think, when she was making love with Owen, about whether she was pleasing him, because she could see it writ large in his face, in his reactions.

Had she been too bold? She had been so carried away, entranced by the effortlessness of it, and the depth of the pleasure, and the sheer delight of it, but what if Owen thought differently? What if he thought her confidence came from her experience? The idea was like a dousing of cold water. Ought she to have pretended ignorance? But tonight had shown her she *was* much more ignorant than she'd realised. And she was in danger of spoiling it, with her insecure doubts.

So she would cast her doubts away, confine those to the past, and enjoy the present. Well, she might just think about the most recent past again, just until she fell asleep. *'I have never felt like this, Phoebe. Never.'* Owen's words. Phoebe could only echo them.

Chapter Nine

Phoebe gazed around the vast space that was earmarked for the main dining room of her new restaurant. The ceilings were picked out in white and gold to match the wall panelling. The windows were tall, French-style. The basement kitchen needed a lot of work, but it had running water and more importantly, the passageway to the dining room was wide and short. There were even a number of small rooms which could be converted for private dining. 'It's perfect,' she said, 'if I want to compete with Monsieur Ude. We could easily seat fifty people in here—double that if we put the tables closer together.'

'I never did go to La Grande Taverne,' Owen said, 'but I'm assuming it looked something like this?'

'Yes.'

He watched her, pacing out the floor, and when she departed to take another look at the basement space, Owen occupied himself with rereading the lease. There was a great deal of leeway, he reckoned, for renegotiating the terms, but the many clauses and sub-clauses failed to hold his attention. It was over a week since that night at Crockford's changed everything for him. And, he hoped, for Phoebe too.

It had borne fruit in a different way too. The *Town Crier* had stopped digging into Phoebe's past and was now breathlessly speculating about the unconventional couple's possible assault on London's gourmands. All excellent advance publicity as far as Owen was concerned.

They hadn't discussed their feelings, but every time they made love, their bodies spoke for them. He had never felt like this before. It might be a cliché, to say that the two of them became one, but it was also true. He shook his head wryly. Who would have thought it!

He was in love with Phoebe. Bloody hell! Owen stuffed the documents back into the leather portfolio, and headed for the window. The glass was icy on his forehead as he leaned against it. Outside, the leaden sky looked ominous, heralding a dusting of snow. Was he really in love? His foolish smile was answer enough, but he still couldn't quite believe it. He wasn't only in love, he was well. Love had cured him, Owen thought, mocking his own mawkishness, but once again, the cliché seemed to be true. He hadn't lost a second to those peculiar lapses for some time. He was still haunted by the asylum nightmare, as he now referred to it in his head, but each time it occurred, the dream moved further on. He had now located the source of the high-pitched wailing, when he opened a door and found himself not in the usual empty room but some sort of crèche. Though as far as he knew, the asylum where

he had first come to his senses after his accident had
not been a lying-in hospital, his memory of those agonising days was hazy to say the least. He had decided
that this nightmare was in fact based on some vague
memory. Though he still couldn't understand why he
awoke feeling so racked with guilt and sorrow, he believed he was making progress and hoped that one day
he'd have progressed far enough to be able to spend
the night sleeping in Phoebe's arms. Not yet, but soon.
What mattered is that he wanted it, that it was an ambition he believed he could one day realise. His appetite for life had returned, thanks to her.

And here she was, his lovely, funny, brave wife,
with dust on her nose and a worried frown. Now was
not the time for a declaration. She knew, she couldn't
doubt the depth of his feelings, but he wanted the first
time he told her to be special. And though he was
pretty certain she was in love with him, he wasn't sure
that she realised it quite yet. It was too fragile and too
new for them to talk about. And besides, she was distracted by her restaurant. So he'd wait until after the
opening night—however long away that might be. It
would be worth it. There was no rush. They had the
rest of their lives to spend together.

Owen had been staring out of the window, but as she
came back into the dining room, he turned and smiled,
and Phoebe forgot her worries for a moment, stepping
into his embrace, resting her cheek against the rough
wool of his greatcoat. Every day, she came to care more
for him. Every time she saw him, her heart did a little

leap and she felt as if the sun came out inside her. She had never been so happy, but she was determined to look no further ahead than today, and then tomorrow and the next day, to enjoy and relish every moment. She was terrified it might end, and so she would not tempt fate by putting a name to her feelings. She wrapped her arms around her husband's waist, reassured by his now familiar shape, then let him go.

'You've got dust on your nose,' he said, wiping it with his kerchief.

'The kitchens haven't been used for some months.'

'It was a town house. When the last lease expired, it was parcelled up into smaller premises. I think this must have been the drawing room. What do you think?'

She took a deep breath. 'I'm sorry. If you'd asked me back in October, when we were first married, I'd probably have said it was perfect. But now...'

'What has changed?'

She smiled at him, suddenly quite sure. 'Everything.'

Owen laughed. 'I think you need to explain.'

'That visit to Crockford's, it was the turning point for me. The food was superlative, exactly what I expected. Even the mackerel roe dish that he is most famous for lived up to my high expectations, and as for the *boudin de cerises a là Bentinck*—who would have thought that cherry pudding could taste so heavenly.'

'You don't think you can compete with that? I can't say I share your enthusiasm for the mackerel concoction, there was so much butter and cream it gave me indigestion just looking at it, but I am not a gourmand.'

'No, but you do like to eat, don't you, Owen?'

'I like to have dinner with you, but the company is far more important than the food—forgive me, I know that's tantamount to heresy for you.'

'But it's not!' Phoebe clapped her hands together, beaming at him. 'You have hit the nail exactly on the head.'

'If I have, it was an accident. What nail?'

'I don't want people to come to our restaurant to worship the food—I want them to enjoy it, but I don't want it to dominate. I can see from your expression that I'm still not explaining it very well. Bear with me.' Phoebe wrapped her cloak more tightly around her, shivering. 'Do you remember the first meal I cooked for you?'

'Of course I do. Venison stew.'

'And when I asked you what was in it, you didn't much care, did you? As far as you were concerned, it was delicious, and that was all that mattered. At La Grande Taverne each ingredient would have been dissected and discussed endlessly. The diners would not have commented on how delicious it was, but how extraordinary or unusual it was, whether it was the *amuse-bouche*, the *entrée* or the dessert. Honestly, Owen, when they were presented with Pascal's *rôti sans pareil*, they were expected to swoon.'

'I know I'm going to regret asking, but what is a *rôti sans pareil*?'

'It is when a series of birds are stuffed inside each other, smallest to largest. The culinary term for it is *engastration* which doesn't sound particularly appetising.'

'It sounds more like a surgical procedure.'

Phoebe chuckled. 'It *is* a surgical procedure. You have to debone each of the birds, and tie them together, as if you were wrapping it up like a present, with a layer of stuffing in between. Most chefs are content with four or five birds, but Pascal insisted on serving twelve.'

'I am not remotely surprised to hear that.'

'The customers loved it. Pascal always came out of the kitchen to carve. If he had not been a chef I think he would have been on the stage.'

'By the sounds of it, he treated the restaurant as his stage, and his customers were his adoring audience. What happened if they didn't adore him?'

'He would have them summarily ejected. How dare they question his cooking! His notoriously temperamental nature added to the sense of theatre, much as like Monsieur Ude.'

'Do you intend to be equally volatile?'

Phoebe rolled her eyes. 'You know that I am not a performer, I want my food to speak for me. Now I've completely lost the thread of what I was trying to explain to you.'

'*Engastration.*'

'Oh, that was just an example. In fact, it was not Pascal's invention, though he claimed it was. The recipe was published in the *Almanach des Gourmands*, which is a sort of gastronomist's periodical, about ten or fifteen years ago. Pascal had a complete collection of them, and I read them. I didn't tell him that I knew he'd purloined the idea for his own though.' She waved her hands dismissively. 'What I'm trying to explain, Owen, is that I don't want to cook that kind of food. I don't want to prove Pascal wrong by imitating him—though Crockford's demonstrated very clearly to me, that in fact Pascal has been imitating Monsieur Ude. But I don't want to give London another Crockford's either. I want our restaurant to be the very opposite of both of those establishments. It will be a place where people will feel comfortable, as if they were sitting down to a meal in their own dining room. The food will be excellent…'

'Of course!'

'But it won't be like a piece of art to be admired. I would like us to have restaurant more like a Parisian café, you know, with a real mix of people. What do you think?'

'Well for a start, we'll have to look at rather different premises.'

'I know, I'm so sorry I've wasted your time.'

'No, don't be sorry, my little revolutionary.'

'Is it so radical? Too radical?'

He laughed. 'I have no idea, but my eye for a business opportunity is telling me that London is ready for something new and different.'

'I thought you only had eyes for me.' Owen smiled down at her, and her heart skipped a beat. 'So, we are decided then,' Phoebe added, feeling not a single twinge of doubt.

'It seems we are,' Owen said, kissing the tip of her nose.

'Such a huge decision merits a proper kiss, don't you think?' she said, laughing.

He swept her into his arms, and her laughter faded immediately as their lips met, to be replaced with desire. 'As ever, my lovely wife, you are absolutely right.'

Christmas Day

The house was unnaturally quiet, since all the servants were enjoying a rare official holiday, leaving Owen and Phoebe to their own devices. Which suited them very well indeed. The festivities began with Owen bringing Phoebe breakfast in bed, before snuggling in beside her to share the simple repast. The tea had grown quite cold by the time they were ready to drink it.

It had been very tempting to remain in bed all day, but the snow which had been threatening for the last week finally started falling so they had ventured out, walking through St James's park then round Hyde Park and on to Regent's Park, following Owen's old running route. Their footsteps were muffled on the snow-covered footpaths, the vast expanses of grass a smooth carpet of white, the trees decorated with clumps of snow clinging to branches.

On their return, they had drunk mulled wine in the kitchen, Owen sitting at the table inexpertly but happily carrying out the more menial tasks, Phoebe bustling about happily in her element, preparing Christmas dinner. Now, with the feast over, they had decamped from the dining room to the parlour, curled up together at either end of the sofa like bookends, Phoebe's stockinged feet resting on Owen's lap.

'My parents always spent Christmas in Dublin when we were growing up,' she said. 'So we never exchanged gifts or made much of a fuss. It was different at Elmswood Manor, Aunt Kate held a big party for all the tenants, and there was a village fayre too. Last year in Paris, Christmas was a working day, cooking other people's dinner. Now this year, I'm here with you.'

'Still cooking dinner, too! My compliments to the chef.'

'My compliments to the *sous-chef.*'

Owen laughed. 'You re-chopped every diced onion I handed you, and you had to dig the eyes out of the potatoes.'

'I hoped you hadn't noticed.'

'I notice everything about you. It really was a delicious dinner, Phoebe, thank you.'

'It was a pleasure. If all our customers are as easily satisfied as you, then I shall have a very straightforward time of it in the kitchen.'

'You think me easily satisfied?'

Her eyes had drifted shut, for he had been playing with her toes, but now they flew open. He was smiling at her, one brow slightly raised, that smile of his that instantly made her pulse race. She wriggled her foot free, to rest it on the top of his thigh. 'On the contrary, I think you might be insatiable.'

He ran his fingers up her calf, stroking circles at the backs of her knees, something which he had discovered made her giddy with delight. 'I don't think I'll ever be able to get enough of you. Not even if I live to be a hundred.'

She was stroking him with her foot, the ridge of his arousal clear through the material of his trousers. He gently pulled her towards him, sliding his hand up her thigh, finding the gap in her drawers, to cup her. She pressed against his hand.

'I'm not the only one who's insatiable,' Owen said, teasing her, lightly stroking her.

Phoebe bit her lip, trying not to moan, and he slid his fingers inside her. Sometimes she enjoyed making love slowly. Sometimes, like now, there was an urgency in her that took her breath away. Always, Owen seemed to know exactly what to do, to read her body as if she had given him a recipe for every occasion. She rushed towards a climax, and it was barely over when he helped her upright, where she was more help than hindrance tugging at his clothes, smoothing the sheath which he had procured over his throbbing arousal, then taking him inside her quickly, deeply, with a harsh groan of satisfaction. Though she was on top, once again he sensed her needs, taking charge, encouraging her to thrust, fast and hard, sending her spiralling out of control, as he came, pulling her tight against his heaving chest, saying her name over and over.

Later, making the most of their deserted home, they returned to the kitchen, where Phoebe warmed the last of the mulled wine and Owen sat at the table watching her. She was wrapped in one of his dressing gowns, a dark green velvet quilted affair which was far too big for her, and made her impossibly endearing. He turned the little box over in the pocket of his own dressing gown, unaccountably nervous about giving her his gift, for it was such an obvious token of love. He had kept his promise to himself not to declare himself, but there were moments every day when he was tempted.

It was never in the aftermath of lovemaking, there was no need for words then. It was when she handed him his breakfast plate, a dainty montage of choice morsels set out with such care and precision, for she knew he had to be tempted to eat in the morning. Or when she was perusing one of the regular letters she received from Eloise, her face an ever-changing picture of emotions, so that he could guess almost every line of it without her reading it out. Or when she was sitting with her precious book of recipes, staring into space, tapping the end of her pencil on her nose, then she would suddenly smile to herself with such glee, and begin to write furiously. Or sometimes it was simply seeing her face light up when he walked into a room, so transparent with love that he thought his heart might burst.

He knew she loved him, but he sensed that she was still fragile. She might not have loved Solignac as she had thought, but she had still been hurt, damaged by the experience. She needed time to become confident in his love for her, and he was still determined to give her as much time as she needed.

But his love token was like a hot coal burning in his pocket. As he took the glass of wine from Phoebe, chinking it to hers, he decided. This had been such a perfect day, he wanted it to end perfectly. 'Close your eyes,' Owen said, 'and hold out your hands.'

'Why?'

'It's a surprise. That's why I told you to close your eyes.'

'A nice surprise?' Phoebe asked, sounding suspicious, though she did as he asked her.

'I'll let you be the judge of that.' He placed the small box in her outstretched hands. 'You can look now.'

She looked at him first, her mouth trembling, though he wasn't sure if she was on the brink of smiling or crying. His stomach cramped with nerves, anticipation making him feel as if he might actually be sick. Had he done the wrong thing? Phoebe opened the box and stared at the ring. She took it out, tracing the heart shape of the rubies which surrounded the central diamond, holding it up to the light to admire the delicate pierce work on the gold band.

'Do you like it?' he demanded, unable to contain himself any longer.

'Oh, Owen.' To his dismay, she burst into tears. Then she threw her arms around his neck. 'Oh, Owen, I've never seen anything so utterly beautiful. Thank you so much.'

'Here, let me put it on.' Weak with relief, he slipped the ring on to her finger above her wedding band. 'Does it fit?'

She splayed her fingers out, gazing rapt at his gift. 'It might have been made for me.'

The truth was, it had been, and at great expense. Now was the perfect moment to tell her he loved her. He was sure of it. There was no point in waiting. She had his heart, that's all he needed to say, and this was a token.

'Phoebe, I...'

There was a rushing in his ears and the stone floor seemed to swoop up to meet him. His knees gave way. As he pitched forward, he saw her face, stricken with horror. And then there was nothing.

'Owen?' Fighting back her rising panic, Phoebe dropped to her knees, easing him down with her, placing his head on her lap. How she had managed to catch him as he fell she had no idea. 'Owen', she said again, leaning over him, listening with her heart pounding for a breath, holding her own, until she heard him, shallow and faint, but he was definitely breathing. She laid her hand on his forehead. His skin was cold, clammy. Feeling helpless and foolish, she placed her hand over his heart under his dressing gown, trying to time her own breathing with his heartbeat. Just when she was beginning to wonder if she should try to rouse him, he opened his eyes, staring blankly at her.

'You fainted,' Phoebe said.

Owen heaved himself to his feet, staring around him as if he had no idea where he was.

'Sit down for a moment. I'll get you some water.'

But he was already pushing past her, heading out of the kitchen.

'Owen?' She ran after him, grabbing his arm.

He shook her off with a snarl. 'For pity's sake just let me be!'

* * *

'Is there something wrong with your tea?'

'What?'

Owen smiled at her, indicating her full cup. 'You've normally emptied the pot by now.'

Phoebe picked up her cup, taking a quick swallow of the cold tea. 'How are you feeling?'

'That's the second time you've asked me that. I'm fine.' She was not fine, she was at a complete loss. After Owen had stormed off last night, she had crept with the stealth of a thief to his rooms. Unable to summon the courage to face him, she had listened intently, until she heard him moving about. After that, she'd sat for over an hour in the kitchen, waiting in vain for him to return.

A sleepless night had brought her early to the breakfast parlour, waiting on tenterhooks for him to join her. Which he had, acting as if nothing untoward had happened. If she hadn't caught him as he fell, she'd have been worried that he'd hit his head. But she had caught him. Had he suffered some sort of apoplexy that had affected his brain? But aside from the fact he was quite oblivious of how the night had ended, he seemed perfectly sane.

Was he *pretending* that he didn't remember because he was embarrassed? 'Did you sleep well?' she asked helplessly.

'I don't know what you put in that mulled wine, but it knocked me out.'

But he hadn't actually touched the mulled wine before he fainted. He wasn't pretending, he really didn't remember, she was certain of that much. Could this be some new phase of his illness? Her blood ran cold at that thought. But, no, why should it be, when there had been no other signs whatsoever? Whatever had happened was an aberration of some kind.

Could one have a surfeit of lovemaking? They had been making love at least once a day, often more, almost every day. And Owen had been celibate for over two years, after all. Was it possible to have an excess? Did it deplete some vital bodily humour? She had no idea. What she did know was that she was clutching at straws.

'Phoebe?'

She blinked.

'Do you like it? The ring?'

So he had noticed she was wearing it, and he did remember giving it to her. 'Oh, Owen, it's beautiful. I've never seen a design like it. The heart, I mean.' Just before he fainted, she had been so sure he was going to tell her that it represented *his* heart. She waited, hoping, longing for him to take the opportunity now. But he was staring at the ring as if he had never seen it before.

'I'm glad it fits.'

'Yes,' she said, struggling to hide her disappointment. 'It's a perfect fit.'

'I'll get you a fresh pot of tea. If you're up to it, I have a new list of premises for us to explore, but if not…'

'I'm fine, Owen. I'm keen to find the right place, now that we have settled on a café-style restaurant.'

* * *

'I think this might be the one,' Phoebe said, gazing around the room, her eyes shining.

Owen smiled at her enthusiasm. 'You've only just walked in the door.'

'I know, but I have a good feeling about it.'

The premises was low-ceilinged, and had clearly been some sort of shop, with panelled walls and wooden floors, and two bow windows facing on to the street. Phoebe was right, there was something very reminiscent of Parisian cafés about it. It was certainly not grand, but it could be made to feel extremely comfortable.

'I can already see it,' Phoebe was saying. 'We'll put seating all around the walls, and rows of little tables—though not crammed as close together as they are in Paris. Then over here, we'll have some more private seating, tables for four or six. And here, the front desk—see, it's an excellent position for the waiters to view the whole room. Come on, let's look upstairs.'

He followed her up the rather narrow staircase.

'Owen! I think the fates must be telling us something.'

The room was built into the eaves and stretched the full length of the café. The floor was bare boards, rather than black and white tiles, the walls painted an unappealing brown rather than red, but the resemblance to the top-floor room at the Procope was nevertheless striking. 'We'd better work out where we might locate the kitchens first,' he cautioned.

Phoebe caught his hand, pulling him down the room. 'Do you remember?'

'Of course I do. Our table was about here, I think.'

'I think you're right. Oh, Owen, this is it. This is our restaurant.' She whirled around, her arms spread, her skirts flying out. 'This really is it.'

He watched her, rooted to the spot, as she danced around the room, opening cupboards, brushing the dust from the window panes to peer out. She was so lovely, and he loved her so much. Seeing the ring on her finger the morning after Christmas had been a shock. He had no recollection of giving her the present. Phoebe had behaved oddly over breakfast, she'd seemed unsettled, though when he asked her, she said there was nothing wrong. The loss of memory panicked him, but six days had passed without further incident. If he'd had a relapse, it was a minor one. He had been premature, he'd concluded, in giving Phoebe such an obvious token. He should have waited, as he'd planned, until after the restaurant was open. Time to make sure too, that he really was cured.

'Kitchens,' Phoebe said, taking his hand again, leading him back down the stairs and then down again, to the basement, where she exclaimed at once, 'This will do nicely.'

Owen, unconvinced, gazed around the empty room.

'Trust me, it's the perfect space,' Phoebe said earnestly. 'You just have to use your imagination.'

'That's your job.' He took out his notebook and pencil. 'You imagine away, and I will make a list.'

'You do like it as much as me, don't you?' she asked, her expression becoming troubled. 'You aren't having second thoughts?'

'Of course not, why would you think that?'

'No reason. You've been a little distracted, that's all.'

Owen had, once again, underestimated his wife's powers of observation. 'I'm not having second thoughts, Phoebe. I've not been sleeping very well, that's all.' Which was true. 'There's so much to think about, if we are to be up and running for the new Season,' he added. Which was also true, but it was not what kept him awake. Or more accurately, prevented him from going back to sleep. Resolutely, he put the latest development in his asylum nightmare to the back of his mind, and smiled down reassuringly at his wife. 'If you are happy with this place, then I am delighted.'

She wrapped her arms around his waist. 'We'll remember this moment in the future, when we are the toast of London, won't we? We'll remember the day when we first walked into this place and we just knew. Don't you think?'

'I don't think, I know we will.'

'Tomorrow is the first day of the new year. It's an omen, isn't it? Everything is falling into place. It's going to be perfect.'

He couldn't bear to disappoint her. He so desperately wanted her to be right. 'Perfect,' Owen said. And kissed her.

'Good morning.' Phoebe forced herself to remain seated as Owen walked into the room. It was better, she had learned these last three weeks, to gauge his mood before rushing into his arms for their first kiss of the day. Today, his smile was forced. Today, he kissed her cheek as he pulled out his chair. So instead of an embrace, the day began with her putting together a small plate of breakfast which she knew, with a sinking heart, that he would only pretend to eat.

She poured him a cup of coffee, trying to assess his mood. There were dark shadows under his eyes, but he hated her to ask him how he had slept and she hated this constant reminder that though they made love as frequently as ever and if anything even more passionately, they had never actually spent the night in the same bed.

'There you are,' she said, putting the plate of food down in front of him.

'What is that?'

'Smoked haddock and a poached egg.'

'No, that noise.'

'I can't hear anything.'

Pushing his chair back, he threw open the door to the breakfast parlour, standing stock still in the doorway for several painful seconds before returning to his seat.

'What did you hear?' Phoebe asked.

'Nothing.' Owen picked up his fork, stared at his plate, then put his fork down again. 'Has the kitchen cat had kittens?'

'No. Did you think you heard…?'

'Nothing!' He sighed heavily, then reached over the table to cover her hand. 'Sorry. I'm a little tired, that's all. This looks lovely. Tell me what your plans are for the day while I eat it.'

She did so, pretending to concentrate on her own breakfast as Owen forced his down with grim determination, finishing with an equally grim smile. 'So, what are your plans?'

They had not changed in the last ten minutes, but he clearly hadn't heard a word she'd said. 'The usual,' Phoebe said brightly. 'Check on progress at the café. Listen to our foreman's reasons for why progress has once again failed to be as expected and as he predicted. Extract yet another promise that he will make up the time.'

Owen threw back the last of his coffee. When he smiled this time, the stranger who had been sitting beside her vanished, and she was once again breakfasting with her husband. 'I'd offer to sort him out for you,' he said, 'but I don't think the threat of a kick up the backside from me will be nearly as effective as one of those little smiles of yours. "Oh, Mr Gilligan, if you can see your way to making up time, it would make me so happy,"' he teased, clasping his hands and assuming a saintly look.

Phoebe giggled. 'I do not sound so pathetic.'

'Tragic, not pathetic. And it works too, so I won't interfere.'

'Wouldn't you like to come with me all the same? The new stoves are arriving.'

'It's a tempting offer, but I've a ton of paperwork to catch up on. I'll see you at dinner.'

As he got to his feet, Phoebe with difficulty refrained from asking him yet again if he was worried about something or if she had offended him, knowing that he would either tell her to stop being foolish, or to have a little faith in herself. And if she asked him if he had a headache, he'd snap at her, though she was sure that his head had been paining him. He was drinking more. Could that be the cause? Could he be drinking because he'd taken on too much? But when she'd asked him that the other day, he'd barked at her. *'I'm not an invalid,'* he'd said.

He leaned down to kiss her cheek, and she turned her face so that their lips met. He stilled and her heart skipped a beat as she silently pleaded with him to kiss her. Which he did, but only fleetingly, patting her shoulder as if she were a child needing reassurance.

It had taken another three weeks for the stoves to be delivered. Finally, they had arrived, and Phoebe had come to inspect them. It was Sunday, so she had the place to herself and was intent on assessing the true state of progress as opposed to the foreman's version of it. Her first impression was that Mr Gilligan had indeed made up for lost time. Stepping inside, she was assailed by the smell of fresh paint. The sconces had been fitted in the freshly varnished wood panelling, the floor had received another coating of wax, and the shelves which would hold glasses, decanters and jugs fixed to the wall where the waiters' station would be. The banquettes had been built and were awaiting the upholsterer.

Upstairs, the decor was also done, the walls painted red, the floor tiled black and white, just like the Procope, and the carpenters had begun work on the

seating. But it was in the kitchen where the main trans-
formation was taking place. The two huge stoves were
in position waiting to be fitted. The scullery now had
sinks, and the building work required for the various
pantries, larders and storage cupboards was completed.

Phoebe tested the pump, giving a squeak of delight
when water gurgled out of the tap. Perching on a stack
of planks, she took off her soaking gloves, intending
to check the list in her notebook, but the heart-shaped
ring distracted her. She had been so sure it was the
prelude to a declaration, but it was almost six weeks
since Owen had placed it on her finger, and as her
hopes faded, fear took their place.

Frowning down at the ruby-encrusted diamond, she
tried to persuade herself that her fears were unfounded,
the product of her own insecurities, but her instincts
told her otherwise. Christmas day had not been the
start of something between them but the beginning of
the end. A slow, painful end, but she was coming to
believe it was nevertheless an end.

Owen had changed that night. Whether he had had
some sort of recurrence of his previous condition was
the obvious question, but so far she hadn't had the
courage or the conviction to ask. His accident had
made him morose and numb. He was neither of those
things. They made love ever more frequently. She had
only to touch him, hand him his plate at breakfast,
press his shoulder when he was poring over papers, for
him to pull her into his arms and kiss her—not gentle, teasing kisses, not affectionate kisses, but always
kisses with intent. Sometimes she felt as if he were

trying to devour her, his need was so insatiable. But then so was her own. She craved him, just as much as he craved her. As if a clock was counting down their time together.

Why would she think that? Owen was not Pascal. Owen admired her. He encouraged her. He understood her so well that he'd been able to make her see herself in a whole new light. He hadn't told her he loved her, but he showed her he did, not only when they made love, but in a hundred different ways. He knew how to make her tea just the way she liked it. He knew that she never added milk save to the first cup. He knew just how to rub her feet without tickling them. She had lost count of the number of excursions they had taken to London's markets, all of them initiated by Owen, and though he claimed still to be a culinary philistine, though she knew he would happily have gone the rest of his life without being able to tell a chanterelle mushroom from a cep, he knew the difference now. He even had a book, *Forest Flora and Fungi.* Recalling the day he'd brought it home, flourishing it under her nose, Phoebe smiled. He had promised to take her foraging for mushrooms, but only when he could be sure that he wouldn't inadvertently poison the pair of them.

He had not told her that he loved her, but he did love her. For all her flaws and her insecurities and her scandalous behaviour and her unconventional ambitions, he loved her. Why would he have given her this ring in the shape of a heart, save as a token of that love? He had married her partly to find a purpose in life, and he had found it. He was no longer a recluse. He had not returned to his old life, but that was because he didn't want his old life. Or so he said. She had given him a purpose. He said that too. But he hadn't told her he loved her. And she loved him so very, very much.

There, it was out in the open, no taking it back now. Not that she wanted to. She loved him. She pressed the diamond to her lips. She loved Owen in a way that made her feelings for Pascal seem utterly trite. She hadn't loved Pascal, she'd loved what he represented, and the life she thought she was leading with him. But Owen—oh, for Owen she would live any kind of life, provided she could be with him. Though the sure and certain knowledge that he would never ask her to lead any kind of life other than the one she wanted, was one of the many reasons she loved him so very much. He had changed her—no, not changed, he'd made her a better version of herself. She hoped that was what she had done for him. She had almost come to believe it.

She must not get things out of proportion. This was an anxious time for both of them—and this place, this café-in-the-making, was the reason for it. That was why he was tired, had the headache, was short-tempered. Owen hadn't told her he loved her simply because the time wasn't right. And she hadn't told him because—because she was just a little bit afraid. Quite a big bit, truth be told. Scared that she might be rejected. That Owen's headaches and tiredness and short temper were caused by his not loving her, and he was feeling guilty about it. He could be regretting the change in their marriage, from platonic to passionate, and because he was such an honourable man, he was trying to steel himself to tell her.

No! Phoebe jumped to her feet, catching the note-book which had been sitting on her lap just before it fell on to the dusty floor. She was making a mountain out of a molehill. Owen loved her. She loved Owen. When the café was launched, the time would be right for them both to admit it. Until then, she would have to guard against these pointless and debilitating and destructive musings, and focus on making a success, first of this place, and then of her marriage.

Chapter Ten

'No need to ask you where you've been,' Owen said. 'Your boots are dusty, there's red paint on your cloak, you have soot on your nose and I'm pretty sure that's a cobweb in your hair.'

'I wouldn't have disturbed you here, only Bremner told me you'd been asking for me. I'll go and get cleaned up. I only wanted to let you know that I was back.'

'Don't go yet. Jasper called while you were out. That's why I've only just finished my exercises. I was catching up on some reading while I cooled down before I take a bath. Come in, Phoebe, stop hovering at the door.'

She came in hesitantly, casting him sidelong glances before seating herself nearest the fire, clearly trying to assess his mood. It pained him to see her do this, for he'd half-convinced himself that she hadn't noticed his erratic moods. Just thinking about his other new symptom made his heart begin to race. So the trick was *not* to dwell on it, Owen told himself, taking a couple of deep breaths.

'There's a new piece in the *Town Crier* this week,' he told Phoebe, handing her the copy of the rag. 'Jasper brought it, though apparently it was Olivia who spotted it in the first place.'

'Miss Braidwood reads this!'

'Everyone reads it, Phoebe. They dread finding their name in it, and are disappointed when they don't.'

'I would be delighted if our name never featured again.'

'Nonsense. Read what it says and tell your clever husband that he was right.'

She smiled at that, no longer wary but simply amused. He could not resist that smile of hers—no one could, male or female—and the most charming thing of all about it was that Phoebe was blissfully unaware of the fact. He'd watched her with the tradesmen at the café. She didn't flirt, she didn't play the simpering miss though he teased her about it. In fact she had no airs and graces at all, she simply told them what she wanted done. And smiled. And then gave him the credit when what she wanted was done in double-quick time!

'Well, what do you think?' he asked, seeing that she had finished reading.

'My husband is a genius. "Mixed dining comes to London for the first time. London is set to loosen its stays and mimic the Continental way, with the opening of Mrs Harrington's exciting new venture. Following their landmark appearance in Crockford's dining room, the Harringtons are enhancing their ground-breaking reputation by opening a restaurant whose exclusivity will be determined by the limited number of dining tables rather than the cost, or the gender of the diners,"' Phoebe read. 'I bet I know where they got that from. I told Mr Gilligan that he and his wife could command a table any time. He said they wouldn't be able to afford it and I said that my intention was to serve a menu that any tradesman could afford.'

'By the sounds of it, your Mr Gilligan will have his dinner paid for him by the *Town Crier*. Jasper has asked me to make sure he has a table at the opening night.'

'Of course. I wonder if he'll bring Miss Braidwood as a guest. He seems to be seeing rather a lot of her.'

Owen shrugged. 'Their mothers are school friends.'

'You don't think that it could be more a case of Jasper and Miss Braidwood becoming friends?'

'They are friends—at least they've known each other all their lives. You know, as children, their mothers visiting each other, that kind of thing.'

'I didn't mean that kind of thing,' Phoebe said drily. 'Never mind.'

'Good grief, you don't mean Jasper and Olivia are becoming an item?'

'Would you be upset?'

'Why on earth would I be upset?'

'No reason,' Phoebe said, in a way that meant there was every reason but she didn't want to tell him.

'You can't possibly imagine that I'd be jealous?'

She shook her head, but she wouldn't look at him, pretending to flick through the scandal sheet.

Appalled that his moods had caused her even a moment's doubt, Owen leaned over to pull the newspaper from her grasp, forcing her to look up. 'I'm married to you,' he said firmly. 'Provided it makes Olivia happy, I don't give a damn who she marries.'

'Do I—are you happy, being married to me, Owen? Only these last few weeks—since the start of this year, you've been—'

'I've been like a bear with a sore head,' he interrupted hastily. 'I know, and I'm sorry for it. After two years of inaction, I may have been overdoing it somewhat.'

It was the only believable lie he could think of, but he regretted it the moment he saw Phoebe's face fall, guessing before she spoke that she was about to blame herself.

'It's my fault,' she said, and Owen groaned inwardly.

'No, it's mine. After two years of wrapping myself in cotton wool, I've allowed my new-found enthusiasm to get the better of me. I've overstretched myself, it's as simple as that.'

'So if you rein back a bit, you'll be perfectly well again, won't you?'

He hated lying to her. But was it really a lie, to say what he fervently hoped? 'It's what I intend to do.'

'In that case I won't burden you by reporting the latest progress.'

'I didn't mean I wanted to return to doing nothing.'

'It's Sunday. It should be a day of rest. I'll go…'

'Stay. Please. We should both have a day of rest, you've been working all hours.'

'I'm enjoying it so much, it doesn't feel like work.'

If nothing else, Owen thought, he had given her this. 'Have you given any thought to a name for your exclusive establishment?'

'What about Café Phoebe? Simple and to the point.'

'And a bit too obvious, if you don't mind me saying.'

'The London Procope Café, then?'

'We could have a little brass plaque put on our upstairs table: *Here, in this exact seat, in the Procope Café Paris in August 1828, Owen met Phoebe*.'

'The *Town Crier* would love that.'

'I'm rather fond of it myself.'

'Who would have thought that meeting would turn out to be so momentous?'

'I always had a sense that it might. I would have turned up for our planned reunion if it had been humanly possible,' Owen said.

'I went. And I waited. And you didn't come. But eventually I came to you.'

'And that was the second-best day of my life. The best being our wedding day, in case you were wondering, though it's pretty obvious to me.'

'It was the best day of my life too, Owen. I—I've been worried that you were regret—'

'Don't even say it. I haven't. Not once. And I won't. Not ever. I promise.'

She blinked away a tear, and Owen cursed himself again. He would get over what was currently tormenting him. And if he didn't, he'd make a better job of keeping it hidden. 'So, if not Café Phoebe, or the London Procope Café, what is it to be then?'

'I don't know. I want it to mean something, have significance. A Leap in the Dark! The Fresh Start Café! New Beginnings! No, I know what it should be. Small Steps. Because that's what we've both taken on our journey to reach this point.'

'I like that,' Owen said touched, 'but shouldn't it have a French name, since it's a Parisian-style café and not just a coffee shop?'

'*Petites etapes*,' Phoebe said, screwing up her nose. 'Aux Petites Etapes doesn't really sound right. Oh, I know! *Pas à pas*—that means quite literally step by step. One step at a time. Le Pas à Pas! What do you think? Will people understand what we mean?'

'As long as we do, who cares? It's unusual and therefore memorable. I love it!'

'Le Pas à Pas! It's silly, but it feels much more real, now it has a name. Only a few more weeks and we'll be ready to open for business. Once the kitchen is complete, I'll be able to start cooking.'

She was glowing again, his lovely Phoebe. He'd forgotten himself, talking to her. Looking at her, he was filled with hope. He could conquer this thing that was trying to take possession of him. He'd done it before. He could do it again, with Phoebe by his side. 'We'll toast the name tonight, before dinner.'

'I look forward to it.' She got to her feet, picking up her paint-stained cloak. 'Le Pas à Pas is going to need a thorough clean-up before any cooking gets done there. I'd better go and get changed out of these things now. And you will be wanting to bathe after your exertions on the apparatus.'

'Stay and bathe with me,' he said impulsively.

'What!'

'I have a bathing chamber containing a bath, with hot running water. A very large bath.'

'Owen, you're surely not suggesting we share it?'

'It would save water. And it would save your maid all the effort of carrying your bath water up the stairs.'

'So it would be economical and thoughtful?'

'It would be both economical and thoughtful,' he agreed. A thick curl of her glorious hair had escaped its pins. Owen tucked it behind her ear, letting his fingers trail down the column of her neck, feathering over the skin at her nape, something that always made her shiver with pleasure. 'But I think it might also be fun.'

'Fun?' She smiled at him. *That* smile. She hadn't smiled that particular smile for weeks. 'What kind of fun?'

'Whatever kind we like.' He kissed her gently, at the same time cupping her breast, his thumb slowly circling her nipple. He felt it bud, through her corsets and her gown. He kissed her again, feeling himself stiffen.

'Owen, I have never—I can't imagine...'

'Phoebe, I have never and I can't imagine, but I'd like to try, wouldn't you?'

'Yes.' She placed her hand over his heart, a new and strange little habit of hers. Then she smiled up at him again. 'Oh, yes.'

Owen was different. No, not different. He wasn't different, he was the man she had fallen in love with, the smiling, teasing, irresistible Owen. Not that she'd

been able to resist the darker version of him either, but
Phoebe was immensely relieved to see that the real
one was still there. She followed him, intrigued and
excited, across the small hallway to his bedchamber. It
was a very masculine room, the furniture dark, solid,
the bed much lower to the ground than hers and without posts or curtains. There were books and papers
everywhere, but nothing else by way of decoration,
no pictures on the walls, only a set of silver-backed
brushes on the dressing table.

He locked the door behind them. Needlessly, she
knew. None of the servants came to these rooms unless summoned. Casting her cloak on to the bed, he led
her towards another door. A huge bath dominated the
square room, set into the corner and taking up most
of one wall. The bath was enclosed in white-painted
wood. Fascinated, she watched as Owen fitted a stop-
per to what was presumably the draining hole, and
turned on the brass tap. Air clanked out, followed by a
thin stream of piping hot water, which became a gush
when he made some complicated adjustments.

'Don't imagine that it's always this co-operative,'
he said, smiling at her astonished expression. 'Half of
the time, the water is no more than tepid.'

'It's wonderful. I've never seen anything like it.'

A porcelain sink was built into a marble-topped
table which held Owen's shaving soap, razor and strop,
and this too had brass taps attached to it. A mirror
hung on this wall, already beginning to mist over due
to the steam rising from the bath water. The floor of
the bathing chamber was covered with large black and

white tiles, smaller tiles in the same monochrome design covering the walls. A selection of towels were laid out ready on a wooden rack. There was a dish of soaps set on a wash stand beside the bath, a large loofah, a scrubbing brush and several sponges sat in another dish.

'Are we really going to get into that together?' Phoebe asked, unable to decide whether the prospect was enticing or simply odd.

'I won't drown you, if that's what you're worried about.'

She giggled. 'It does look almost big enough to swim in. Not that I can swim.'

'I can. I used to swim around the Serpentine, in Hyde Park in the summer. In the early hours, obviously,' Owen added, 'lest my semi-naked state cause offence. Fortunately there's no one here for us to offend, so we can bathe completely naked. If you want to, that is? I don't want you to do anything...'

'I want to,' she said, because she didn't really care whether they were in a bed or a bath or the back of a carriage, for that matter, as long as they were together. 'I really do want to,' she said, reaching up to kiss him.

It was a long, slow kiss, the kind of kiss that had been missing for weeks from their lovemaking. This kiss went on and on, breaking only when Owen cursed, and hurriedly switched off the tap to prevent the bath from overflowing. Then the kiss started again, and it carried on as they undressed each other, dropping their clothes heedlessly on to the damp tiles. She watched her own pleasure reflected in his eyes as he touched her, caressed her, stroked her, and she echoed every one of his movements. When they were naked, he helped her step into the bath, joining her with a fluidity that still astonished her, when she looked at the scarring at his hip.

He took one of the sponges from the dish and soaped it. And then he soaped her, slow sweeping strokes, first her back, down to her bottom, then her front, using the sponge to tease her nipples, until she was only just clinging to the edge of self-control. She lost it very quickly when he gently rubbed between her legs, the soft soapy sponge, the warm water, and Owen, watching her so intently, wrenching her climax from her. She clung to him, panting, conscious first of his erection pressing into her belly, then of the delicious sliding sensation of soapy skin on skin. Taking the sponge from him, she set out to tease him as he had done her, watching him, the sinful smile fading to sensual pleasure, his eyes darkening, his breath becoming shallow.

'Phoebe, you have to stop or I'll…'

'I want you to.'

'Inside you,' he said. 'Please, I want to be inside you.'

She dropped the sponge, bracing herself against the wall tiles. They felt cool on her hot skin. He entered her slowly, pushing higher inch by inch, his eyes on hers, and she instinctively angled herself to take him higher. And then he thrust. Slowly, so she wouldn't over-balance. Slowly, because it was what they both wanted. She had never felt so close to him before as this, their bodies slick and sliding, their eyes locked. It seemed to go on for ever. She never wanted it to end. But then she tipped over to the point where she was desperate for it to end, to rush to the ending, and he sensed it, thrusting harder, faster, until she cried out, and he cried out only seconds later, pulling himself free of her, but holding her, their mouths clinging in one last utterly sated panting kiss.

Phoebe woke with a start, completely disoriented. She was in Owen's room, lying on the very edge of the bed, with her husband splayed out beside her naked, the sheets a tangle around his legs. She shivered and was about to claim a share of the bedcoverings back when Owen muttered. He was dreaming. Tentatively, she put a hand on his shoulder to try to wake him, but he shuddered, cowering away from her.

Phoebe edged out of the bed, putting on his dressing gown. His breathing was fast and shallow, as if he had been running hard. There was a sudden stillness to him, then his arms shot out in front of him and he strained, as if he was trying to push away some invisible obstacle.

'Owen.'

She touched his shoulder. He heaved again, then with a cry sat up, his eyes wide open, a blank look of abject horror on his face. 'I can't stop them.'

'What can't you stop?' she whispered.

'If I could get the door open, they would stop crying. I can't get the door open. I can't get them out. I can't get them out.'

He dropped his head on to his hands and broke into wild sobs. Appalled and helpless, Phoebe tried to wrap her arms around him, but as soon as she touched him he pushed her away. 'What are you doing here?'

'Owen, I...'

'Get out.'

'Owen, you were dreaming, I...'

'Get out! Get out! Why can't you leave me alone.'

March 1831

She had put it off long enough. It was almost a month since she had witnessed Owen's nightmare, a month in which his behaviour had become more and more erratic, his moods more and more volatile. Phoebe was treading on eggshells all of the time, never knowing from one morning to the next how he would be, or if he would even remember how he had been the day before.

There were periods of calm, when she persuaded herself that he was improving, but they were getting further and further apart. She couldn't pretend any more, but as she waited, sipping her tea in the breakfast parlour, she would have given almost anything to persuade herself that she could.

It was no use. She had to find the strength to confront him, no matter how painful, because they were already perilously close to the point of no return, a living nightmare where they both pretended that Owen was behaving perfectly normally, and that his 'perfectly normal' behaviour wasn't breaking her heart.

She had tried, a week ago, to talk to him, tried to tell him how upsetting she found his behaviour, but it had only made him worse—not angry, but stricken. Since then, he had retreated into himself, though his efforts to control his emotions at times made him shake visibly. She felt so utterly helpless, watching him suffering, so determined to deny that he was suffering. He had gone from being a man who felt nothing, to someone so full of conflicting emotions he could barely contain them all.

She had shied away from forcing a confrontation because she didn't want to face the truth. If he no longer loved her—but she must not think that. She had to be strong. She had to be positive. If he loved her, then they could conquer whatever ailed him. She loved him so much, she would do anything she could to save their marriage. If he loved her.

'I'm sorry, I've kept you waiting.'

Phoebe forced a smile. 'I was up early,' she said, though Owen was almost an hour later than usual. 'Shall I pour your coffee?'

'Please.'

He sat down without touching her, and her heart sank as he forced a smile.

'Shall I get you some breakfast?'

'I'll get my own. I don't want to keep you back. I know you're eager to try out your new kitchen for the first time.'

'I'm not in such a hurry that I can't stay and have breakfast with my husband.'

'I'm not hungry, Phoebe.'

'Just an egg and some of this—'

'I said I'm not hungry!' Owen swore viciously. 'Look, I'm sorry, but despite what you believe, food is not the cure for all ills. Forgive me, I didn't sleep well. I have the headache.'

She could walk away. He clearly wanted to be left alone. Perhaps he did have a headache. But what if she was the cause? 'Owen.' She angled herself in her chair to reach for his hand. 'Owen, won't you please tell me what it is that ails you?'

'I have the headache, I've just told you that.'

'Is it—didn't you sleep?'

He edged his hand away from her clasp. 'I told you that too.'

'Did you—did you have a nightmare again?'

He stilled. 'What makes you think that?'

'I saw you—don't you remember?' But judging from his blank look, he did not. Though she felt as if she was standing on the edge of an abyss, Phoebe forced herself to continue. 'Last month—after we— it was the last time we made love. In your bathing room—we fell asleep in your bedchamber.' He paled, but said nothing. 'I woke—you woke me up, shouting,' Phoebe said. 'Something about crying. You wanted me to make them stop. I thought…'

He pushed his chair back, stumbling to his feet. 'I don't want to talk about it.'

'But you do remember?' Phoebe persisted. 'The dream, I mean? And when you woke up, sending me away?'

'No. Yes. I don't want to talk about it, Phoebe.'

'Owen, we have to talk about it. Something is wrong, and I can't help you if I don't know what it is.'

'You can't help me.'

He threw himself across the room to look out of the window. She could see his shoulders rising and falling in his effort to control himself. She knew he wanted her to leave, but she had come this far, she couldn't back down now. 'Owen, whatever it is, can't you please tell me?'

'I don't know what the hell it is! I just need you to leave me alone.'

She went to him, wrapping her arms around his waist. 'My love, please won't you tell me? There's nothing you can say that…'

'Don't, Phoebe.' His voice broke. He turned around, pulling her into his arms. 'I beg you, don't say any more. There is nothing to be said. Nothing to be done.'

'But, Owen…'

'No!' Tears tracked down his cheeks. 'I'm sorry,' he said, 'I'm so sorry, but it's simply not possible.'

'What? Owen, please…'

'I can't be with you like this. You have to understand…'

'But I want…'

'Phoebe,' he said, 'sometimes we simply can't have what we want.'

It was the gentleness in his tone that told her all hope was lost. The way he put her from him, so carefully, as if he was afraid she would break. And indeed, her heart was breaking, had been breaking a little bit every day, for the worse he had become, the more desperately she loved him. But it was abundantly clear now that he didn't love her. And it was destroying him, his not loving her. Though she couldn't imagine life without him, for even this Owen was better than no Owen at all, she was going to have to let him go, for his sake.

She ought to have known it wouldn't last. She *had* known. She recalled thinking here in this very room, that she wasn't up to his weight. Why would a man like Owen want to be tied to a woman like her, whose only talent was cooking! But he had tied himself to her, and he was far too honourable a man to admit that he regretted it. Even when he so obviously did.

'Go to the café,' Owen said. 'Go and cook. You're so close to that pot of gold at the end of the rainbow, Phoebe, don't let me ruin it for you.'

She wanted to tell him she didn't give a damn about the café, not compared to him. But the café was what had brought them together. The café had given him a purpose. If she told him she didn't care, she'd only be adding to his guilt.

'Will you still come—tonight, I mean?' she asked, knowing she sounded pitiful, unable to stop herself. It was to be a private dinner for herself and Owen. He had suggested it weeks ago. It was supposed to be a final treat before they both threw themselves headlong into the launch of the café, which was planned for next month. A celebratory meal to toast their future success. Now it was going to be a wake to mark the death of their marriage.

'Of course,' Owen said eventually, forcing another of his rigid smiles. 'The first meal cooked in the kitchen at Le Pas à Pas. Of course I'll come.' He kissed the air a few inches from her lips. 'Go on. I'll see you there later.'

Owen spent the day trying to forget what had happened this morning, trying to eradicate the memory of his brave Phoebe's misguided and doomed attempt to help him. He knew he was beyond help. It was simply a question of holding himself together as best he could until the launch of Le Pas à Pas was complete, and Phoebe's future assured. By the time he arrived several hours later he had himself under control. Or as near as he ever came to that, these days, veering between the feeling that he was no longer part of this world, and the feeling that he could not bear to be part of it. Guilt for some undisclosed crime weighed him down. The wailing was never far away. But the vivid fragments of memory, the latest development in his illness, were the worst. Sudden blazes of light like the limelight they used in the theatre, and then the images would start to flash through his mind. Different each time, nothing seemingly connected, like pieces of a puzzle. They came to him in the night and in the day. He had tried to clutch at the images, to make sense of them, it was like trying to grasp smoke. There was only his palpitating heart, his gasping breath, and the tears streaming down his face. He would not allow them to happen tonight. He would not allow anything to interfere with tonight, for Phoebe's sake.

The café was virtually complete. The tables and chairs were set up, the red-velvet curtains hung in the window, the banquettes upholstered. Phoebe had lit all the sconces and the central chandeliers for his arrival, and laid some of the tables, presumably to give him a sense of how it would look when they were open, simple settings with white crockery, plain glasses and one set of cutlery.

'Well, what do you think?' she asked, smiling nervously as she locked the door behind him.

He took his time answering, knowing how much it would matter to her, wanting to do at least this small thing to please her. He was determined to do everything in his power to make tonight a success, but he was already so terrified of betraying himself, it was like a self-fulfilling prophecy.

'Owen?'

He started, swore viciously, then was immediately awash with guilt as he saw Phoebe flinch. 'It's lovely,' he said, the first anodyne expression he could think of. Take deep breaths! Turning away from her sad, tragic gaze, he forced himself to look. 'Cosy, welcoming. The dark panelling you chose was perfect, it will feel warm, even in the depths of winter. And the banquettes. Very Parisian. It's the sort of place where you could easily picture your builder and his wife at that table, Wellington and a few of his cronies there, perhaps your sister and her husband, the Earl of Fearnoch, tête-à-tête there.'

He was wittering, but Phoebe was either fooled or pretending to be fooled. 'And upstairs?' she asked, leading the way.

'The Procope,' Owen said, a lump rising in his throat as he stood at the top of the stairs.

'And here,' Phoebe said, taking his hand and urging him gently towards the only table which had been set, where a jug of wine stood waiting with two glasses, 'where Owen met Phoebe. There is no plaque, but I didn't think we'd need reminding.'

The lighting up here was dim. Owen swiped at his eyes while Phoebe sat down. 'I won't ever forget,' he said, taking his chair, pouring them both a glass of wine, spilling some of it on to the crisp starched linen which his wife, his precious lovely beloved wife, pretended not to notice. 'To brief encounters that change lives,' he said, raising his glass. 'And to you, Phoebe. For being unique.'

'To Owen, who has made all of this possible. The best and only husband,' she said, touching his glass, her voice husky.

'You've done this, Phoebe.'

'I couldn't have even begun without you.' She clutched at his hand. 'You know that, don't you? In a few weeks, Le Pas à Pas will open, my dream come true, thanks to you. I won't ever forget that.' She jumped to her feet. 'Now, if you will excuse me, tonight I am the chef and the *sous-chef* and the waitress all in one. Sit here, enjoy this lovely wine which, I hope you don't mind, I purloined from your cellar, for our own supply has not been delivered yet.'

'What is mine is yours. Purloin the whole lot if you want.'

'Don't be silly.' She leaned over, as if she would kiss

him, then changed her mind. 'The first course will be served in fifteen minutes.'

She bustled away, disappearing down the stairs, her boots clattering on the polished wood. Then he heard her descend the next flight to the kitchen. Alone, Owen felt bereft. He poured himself another glass of wine, though he knew he'd drunk the first far too quickly.

I won't ever forget that.

Her words sounded portentous. He knew he was hurting her. He was shielding her from his torment for her own good as well as his. But to be confronted with the evidence, to see her face, to witness her trying so hard to act as if he was behaving rationally, as if everything between them was normal—it was agony. She knew. She knew their marriage was over in all but name. That's what she'd been telling him.

He downed the rest of his wine and pushed back his chair. If it must be over, let him please, please, please find the strength to get through tonight. He'd join her in the kitchen, watch her at the stove. It was something he'd done many times before at home, something he'd come to enjoy, seeing her skills with the knife, watching her face as she tasted something, that little frown she gave when the seasoning wasn't quite right, the small smile of satisfaction when it was.

Making his way down the second flight of stairs, he was assailed with a medley of delicious smells. Phoebe, a huge apron enveloping her, was at the stove, using a wire brush on one of the burners on one of the two cast-iron, gas-fuelled stoves. Owen had been wary of this very recent innovation from the start, but she insisted they would prove much more efficient.

'What's wrong with it?' he asked.

'The pipe is blocked, I think. There, that's it done.'

She put the brush down and lit the supply. A ball of flame exploded out of the pipe with a whoosh and a searing blast of heat. Owen was dimly aware of Phoebe leaping out of the way. He could hear her saying something. He could see she was unscathed. But he wasn't. In that split second everything fell into place. Everything that had happened. Everything. The full horror of it all.

'No!' he cried out, tearing at his hair, squeezing his eyes tight shut. 'Dear God, no!' But it wouldn't go away. He dropped to his knees, covering his face with his hands. He couldn't breathe, his heart was pounding so fast.

'Owen.'

'Phoebe.' She was kneeling on the floor beside him. 'Phoebe.' He clutched at her shoulders, begging her silently to save him, but the images were playing out again in his head, the whole dreadful scene from start to finish.

He struggled to his feet.

'Where are you going?'

He made for the stairs.

'Owen, you are not fit…'

'You're right. I'm not fit.'

'Owen!'

He had to get away. He had to get out of this place, into the open air and he had to run, as fast as he could, run for his life. And never look back.

He heard her shouting his name from the door of the café, but he was already off. Not running the way he once had, he would never be able to do that again. But running, through the searing pain that now tore at his hip, he ran out into the fading light and into the streets of London, where he prayed he might lose himself. For ever.

Chapter Eleven

Phoebe waited for more than two hours at the café, at a loss to know what else to do, but Owen didn't return. Stripping the table upstairs, putting what was salvageable of the dinner, which she hadn't even finished cooking, away in the larder, she extinguished all the lights and locked up. She had sent the carriage home, expecting Owen to escort her back. Thinking to pick up a hackney nearby, she made her way out into the dark London streets, clutching her cloak around her, the hood covering her face. There were no hackney cabs at the stop. She knew her way to Covent Garden from here, but at this time of night, she didn't think being on her own in Covent Garden was a good idea. So she walked, trying to keep a steady pace, resisting the urge to look over her shoulder, far more concerned about Owen than herself.

The front door of the town house was not locked. A sconce burned in the hall, but the servants had all retired as usual. Heart thumping, the acrid taste of fear in her mouth, Phoebe lit a candle and made for the door to Owen's apartments. Thick silence greeted her. The main room was in complete darkness. Holding her candle high, she could see that the gymnastic equipment had been recently used, the polished bars covered in the chalk Owen rubbed into his hands to give him grip, now that he no longer wore gloves. But the room was desolate. So too was his study. And his bedchamber.

She perched on the edge of his bed, wondering if she dared wait here for him. Where was he? Though her instincts were to search the streets for him, she knew that was about the most foolish and dangerous thing she could do. If anything happened to her, Owen would add that to the burden of guilt that was already crushing him. She could have a note sent round to Jasper. Jasper knew Owen's old haunts, but Owen didn't look like a man in search of company. He had looked like a man in search of oblivion.

Where was he? He wouldn't have harmed himself, surely? He must know how worried she would be. But when he'd run off, he was beyond reason.

Where *was* he? Phoebe, who never prayed, sent up a silent prayer to keep him safe. And then another. If he had not returned by daylight, she'd have no option but to send for Jasper. Her isolation struck her for the first time since she'd left Paris. She didn't have any friends. She had kept herself apart from her family. Without Owen…

She was going to have to live the rest of her life without Owen. Dear heavens though, it was one thing to live apart from him, but for him not to be in this world—no. She would not allow herself to go down that path. She must not linger here either, waiting for him, ready to confront him in whatever state he came home, when he would prefer her not to see him in his distressed state. And she mustn't cry either. There was no point in feeling sorry for herself. Whatever help Owen needed, whatever he wanted or didn't want from her, she had to be prepared to do it.

Phoebe was asleep, still fully dressed save for her boots, on top of the bedcovers, when Owen finally returned, but the creaking of her bedchamber door woke her. She leapt up, saw him, and threw herself at him.

'You're back.' She pressed herself against him as if she was trying to burrow into his body. 'I've been so worried.'

He wrapped his arms around her, resting his chin on her tousled hair, closing his eyes for just a moment to drink in the familiar scent of her, to enjoy the familiar shape of her. And then he let her go.

She stepped away from him, her eyes huge, her face pale and ghostly, determinedly set. 'Before you say anything, I want to tell you that I understand. I won't make a fuss.'

'Phoebe, I don't think you can possibly understand.'

'You're such an honourable man, and I—I've made it pretty obvious what I feel for you, but you can't make yourself feel something you don't, Owen. You can't pretend that you—that you still care for me. I think I've known for a while that you don't, but I didn't want to face it. Today has proved to me that I can't hide my head in the sand any longer. I have to set you free. I'm so sorry I didn't act sooner. I was—well, it doesn't matter what I was. You're free now.'

Her words made him want to sob. They made him want to pull her back into his arms and tell her, finally, once and for all how much he loved her. 'You think that I don't love you,' he said, feeling as if his heart was tearing apart inside his chest.

'I know you don't. Perhaps you thought you did for a while, perhaps you were trying to persuade yourself that you did…'

'Phoebe! Oh, Phoebe, why on earth would I do that?'

'Because you knew it was what I wanted. When you gave me this.' She thrust out her left hand. 'When you gave me this ring, I thought that—I hoped that it was because—that you were giving me your heart. For the next few days, after Christmas, I kept hoping that you'd say the words I was so sure you were about to say before you fainted.'

'I fainted,' he said fatalistically, as his fears were confirmed.

'You simply couldn't bring yourself to lie.'

'I don't remember.' But he did, now. He remembered being so full of joy, so sure that the time was right to tell her. And then the joy turning to blackness.

Phoebe took the ring from her finger and held it out. 'You can have it back, Owen. You're free.'

He hesitated. Wouldn't it be easier for both of them, to let her believe he didn't love her? He could make up some story about tonight's debacle, some sanitised version of the truth, spare himself the agony of recounting the harsh reality. And leave Phoebe imagining she wasn't good enough for him, when it was he who was so unworthy of her.

'No,' Owen said, to himself and to Phoebe. 'You've got it all wrong.' His hip was burning from the amount of walking he'd done. And running. All to no avail. He couldn't run from himself. He waved vaguely at the hearth where the fire smouldered and the chair Phoebe liked to sit in to read was pulled close. 'Sit there. I'll…'

He staggered, lurching like a drunk towards the hearth. 'I'll sit on a cushion.'

'You'll sit there. I'll sit on a cushion.' Phoebe pushed him on to the chair. He was too tired to resist. 'Shall I order some coffee?' she asked, stacking several pillows on the floor. 'Brandy?' she queried, when he shook his head.

'Nothing. Just sit and hear me out, please.'

To his utter relief she did, sensing that he didn't want her to touch him, tucking her legs under her out of reach of his. 'Tonight, in the kitchen, when the stove exploded, I finally remembered,' he began, launching quickly into the story before he could have second thoughts. 'My accident, I mean, everything about it.' He curled his fingers around the arms of the chair to stop himself shaking. 'It's been coming back to me in fits and starts but until tonight, I couldn't—it made no sense.'

'When did you start remembering?'

'After Christmas.'

'After you fainted, when you gave me the ring.'

'Yes. Not straight after. It started with random episodes—that's what I've been calling them, episodes.'

'When you lose your temper?'

'Or pass out. I've lost consciousness a few times.'

'Oh, Owen! I had no idea. I'm so sorry…'

He held up his hand to silence her. 'You had no idea because I didn't want you to know. It was bad enough, pushing you away, seeing you so hurt when my temper snapped, seeing you trying so hard not to upset me. And besides, I didn't remember after—when I fainted, I mean. If I'm honest—and after today, I have no option but to be honest—I was trying to fool myself.'

'Oh, Owen, so was I. If only I'd spoken sooner, perhaps…'

'No,' he said firmly. 'You have to stop thinking like that. This is not your fault. It's mine. Mine completely. I thought for a while I was going mad. The nightmares, and the memories, they jump out at me when I least expect it. I feel possessed. By grief. And by guilt. The guilt has been the worst. I didn't understand until tonight. And now…'

He began to shake again, so hard that he had to dig his heels into the rug, clench his belly tight, just to hold himself steady on the chair. Deep breaths, remember. Stay still and take deep breaths.

Finally it passed. Phoebe hadn't moved towards him, though he could see she was braced to leap into action at the least sign from him. 'Thank you,' Owen said gruffly. Another deep breath, and he was as ready as he'd ever be. Get it over with, he told himself. As quickly as possible.

'There was a fire,' he said. 'You already know that. In Marseilles. In the Panier district, which is the oldest part of the city. The buildings there are tall, tightly packed, tiny windows, narrow alleyways, steep staircases, divided up into homes for heaven knows how many families. I was walking there. Just walking. Thinking. Then I saw the flames. The whole building was in flames, and there was a chain of people passing buckets of water which snaked around the side of the building. They were tackling it from the back. But it was futile. Anyone could see the fire had taken too strong a hold.'

He spoke quickly, urgently, desperate to get the words out, to reach the end. 'I went to help regardless. I was about to join the chain when I saw her. A screaming woman, trying to get into the building. Another woman—her sister, a friend, a neighbour, it doesn't matter—was trying to pull her back. But the first woman was frantic, and all the men were distracted, concentrating on trying to contain the fire. She got free, and she launched herself into the doorway and into the stairwell. I didn't think. I simply acted instinctively. I went in after her.'

'Owen! Oh, dear heavens, Owen.'

'I got to her halfway up the first flight of stairs.'

'You saved her!'

'She was trying to get to her baby. The child was trapped in their second-floor apartment, left behind in the panic and confusion.'

Phoebe had her hand over her mouth. Her eyes were wide with horror. 'You told her you would rescue it.'

'I couldn't let *her* attempt to.'

'No. No, you wouldn't. Of course you wouldn't.'

'The baby—I still don't know if it was a boy or a girl—the baby was in the room at the front of the second floor. I wrapped my kerchief around my face. My one solitary act of self-preservation. I'm surprised I did that much. I got as far as the door. I could hear it crying. The fire had taken hold of the rafters. The ceiling was about to come down, there was plaster crumbling, smoke, flames—but I could hear the baby crying.'

'The crying. "Make it stop", that's what you said in your nightmare. "Make it stop." Was that what you were dreaming?'

'Not exactly. In my dream there wasn't a fire. It was a crèche. A hospital. I couldn't get out, in my dream. What really happened is that I couldn't get in. I could hear voices behind me, pleading with me to turn back. But I was so sure I could reach the child.'

The shaking possessed him again, but he ignored it. 'I thought myself invincible, you see. I could run faster than anyone. I could perform acrobatics to a standard that would allow me to make a living on stage if I had chosen to. I had never been bested in the boxing ring or any sort of race or any sort of competition. I'd never even suffered more than the most superficial injury despite my many hair-raising escapades. It wasn't that I was unaware of the risks, more that I thought myself impervious.' He held up his hands. 'I wasn't. The lintel from the doorframe fell on me, trapping me under it when I was feet away from reaching the child.'

* * *

Owen was trembling violently. Phoebe watched him, numb with shock, his suffering unimaginable, unable to offer any comfort save to listen, to hear him out until the tragic end.

'I could hear the poor little mite crying while I was lying there under the beam,' he continued, 'half in and half out of the apartment. I could hear it crying and I could see the fire creeping towards me.' Tears were streaming down his face. His eyes were wide open, but he wasn't seeing her, he was lost in the unfolding horror. 'Before, before I could remember, before we were married, I had a nightmare. My reaching dream, I'd call it. I'd wake up knowing something terrible had happened, that it was my fault, but I didn't know what or why. Now I know and I'll never be able to forget it.

'When it stopped, when the crying stopped, it was worse. All I could hear then was the fire roaring, see it licking its way towards me. I couldn't move. I didn't feel anything, I didn't know that my hip had been crushed, all I wanted—all I wanted was to crawl forward, even though I knew it was too late.' Owen lifted his head to look straight at her. 'You have no idea how that felt. Knowing how close I was and that I'd never get any closer.'

'Owen...'

He shook his head violently to silence her. 'They pulled me out just in time. Two men took their lives in their hands to rescue me. They should have left me.'

This was too much for her. Phoebe closed the space between them, kneeling in front of him to wrap her arms around him. He let her hold him, but she had the impression it was for her benefit, not his. He had stopped shaking, stopped sobbing, sat rigid in her arms, silent. 'You tried, Owen,' she said. 'That's so much more than most would have done.'

'I failed. That's all that matters.'

'No! You spared that poor woman the agony of heaven knows what.'

'I delayed her. Time was of the essence. If I'd let her go, she might have…'

'You can't think like that. She might well have perished herself, as well as her child. You probably saved her life.'

He disengaged himself from her hold, getting up from the chair. 'We'll never know. All I know is that I failed to save the baby and my recklessness cost me dearly. Don't tell me what I can and can't think, Phoebe, you weren't there.'

'No, I wasn't. I'm sorry, I…'

'I told you so that you'd understand—not what happened then but the impact it's having on me now.'

She stared up at him, dazed. 'But now you have remembered…'

'It makes no difference.' He helped her to her feet, putting his arms around her, but the gesture was wooden, forced. 'Now I have remembered, it will never leave me. What you have seen these last few weeks is who I am now.' He took a step back from her, holding her at arm's reach. 'I've had time to think tonight, you haven't, but when you have, you'll see.'

'See what?'

'I thought I was getting better.'

'You were,' she said fiercely.

'No, Phoebe. I was getting worse.' He was focusing on her now, and the expression on his face filled her with a sense of dread for what she saw there was a firm resolve. 'I wanted to believe I was getting better. I wanted so very much to believe that, because I love you.'

'Oh, Owen.'

'No, don't cry. Please, don't cry. You have to be brave, Phoebe.'

'I didn't understand. I thought you didn't love me. But if you do...'

'I do. Please don't look like that.' He shuddered, pulling her close once more, holding her tightly, smoothing her hair. 'I love you with all my heart, but it's no good, my darling.'

'You got better once, you can get better again.'

'No. I didn't get better, that's what you don't understand. I blocked it all out for a while, that's all. But I think that loving you, being so happy, I think it—' He broke off, swearing. 'This is so difficult to say. I got by before by blocking out the truth, by somehow hiding it from myself because I wasn't able to deal with it. Then you came along, and I fell in love with you, and thanks to you, thanks to the hope you gave me, the reason for living you gave me, I grew stronger. Strong enough to let my defences down. Strong enough to remember.'

'But then if it hadn't been for me, you wouldn't have remembered and...'

'No,' he said firmly, giving her a tiny shake. 'What

I'm trying to say is that you helped me. The dam had to be breached, Phoebe, sooner or later. Tonight it burst completely, and the genie is well and truly out of the bottle. I can't put it back. I don't want to. In a way, it's a relief, don't you see, understanding the grief and the guilt, knowing why I've had all those other symptoms— the tears, the fainting, the nightmares, the temper. At least I know I'm not mad, even though I also know I'm no fit husband for you.'

There was a sense of inevitability in his words, a horrible logic, but she didn't want to hear it. 'You're the only husband I want.'

'Please don't say that,' he said, looking quite wretched. 'Please, I beg you, try to understand. It's going to be hard enough coming to terms with what I've done, trying to find a way to live with myself, without inflicting all my suffering on you.'

'I don't care, Owen, I'd gladly suffer with you.'

'I know, but I couldn't bear that.' He smoothed her hair back from her face. 'Look at you, so lovely and so brave and so defiant. Look at how much you've changed these last five months.'

'Because of you.'

'No. I gave you the means, that's all.'

'You didn't just give me money, Owen. You've made me believe in myself.'

'Then that's one good thing to come of our marriage. I want you to succeed, Phoebe. Do you remember, back in October when you first came to me, I told you that if you succeeded, if I could help you realise your dream, then it would make up for having lost mine?' He let her go. 'I need you to see it through for both our sakes. I deserve to suffer, that's the price I have to pay for having failed. But I cannot—I will not—make you suffer too.'

'You don't *deserve* to suffer. You tried everything humanly possible...'

'And still failed. As I said, I've had time to think about this, you have not. I told you because I didn't want you to think I didn't love you. But it's not good enough. I don't deserve you. You said you were willing to release me...'

'Because I thought you didn't love me, but you do, and I love you—I'm sorry, I know you don't want me to say it, but I love you so much.'

But he simply shook his head, his lips set. 'I will do my best to support you until the launch, but after that— it's over. I will have my lawyer sort out an agreement.'

'I don't want an agreement! I want you, Owen.'

'When you've had time to think it over, to reflect, you'll realise that is impossible. We would both be miserable.' His mouth quivered. His shoulders shook. 'Let me go, Phoebe. If you love me that much, do as I ask. I beg you.'

There was nothing more to be said. She loved him too much to care about her own suffering. 'You don't need to beg,' Phoebe said. 'You're free.'

April 1831

The special celebration menu for the grand opening of Le Pas à Pas was displayed at the entrance on a

lectern, with a copy on printed cards placed on each
of the tables. The crisp table linen gleamed white in
the soft candlelight. The glasses had been polished to
a spotless sparkle. Accompanied by her head waiter,
Phoebe made a final tour of both the upstairs and the
downstairs dining rooms before returning to the kitchens for a last-minute check that all was ready for their
first proper service. They had practised endlessly, she
and her small team, over the last few weeks, so there
was no reason for her to be anxious, but she was sick
with nerves. Not that anyone would know, from her
demeanour. One of the many skills she had perfected
since she had agreed to put an end to their marriage,
was the ability to hide her feelings. She hoped that in
time practice would make perfect to the point where
she fooled herself, but she was a very long way from
reaching that goal.

She had been unable to prevent herself from begging Owen to change his mind, trying to persuade
him that time would heal his illness. To no avail. Very
quickly she realised that the only outcome of her outburst was to increase his suffering. And his suffering
continued. He grew hollow-eyed, thinner and paler as
the weeks passed. Dinner became an endurance test,
with her talking bright inanities, and Owen sitting silently, closed in on himself. He drank too much. He
ate too little. She came upon him once, glassy-eyed,
muttering, wandering in the garden in the early hours
of the morning, when she had been unable to sleep,
and smelled opium on his breath. She recognised the
drug at once, for there had been a kitchen porter in La

Grande Taverne, a veteran of Napoleon's army, who took it on the days, he used to say, when the past overwhelmed him. It was a turning point for her, seeing that her presence had reduced Owen to seeking oblivion in such a manner. She extracted a promise from him that he wouldn't use it again, and in return, she promised not to try to change his mind again. So tonight, she would launch her restaurant. And tomorrow, she and her husband would part for ever.

She left the heat of the kitchen to snatch a brief moment of solitude in her tiny office, with the door ajar so that she would be able to hear the head waiter greet the first of their invited guests. Owen wouldn't be here for the launch. He didn't want to risk suffering an episode in front of her diners. She understood, but understanding wasn't the same as accepting. This should have been their night. Le Pas à Pas wouldn't exist if it wasn't for him. The guest list had been compiled by him, a carefully constructed mixture of friends with influence and friends who enjoyed food, all friends he had long ago abandoned and had no plans to see again either, cultivated and cajoled into sampling a taste of Paris in London for her sake. Jasper would be here with Miss Braidwood, to whom he had recently become betrothed, and so too would the reporter from the *Town Crier*, for it was better to keep your enemies close, Owen had said. But the guest list was not confined to the upper classes, for Phoebe was determined that Le Pas à Pas would not be the province of the rich, but open to all. So Mr Gilligan, the foreman, and his wife would have pride of place. She wouldn't be meeting any of the diners, distinguished or otherwise, for she would be confining herself to the kitchens. If any of them actually showed up, that is.

Above her, she heard the door open and her head waiter's dulcet tones wishing the new arrivals a very good evening. It was starting. Hearing the sound of footsteps on the stairs, thinking it would be one of the waiting staff, she was about to return to the kitchen when a voice halted her in her tracks.

'Phoebe.'

'Owen!'

He was in evening dress, freshly shaved, and trying to smile. 'Your first night. I couldn't let you endure it on your own.'

'Owen!' Without thinking, she threw her arms around his neck. 'Thank you.'

'You'll have London at your feet, trust me.' He held her briefly, all too briefly, before disentangling himself. 'I know you wanted to wait until you'd made a success of this place before telling them, but I also know how much their support means to you, so I took the liberty of writing to your sisters,' he said, handing her two letters. 'It was presumptuous of me, I have no right—but I hope I did the right thing.'

Both letters were short, loving and full of exclamations marks. Eloise and Estelle were unreservedly delighted and proud. Neither thought she needed luck, but they wished it anyway, and hoped that they'd be privileged enough to dine at what was certain to be the top restaurant in London very soon.

Tears smarted in Phoebe's eyes. 'Oh, Owen, what a

lovely surprise. Thank you. For these. For all this. And most especially for our time together.' She caught his hand, rubbing her cheek against it, the longing to tell him how much she loved him almost overwhelming. But it would hurt him, and he'd been so brave coming here, and she loved him so very much. 'Thank you,' she said instead, turning his hand around to kiss his palm.

The café door opened again, and this time there was the unmistakable clump of several pairs of feet. 'Your first diners,' Owen said. 'Go on, get into that kitchen and work your magic.'

'You're not staying?'

'Le Pas à Pas is your creation. Your very own establishment, with your very own menus, your own dishes. A place where men and women can dine together, as they can in Paris. Just imagine!'

'Did I say that?'

'Your very own words. I've never forgotten them. Enjoy it.'

'Won't you stay, just for a short while?'

His smile faded. 'Not a good idea. You want the *Town Crier* to report on your delicious food, not your lunatic husband.'

The front door opened. Owen heard Phoebe call goodnight to the coachman, heard the clatter of hooves as the town coach headed round to the mews, and the door closed. He had been in two minds all night as to whether to wait up for her, but aside from the sick, jittery feeling in his gut which was his personal countdown to his wife's departure, he could detect no signs of any imminent episode. Not that there were always signs.

He opened the parlour door just as she was putting her foot on the first stair, and called her name. 'If you're not too tired, I'm desperate to hear about your triumphant debut.'

'You seem very confident that it was a triumph.'

'And?'

She edged past him to her usual sofa. 'I am pleased to tell you that your confidence was not misplaced.'

'I knew it!' He resisted the urge to hug her, and resisted the desire to share the sofa with her as he used to do. Phoebe, in the process of taking off her boots, noticed his hesitation before he took the chair, but made no comment. There should be champagne to celebrate a night like this, but champagne was too reminiscent of the halcyon days of their marriage. Besides, he was trying to cut down on his drinking. 'Tell me all about it.'

'Everyone turned up. Every table was filled. The food went out on time. The plates came back empty,' she answered, sounding deflated.

'You're tired. And I've no right—I should have been there. I'm sorry.'

'No, Owen, I'm sorry. I'm not tired, I'm weary, that's all. My head hurts and my feet hurt.' She tucked them up under her.

Owen moved to the other end of the sofa. 'Let me see if I can help.'

She stretched out cautiously, putting her stockinged feet in his lap, but as soon as he began to knead her toes he felt her relax.

'That is so good. Those stone floors are the one thing I'd change about Le Pas à Pas. That, and the staircase from the kitchens. Our waiters had a couple of narrow escapes with the soup tureens.'

'How did they cope? You were worried about one of them.'

'John. I spoke to him yesterday. He was fine. The terrine was very popular. And the confit egg with the smoked fish—that went down very well too. I'm thinking I might try it with asparagus when it comes into season next month, and a little toast.'

'How was the venison received?'

'I think they might have loved it almost as much as you do, judging by the empty plates.'

'Not possible.' Owen kissed the tip of her big toe, the usual sign that she should swap feet. Phoebe's eyes flew open, but he simply continued with the massage, pretending the intimacy hadn't happened. 'Did you speak to Jasper? What did you think of Olivia?'

'I didn't venture out of the kitchens. There were any number of compliments sent down, but I—well, you know I've always believed my food should speak for itself.'

And he'd been adamant that it would be good publicity if people could see the beauty who presided over the pots, but he had no right to say so now. Le Pas à Pas was in Phoebe's very capable hands.

'I know you don't agree,' she said, reading his thoughts.

'I can be wrong. It's not unknown.'

'But you don't think you're wrong about us?'

There was a break in her voice that pierced his heart. 'Nor do you, Phoebe.'

'No, I don't. I don't want you to suffer any more than you have to.'

'I've decided to go abroad. It will be easier for both of us, to resist the temptation to see one another, and I think it will be good for me, to travel.'

'To experience what you missed out on, two years ago?'

'Not exactly. A little. To try to discover if a change of scene will change how I feel, too.'

'You mean you think you might get better? That distance will—'

'I don't know, Phoebe,' Owen interrupted hastily. 'I dare not hope, but I have to act. I won't let myself become what I was when you walked back into my life. I won't undo all the good you've done for me.'

'I could come with you?' But before he could answer, Phoebe was already shaking her head. 'You don't want me to. You don't need to say it.'

'It's not that I don't want you to, it's that I need to do this myself.'

'Will you come back, Owen?'

He wanted to say yes, more than anything else in the world. 'Eventually. But I don't want you to wait. Don't wait. Don't hope. Don't do what I did, and live in limbo. It's such a cliché, but it's true, my darling. Life's too short. Promise me you'll make the most of it.'

Her eyes were bright with tears, but she held them back. 'You ask so much of me.'

'Never anything I know you can't do.'

She closed her eyes, laying her head back. He had ceased kneading, but now she wiggled her toes. 'Don't stop.'

He closed his eyes too, working his way up to her calf, giving himself over to the familiar sensation of her silk stocking sliding over her skin, his fingers working into the muscle until the tension was relieved, and then the sweeping, soothing strokes she liked when he finished. He changed his attention to the other leg, and she rested her foot at the top of his thigh. He started kneading, and she began to stroke his groin with her toe.

Owen groaned. His hands slid up her leg, to the top of her thigh, to cup the heat between her legs. He ached for her. He already missed her, as if a part of him had been severed. If they could just make love one last time—he was trying to close the thought down when she reached for him.

'One last time, Owen. So we can remember it this way.'

It was impossible to resist. He pulled her on to his lap and their lips met in the sweetest, most delicious of bittersweet kisses. She murmured his name over and over as they kissed, as they stroked each other in that familiar way, and he said her name too, over and over, because he couldn't tell her that he loved her, but he could demonstrate that he did. When he entered her, tears leaked from her eyes and he licked them away, and then the sheer delight of being inside her, of having her arms wrapped around him, their partially clad bodies entwined, took over, and the knowledge that it would be the last time, which should have made their lovemaking slow, instead made it frantic. It was over far too soon.

'Phoebe.'

She shook her head, putting her finger over his mouth. 'Don't say it. Don't look for me in the morning.' She kissed him lingeringly one last time. She quickly gathered up her clothes. Then she was gone.

He sat up all night, wide awake in his work room, counting down the hours until she left. She had taken a suite at a hotel in the short term. Now that he had decided to go abroad, there was no reason for her to leave the town house, save that he didn't want her to wait for him. And she had promised him not to.

Was he truly without hope? It was after six and the servants were stirring when Owen finally accepted that he was not. Hopelessness would keep him here, retiring back into solitude, giving up on the world, making a recluse of him again. It was hope that was taking him out into the world, though he dreaded all that entailed, for he would be exposed, raw, and able to rely on no one but himself. He hoped that somewhere in his travels he would find a way to live with himself. Because then, and only then, could he hope that he'd be able to find a way also to live with Phoebe.

Chapter Twelve

One year later, April 1832

Owen stood at the foot of the steps outside Fearnoch House, the London residence of Phoebe's sister, Eloise. Phoebe had moved there shortly after he had left England, according to his lawyer, who also acted for her in matters of business. The man had been astounded when Owen arrived at his office an hour ago demanding to know the whereabouts of his own wife. He'd have been even more astounded if he'd known that the only thing that prevented Owen tracking him down as soon as he arrived back in London last night, was the fact that he had no idea where his lawyer lived.

He had not slept in the hotel where he'd been forced to stay, his own house being locked up, but he had bathed and changed. Now here he stood on the steps outside a London town house he'd never been in before, his stomach churning with nerves. Almost exactly a year and a half ago, Phoebe had stood outside his town house, uncertain of her own reception. Only now did he realise just how brave she had been, simply to knock on the door and beg an audience. How close he'd come to refusing her. Please to all the gods in heaven, she did not refuse him now.

She would be perfectly with her rights to do so. He had asked her not to wait. He had refused to give her any hope. His lawyer had told him enough to assure him that she had made a resounding success of Le Pas à Pas, enough to fill Owen's heart with pride. And now with doubt. Would she want to make room in her life for him? He thought she'd understood his reasons for leaving, but a year was a very long time. What if Phoebe had found someone else to fill the hole he'd torn in her heart?

The very notion of it made him feel dizzy. He told himself staunchly that he would endure such a blow with dignity, that he would understand, that he would be happy that she was happy. That's what he told himself. He didn't believe a word of it as he rang the bell, for the one solid truth he had known all along was that he loved her, and that he wanted to spend the rest of his life loving her. 'Let her see me. Let her listen. Let her give me a chance,' is what he said to himself. 'Let her still love me.'

Phoebe picked up the copy of the *Town Crier*, which had been sent to her courtesy of the publication's editor.

The first anniversary of Le Pas à Pas, our favourite London eatery, was celebrated last night with the usual muted panache we have come to associate with Mrs Harrington, the chef patroness.

*Regular diners will be relieved to know that
the renowned venison ragout still features on
the new menu, though it is now served with an
Italian concoction called macaroni served with
cheese, rather than the potato gratin that is a
particular favourite of Yours Truly.*

*Is this innovation, which Mrs Harrington
credits to Signora Sarti, her Italian* sous-chef,
an improvement? It is certainly different!

In other words, he hated it, Phoebe thought, setting
the rag aside. Which was a pity, because Gina was an
excellent chef who deserved a reward for her loyalty.
Having her name in print and her first dish on the menu
was only the start. Phoebe intended to introduce several more in the coming months, and to delegate more
too, with her plans to open a sister café to Le Pas à
Pas well in train. There was another pasta dish Gina
made, with asparagus and fresh peas, that would eat
beautifully paired with pork.

It was Sunday, her day off from the stoves, and a
lovely spring day, perfect for a walk in the park. She
checked her little enamel watch. Work first. She'd had
no idea there was so much paperwork involved in rent-
ing and fitting out a new premises. Owen had taken
care of that side of the business the first time around.
The familiar pain made her heart clench, but she was
used to it now. She had promised him not to hope. She
had promised him not to wait for him, to make the
most of her life. She had been true to both vows, but

she loved him every bit as much now as she had done the day she had forced herself to walk away from him.

The distant clang of the doorbell a few moments later made her frown. It was only just after eight in the morning. 'You know I don't like to be disturbed on a Sunday,' she said, frowning at Wiggins, Eloise's butler.

'Indeed, Mrs Harrington, but I think you may wish to make an exception for this caller.'

'I hope you will,' came a voice from behind the butler's back.

'Owen?' The room began to spin. Phoebe clutched the edge of the dining table.

'May I come in?'

'Owen? What are you doing here? You're supposed to be abroad.'

'I came back.'

Wiggins had tactfully disappeared, but Owen was still hovering at the door. He was tanned. His hair had been bleached gold. He looked older, but younger. Different, but the same. And just looking at him, she felt the same too—the tug of attraction, the ache of unspoken love in her heart. Which must remain unspoken, she cautioned herself. It had been a year. She would embarrass the pair of them by throwing herself at a husband who had come seeking a formal separation.

'Come in. Would you like some coffee?'

'No, thank you.' He stepped warily into the room, as if unsure of his welcome. 'I'm sorry to surprise you like this. I only got back last night. I'd have called then, if I'd known where you were.'

'You look very well, Owen.'

'Do I? I feel—I wasn't sure you'd see me. You look lovely, as ever.'

'I've been working hard. The café...'

'Phoebe, I don't care about the café. No, that's not true, of course I care, but not right at this moment.' Owen finally crossed the room to her side. 'I've had nearly a month to rehearse this, the whole journey home, and now I can't think of a thing to say, except that I love you with all my heart and I've missed you with all my heart, and I'm not cured and I may never be, but I don't want to spend another minute of my life without you.'

She stared at him, open mouthed, her heart leaping ahead of her brain, fluttering wildly with joy while she tried to assimilate what he had said.

Owen made to take her hand then changed his mind. 'I know this is a shock. When I left England, I had no idea how long I would be gone. I was lost, I was scared, I didn't know who I was. I thought the worst thing that could happen to me had happened that night, when I remembered my accident, but I knew even then that the worst thing that could happen was losing you. I know I told you not to hope, but I hoped, I never stopped hoping, that I'd find a way to come back to you.'

'Why didn't you tell me?'

'Because I've lived a life in limbo, Phoebe. Before you came into my life, that's what I was doing. Yes, I was working away on my investments, but that was never anything other than a way to kill time. You gave me a purpose, but I've never forgotten what it was like *not* to have one—or rather, what it was like when my only purpose was waiting for something to happen—

waiting to remember, is what I was doing. Instead, you happened. And you changed everything for me.'

She wanted so much to have his arms around her, but she wanted even more to hear him out, because the hope that she hadn't ever fully repressed either, was blooming so quickly inside her. 'Go on,' Phoebe said, indicating a chair.

'Are you sure? I have no right to expect you even to listen to me.'

'Owen, almost exactly eighteen months ago, I called on you. You saw no one, but you saw me, and you listened to me. At the very least, don't you think I owe you this?'

'Is that the only reason? If you would rather not hear what I have to say, if you've made a new life for yourself...'

'Would you leave?'

He laughed shortly. 'I asked myself the same question while I was on the doorstep a few moments ago. I told myself I would, but I know I wouldn't. I love you with all my heart, Phoebe. That's the one constant that's been with me for the last year, and I'm going to do my damnedest to persuade you to give me another chance.' He swallowed, took a visible breath. 'But you found the strength to let me go when I needed you to. Hear me out, that's all I ask. If you decide, after that, that I won't make you happy then I promise I'll find the strength to leave you.'

Once again, the urge to throw herself into his arms and tell him that nothing mattered save that he was here was overpowering. She loved him, she didn't doubt that he loved her, but the last year had proved to her that he'd been right to go, that if he'd stayed, they would have torn each other apart. So Phoebe didn't throw herself into Owen's arms, instead she ordered him a pot of coffee and herself a fresh pot of tea. And when she had poured their drinks, she nodded to him, permitting herself a very small smile. 'I'm listening.'

Owen took a sip of coffee, trying to collect his thoughts. Phoebe had changed. She was still his beautiful, desirable wife, but there was an inner strength about her that hadn't been there before. The old Phoebe would have either thrown herself into his arms or shown him the door. This Phoebe was determined to make a more rational decision, and by the sun and moon and stars, he admired her for it. He loved her so much, but he had a lot to prove. He finished his coffee in one gulp. He was determined to do just that.

'You know why I left,' he said. 'First of all, I thought if I got away from England, it might help my condition, but it didn't. I still had episodes, and I had the additional misery of missing you. Which I came to realise very quickly, was making me much more miserable than the episodes.'

'But you didn't come back, because you were determined not to make me miserable too?'

'That was a big part of it, you know that, but the other part of it was…'

'You needed to be alone.'

'Yes,' Owen said gratefully. 'I knew you understood that.'

'I did, eventually. It hurt, Owen, because at first I thought you didn't want my help. Then I realised that I simply couldn't help.' Phoebe smiled sadly. 'And that hurt too, but in a different way.'

'I didn't know who I was any more, but I knew I wasn't the person I thought I was. When you're alone and no one knows you and no one knows where you are, it does clear your mind. Remembering what happened the day of the fire—' Owen broke off, shuddering. 'The horror and the tragedy of that won't change. But I did start to question how I viewed my part in it.'

'You saw that it wasn't your fault that the poor little baby died?'

He sighed heavily. 'I truly don't think anyone could have saved him.'

'Him?'

'It was a little boy. I know, because I went to Marseille and I tracked down his mother.'

'You did!' Phoebe caught his hand, lifting it to her cheek, pressing a kiss to his palm, a familiar, tender little gesture that was one of the things he'd missed the most about her. 'That was very brave.'

'I almost didn't go through with it,' he admitted. 'But I'm glad I did. I wasn't even sure Madame Le-Brun would want to meet with me. It was her husband, in fact, who came to the café where I was waiting. I thought he was going to attack me, but he took my hand and he…' Tears sprang unbidden. But he was used to tears now, and no longer ashamed of them, so he didn't apologise. 'He embraced me and said he had waited a long time to thank me for saving his wife.'

Phoebe smudged the tear which tracked down his cheek with her thumb. 'I always knew you were a hero.'

'I'm not. I was a fool. I don't think anyone could have saved that child. I may have saved Madame Le-Brun, but I risked my own life doing so. It was mine to risk, but the two men who saved me—their lives were not mine to risk. I was lucky, very lucky, that they were so brave.'

'Did you meet them too, in Marseille?'

'I did. And invested a little money in their fishing boats—I now know a great deal more than I will ever need to about the fish of the Mediterranean. Perhaps even more than you.'

'You're a good man, Owen Harrington. You knew they wouldn't accept money.'

'It's a good investment. More importantly, meeting them, all of them, returning to Marseille as I did, it made me finally see things differently.'

Owen poured himself another cup of coffee, forcing himself not to rush. Phoebe, his lovely, patient, strong Phoebe, was such a distracting presence, but he had to get this right. 'I saw that I'd been looking at my accident the wrong way round, you see. I thought it had deprived me of my second chance. Before you came along, I was wallowing in self-pity, I was miserable.'

'In limbo.'

'Exactly. You dragged me out of the pit of despair. No, don't tell me that I did it myself. I did, in the practical sense, but if it hadn't been for you, for wanting to be better for you, then I wouldn't have done anything. Then I fell in love with you. I was happy, I thought I couldn't be happier, but I was wrong about that. It was still there, the guilt and the grief, waiting until I was well enough to deal with it. You made me well enough.'

'And have you dealt with it?'

'I'm not better,' Owen said. 'I won't lie to you, Phoebe. I may never completely recover. I still have episodes. But I understand them. There's less of them, much less. And because I understand what happened, I can bear them.' He took a last sip of coffee. 'I hope that they are symptoms of progress. Like lancing a boil, the poison has to come out, do you see?'

'I think so.'

'But I could be wrong, Phoebe. I know—don't ask me how, I simply do—that they won't get worse, but I may never be clear of them. I'm asking a lot of you. I'm asking you to take what I say on trust until you have the evidence that I'm right. If that means you want me to wait until you are reassured, then I'll wait for however long it takes. But I can promise you two things, hand on heart. The first is that I won't be going away again. And the second is that I love you. Always.'

He dropped to his knees beside her, finally allowing himself to take her hand. 'That fire didn't deprive me of a second chance, it gave me one. I could have died. I didn't. I have a life to live, and I want to live it with you. Every single second of it. I have made my peace with the tragedy that I was part of, but I want more than that. I want happiness. And the only true happiness for me is with you. But if you don't feel the same...'

'I do.' Phoebe fell on to the floor beside him and

threw her arms around him. 'I love you so much, Owen, so very much.'

'It won't be plain sailing.'

She laughed. 'No, it certainly won't. For a start I'm about to open a second café.'

'Why stop at a second! Why stop at London! You are magnificent. I love you so much.'

'And I love you. I haven't stopped loving you but, Owen—are you absolutely sure?'

'Completely and utterly sure. The whole time I was away, I carried you here.' He touched his heart. 'This is yours, if you want it, my darling. Will you take it?'

He drew the ring from the inner pocket of his waist-coat and held it out to her.

'I left that behind,' Phoebe said.

'And I took it with me. Will you take it?'

'For ever.'

He put the ring on her wedding finger above the wedding band. He kissed the ring. Then he turned her hand over to kiss her palm. Then finally, he pulled her into his arms. Their lips met. Their kiss was awkward, tentative at first, but it deepened quickly and they clung together, kissing until they had to stop for breath.

'Are you really here?' Phoebe asked, touching his tanned face, the rough stubble on his chin.

'For ever.' He kissed her again, and knew without a shadow of a doubt that he had finally found the place where he belonged. 'For ever,' he repeated, then he kissed her again. 'I promise.'

* * * * *

Historical Note

The Procope, where Phoebe and Owen first meet, is one of Paris's oldest cafés. Situated in St Germain on the Left Bank, it's a fabulously atmospheric place where everyone who was anyone—or more accurately every *man*, in the early days—met to talk, drink and eat. Benjamin Franklin, whose 'I eat to live, not live to eat' quote I purloined, was one of many famous Enlightenment regulars there.

Antoine Beauvilliers was a pioneering chef whose restaurant, La Grande Taverne de Londres, which I've borrowed for Pascal—who *isn't* real—was located in the Palais Royale. His style of cooking went out of fashion in the eighteen-twenties, when his restaurant closed, but his recipe book, *L'Art du Cuisinier*, became a French classic and was translated into English around about the time that Phoebe's sister Eloise bought her a copy as a present.

Two other chefs feature in this book. Monsieur Salois, whose recommendation got Phoebe the job with Pascal, is an invention of my friend and fellow writer

Bronwyn Scott, who introduced him in the first of our joint Brockmore stories, *Scandal at the Midsummer Ball*. Eustache Ude, on the other hand, was very real. I couldn't do justice to the man who really did make a theatre of cooking and dining, threatening customers with a cleaver who failed to appreciate his food as much as he thought they should, so I most reluctantly kept him off the page. Imagine a combination of Gordon Ramsay and Marco Pierre White, multiply it by ten, and you'll be close.

Ude was employed at Crockford's club for the phenomenal salary of one thousand, two hundred pounds a year, when a top-class chef would normally be paid about fifty pounds. I first read about him in Nicholas Foulkes's excellent *Gentlemen and Blackguards*, when I was researching gambling clubs for another book, *Rumours that Ruined a Lady*, where another of my heroines breached that all-male bastion for a very different reason.

Alexis Soyer, another renowned chef who worked at the Reform Club and who doesn't appear in this book, was responsible for making gas stoves popular. This was about ten years after Phoebe's time, but the stoves were patented in 1828, so my heroine is in this, as in so many things, an innovator.

I read about the tradition of running footmen in Karl Shaw's *Mad, Bad and Dangerous to Know*. The Fourth Duke of Marlborough really did race his footman from Brighton to London, the servant on foot, the Duke in a carriage and four. And the poor servant really did come close to winning before expiring.

Regular readers will know that I'm fond of re-using my characters. Jean-Luc Bauduin, Duc de Montendre, who supplies Owen's wine, is the hero of *From Courtesan to Convenient Wife*. The Flying Vengarovs make a cameo appearance in that same book, but they originated in *Scandal at the Midsummer Ball*, along with Monsieur Salois.

Rules restaurant is still going strong to this day. Serving pretty much the same fayre too, so you can enjoy a taste—quite literally—of Regency life if you go there.

And last but certainly not least, I'd like to say a huge *merci* to my lovely French neighbour Hélène, for helping me to name Phoebe's restaurant. *C'est parfait!*

LET'S TALK
Romance

For exclusive extracts, competitions
and special offers, find us online:

JOIN THE
MILLS & BOON
BOOKCLUB

* **FREE** delivery direct to your door

* **EXCLUSIVE** offers every month

* **EXCITING** rewards programme

50% OFF
YOUR FIRST
PARCEL

Join today at
Millsandboon.co.uk/Bookclub

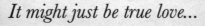

GET YOUR ROMANCE FIX!

Get the latest romance news,
exclusive author interviews, story
extracts and much more!

MILLS & BOON

MODERN

Power and Passion

Prepare to be swept off your feet by sophisticated, sexy and seductive heroes, in some of the world's most glamourous and romantic locations, where power and passion collide.

MILLS & BOON
MEDICAL
Pulse-Racing Passion

Set your pulse racing with dedicated, delectable doctors in the high-pressure world of medicine, where emotions run high and passion, comfort and love are the best medicine.

MILLS & BOON
Desire

Indulge in secrets and scandal, intense drama and plenty of sizzling hot action with powerful and passionate heroes who have it all: wealth, status, good looks…everything but the right woman.